The Tsarina's Daughter

Also by Carolly Erickson

HISTORICAL ENTERTAINMENTS

The Hidden Diary of Marie Antoinette
The Last Wife of Henry VIII
The Secret Life of Josephine

NONFICTION

The Records of Medieval Europe
Civilization and Society in the West
The Medieval Vision
Bloody Mary
Great Harry
The First Elizabeth
Mistress Anne
Our Tempestuous Day
Bonnie Prince Charlie
To the Scaffold
Her Little Majesty
Arc of the Arrow
Great Catherine
Josephine
Alexandra
Royal Panoply
Lilibet
The Girl from Botany Bay

The Tsarina's Daughter

CAROLLY ERICKSON

St. Martin's Press ✖ New York

This is a work of fiction. All of the characters, organizations, and events portrayed in this novel are either products of the author's imagination or are used fictitiously.

www.stmartins.com

ISBN-13: 978-0-312-55122-3
ISBN-10: 0-312-55122-3

First Edition: September 2008

10 9 8 7 6 5 4 3 2 1

The Tsarina's Daughter

PROLOGUE

November 15, 1989

My name is Daria Gradov and I live in Yellow Rain, Saskatchewan. I am a widow. My dear Michael has died but my family is close by. They look after me, especially my son Nicholas and his boys.

They believe their name to be Gradov, like their father's. But their true name, their true heritage, is Romanov. They don't yet know it, but they are heirs to the throne of the tsars.

Now that the world is celebrating the fall of the Berlin Wall, and I am celebrating my ninety-third year of life, the time has come for me to tell the story of my true family, as a gift to my son and grandsons. As an act of penance, perhaps, for turning my back on my birthright and disguising the truth of my origins for so many years.

For I only became Daria Gradov in 1918, when Michael and I boarded the train that took us to Murmansk. I had false papers. No one suspected that I was really Tatiana Romanov, second oldest daughter of Tsar Nicholas and Tsarina Alexandra. That girl was dead, shot with her mother and father, her sisters and brother in the basement of a shabby house in Siberia. Only Michael and I and a few trusted others knew that the girl who died in the basement was not Tatiana.

I am Tatiana.

And now I must tell my story, and my family's story, so that old wrongs can be righted and the world can know the truth.

One

My *story begins* at the extreme edge of memory, on a snowy January afternoon when I was six years old, and it seemed as if all the bells in all the churches of St. Petersburg were ringing at once.

I remember my father lifted me up so I could see over the top of the balcony railing, and I felt the freezing wind on my face and saw, through the greenish-yellow fog, a crowd of people such as I had never seen before.

The mass of people, all singing and shouting and waving flags and banners, seemed to stretch as far as I could see, all across the Palace Square and beyond, out toward the corners of the avenues and even along the bridge across the river.

"Batiushka! Batiushka!" they were shouting. "Little Father!" Though the noise of their shouting seemed to dissolve into the resonant clanging of the bells and the singing of "God Save the Tsar."

It was my name day, or near it, the Feast of the Holy Martyr Tatiana of Rome who lived in the time of the Caesars, and at first I thought they were all shouting and singing to celebrate my name day feast, so I waved and smiled and thought, how kind they all are, to show such joy at my feast day.

But of course it was not my name day that they were celebrating, it was something much more important, as I found out later.

My father put me down but I could still see through the open stonework of the balustrade and I could still hear the tremendous commotion. People began singing "Holy Russia" and chanting "Hail to the Russian army and fleet" and clapping as they chanted, though their poor hands must have been raw from the cold. Mother led us back through the glass doors into the White Hall and we thawed ourselves in front of the fire.

She smiled at us and gave us hot milk and plates of warm buns with honey and icing. We were all happy that day because she had just told us a wonderful secret: that we would soon have a baby brother.

There were four of us girls in the family, in that winter of 1904. I was six, as I have already said, Olga had just turned eight, fat little Marie was four and the baby, Anastasia, was two and a half. Everybody said we needed a brother and mama assured us that we would soon have one, no matter what stories our Grandma Minnie told. (Grandma Minnie was unkind to mama, and always said she could only have girls.)

"Is it because our little brother is coming that all the people are shouting and all the bells are ringing?" I asked.

"No, Tania. It is because they love Russia and they love us, especially your dear papa."

"I heard Chemodurov say it was because of the war," Olga said, in her most grown-up, know-it-all voice. Chemodurov was my father's valet and the source of all Olga's information at that time.

"Hush! We leave such things to your father." Mama spoke crisply, and gave Olga a look that made her frown and sulk, though she did obey and said nothing more.

"How was your dancing lesson, Tania?" mama asked, changing the subject. "Did you manage to avoid stepping on Olga's feet?"

"Professor Leitfelter says I am a good dancer," I said proudly. "I keep good time with my feet."

Olga and I went to dancing class twice a week at the Vorontzov Institute for Young Noblewomen. With forty other girls, all of us dressed in identical long white pinafores and pink linen underskirts, we stepped and twirled, promenaded and bowed to the music of a grand piano, while our dancing master walked up and down, correcting our form and clapping his hands irritably when we failed to keep in step.

I loved dancing class. Everything about it pleased me, from the beautiful high-ceilinged immaculately white ballroom in which it was held, with its grand marble columns and its immense chandeliers, to the gold-framed portraits that looked down on us from the walls while we danced, to the grace of the best dancers and the carefree feeling the movements brought out in me.

Among those other girls I was no longer a grand duchess, fussed over by nursemaids and servants. I was just one of forty identical girls, treated no differently from the others just because I was the emperor's daughter. (Professor Leitfelter was equally strict with us all.) For as long as the class lasted I yielded, happily, to the flow of the music and drifted away.

On the following day the immense crowds formed again in Palace Square and out beyond it. Once again the church bells rang and the people sang and shouted, and my father led us all out onto the balcony to receive their tribute.

"I've never seen anything like it," my father said to us all at tea that afternoon. "Such huge demonstrations of support, such outpourings of love and affection for the nation—"

"And the dynasty. Don't forget that," my mother interrupted. "It is for the house of Romanov, and for you, Nicky."

My father smiled gently, as he always did when reminded that he, the emperor, was the focus of veneration.

"My people are loyal," he said. "They may complain, they may go on strike and march in protest and even throw bombs, but when the nation needs them, they respond. I'm told there are crowds like this in every town," he went on. "Men are rushing to volunteer for army service. Contributions are pouring in, tens of thousands of rubles. And all because we are at war with Japan."

"We will win, won't we, papa?" I asked.

"Of course, Tania. Only the British have a finer navy than we do. Though Cousin Willy has many fine ships as well." Mama's cousin Willy was Kaiser Wilhelm, ruler of Germany. I had seen pictures of him in mama's study, a burly, angry-looking man. Mama didn't like him.

For many days the crowds came to cheer and sing, and we all went out on the balcony to smile and wave. But papa, who always looked a little sad except when he was taking a long walk or riding his bicycle or chopping wood, began to look very sad, and before long the noise and the singing stopped, though there were still many people in Palace Square, looking up toward the balcony or talking among themselves.

Olga told me that some of our big Russian ships had been sunk by the Japanese. A lot of men had drowned, she said, and I thought, no wonder papa looks sad.

"There is a war. A terrible war. And we are losing. Chemodurov says so."

I remember being confused, and being sorry to see my father's sad face (for he could be very jolly), and the next thing I remember was the day my baby brother was born.

On that day, in the morning, we children were sent upstairs to the nursery, out of the way, and were told that mama had gone into Grandma Minnie's bedroom, to lie in her bed.

"All the tsars of Russia have been born in that bed," our nursemaid told us. "Your father, and your grandfather, who was strong as an ox, and your sainted great-grandfather, the one who was blown all to pieces by that awful man."

It was not long before the guns in the Peter and Paul Fortress began going off and we knew that our little brother had come into the world. We were allowed to go downstairs to see mama and the little baby. Mama was lying back on the soft pillows of the bed and looking very tired, the way she looked when her head hurt. Yet she looked beautiful, with her lovely face softened by fatigue and her rich dark blond hair spread out all over the lace-trimmed pillow. She smiled at us and held out her hands.

Beside the bed a golden cradle flamed in the sunlight. Next to the cradle sat one of the nursery maids, gently rocking it with her foot. I remember peering down into the cradle and seeing there, beneath a purple velvet coverlet embroidered in gold, our new brother, asleep.

"Alexei," mama said quietly. "We are going to call him Alexei. The eighth Romanov to sit on the throne of all the Russias. Now, that is something to celebrate."

Two

The wicked contraption was brought up to the nursery by our manservant Sedynov not long after Alexei was born, the awful device that was supposed to make me learn to sit up straight.

In those first days after my brother's birth, mama was ill and in bed downstairs and Grandma Minnie took charge of us in the nursery upstairs. Grandma Minnie was not kind and loving like mama, she slapped our hands with a stick when we displeased her and once even raised her riding crop like a whip when Olga refused to mind her.

"You girls have been too indulged," she said the day the device was brought into the nursery. "Now you will be made to behave like well-bred young ladies, young ladies who do not speak out of turn or cross their legs or slouch." She glared at me. "Yes, Tatiana, I am talking about you. You slouch. You must be trained to sit up straight."

She had Sedynov bring the contraption over to where Olga and I were standing. It was a long steel rod with leather straps at the top and bottom. Following her instructions he fastened the rod to my back, along my spine, buckling the straps at my waist and around my forehead.

I couldn't move, it was hard even to breathe at first, so tightly was I bound.

"No! No! Take the horrid thing off!" I shouted, wriggling and struggling, trying to loosen the leather belt, all the while growing very red in the face. I could hear Olga laughing as she watched the spectacle.

"Sedynov! Take it off at once!" I cried out again.

The manservant, who was fond of us and had served us all our lives, looked up from under his beetle brows at Grandma Minnie, who frowned at him, and then at me. Of course he had to obey grandma, who was, after all, the Dowager Empress.

"I'll stand straight, grandma, I promise, just take this thing off me!"

"You'll wear it for four hours every day until your spine straightens, just as I did when I was little. My sister and I both," she said with a glance at Olga, who immediately stiffened her back and held her chin high, in hopes of avoiding the torture I was undergoing. Grandma Minnie had been Princess Dagmar of Denmark before she married my grandfather Emperor Alexander, and her sister had been Princess Alexandra, now Queen Alexandra of England. Grandma Minnie often said that the reason she and her sister had married so well was that their posture was beyond reproach—though in fact, as I now know, it was because, besides being princesses, they were both very beautiful women.

The steel rod became the bane of my existence for the next few months. I was forced to wear it for many hours every day, and even when it was taken off my back felt stiff and sore and I could not bend my head down without pain.

"I'm sorry to have to do this, mistress," Sedynov murmured whenever he strapped the steel rod on. "But it is your exalted grandmother's command."

"Yes, Sedynov, I understand. You must do as you are told."

"Thank you, mistress. I will pray for you."

The maidservants also felt pity for me, sly Niuta giving me sympathetic looks and kind Elizaveta putting sweets in the pockets of my pinafore when she thought no one was watching. Shoura, our chief maid and dresser, sometimes unfastened the cruel rod for an hour at a time when she knew for certain that Grandma Minnie would not be coming into the nursery to see what was going on.

We were accustomed to discomfort in the nursery. Olga, Marie, Anastasia and I all slept on narrow, hard camp beds—the kind of beds soldiers sleep on in their barracks. It was a tradition, Grandma Minnie said, and tradition had to be maintained. All the imperial daughters of the Romanovs—though not the sons—had slept on hard camp beds for many generations, ever since some long-ago emperor decreed that his daughters would not be allowed to sleep in comfort on featherbeds until they were married.

"I don't see why we have to suffer just because some ancestor of ours made his daughters suffer," Olga remarked one night as she got into her narrow bed next to mine. "After all, we belong to ourselves, not to the past."

But the force of tradition was strong, and the camp beds remained in the nursery.

In truth, all that went on in the upstairs nursery, where we four sisters spent most of our waking and all of our sleeping hours, was just then far less important than what went on in our new brother's nursery downstairs. All attention was on him, as the long-awaited heir to the throne.

And there was a secret about him, an alarming, potentially fatal secret, that only the family and a few trusted others knew: Alexei had the bleeding disease—what the Russians call the "English disease"—and was very ill.

When he was first born he began bleeding from his tiny navel, and had to wear a bandage across his belly. The bandage kept turning red with his blood, and had to be changed every half-hour. Whenever I was taken in to see the baby and mama I watched the nursemaids changing his bandage, again and again, and I thought, soon he will have no more blood in him. But I didn't say that to mama, for she was so pale and so filled with worry that I didn't want to add to her fears.

Dr. Korovin and the surgeon Fedorov hovered near the cradle, watching Alexei and talking to one another. I heard them use the word "grave" a lot, and I imagined that they meant they were digging a grave for Alexei. As it turned out, they were saying that his condition was "grave," but I was too young to understand this, and thought the worst.

I had two cousins with the bleeding disease, Aunt Irene's sons Waldemar and Henry. They had come to visit us at Tsarskoe Selo several times, and they were both pale and thin, though Waldemar was very lively and liked to jump on the net with us and run fast when we played ball. A few months before Alexei was born, mama told us that Henry had died, and she asked us to pray before the icon of the Holy Mother of God for Waldemar, who she said might die too.

Henry, mama said, fell down and bumped his head on a chair, and his head began to bleed inside and would not stop. I imagined his head swelling up like a balloon, growing bigger and bigger and finally exploding, with all the blood flying out in all directions. It was horrible, I had nightmares about it. I wondered, would Alexei's head swell up too, and explode? Whenever I went into the nursery I watched for signs that his head was growing bigger. But all I saw was the bandage around his middle, and sometimes he seemed to hold one leg straight out and one of the nursemaids would massage it.

My father's uncles were often in the nursery, especially the tall, thin, rather sour Uncle Gega and the imposing Uncle Bembo, bespectacled and bewhiskered, who had a little silver-backed notebook that he took everywhere and was always writing things down in it. Uncle Gega said little but when he did speak, he shouted, jarring mama's nerves and making her wince. Uncle Gega was married to Aunt Ella, mama's sweet-faced, affectionate older sister who always looked beautiful though Niuta said she made her own clothes—something no well-bred titled lady ought to do.

"That child has something wrong with it," Uncle Gega shouted, peering down into Alexei's golden cradle. "Look at the way its leg sticks out! As if it were broken. Can't it be fixed?" He glared at the surgeon Dr. Fedorov, who shrank from his sharp gaze and turned to his colleague.

"Stop that muttering and give me an answer!"

"Your Excellency, the tsarevich's limbs are—are—"

"Are what?"

"Are still developing," Dr. Korovin said with an air of professional finality.

"I don't like the look of him," was Uncle Gega's parting remark, as he swept out of the room without so much as a nod to mama.

Alexei cried a lot. I could hear his wails even in the night nursery upstairs, and I imagined that his head might be filling with blood and hurting him. I wondered if his pain could be as great as mine, when day after day I had to submit to the strapping on of the cruel steel rod and the sharp, torturous straightening of my spine.

Three

We were standing in the Blue Salon of the Winter Palace, in front of the high arched window that looked out across the icebound Neva toward the looming Peter and Paul Fortress on the opposite bank. I stood next to Grandma Minnie and could feel her eyes on me, inspecting my posture, my behavior, my expression.

"Smile, Tatiana," she often said. "Well brought up girls don't frown. Girls who frown never find husbands."

I knew that she was examining me from the crown of my head to the felt boots I wore—peasant boots—because the palace floors were ice cold and without my felt boots my toes turned blue.

We were all there, standing in a row in front of the tall high window, my three sisters and I and Aunt Olga and Grandma Minnie and Uncle Vladimir and Auntie Miechen and the palace marshal and some of the servants who had come with us from Tsarskoe Selo to witness the ceremony. Mama and Alexei were not with us, mama had a headache and Alexei, still only a baby, was much too young to watch the events on the river.

We had all been to mass and had come from the service to witness my father perform the Blessing of the Waters, the sacred ceremony that sanctified the Neva and invoked divine aid on the city for the coming year.

He stood out on the pale blue-green ice, a lone small figure in his thick fur coat and hat, watching as a hole was cut in the frozen surface of the river. A small detachment of marine police came up to stand behind him, at a respectful distance, and as we watched, the Bishop of Petersburg in his gleaming gold vestments walked slowly toward the newly made opening in the ice and prepared to dip his staff into the dark water.

The scene unfolded in silence before us, we were too far away to hear the prayers that were being said, or to see, until it was much too late, that some of the marine police were turning and pointing in the direction of the fortress and running out across the ice as if in panic.

Then the pop and pounding of distant guns firing reached us, and we saw men begin to fall, struck by bullets and cannonfire, until only my father and the bishop were still standing. I heard Uncle Vladimir shout for the guard and Aunt Olga screamed as the window glass in front of us shattered into a million splintered crystals. I drew back in alarm just as Grandma Minnie put her hand to her forehead and sank down toward the floor, blood on her hand and gown. I was aware of cold air pouring in around me, of a confusion of voices and of men streaming into the immense room.

A uniformed officer grabbed my arm.

"Come, Your Highness."

"Papa—is papa safe?" I turned my head to look back at the scene on the river but all I could see was a blur of swiftly moving bodies. I let the officer who had taken my arm lead me away, down a long corridor toward one of the guardrooms.

"Here, Your Highness. Stay here. You will not be disturbed here." I was in a small, dimly lit, musty-smelling cupboard lined with shelves. I was alone. I heard the sound of the door being shut and locked.

Was papa all right? Where were my sisters? What had happened, out on the ice? I tried to open the cupboard door, but it would not yield. Would I be left here, forgotten, until I starved?

"Mama!" I screamed, knowing that she couldn't hear me. "Sedynov! Shoura! Niuta!"

But no one came, and soon the only sound I heard was the sound of my heart beating, the blood pounding in my ears, and the faint scratching of a rat in a far corner of the dim room.

Four

Not long after these frightening events I remember sitting in mama's lavender room, the room that always smelled of lilacs and of her favorite perfume, called "White Roses." She was stretched out on her white chaise longue, with a pale pink shawl covering her legs—her legs hurt her a lot—knitting a balaclava out of grey wool for one of her charities.

I liked going into mama's special room not only because I loved her but because it was always peaceful there, with the little white-and-gilded clock ticking, the clock her grandmother Queen Victoria gave her when she was a little girl, and the pictures of St. Cecelia and of mama's mother Alice on the wall next to the icon of the Annunciation. She had pictures of me there too, and my sisters and brother, and a big one of Queen Victoria when she was very very old and small and wrinkled, wearing an old-fashioned white lace cap over her grey hair. I always thought, when I was little, that the elderly queen was smiling at me out of that picture.

Mama lifted her needles and looked over at me, the look in her dark blue eyes warm.

"And how is my Taniushka? Did you have dancing class today?"

"I am well, mama. But dancing class is canceled. Professor Leitfelter says the streets are too dangerous. Everyone should stay home."

It was true. There was much turmoil in the city just then, with all the workers on strike and rioting and soldiers everywhere. Everyone said it was a miracle my father had been spared on the day he was shot at, standing there in the open on the river. He had not gone out of the palace since that day, except to travel, surrounded by guardsmen and cavalry, to our country palace Tsarskoe Selo.

"The Lord has let him live," I heard Grandma Minnie say when she visited the nursery. "His life has been saved so that he can preserve Russia from the wickedness of the ungodly masses." She wore a bandage on her forehead to cover the wound she had received on the day the shots were fired at papa; she covered it with a veil but I could still see it.

I looked over at mama, her needles swift in her hands. She was wearing the rings she often wore these days, a ring with a single large pearl, and another little ring with the sign of the swastika engraved on it, which she had told me was an ancient Indian symbol meaning "well-being."

Her hands were turning red, and her cheeks too were becoming pink. I knew what that meant. She was uneasy. She held out her hand to me, the hand with the swastika ring.

"Taniushka, do you know what this symbol means?"

"Yes, mama. You told me. It means 'well-being.'"

"And do you know why I wear it?"

"No, mama."

"Because it was given to me by a wonderful man, a teacher named Philippe, who came to us from France. When he gave it to me he told me that I must always remember, whatever happens, I will have a feeling of well-being, because I am a blessed child of God, and nothing truly bad can ever happen to me."

I looked at her, unsure what to say.

"Now, there is something I must tell you that is very sad and distressing, but I still feel well-being inside, and I want you to feel that too. Nothing that happens can ever touch us, deep down inside. Will you remember that?"

"Yes, mama. It isn't about papa, is it?"

"No, dear. It is your Uncle Gega." She swallowed, then went on. "A bomb was thrown into his carriage. He was badly hurt—in fact, dear, his life has ended." She crossed herself.

"Oh! Poor Aunt Ella!"

"It is because Aunt Ella is going to come to visit us, all the way from Moscow, that I am telling you this. She will arrive in a few days. She will be protected here with us. We must be especially kind to her."

I did not love Uncle Gega, in fact I disliked him, and even thought that he was faintly ridiculous because he wore corsets under his linen shirts to make his waist smaller and when the shirts were tight Olga and I could see the bones of the corsets very clearly and we always laughed—though never when he was nearby, of course.

"Will we go to Uncle Gega's funeral?"

"No, dear. He will be buried in Moscow and it would not be safe for us to go there now." She paused. "Just remember, Tania, that you always carry your well-being deep inside. When Aunt Ella comes, you must not show your distress."

I nodded. "I will do my best."

But when Aunt Ella arrived, her face tear-stained and her usually immaculate grooming and dress in disarray, I could not contain my feelings. I couldn't help but run to her and weep in her arms. She hugged me and told me how big I was getting, and hugged my sisters and baby Alexei too.

"Dear ones," she told us, "try not to grieve. My dear Serge is in paradise with the angels. He knew that the wicked bomb-throwers were after him. He tried to evade them. He even slept in a different palace every night, in the strong fortress of the Kremlin, so they wouldn't be able to find him."

I wondered, will we all have to start sleeping in a different palace every night? For I had heard it said that the bomb-throwers were going to kill us all, every one of us in the imperial family. Uncle Gega was only the first to go. Did Aunt Ella believe that she too would soon die?

My sister had a copy of a newspaper, *The Russian Word*, that Chemodurov lent her. It told all about what happened when the bomb hit Uncle Gega's body, how his head was destroyed along with both his arms and one of his legs, so that when Aunt Ella went looking for what was left of him in the bloody snow she could only find his chest and one leg and one of his hands that was lying all by itself. I didn't expect anyone to bring up any of that, but to my surprise Aunt Ella told us all how she took all that was left of Serge and put it in a very large hollow wooden cross that she hung on the wall. She put what was left of his bloody clothes inside the cross too, but kept the medal that he wore for protection and now wore it around her own neck on a gold chain.

"I feel he is still here, with me," she told us one afternoon as we all were gathered for our tea, fingering the medal as she spoke. "He watches over me."

"Someone should have watched over him," I said, without thinking, and Grandma Minnie said "Shhh" and glowered at me over her teacup.

"I only meant the police and the soldiers, grandma. They should have kept him safe."

"But how could they," Ella asked mildly, "when they didn't know who the bomb-throwers were going to be? They can't guard all of us against an unknown enemy. You've had a narrow escape yourselves, I understand. Despite all the soldiers here in the palace, you yourselves were shot at—and then there were those choristers who turned out to be bomb-throwers. You were fortunate to escape them."

"What choristers?" Olga wanted to know.

"Oh, so you didn't tell the children," Ella said to mama. "Well, I suppose that was right. No need to frighten them."

"Tell us now," Olga said, turning to mama who reddened and said nothing.

"We had some unwanted guests among us not long ago," my father said with a slight smile. "They were caught in the chapel, dressed as choristers, about to begin singing the evening service. An alert guard—I gave him a medal for this afterward—saw some suspicious bulges under the robes these men were wearing. They were arrested, and the police found that they had explosives strapped around their waists."

I heard Olga's sharp intake of breath, and I too felt shocked—and frightened.

"They were going to blow us up," I said.

"That may have been their plan," was my father's firm response, "but we are well guarded, and their plan did not succeed."

I glanced over at Aunt Ella, who had a withdrawn look, like one who is lost in her own thoughts. Now that she was a widow she had changed, I thought. The cut of her gown was simple, her headdress less like that of a member of the imperial family and more like that of a woman from the countryside. She was still as beautiful as ever, with very fair skin and light blue eyes that had a distinctive flaw—her left eye had a very noticeable spot of brown amid the blue. She was beautiful, but she was downcast, and I could not help feeling sad as I watched her face with the tracks of tears visible down the center of both cheeks.

"If the bomb-throwers mean to keep us from living our daily lives, they are sure to be disappointed," mama said, reaching into her deep knitting bag and bringing out a ball of grey wool with her knitting needles protruding from it.

"I for one mean to go on with my daily tasks, one of which is to finish this balaclava so that it can go on sale at the next charity auction."

"Which of your charities is it this time?" Grandma Minnie asked witheringly. "The Widows of German Wars, or the Queen Victoria Memorial Fund?"

"Mama—" papa began weakly, but broke off.

I got up and went to sit beside mama. "Let me wind your wool, mama. I hope you will teach me to knit one of these days. And I think your charities are good. They help people." I looked, as pointedly as I could, at Grandma Minnie as I said this. I heard Olga begin to snicker.

"Why don't we start a new charity, the Naughty Little Girls' Good Posture Fund?"

It was a threat. Grandma Minnie was threatening to make me wear the hated steel brace for even more hours every day. I burst into tears.

"Tania, Tania, what is it?" my father said, and mama echoed him, "Taniushka, what is upsetting you?"

"I can't tell you. She made me promise not to."

"Who made you promise? What on earth is this about?" I didn't answer. "You must tell me, Tania." I could never resist my father, I could hear the concern in his voice.

I sniffed, looked over at Grandma Minnie and slowly raised my hand, pointing with one finger in her direction.

"It is impolite to point, Tatiana," Grandma Minnie said sharply. "I have told you that a hundred times, and so has your governess."

Now my father stood up, and confronted Grandma Minnie. "Just what is going on? Have the courtesy to tell me."

Grandma Minnie shrugged and turned away. "Your daughter is impudent. And she slouches."

Ignoring this response, my father continued to question his mother. "What can't she tell me?"

There was no response from Grandma Minnie. The tension in the room rose. Eventually Ella got up from her chair, came over to me, and took my hand.

"We're going to go for a walk," she said quietly and led me out of the room and into the greenhouse, with its fresh smell and array of blooming, green-leaved plants. We walked there for a time, in silence. Eventually we came to a bench and Ella sat down. I sat beside her.

"When I was a little girl," she said, "and I was upset about something, my mother always took me for a walk. It helped. Now, are you ready to talk about what is upsetting you so?"

"If I tell I'll be punished."

"By your grandmother?"

"Yes."

"But I imagine she didn't make you promise not to tell me, only your parents. Am I right? After all, she didn't know that I would be here."

"Yes. She said, if you tell your mama or your papa about this I will make you wear it twice as long."

"Wear what?"

"The contraption."

"What contraption?"

"I don't know the name of it. Sedynov straps me into it nearly every day, and I have to wear it for four hours. Or more."

A look of consternation passed across Ella's lovely features.

"Where is this contraption now?"

"In a closet in the nursery."

"Show it to me."

"Do you promise to protect me if Grandma Minnie punishes me?"

"Yes. Never doubt it. And I have a feeling Grandma Minnie won't be given a chance to punish you any more after today."

I took Ella up to the nursery and showed her where Sedynov kept the horrid device with the steel rod and leather straps. I described my torture with the thing strapped to my back.

Aunt Ella said only one word: "Barbaric!" She left me there in the nursery, under Niuta's eye, and went out.

Nothing more was ever said about the horrid contraption, but the next time I dared to look in the nursery closet it was gone, and I was never punished for telling Aunt Ella about it, and from then on, I noticed, Grandma Minnie hardly ever came into the nursery and I was free.

Five

After Uncle Gega died my father smoked a lot and stroked his beard a lot and went for long walks by himself on the small island in the lake at Tsarskoe Selo that we call the Children's Island. The woods are thick there, it is a good place to hide. He stayed there for hours at a time, even though I heard Grandma Minnie say he was keeping his ministers waiting and failing to meet with the messengers who were constantly bringing him bad news about the war, the rioting and the bomb-throwers.

Poor papa! Mama was always telling us to pray for him as he had a heavy burden to bear. I know he was worried about Alexei's safety. He had Alexei's nursemaids put him to sleep in a different room every night and a doll was put in his golden cradle in the first floor nursery, to take his place in case there was an attack.

How could papa help feeling worried when every day big heavy bags full of telegrams were delivered to his study, telegrams from all over the world, more than any one man could ever possibly read, let alone answer.

"I know what they all say," he would remark as more and more bags were brought in. "I don't have to read them. They are full of criticisms. 'Give up your crown,' they say. 'Give Russia to the people.' But if I did step down, would the Russian people be able to govern themselves? I think not."

Each day more bags were delivered, and each night, Niuta told me, she saw them loaded into a cart along with the night soil and dumped into the Fontanka Canal.

Sometimes papa could forget all his worries and be very silly, especially with Uncle Sandro. He and Sandro liked to chase each other around the room or wrestle like boys or push each other off the sofa, laughing and punching each other. But Uncle Sandro was frightened too, in those hard days after Uncle Gega died, and Aunt Xenia his wife was frightened along with him. I heard them talking to papa and mama about their yacht, and their plan to sail her to Greece and live there.

"Leave Russia!" I heard Papa say. "Never. Only a coward would leave." But despite his bold words he still hid on the Children's Island, and young as I was then, I could see fear in his eyes.

We had a new tutor just then, Monsieur Pierre Gilliard, who gave us lessons in French and history and told us wonderful stories about places he had been and things he had seen. He was a serious man, and when I was little I thought him very wise. His dark grey suits and striped ties worn with a stickpin, his knowing light brown eyes and thick brown beard gave him the air of a professor, which he had once been. He spoke French and German with us, though he only knew a little Russian. He read plays to us, taking all the parts, and he even wrote plays himself.

On the first day he came to Tsarskoe Selo and mama brought him into the nursery to meet us, I offered to take him to see the elephant.

His eyes brightened at this suggestion, and I took his hand and we all went together, even little Anastasia, to the zoo in the park near the Children's Island where the sad old beast lived in his own elephant house. My younger sisters' nurse went with us.

No one could remember how long the elephant had been at Tsarskoe Selo, but it was said he had been brought from India as a gift to papa's grandfather. He was very shaggy and dusty—he liked to shoot dust out of his trunk high up into the air and let it fall down his back—and the water in his small pond was always dirty and smelly.

"Do you know where India is?" Monsieur Gilliard asked us after he had gazed at the animal for a few minutes.

"I know!" Olga said. "It is right below China, and above Australia."

"Capital, Olga, capital!" He liked this English expression, and used it often, rubbing his hands together.

"And can you tell me something about India, Tatiana?"

"I know there are elephants there, and tigers. Papa shot a tiger in India once."

"No he didn't. That was Uncle Vladimir."

Monsieur Gilliard ignored Olga's interruption. "And what of the climate, Tatiana? Is it very hot there, in India, do you think?"

I shrugged. I didn't know.

"Silly, of course it is very hot there. It is all desert. No one can live there in the summer."

Monsieur Gilliard was peering into the elephant's enclosure. The dusty elephant was shaking his head and stamping one foot.

"I imagine he must be very cold, here in Russia. He is used to lots of hot sun. And I imagine he is very lonely." He lowered his voice as he spoke.

"I like him," Marie said loudly, almost shouting. "I want to ride him!" She ran up to the bars of the enclosure and, grasping them, began shaking them.

"Marie!" The nurse pulled her back from the ironwork and chided her.

Monsieur Gilliard continued to talk to us, very naturally and pleasantly, for half an hour before we went in to tea. We warmed to him, and our French improved, listening to him speak, though we all began to speak French the way the Swiss do and not the way the Parisians do.

It was Monsieur Gilliard who explained to us, briefly and in a way Olga and I could understand, why we had to stay at Tsarskoe Selo and why everyone was so frightened. He told us about the defeat of our Russian fleet and the shameful way some of the sailors behaved, rising up and rebelling against their captains and even murdering some of them. He talked in a calm, reasonable way about these terrible events, and he made us see them as part of history rather than as sudden, shocking blows to our dear Russia.

"Nearly anything can be understood," he said reflectively, "provided it is seen in the light of history. We are all a part of history, we add to it every day."

I thought of this on the day papa was about to leave Tsarskoe Selo to ride at the head of a cavalry parade in Petersburg. He wore the green trousers and red and gold jacket of the Grozny Hussars, and was mounted on a splendid prancing roan. We all came out onto the terrace of the palace to watch him as he took his place at the head of a mass of mounted riders, even mama, who was having trouble walking as her leg was very sore.

Just as the gates were opening to let the horsemen out, with my father leading them, a messenger arrived on a lathered horse, panting and shouting.

The riders halted, and for a few moments we continued to stand and watch, not knowing what was happening. Then we saw the great iron gates swing shut, and papa turned his horse and rode at a gallop back toward the stables.

Later we learned that the messenger had brought a warning, from one of the ministers. The bomb-throwers were waiting along the parade route. They had three carts loaded with bombs. They meant to kill papa.

"A hellish plot!" Grandma Minnie said. "A wicked, hellish plot!"

Still later, at dinner, we learned that they had thrown their bombs, but that only one man, the old doorman at the Mariinsky Hotel, was killed.

Papa knew him, he had often been taken to the hotel as a child, and remembered him. I saw papa walking on the Children's Island at twilight and gathering lilies of the valley, and I knew that he was thinking of the poor old man and it made me sad.

"Children!" mama said to us the following morning, her smile bright, "I have something to show you." She held up a small icon, painted in bold colors and with a thick gold frame. "A wise starets—a holy man—from Pokrovsky has sent papa this wonderworking icon of St. Simon Verkhoturie. It was this icon that saved his life yesterday. It will protect him from now on."

She carefully hung the icon on the wall, and nodded to a servant to light the candle beneath it. We all knelt and prayed for papa's safety. Monsieur Gilliard's words came back to me as I knelt there. We are all a part of history. We add to it every day. What, I wondered, would the next day bring, and the next?

Six

It was just after we returned from our summer cruise aboard our yacht, the *Standart*, that I first met Daria.

For a month and more we had been cruising in calm Baltic waters, winding in and out among the small islands off the Finnish coast, the weather fair and warm, the winds soft. We went ashore and waded along the rocky shoreline, our skirts tucked up under our belts, our petticoats wet and bedraggled, trying to catch fish with our nets while papa shot at ravens and sea birds and looked out across the water through his binoculars.

Mama, who was always at her most relaxed and at ease on our yacht, sat in her deck chair with a warm shawl around her legs and took pictures of us all, now smiling when we posed for her, now growing cross with us when we made faces or turned our backs to the lens. Anastasia ran up and down the deck too quickly to be photographed at all, and Marie stuck out her tongue at the camera and then tried to climb the ropes and the mast.

Those were carefree days, except that mama and papa were always watching Alexei, looking for signs that he was bleeding again. His left leg stuck out all the time, he could never bend his knee because there was too much blood inside it. He couldn't really walk, so he hobbled, but then he fell down a lot so one of the sailors, a big sturdy one called Derevenko, had to carry him. Mama took a lot of pictures of Derevenko on the yacht with Alexei in his arms.

It was just after we got back to Tsarskoe Selo, as I said, that I met Daria for the first time.

Niuta was removing my slippers to have them cleaned when a kitchen maid came into the nursery and handed her a note. She read it and put it in her pocket. I saw at once that whatever was in the note alarmed her.

She handed my soiled slippers to a waiting valet and hurriedly put new ones on my feet.

"Come!" she said, taking my hand. "We're going to the kitchens."

I was pleased at first, thinking she was going to offer me a treat—some freshly baked pastries, or a jam roll of the kind mama loved or perhaps a tart—but instead we went right through the furnace-hot palace bakery without stopping and on down the stone steps into a pantry lined with shelves full of jars and pots and cans.

In one corner was a young girl crouching as if in fear, her face black with soot and her clothes grey rags covered in soot and ash. She clutched a basket. Inside the basket was a small dog, its fur as black with soot as its mistress.

"Daria!"

Niuta ran to the girl, helped her to her feet and put her arms around her.

"Dariushka! What happened to you?"

"Fire," the girl said, her voice little more than a whisper. "Fire all around."

"Where?"

"The factory. All the factories." She choked and coughed. "So many people—all running—the police chasing us—" She broke off, unable to speak further.

"There there, I'll take care of you now."

Niuta turned to me. "Tania, dear, would you please be so good as to go back to the bakery and get some wet cloths and a few rolls and a glass of tea for my little sister?"

"Your sister?"

"This is my sister, Daria. Daria, this is the Grand Duchess Tatiana."

"How do you do," I said politely. The girl glanced at me suspiciously, and gave me the barest nod.

Of course I thought the situation very odd, because I was never asked to do such menial tasks and it was unheard-of for servants to bring their relatives into the palace. Still, Niuta was someone I loved and trusted, for she was my mother's principal dresser and was often in the nursery and I had known her all my life, and her sister was obviously in need of help. I went into the bakery and asked if I might have some rolls and some tea. While the food was being brought I found some cloths covering fresh loaves of bread and dipped them in a pan of water. Then I took everything back down the stone steps into the pantry.

"Thank you, Tania. I think you ought to go back to the nursery now."

"I want to stay. I want to help."

"You? The tsar's daughter? You want to help me?" Daria's voice was hoarse and accusatory as she tried to talk. Niuta handed her the glass of tea I had brought and she took a long swallow.

"Yes. Why shouldn't I?"

Daria spat.

"Do you know who set the fire that nearly killed me? Your father's police, that's who."

"Why would they do that?" I wanted to know.

Daria had begun wolfing down the rolls I had brought, and feeding some to the dog, who gobbled up the floury morsels she held out to him as if he hadn't eaten in days.

"Because we're on strike," she said with her mouth nearly full.

"Daria is employed at the Phoenix metalworking plant," Niuta explained. "All the workers there are on strike."

"All the factory workers in Petersburg are on strike," Daria said with some vehemence after she swallowed what was left of her roll. "We want fair wages. We don't want to work sixteen hours a day, until we drop from weariness or walk into the machinery and die."

She drank her tea and rubbed her swollen eyelids, then went on.

"It started in the Shchukin Arcade. A big fire. The police did it. My friend saw them. They put a torch to some old dry wood, and threw on some rags to make it burn faster."

Fear came into the girl's eyes as she went on, reliving the terror of what she had seen and experienced.

"It was like hell, the flames of hell. The heat! The smell of all the burning wood! The screaming! So much screaming!

" 'The plant's going up,' I heard a man say. It was the rubber plant not far from us. We smelled the tires burning. That's when they unlocked the doors and let us all out."

"You mean you were locked in?"

Daria looked at me with contempt.

"We are always locked in. Aren't cattle always locked in, to keep them from running away?

"Everybody began running," she resumed after a moment. "I was thrown against the wall. I was lucky. Some people got trampled."

"Did no one try to help you? Not the police or the soldiers? They must have tried to help the women at least—" I began, but Daria's glare silenced me.

"She is too young to understand," Niuta said to her sister. "We mustn't speak of this any more now."

"No, no. I want to understand. I want to know," I insisted.

"What if she tells somebody?" Daria asked Niuta, suddenly fearful. "You'll be put in prison."

"I don't think so. The empress has always been kind to me."

"Except when she yells at you," I put in, for mama did get very excited and angry at times and shouted at the servants. "Remember when you forgot to lock the lace cabinet that time."

"Great ladies forget themselves sometimes," Niuta said archly. "It is overlooked."

Daria's little dog gave a sharp bark and Niuta looked around the pantry warily.

"Keep him quiet! We don't want anyone coming in and finding you here." As she spoke Niuta handed her sister one of the wet cloths I had brought. "Here, wash your face and hands. I'll try to get some of this soot off your clothes. Then I'll take you upstairs."

In a few moments, as I watched, Daria was transformed from a grimy factory worker into a round-faced peasant girl, her colorful red kerchief rinsed out and replaced over her fair hair, her complexion sallow but still with a hint of freshness from the countryside. The change in her appearance was striking, but there was no change, I noticed, in her eyes. They were filled with hostility, fear and deep distrust.

Niuta began brushing the soot and ash from Daria's full skirts and then cried out.

"By all the saints! You're pregnant!"

Daria held her head up proudly. "What if I am? I can have a child if I choose!"

Niuta crossed herself. "But Daria, you're so very young, and you have no husband!"

"I was going to have one, until the Cossacks cut him to bits!" For the first time I saw her eyes fill with tears, though her hoarse voice remained raised, her tone defiant.

"It was the day we went on strike," she went on. "We marched, thousands of us, down Schlüsselburg Road past the factories and mills. We were singing. We joined hands. We felt so strong that morning! Then we heard them coming. Hundreds of them, Cossacks on big horses, riding toward us with their swords up, and yelling as they came. My Sasha stood up against them, but they cut his head open. He fell down and never got up."

I listened, horrified but at the same time intrigued. I was ashamed of myself for being so interested in such dreadful events.

"We were going to go home to Pokrovsky and get married. Instead I am a widow before I even became a wife! And I'm going to have Sasha's baby!"

Niuta helped her trembling sister back up the steps and I brought along the little dog in his basket. Daria was sheltered, temporarily, in Niuta's tiny attic room—all mama's personal servants slept in the attic—and was given work in the ironing room, the vast workroom where dozens of servants ironed mama's gowns and removed and ironed their yards of trimmings.

Later, after Niuta and I had returned to the nursery, she sat me down and talked to me seriously.

"Tania, I trust you not to say anything to anyone, not even your mother and father, about what you have seen and heard today."

I readily gave my word, sensing that I had been entrusted with a glimpse into a world I had never known existed, and feeling privileged that Niuta trusted me.

"I love my baby sister, but she can be very difficult. We came here from Pokrovsky together and were helped by a priest to get work. I have been very content. Your mother is a good mistress even if she does get angry sometimes. But Daria chose to work in the factory and has been angry and unhappy ever since. I wish she had been able to marry and go back home."

"I have been saving my pocket money," I said. "If I gave it to her, could she go back home?"

Niuta smiled. "You are a kind girl, Tania. But I'm afraid it would cost much more than you have to send her back. And I'm not certain she would go. But at least, for the time being, she will be all right. Once her baby is born, however, everything will change. I don't know what she'll do then."

That night after Olga and I had taken our baths in our silver tub, the hot bath water scented with oil of almonds, I longed to tell Olga about Daria, and especially about what she had said about the police starting a fire and attacking and killing the striking workers. Was it possible? Were my father's proud, handsome Cossack regiments murdering people? Or were they merely keeping order? Surely order had to be preserved.

Troublesome thoughts preyed on my mind when I tried to sleep, and I tossed and turned in my uncomfortable camp bed.

"In the name of all the saints, Tania, stop your thrashing!" Olga snapped. I heard her pounding her pillow. "I'm going to ask papa if I can have my own room!"

Seven

"Mama, can I have my own room?"

I stood watching my mother dress, putting on her pink and white lace corset and looking at her reflection in the high triple mirror while Niuta and Elizaveta tied the corset tightly around her waist. The dressing room was full of the scent of verbena, mixed with the perfume of the rose petals that floated in mama's bath water. The tables and chairs in the large, open room were draped with silk stockings, filmy net petticoats, dozens of pairs of slippers for mama's rather large feet, and four gowns from the fashionable couturier Lamanov.

"Which gown will you have, Your Highness?" Shoura, mama's pretty, auburn-haired second dresser, held up a lavender silk gown with a bodice of purple velvet and full sleeves. "This one suits you very well."

Mama took the gown and held it up against herself, twisting this way and that so that the skirt swung from side to side.

"Mama—" I said again.

"In a minute, Tania."

Dropping the lavender gown, which fell to the floor in a heap, she pointed to a pale yellow gown draped over a satin-lined basket. Niuta lifted the delicate creation and brought it to her. Once again mama held the gown up against herself and scrutinized the effect in the triple mirror.

"I never could wear yellow," she muttered. "Only brunettes can wear yellow. Lamanov was wrong."

"Your Highness is beautiful in gowns of all colors," said Elizaveta, youngest of the dressers and the one who fumbled the most with buttons and hooks and ribbon ties.

"Nonsense," said mama brusquely. "Bring me the mauve."

Mauve was mama's favorite color and I was not surprised when she chose to wear the mauve gown, with its girlish white lace trim and its chaste high neck. The three dressers set about fastening mama into the beautifully made bodice and skirt.

"I know what they're all going to say when they see me in this. Oh yes, I know. I can just hear them all, that domineering Minnie, and fat old Miechen, and Xenia—oh yes! Xenia has her spiteful side!—and all the others.

"Stuffy Englishwoman! That's what they call me. Stiff, prissy Englishwoman!"

She took a cigarette from an ivory box on a nearby table and Elizaveta lit it for her. The stink of tobacco replaced the perfume of verbena and roses.

"Mama, I really need my own room. Olga asked papa for her own room, so can I please have my own too?"

"Tania, you can see that I am trying to get ready for my reception. I have never before given a reception of my own, Minnie has never allowed it, and this is very important. Everyone is invited, not only the family but all the people who count. All those snobs who go to the ballet every Sunday and to the theater every Saturday and dine out at the Bear and that den of vice that calls itself a Cuban restaurant."

"But mama, it will only take a minute for you to say yes or no."

"Not now. Right now I have other things on my mind."

Niuta brought a pair of mauve satin slippers and held them out to mama.

"How many times do I have to tell you, Niuta, I can't bear satin shoes! They worry me too much! Bring the suede ones, the comfortable ones.

"There, that's better," she said as she sat down and slipped on the scuffed shoes. "Now they can say, 'There goes the stuffy Englishwoman with the frumpy shoes!'"

I had to laugh at that, and even Shoura and Niuta smiled. Elizaveta had begun dressing mama's hair and mama was smoking her second cigarette when one of her ladies came in.

"Your Highness, Dr. Korovin is asking for you in the nursery. The tsarevich is ill again."

With a swiftness that startled me Mama jumped from her chair and hurried out into the corridor and down the stairs and along the hallways that led to my brother's nursery. I ran after her. She limped on her sore leg but half-walked, half-ran very quickly despite her limp.

We could hear Alexei screaming far down the corridor. His screams when in pain were heart-wrenching: loud, piteous cries that went on and on for hours, until he lost his voice and could only utter hoarse sobs. Judging from the sound, he hadn't been in pain very long. Mama rushed into the nursery and stood beside Alexei's small bed, murmuring to him and feeling his pale forehead with her hand. I stood beside her, wishing there was something—anything—I could do.

"Tell me what happened," she said to the flustered, frightened Dr. Korovin.

"There was nothing. He did not fall or injure himself. It was very sudden. He just yelled 'my back!' and then began crying, then screaming."

Papa, looking very distracted, came in and stood beside us, watching the screaming Alexei, whose pain was so great that he took no notice of us and drew no comfort from our presence.

"For God's sake, is there nothing you can do?" papa shouted to Dr. Korovin over the bedlam.

"I can summon my colleagues from Petersburg, as I did last time, but they would have nothing new to suggest. Nothing has any effect, not hot packs or cold packs, not mustard plasters or leeches. I regret to have to tell you this, Your Imperial Highness, but medical science can do nothing for your son."

As the doctor spoke, Alexei's screams seemed to become louder and more urgent and mama's face got very red.

"Get out!" she shouted to Dr. Korovin. "If you can do nothing, then leave the room this instant!"

With a disparaging glance at mama, the physician bowed and walked out of the room, his two assistants following him, leaving only the medical orderly behind.

Papa put his hands over his ears and turned aside, away from Alexei and his pitiful cries.

Mama grasped papa's arm. "What about that healer from Pokrovsky, the one who sent you the icon of St. Simon Verkhoturie?" She practically had to shout to make papa hear her.

He turned toward her, bemused. "We know nothing of him."

"They say he can bewitch the blood."

"What's that?" I asked, but no one heard me.

Mama continued to tug on papa's arm until he cried out in exasperation.

"Oh, very well, send for him! Send for whomever you like! I'm going to my study." He wrenched his arm away from mama's strong grip and walked swiftly out of the room.

Mama beckoned to Sedynov, who stood nearby, and told him to fetch the Siberian and gave him the man's address.

"How is it that you know where to find this man, mama?"

"He left his card, when he brought papa the icon."

"But you have no card now, at this moment."

"I remembered the address. I thought we might need this man's help one day. After all, his icon saved papa's life."

Sedynov went out and then returned almost at once, a look of astonishment on his ruddy, wrinkled face.

"Your Highness," he said, "the man is already here, in the palace. He is on his way to you now."

A murmur passed through the room. I heard whispers of "How did he know to come here?" "What is he doing here?" "Who is this man?"

Suddenly I felt a change in the room. A ripple of calm, a sweetness. I cannot describe it otherwise. Everyone felt it. The servants stopped talking and fussing around Alexei's crib. Mama stopped her eternal fidgeting and became quite still. The medical orderly who never left Alexei's side, and who was a very religious man, dropped to his knees and bowed his head. And Alexei, who had been screaming without interruption, whimpered and sobbed a little, and then was still also.

There came into the room a most extraordinary man. He was dressed like a peasant, in a long black coat, shiny from much wear. His hair was long and unkempt, greying at the temples, and his beard was in need of combing. He wore no adornment save a large copper cross on a leather

34

thong around his neck. But his face was unlike any other I have ever seen. It seemed lit from within, radiant with a faint glow. I could not take my eyes from his face. His eyes, a soft grey color, sparkled with life and with an almost palpable force.

He brought something into the room with him, something for which none of us had a name. Something that drew us and held us in its warm, benign embrace.

"No sorrow!" he said as he came in, lifting his hand in benediction. "All sorrow forgotten! Only the joy of the day!"

He went to Alexei's crib and stood over it, smiling and shaking his head.

"No more, no more," he said softly, fingering the simple copper cross he wore around his neck, looking down into Alexei's tear-stained face.

Alexei blinked rapidly, then stretched out one small hand toward the stranger, who grasped it and said, in old-fashioned language, "Be thou whole, little wayfarer!" And he began humming to himself. After a moment Alexei, soothed by the sound, slowly closed his eyes and went to sleep.

"Tomorrow he will be whole again."

Mama broke the stillness in the room by saying to the stranger, "How can we thank you?"

"By being good to one another. By loving one another."

"How did you know to come here today?"

He shook his head. "I try to go where I am needed. Where I am led."

"You are the starets, the holy man, are you not? The one that sent my husband the icon of St. Simon?"

He nodded. "My name is Novy. In my village I am called God's rascal. The naughty one. Rasputin." His face changed. He looked distracted. "You have a pain in your leg," he said to mama, using the old-fashioned "thee" and "thy."

She nodded.

"Sit," the stranger commanded.

Mama sat down on the sofa.

He stood before her, and once again I felt the curious sensation of a change in the room. I said to myself, he is summoning his powers.

"Be thou whole, wayfarer!" he said to mama, who clutched her trembling leg. Then, humming to himself, the stranger turned and walked out of the room, ignoring the hands that reached out to touch him as he passed.

The next day, as the stranger who called himself Novy predicted, Alexei's pain was gone though he was not cured of the bleeding disease. Mama, on the other hand, still had her sore leg and was in a bad temper. The reception she had held the night before, which she had arranged with such care, and to which she had invited all her in-laws and much of Petersburg society, was a spectacular failure.

No one attended. When the hour came for the reception to begin, Mama stood in her beautiful mauve gown at the center of the grand salon, the room decorated with flowers sent all the way from the Riviera, the tables laden with delicacies and wines, punch and cakes. Dozens of white-gloved valets in spotless livery stood waiting to serve the hundreds of expected guests. The orchestra played. The tall ornate doors of the salon stood open. But not a single person came through them.

Ten minutes passed, then twenty. After half an hour mama, her face and hands beet red, her mouth set in a grim line, held out her arm to the nearest valet and was escorted out of the room.

It was Aunt Xenia who told mama why no one had come to her reception. Grandma Minnie had held a reception of her own at the very same hour and had insisted that the entire court attend. And because mama was disliked, and Grandma Minnie was feared, everyone had obeyed her.

I felt very sad for mama, watching from my perch high up on the balcony on the day of her reception, hidden from view. I imagined how angry she must be—and yet, at the same time, how happy she must feel about Alexei and his encounter with the remarkable Siberian healer. What was one failed reception when compared to the hope that my brother might not have to suffer any more, the hope that he might survive?

Eight

There was a violent thunderstorm on the night the entire family gathered in the malachite banqueting hall to dine and watch *The Pride of Messina*, KR's new play. KR was my father's cousin, Grand Duke Constantine, but no one ever called him anything but KR, not even Olga and I. As a mark of honor KR was seated to my father's right at the head of the long banqueting table, and he preened and gloated throughout the dinner, lifting his glass again and again to offer toasts, telling jokes, talking loudly to papa and winking and flirting with the women and girls, especially my sister Olga, who was just then being considered as a bride for the Crown Prince of Romania and was feeling very grown-up and special, though she was only fourteen years old.

Thunder rumbled like cannonfire and rain beat against the tall windows as course after course of tantalizing entrees was brought in: shrimp bisque and Cassolettes Pompadour, Loire trout braised in sauternes, lamb fillet and roast bartavels and ortolans garnished with truffles. Each course had its own wines, and the longer the dining went on, and the more wine was drunk, the louder and more expansive the family became.

There must have been at least twenty of us around the table that night, if memory serves, papa and KR and Olga, Marie and I (mama was not present, she hated dining with Grandma Minnie and held a grudge against her for causing the failure of her grand reception) but not

Anastasia or Alexei, they were too young, Grandma Minnie presiding at the far end of the table, Uncle Vladimir and Auntie Miechen, Aunt Xenia and Uncle Sandro, and old Uncle Bembo, looking sour because he disliked KR's fanciful plays and thought them unworthy of a Romanov.

Aunt Olenka was there—she had a role in KR's play and did not stay through dessert, having to go and put on her costume and makeup— along with her husband Petya, who everyone said in hushed tones was no husband to her and who ate very daintily and picked at his food.

Aunt Olenka could be very jolly when she chose to be, she was my favorite aunt though I loved Aunt Ella very much too for her kindness and goodness. Aunt Olenka was my father's youngest sister and unlike his other sister Xenia, Olenka was quite plain, with buck teeth and large ears that stood out from her head and a somewhat ratlike face. She was a large, rather shapeless woman with an impish smile and a taste for elegant, costly clothes, especially furs. No one in the family had furs like Aunt Olenka's, not even Grandma Minnie. Mama said it was wicked to spend so much money on furs when so many in Petersburg were poor and cold all winter long, but she never said it was wicked to spend money on diamonds (which, after all, cost much more than furs) and she herself had a ring with an enormous pink diamond that Niuta said must have cost a king's ransom.

As a rule Olenka spoke up a lot at family dinners and laughed a lot too, but on this night she was unusually quiet, probably because only a few days earlier she had suffered a great shock and had a lucky escape from death. She was riding with Petya in their brand new automobile. At that time automobiles were a rarity in Petersburg, only a few very rich people had them. My father was suspicious of mechanical things and still drove a carriage and I heard him say to mama more than once that automobiles were just a dangerous fad and would soon pass and everyone would go back to using only horses.

But Aunt Olenka and Petya always had to have the newest and latest thing and Petya boasted that his automobile went at the unheard-of speed of thirty versts an hour. However, Petya was a poor driver—so Grandma Minnie told everyone—and the roads were very poor in those days as well, muddy and rutted and full of deep holes, so it may be that the accident wasn't really Petya's fault. At any rate, the car was speeding down a narrow road through the forest and it smashed into a tree.

Everyone at the banquet table that night knew about the accident, but no one was talking about it. Instead they were just staring rudely at Olenka and Petya while talking of other things. Meanwhile the thunder was pounding and roaring and the rain continued to lash against the windows, and once or twice I saw Grandma Minnie wince when a loud crack was heard overhead followed by a furious burst of rain.

Presently Aunt Xenia spoke up, teasing my sister.

"Tell us, Olga, when is the Romanian crown prince coming to visit us?" Olga blushed.

"I hear he is eager to get married—very eager—and that he has his eye on a certain Russian grand duchess." Laughter followed this remark.

"Well," said Olga, putting down her fork, aware that all eyes were on her, "I believe it is time he got married. He is twenty-four. Or is it twenty-five?"

"Nothing is concluded yet," papa said. "There is plenty of time to consider what is best—not only for Olga but for all my children."

"Is he handsome, Olga, this crown prince of yours?"

"I have heard that he is."

"Hah! Then he won't take her. Her forehead is too high," said Grandma Minnie. "And she is too much of a know-it-all." In fact Olga was very good at her lessons, very clever. Monsieur Gilliard was pleased with her.

"I am very proud of Olga's intelligence and good sense," papa said, smiling at Olga. "You know that, mother."

"But Tatiana is prettier," put in KR. "Just like the ingénue in my play. A true Russian rose, a Red Maid. Why, in the second act of *The Bride of Messina*—"

"We don't want to hear about it!" Uncle Bembo snapped. "It's bad enough we have to sit through the damnable play!"

"Olga!" Auntie Miechen suddenly cried, "throw your slipper!"

It was a traditional game played by peasant girls. They threw their slippers over one shoulder, and then looked to see what letter the fallen slippers formed. That letter was thought to be the initial of their future husband's Christian name.

Olga looked over at papa, who shrugged as if to say, do it if you like, it doesn't matter to me.

What happened next happened so quickly, and was so unexpected, that it took us all by surprise. Olga removed her slippers, stood with her back to the table, and threw the slippers over her left shoulder.

One landed in Grandma Minnie's plate and the other overturned her wineglass, splashing red wine all over the front of her pale blue velvet gown and making her shriek with vexation.

"Oh you wicked, wicked girl! See what you've done! It's all your horrid mother's fault, raising you with no rules, no morals, no reverence for anything or anyone—"

"Mother!" papa said, "you forget yourself! I suggest you go and change your gown and take some of your Quiet Drops. Olga, apologize to your grandmother."

"If she will apologize to me for what she said about my forehead, and my being a know-it-all," Olga replied staunchly. At that moment, I have to say, I felt proud of my sister. And as if in response to the confrontation in the room, a powerful crack of thunder broke over our heads and rolled on for a long minute.

Sighing and shaking his head, papa stood, looking down the long table. "Can't we have peace and order within our family, at least, even if we have nothing but disorder and violence in the world at large? Can't we come together as a family, in love, and support each other? Not so long ago Uncle Serge was among us, and now he is gone, blown to bits by a bomb. I have been shot at and threatened by bomb-throwers. We all know what it is to live in fear and uncertainty. Let us join hands and exchange a kiss of peace, and forget our petty quarrels."

He reached out and grasped KR's hand on his right, and Uncle Sandro's on his left. One by one the rest of us did as he asked, until everyone around the table was linked to everyone else. Then we each reached over to kiss the cheek of those to our right and left. I kissed old Uncle Vladimir and Petya, and heard KR cry out, "Long live the house of Romanov!"

I will always remember that moment, the candlelit dining room, the gilded mirrors and shining silver and gold-rimmed plates, the white linen and bowls of flowers, the gleaming columns of rich green malachite around the walls, the sound of the thunder and the pounding rain.

Papa gave the order for the stage at one end of the room to be illuminated and led us to our seats to watch KR's play. I got up to leave the table but as I did so I glanced at Grandma Minnie's place, and at Olga's slippers. They had fallen into a neat "V." Would she marry someone whose name began with V? If so, I thought, then there will be no betrothal to the crown prince of Romania, whose name, I had heard mama say, was Carel.

Nine

There was a great deal of food left over from the banquet, and I asked Sedynov to go down to the kitchens and put together a hamper of leftovers. Together we took the hamper up to the ironing workroom where I hoped to find Niuta's sister Daria. Though it was long past midnight the room was brightly lit and several dozen women were hunched over their ironing boards, pushing heavy irons across lengths of fabric and lace. The ironers never stopped working, Niuta had told me. When some of them left to eat or rest, others were always waiting to take their places. The irons were kept hot, and the gowns, petticoats and yards and yards of trim kept arriving to be ironed, at all hours of the day and night.

I found Daria at once as she was wearing the same bright red head scarf she had on the day she came to the palace fleeing the fire. She was startled to see me, yet her look of surprise quickly turned to suspicion as she took note of my pale green silk gown and carefully arranged hair, tied back off my face with a green silk ribbon. Around my neck were the gleaming pearls mama had given me on my birthday. I looked like someone who had just come from a sumptuous banquet or a lavish party, as indeed I had.

The other ironers, seeing me, curtseyed and stood back from their boards, as a sign of respect. But Daria set her heavy iron down noisily in its metal cradle and stood where she was, confronting me.

"What are you doing here?" she demanded.

"See here, girl!" cried Sedynov angrily. "Remember who you are addressing! This is the Grand Duchess Tatiana!" He moved toward her, as if to strike her or grab her arm.

"No, Sedynov," I said. "Daria and I know each other. She is fully aware of who I am."

"Then why isn't she showing you respect?"

"For the same reason she chose to work in a factory rather than at the palace when she first came to Petersburg. She disapproves of my father and his government."

"And who is she to disapprove? A girl, nothing but a girl. A girl whose husband cannot provide for her, by the look of things. If he could, she would not be here, she would be at home, in her kitchen, or in the nursery." His eyes swept Daria's figure, pausing at her bulging belly. Sedynov rarely said very much. His sharp words surprised me, though his fierce loyalty did not.

Daria turned toward Sedynov. "I have no husband," she said. "I had a fiancé, but the tsar's Cossacks killed him."

"No doubt he deserved it," Sedynov replied with a sneer. "That wouldn't happen to be a bomb under your skirt and not a baby, would it?"

At this the other ironers shrieked and ran for the door. Before I could try to stop him Sedynov had grabbed Daria and begun squeezing her belly. She cried out in pain.

"How dare you! Stop that! You're hurting my child!"

Sedynov shrugged and let Daria go. "We can't trust anyone, not any more," he said. "Only the other day there were twelve bricklayers arrested here at Tsarskoe Selo. Two of them had bombs in their carts instead of bricks."

"Daria," I said, "I've brought you some food. From the banquet my family held tonight. I thought you might want to take it back with you to the quarter where you used to live. Niuta says you have friends there who are in need of food."

With obvious reluctance, Sedynov brought the hamper over and set it down in front of Daria. She barely glanced at it.

"And how many starving workers did you imagine could be fed from that puny basket? Five? Ten, if they took small bites?"

"Isn't it a good thing if even a few are fed?" My voice rose as I spoke, for Daria's rebuke stung me and made me feel both contrite and irritated at the same time.

She did not answer, but picked up her heavy iron and resumed her work. Sedynov moved to pick up the hamper.

"Leave that, Sedynov. She may get hungry in the night."

We approached the door. Just before we reached it I heard Daria's voice.

"If you really want to be of use, bring ten hampers to the milk door of the pantry at dawn. Find the milk woman called Avdokia. She will take them. She will see that they are given out."

"I will if I can," I said, and went through the door Sedynov held open for me.

Only the candles beneath the icons on the walls lit the nursery when I returned to it. The servants had gone to bed, Niuta was presumably in her attic room and only one of the sleepy young maidservants was waiting up to help me undress.

"Wake me at dawn," I told her as she slipped my gown over my head and helped unfasten my petticoats. I asked the weary Sedynov to make up some more hampers and leave them near the milk door.

"It's no use, Your Highness," he said to me. "You cannot do much, no matter how hard you try. There are too many hungry mouths. And this girl, this sister of Niuta's, she is filled with hate."

"Good night, Sedynov," I said politely but dismissively. "Please do what I have asked."

He went, grumbling, and I lay down to get what sleep I could.

I was awakened before dawn and quickly washed my face in the marble basin. As rapidly as I could I put on a peasant costume my father had bought for me the previous summer; he had outfitted all of us in colorful embroidered skirts and vests and flowered blouses from an outdoor market on one of our rare expeditions into the countryside. He had bought himself a pair of bright red pantaloons and a green shirt made of some coarse material. In it he looked every inch the earthy, goodhearted farmer fresh from his sunflower fields. I braided my hair and tied a bright kerchief under my chin, then, doing my best not to wake the sleeping Olga, I slipped out of the room and down into the kitchens and the adjacent pantries.

There was no one in the cool, dim milk pantry, with its big earthenware jars and churns around the walls, and I went to the high wooden double doors and opened them a crack—just wide enough to peer out into the courtyard beyond.

It had been raining, and the black ground was soggy and full of rivulets of dirty water. Puddles here and there reflected the pinkish light in the sky, as birds swooped down to peck at bits of straw, only to rise in a flurry of wings when carts came and went, loaded with baskets and sacks of goods for the palace.

Sedynov had followed my orders and I counted ten hampers stacked just inside the doors of the milk pantry, waiting to be picked up.

Presently a ramshackle cart rolled into the courtyard, pulled by a broken-down speckled grey horse.

"Whoa there, Folya! Not so fast!"

The driver of the cart pulled on the reins and grunted.

"There now, stay there!"

Slowly, so as to accommodate her great girth, she climbed down from the cart and stepped into the mud, her boots sinking deep beneath her. She is as big and tall as a man, I thought, and she has a man's voice too. Yet her broad, ugly face, with its jowly cheeks and large nose, its deepset eyes and small, almost prim mouth was unmistakably a woman's face, and there was just a hint of coquetry in the way her lank thick black hair curled around her ears with their small gold earrings.

Hoisting two large containers of milk out of the cart she stomped rather than walked toward me, splashing through the puddles, completely heedless of the dark splotches the water left on her grimy yellow skirt. When she reached the doors she pushed them open forcefully, nearly knocking me over, and set her burdens down. She hardly gave me a glance, however, before spying the hampers and reaching for them. She took as many as she could carry and, having put them in the cart, came back with more milk.

"Are you Avdokia?" I asked, with a slight tremor in my voice, for she really was formidable, especially to me as I was then, still a child.

"Avdokia Stepanovna Novy," she said in her deep, husky voice, lifting the rest of the hampers and stomping back to her cart.

"Wait! I want to—I want to go with you."

I hadn't planned to say it, indeed I hadn't planned to say anything. Just why I did say it I never knew.

"Daria told me to look for you. To wait for you," I added.

"Daria? You are a friend of my Daria?"

"And of Niuta," I said, only too aware that Daria would certainly not have called me a friend, and that Niuta was my mother's servant.

Avdokia took full notice of me now for the first time, taking in my peasant clothing, my braids and head scarf—and my satin slippers. I owned a pair of felt peasant boots but no leather ones, and so I had simply put on the slippers I had worn to the banquet the previous night.

I saw suspicion in the milkwoman's deepset black eyes, and was aware that she was coming to a decision about me. At last she said, "Get in," and indicated that I should climb up onto the cart with her.

"I will take you to the Vyborg, little daughter," she said. "I will show you things you have never seen before."

Ten

Freight wagons clogged the road as we approached the outskirts of the city, and the air was thick with a choking dust and smoke. I rode in the back of the cart, behind Avdokia's looming form on the driver's seat, and I felt increasingly small and lost amid the slow-moving traffic all around us.

We were in Smokestack Town, as Olga and I called the factory suburbs we had often glimpsed from the windows of the Winter Palace. I had seen Smokestack Town from a distance many times, but had never been near it, nor had I traveled along its narrow streets as I did now, with Avdokia shouting and swearing at the other cart drivers and lashing her broken-down horse with her whip in a vain effort to make him go faster.

There were no fine carriages along these roads, as there were on the broad, wide Nevsky Prospekt on the palace side of the river, and we passed no fine shops or hotels, only row after row of featureless, run-down ugly tenements pressed together, with here and there a tavern or a low house of pleasure, the women displaying themselves in the dingy front window.

There were thin dogs slinking along the streets, and drunks lying along the ditches where a stinking stream of water ran, and here and there a dead horse, covered in flies and blocking the road, that no one had bothered to haul away.

Near the Shchukin market we passed through an area where all the buildings had burned down and only blackened timbers remained. I thought of what Daria had said about the terror of the fire, how the workers locked in the factory had panicked before being released to run outside into the heat and smoke and blazing flames.

Presently we came to a massive building that looked as though it had been partially burned but repaired; the word Phoenix was painted in thick uneven black letters above two massive doors. A dozen or more guards stood at these doors, armed with rifles, and I counted seventeen police and mounted soldiers standing by, watching a milling crowd of ragged-looking people that had gathered in the street, some holding signs that read "Workers Unite" and "Brotherhood." Thick grey ash showered down on us from two tall smokestacks that loomed above the roofline of the building, turning the people in the crowd, the guards, the police and soldiers, even the horses a uniform shade of dull grey.

Avdokia flourished her whip and we passed on, through ever narrower streets where mounds of garbage rotted and human and animal waste were heaped. Where were the nightsoil men, I wondered. Why hadn't they collected all this foul matter, as they did in the streets around the Winter Palace and at Tsarskoe Selo?

The stench was overpowering. I held my nose and tried to tell myself, it's only for a little while. Soon we'll be out of this dreadful place. For the first time I began to feel frightened. What if I never got out? What if I was trapped here, forced to work in a factory the way Daria had, locked in and never released? Would I grow old in this terrible place and die? Would anyone in my family know where to look for me?

Suddenly Avdokia turned the cart sharply and passed under an archway to enter a dingy courtyard. She pulled the weary horse to a stop and got down from the cart, saying "Here we are then" and reaching for several of the hampers, which had become covered in grey ash.

I followed her down a steep set of narrow stone stairs, tottering and nearly falling as there was no handrail to cling to. There was no light to see by either, and as we descended it became harder and harder to discern the steps, though we could hear voices—many voices, some of them raised in sharp argument—and they became louder and louder. Finally we reached the bottom of the steps and, without bothering to knock, Avdokia threw open a heavy wooden door.

Inside was a scene of indescribable squalor. More steps led downward into a filthy room where a few dim candles burned in sconces on the grime-streaked walls. A dozen people stood, some up to their ankles in reeking water, carrying on a loud debate while in an alcove beneath the stairs a man and woman tried to sleep on a narrow cot, a tiny child between them.

I had thought the streets outside nauseatingly foul, but the stench in this dark room was much worse. The sour smell of old cabbage soup mingled with the sickly sweet tang of alcohol and the stink of unwashed bodies and unemptied chamber pots. In one corner of the room a woman was washing clothes in a tin bucket, in another a man smoked a long pipe filled with cheap tobacco of the kind Sedynov favored.

Avdokia stood in the open doorway, holding out several of the full hampers.

"Food!" she shouted. "I have brought food!"

A cry arose, a startled cry of surprise and disbelief.

One of the men, ruddy-cheeked and thick-set, sprang up the stairs clumsily in his wet boots and tried to embrace the milk woman.

"Avdochka, sweet Avdochka, give me a kiss! Uglier than ever, aren't you my girl! Come here!"

"Guard your nuts, Mihailik! I have a knife!"

Both laughed and the man, taking one of the hampers, went back down the stairs as the others crowded around him.

The food was set down on a low bench and all present tore into the hamper greedily, their former talk and argument forgotten. Avdokia went back outside for the rest of the hampers and her goings and comings attracted attention. Soon other residents of the building were swarming into the basement to share in the feast.

I stayed close to Avdokia, who ignored me, and stared at the faces of the people who were devouring the delicious food we had brought. Food from the tsar's table, if only they had known it.

They were grey, haggard faces for the most part, the eyes over-bright with greedy hunger, the cheeks pinched. Of the men, only Mihailik, the one who had spoken to Avdokia, had the filled-out frame of a mature man; the others had the stature and limbs of boys, though their faces showed that they were clearly much older.

"Where's the vodka, Avdokia?" shouted one of the men. "We must have a toast!"

"It's water for you, Drozya. Water is all you deserve!"

"I deserve only the best!"

"Somebody get some water!"

"Here, girl, run upstairs and fetch water!" I felt a pitcher being thrust into my hands. I did not know what to do. In the palace, it was the servants who fetched all the water, I did not know from where.

"Don't just stand there, girl, bring us some water!"

I opened my mouth to speak, but before I could say anything the man who had given me the pitcher was shouting to Avdokia.

"Is this one of yours, Avdokia? I hate to tell you this but she's a bit of a sluggard." He looked at me again. "No, she can't be one of yours. She looks too clean."

Laughter followed this remark and I realized many of the people in the room were looking at me.

"She came with the food," Avdokia said gruffly. "From the palace."

The man next to me bent down toward me, pretending to glower. "Maybe we should roast her then," he growled.

"No. She's too skinny."

I realized I had to say something, but of course I did not want anyone to know who I really was. Besides, I thought, if I tell them I am the tsar's daughter they will only laugh at me again and think I am mad.

"My mother works in the ironing room at the palace—with Daria," I said. "In the palace we are required to bathe at least once a week." I realized that my voice, thin and reedy with nervousness, must sound too prim to be the voice of an ironer's daughter. "I hate the bath," I added insincerely, thinking just the opposite, that I would give anything, at that moment, to be able to step into the silver tub I shared with Olga and smell the almond-scented soap we used.

"Whoever you are, I'm thirsty!"

Avdokia came toward me with a pitcher in her hand and led me out of the apartment and back up the dim stairs to the courtyard where her cart waited. At the far end was a spigot. Above it a sign had been nailed in place. It read: BOIL ALL WATER BEFORE DRINKING.

Avdokia showed me how to turn the spigot on and fill my pitcher, then filled her own.

"Why must the water be boiled?" I asked her.

"By all the saints, what an innocent you are! Surely you know that water makes you sick!"

I did know that a lot of people in Petersburg got sick, thousands and thousands of them, mama said, but from drinking water?

"The people in this building are lucky," Avdokia was telling me. "They can come up here to this spout and get water whenever they want it. The poor wretches next door don't have any. They have to go to the river."

I thought of all the times I had seen night soil and garbage and dead animals being dumped into the river—along with all those telegrams my father received. There were all sorts of awful things in the river. How could anyone drink from it?

By the time we got back to the apartment and Avdokia had put the water in a kettle to boil over the blackened stove, someone had brought in vodka and bottles were being handed around.

"Here, girl, take a sip. It won't hurt you!"

Feeling reckless, I let a little of the fiery liquid roll over my tongue—and immediately began coughing. A dozen arms patted my back.

"There there, little palace-girl, little bath-girl. Take another sip. It'll do you good. And here! Have some of this food! I'll bet you never tasted anything so good in all your life!"

With that, I took a piece of lamb and began to eat, while all around me toasts were drunk to the strike, to workers everywhere, and to Avdokia, who drank so much that she fell asleep on the drive back to Tsarskoe Selo and it was left to the tired grey horse Folya to find our way home.

Eleven

It was about this time that I began to see Grandma Minnie and our tutor Monsieur Gilliard talking together quite often. They walked side by side in the gardens at Tsarskoe Selo and she invited him to take tea with her in the summer house or the Chinese pagoda by the lake. I could not help but notice that they talked for a long time and Grandma Minnie looked very serious.

I hoped they were not talking about me. I knew that Grandma Minnie thought I was a lazy slouching girl and that she was convinced I was not doing as well at my lessons as Olga was, which was true. Olga was much more clever than I, though Grandma Minnie was always criticizing her for having a big forehead and disapproved of her for being too bold in her manner.

I began to worry whenever I saw Grandma Minnie and Monsieur Gilliard together. Was she planning some terrible punishment for me? Would I be given extra schoolwork, or confined to the schoolroom for extra hours every day?

I suppose I felt nervous and guilty about my secret trip to Smokestack Town with the milk woman Avdokia. No one in my family found out about my few hours away from Tsarskoe Selo; only Daria and Niuta knew where I had been and what I had done, and they had every reason to be quiet about it. I was afraid that somehow Grandma Minnie might find out and try to confine me so that I wouldn't wander away again. I even had a nightmare in which she chained me to my bed, and I woke up crying out to be freed.

By this time my pleas to be given my own room had been heeded and I did have my own small pink and yellow bedchamber with my uncomfortable camp bed and a cot for Niuta, who slept nearby in case I needed anything during the night. My beloved wolfhound Artipo slept on my bed, whining a lot because of his sore and swollen paw. I did my best to comfort him, putting a healing salve on his paw and wrapping the paw in soft felt, but he went on whining and I knew he was in pain.

Monsieur Gilliard was teaching us about the gods and goddesses of the Greeks and Romans. The palace gardens were full of classical statuary and he gave me the assignment to take my sketchbook outside and draw the statues, attempting to identify each one. I was preoccupied with sketching a marble Zeus with a bushy beard when I heard Grandma Minnie's shrill, commanding voice and Monsieur Gilliard's measured, lightly accented baritone. I ducked behind the statue and found a hiding place between two rows of rosebushes, hoping they would not see me. They walked by, passing quite close to me, and then sat side by side on a wrought-iron bench. I held my breath, dreading that they might discover me. But quite soon I became caught up in what Grandma Minnie was saying, and listened intently.

"What a state she is in, Pierre! I tell you, she is worse every day. She has such an odd look in her eye, haven't you noticed? As though she distrusts the whole world. She stays in that room of hers night and day, won't go out, always has a headache or a sore leg or else she's staying up night after night with the boy, or doing God knows what with that filthy Siberian Novy. The one who calls himself God's rascal, Rasputin. Now honestly, I ask you, Pierre, what do you think of him?"

"I have never encountered anyone like him. I don't really know what to make of him. It's almost as if—he belongs to another race of men."

"Another race of thieves, more likely! Do you know the police are watching him? I asked them to."

"Has he done anything suspicious?"

"He was in jail in Tobolsk, so they say."

"Are you certain of that?"

"I am attempting to make certain of it, yes. I want to find out the truth, so I can make Nicky believe it, so I can break this hold she has over him, and that filthy Siberian has over her."

They were talking about mama, of course, and the Siberian, whom they called Father Gregory. I confess that my first reaction was, thank the Lord they are not talking about me! Yet as I listened to Grandma Minnie, I realized that what she was saying was quite true. Mama had become more withdrawn, and distrusted others more. But that was because she was disliked, because hardly anyone in the imperial family sought her out or wanted to be with her, indeed they went out of their way to criticize and insult her.

"Do you know, the other day, when it was raining so hard, she started screaming when no one could find her waterproof cape. She kept at it for half an hour, shouting at her maids and throwing things. She was like a madwoman. Then it turned out she had given the cape away to her sister Irene, when she was here visiting, but she had forgotten that and blamed her dressers for stealing the cape and selling it! Imagine!"

"She has become forgetful. I think it must be that medicine she takes to help her sleep. It leaves her groggy and clouds her mind."

I heard Grandma Minnie sniff.

"Is it that medicine that makes her see her dead mother?"

"What?"

"Niuta told me. Alix claims she sees her dead mother, walking down the corridors of the palace."

There was a pause, then I heard Monsieur Gilliard say, "I wasn't aware of that," in a way that made me think he found this disturbing. It didn't disturb me, as I had been hearing mama talk about seeing her mother for as long as I could remember. I thought it was normal, seeing ghosts. The servants were convinced that the ghost of Emperor Paul walked the hallways of the Alexander Palace and I heard them whisper other stories about spirits. I had never seen one myself.

When Grandma Minnie spoke again it was in a different tone, a more cautious one.

"Have you heard of a Jewish doctor in Vienna who treats unbalanced minds? Many people go to him, some of them quite well connected people, even royals. He's not a quack like the Siberian, though some of his ideas do seem farfetched."

"If you mean Dr. Freud, yes. I have heard of him."

"I have been making inquiries. I believe I could convince him to treat Alix, if she would cooperate."

"But surely—you don't believe the tsarina is insane."

"I believe she is unbalanced, yes. And so do others."

"What does the emperor say?"

"I haven't discussed it with him. But I will. And I think I can persuade him that his wife is ill, and needs care."

They rose from the bench and walked on together toward the Children's Island, still talking of this doctor and of mama. Was this a trick, I wondered? Was Grandma Minnie up to something? I did not trust her. I felt protective toward mama.

No, I thought. I won't let this happen. I knew that mad people were shut away in dark rooms and mistreated, maybe even tortured. I couldn't let that happen to dear mama. I would protect her, defend her.

After Grandma Minnie and Monsieur Gilliard left I tried to go on with my sketch of the bearded Zeus, but my troubled thoughts kept getting in the way. Instead of the statue of the god I kept seeing a Viennese doctor, a doctor with eyeglasses like Dr. Fedorov and a dark suit with a waistcoat like Alexei's other doctor, Dr. Raukhfus. He had a big butterfly net in his hand and he was chasing mama across the lawn, only mama, with her bad leg, couldn't run fast enough to escape from him.

I shook my head, trying to dispel these awful images, but my fears for mama's safety haunted me, and when I finally completed my poor sketch of Zeus and handed it to Monsieur Gilliard the next day he looked at me in surprise.

"You have captured the fierceness of the great god, Tania, but where is his benevolence? Where is his wisdom?" He shook his head. "There is a statue of Daphne on the Children's Island. Why don't you try sketching her? You remember the story I told you, of how Daphne was pursued by Apollo and she prayed to Zeus to rescue her and he changed her into a laurel tree? The statue is well devised, the sculptor has created a woman who is being transformed into something else entirely. She is half woman, half tree. Let me see whether you can capture this transformation in your sketch."

I did as Monsieur Gilliard asked, and took my sketchbook out into the gardens again. But as I stared at the statue of Daphne, and tried to focus on the way her arms were turning into limbs, her legs into a tree-trunk, her tortured, open-mouthed face into the bark of a laurel tree, all I could think of was mama. Was she too in transformation, as Grandma Minnie seemed to think, from my beautiful loving mother into a screaming madwoman with an odd look in her eye, distrustful and afflicted, too frightened to face the world and haunted by the ghost of her dead mother?

Dear mama, I thought, how can I help you? What can I do for you? I resolved, then and there, to do all I could to keep her from harm.

Twelve

The sparkling blue waters of the Solent flashed in the sunlight as dozens of sleek yachts rode at anchor in the gentle swells. Our yacht, the *Standart,* stood out among them for its size and magnificence, and for the large number of launches that came and went between it and the splendid pier that extended from the even more splendid Royal Yacht Squadron with its fanciful turrets and wide canopied porch facing the lovely view of the water.

We had come to Cowes, on the Isle of Wight off the coast of southern England, at the invitation of mama's uncle King Edward VII and Grandma Minnie's sister Queen Alexandra.

"You must come for the races, Nicky," the king had written to papa. "You must watch me trounce that arrogant nephew of mine, that Willy! He may have a bigger navy than I do but by all that's holy he doesn't have a faster yacht!"

The *Standart* was not a racing yacht, she was not going to take part in the race meet. Being much older and much heavier than the others, she had a tendency to wallow—so I heard the sailors say—and did not handle with the ease of the lighter, faster craft, which were, after all, built for speed and not for comfort or elegance. Besides, papa was not a sportsman like Uncle Edward was; he liked shooting but not competing. He would not have raced his yacht no matter how fast it went or how lightly it skimmed over the water. Uncle Edward, on the other hand, was always racing against somebody or something, as mama told me with a slight air of disdain. "Cousin Bertie is a man of shallow tastes—and he was a great disappointment to his mother, as she often told us when we were children."

Standing at the railing, looking out across the wide expanse of yachts and smaller boats, I could easily make out the two yachts belonging to Uncle Edward and mama's cousin Willy, who was the German Emperor Wilhelm II, the much-talked-of belligerent little man whose face I recognized from the photograph in mama's room, known for his angry outbursts and his withered left arm.

"Willy always has to win," papa said, standing beside me and smiling his sweet smile. "Look at that yacht! The newest, finest product of the Kiel shipyards. Bertie's boat will never catch it."

Our visit to Cowes, in addition to being a family visit was, of course, a state visit and the newspapers were full of photographs of the three sovereigns, Uncle Edward, mama's cousin Willy and papa, all looking friendly and cheerful and not in the least like rulers about to plunge their countries into war.

But that was what the newspapers printed, below the convivial photographs: Relations Worsen, Kaiser at Odds with Great Britain, Russia and France. Isle of Wight Visit a Prelude to War. Marine Conclave a Failure.

It did not matter what the headlines said; we were eager to have a good time. There was a ball every afternoon, it seemed, and one of the balls was in our honor. I wore a gown of blue and ivory striped silk, with puffed lace sleeves and rose-colored ribbon trim. It was my first gown with a fitted bodice, not the shapeless bodice of a little girl's dress but a bodice made for a young woman, with added fullness for my new breasts, which were just beginning to emerge from my formerly flat chest. I was both proud and embarrassed by my changing body. I kept nervously expecting that any day blood would gush out from between my thighs, as mama had explained it would. Olga had begun experiencing her bloody days, and she was very superior about it, even bringing her stained underclothes into my room and flaunting them, which was extremely immodest.

"Don't worry, Tania, it won't happen to you for ages," she said. "You're always behind. Behind in growing up, behind in your schoolwork, behind in your understanding of the real world. You're still a child. You belong in the nursery."

But when Prince Adalbert asked me to dance at the ball, I did not feel as though I belonged in the nursery any longer. The prince was cousin Willy's son and much better looking than his fidgety father, who when I was introduced to him barely looked at me and kept shifting his weight nervously from one leg to the other. The Kaiser had a small, comical gnome-like face and a huge dark upturned moustache, but Adalbert was fair, with lovely blue eyes and a soft-looking blond moustache that adorned his upper lip in a very manly fashion.

He took my hand and led me out onto the dance floor with a smile that won my heart at once in a schoolgirl crush. The light touch of his hand on my waist, his fingers holding mine as we waltzed together, his kind words caught me up in mild confusion, so that I stumbled over my replies and forgot my dancing-school lessons about how to follow my partner gracefully. He appeared to find my clumsiness charming, and told me what a pretty girl I was.

He took me aboard the *Meteor*, his father's enormous yacht, pointing out its sleek design and feather-light balsawood decking and planking, its lightweight steel frame and its nearly eleven thousand feet of canvas.

"My father's boat is much faster than the king's *New Britannia*," he said with some pride. "*Meteor* won the Sultan of Johore's challenge cup last year. She left all the others far in her wake."

"Do you race too?" I asked Adalbert, thinking how very handsome he was with his light blue eyes and curling blond hair, his pink lips and white teeth. I had never been kissed, but I wanted to be now. I had to remind myself that Adalbert was my second cousin, and much older than I was.

"Of course. I have my own yacht, the *Mercury*. She is much smaller than the *Meteor*, naturally. Only a fourth-class vessel. But her sails are wings. She flies!"

Adalbert was not present at the grand ball held on the following night in our honor at the Royal Yacht Squadron. Cousin Willy had declined his invitation on hearing that Uncle Edward had accused him of wanting to be the "boss of Cowes," and Adalbert had been forced to decline his invitation as well.

"Not only am I the boss of yacht racing," Cousin Willy said, according to Grandma Minnie, "but I will soon be the boss of all the world's oceans besides."

"The braggart!" mama exclaimed when she heard this, as we completed our toilettes for the ball. "Who does he imagine he is, to speak so?"

"His navy is the largest in the world, so I am advised," papa remarked, reaching for his champagne glass. He was reclining in a soft chair in mama's dressing room, smoking a cigarette and blowing smoke rings.

"The largest perhaps, but certainly not the finest. That honor still goes to Uncle Edward's fleet, surely."

"It certainly does not go to ours," papa said with a sigh. "Not after all the damage we suffered when the Japanese attacked. So many good ships and good men lost!"

"Never mind! The Russian navy will be great again one day!"

Mama did her best to keep her voice bright with confidence, but it was evidently an effort for her, and I could tell she was under a good deal of strain. Her face was getting red and there were blotches on her cheeks that always appeared when she was tense. Her dread of public occasions was causing her anxiety. She smoothed her gown and patted her high-piled hair.

"Olga! Tania! Come here, girls, and listen carefully. There are rules at Uncle Bertie's court that are different from ours. First, never stare at his belly."

I burst out laughing. I couldn't help it.

"He is sensitive about his weight and likes to pretend he is still young and good-looking. Let him pretend. And when we sit down to supper, don't touch the Bar-le-Duc jam. It is his favorite. Don't ask him anything, or say anything unless he speaks to you first. Remember, he is a king."

"But we are grand duchesses!"

Mama couldn't help smiling, though she tried not to.

"Don't disgrace your family, either of you. Besides, if you giggle or make fools of yourselves, you will surely make me and your papa laugh, and that would never do."

When we were presented to Uncle Edward and Queen Alexandra I had to blink several times to assure myself I wasn't imagining things. The king was an old man with white hair and a full white beard, immensely fat, wearing a red plaid waistcoat beneath his formal evening dress. He sat in a wide thronelike chair at one end of the ballroom with the smiling, pretty, dark-haired Aunt Alexandra beside him, and he had the Racing Form folded on his lap.

Olga's name and mine were announced, and we approached the royals and curtseyed.

The king looked at us gravely, and then said, in a throaty bass voice loud enough for mama to hear, "Two fine Russian fillies from your stables, Sunshine. Where are the rest?"

I had never heard mama called by her childhood nickname of Sunshine before. She blushed at the name, her blush a fiery red. But she did not look entirely displeased, and I heard her reply, in her soft voice, "They are on the *Standart*, Pudge."

The king looked startled, then burst out with a laugh so hearty and so infectious that it brought smiles to many faces.

"Pudge! Ha! Pudge!" His laugh made his old man's features look boyish and gleeful. "Now there's a name I haven't heard in years. The dear old queen's name for me. Pudge!" He peered at mama. "You must come out with me, Sunshine, in my new Daimler. Will you?"

"Gladly, if Your Majesty wishes."

"Come now, Sunshine, none of this Your Majesty nonsense. I prefer Pudge!"

The king seated us near him at supper and continued to look jolly and merry as he worked his way greedily through course after course of lavish dishes, each course washed down with a different fine wine. At his elbow, as he ate, was a jar of Bar-le-Duc jam which he smeared liberally across the meats and fish, the lobster and even the subtly flavored side dishes. At times the king paused to listen to the lively band—the Blue Hungarian—and waved his fork in the air in time to the music.

The ballroom was splendid with oversize epergnes filled with orchids and white lilacs ornamenting the supper tables, and we ate off beautiful Sèvres china and drank from sparkling crystal goblets that shone as brightly as the women's crownlike tiaras. Tall footmen in yellow jackets and green breeches stood behind each chair, ready to remove plates, fill goblets, even pick up stray flowers that fell from the women's white tulle gowns.

My thoughts could not help wandering to the scenes I had witnessed in the Vyborg, that horrifying yet fascinating world of want and overcrowded wretchedness at home in Petersburg. What would all these beautifully dressed, well fed people think if they could see what I had seen there? What would my family think if they knew that I had gone to Daria's basement apartment with Avdokia the milk woman not only once but several times, each time taking food and castoff clothing and, on the final time, medicine for the woman in the filthy apartment who had such a bad cough.

My musings were interrupted by the strident voice of a woman across the table from me, an American.

"I had it made in Paris," she was telling her neighbor. "It is an exact duplicate of a crown made for a Spanish queen."

"Mine is a replica of one worn by the Empress Josephine at her coronation," came another female voice.

"Some, of course, are more authentic than others. I'm told the pawnshops are full of tiaras with false gems. After all, royalty has its tawdry side."

This ill-advised remark was greeted by a hush. Everyone looked at the king, to see if he had taken offense. But he was concentrating on the plate of partridges being set in front of him, and appeared not to have heard the offensive remark.

While we watched, he took a knife and spread Bar-le-Duc jam over the roasted birds. Then he took a bite. At once the corners of his mouth turned down and his nose wrinkled in distaste. He spat his mouthful of partridge onto the delicate china plate.

"This sauce tastes like old shoe leather!" he cried out. "And the birds are tough. Bring me my prune soufflé." And taking the plate of partridges he tossed it onto the carpet and reached for his goblet of wine.

Thirteen

Preparations for the race went forward feverishly. Mama's cousin Willy held race practices for his crew every afternoon, whether or not the wind was favorable, conducting them himself, and had the *Meteor* hauled out of the water and her bow scraped again and again, lest the smallest bit of dirt or weed or barnacle mar the smooth fast surface of the narrow hull.

Uncle Bertie did not go aboard the *New Britannia* himself, but had a superb crew—so everyone said—and watched them sailing up and down in front of the Royal Yacht Squadron when he was not preoccupied with driving his Daimler or organizing torchlight parades or talking about his hopes for his race horses Persimmon and Witch of Air.

There were to be five yachts in the upcoming race, though it was agreed that either the *Meteor* or the *New Britannia* would surely win, the other boats being inferior in design and operation.

"Besides," mama said to Olga and me when we were alone, "they wouldn't let any really fast boats enter the race. It wouldn't do to have some boat owned by a commoner beat a royal yacht."

As race day approached mama became more and more weary of all the racing talk and tired of waiting on the lawn in front of the Royal Yacht Squadron to watch the afternoon's trials.

"I think I'll invite the ladies to tea aboard the *Standart,*" she said. "Yes.

A party just for the ladies. We can have lobster and caviar, tea cakes and pastries."

"But mama," I reminded her, "remember what happened when you gave your last party. Ladies can be very unkind."

"Don't talk foolishness, Tania. These are my relatives, here at Cowes. Good kind English and German folk, most of them, not haughty Russians!"

"Grandma Minnie will be there," I reminded her. I could not help thinking about Grandma Minnie's harsh, critical words about mama and what she had said to Monsieur Gilliard about her. I was convinced that Grandma Minnie wanted to put mama into a home for mad people, or a dark dungeon.

"But she will be with her sister the queen," mama replied. "She would not be unkind to me when Queen Alexandra is with her, surely. The queen is so gentle and thoughtful."

"Don't listen to Tania, mama," Olga said. "She is only a child. She cannot yet understand women as we can."

The tea was held as mama wished, and if she had been worried that the women she invited might not come to her party, she was soon able to relax as launch after launch came up to the *Standart*, delivering silk-gowned, white-gloved, straw-hatted ladies in twos and threes.

Among them were Queen Alexandra and her three daughters, pop-eyed Victoria, plain Louise and Maud, whose ears stuck out; mama's older sisters Victoria and Irene (my third favorite aunt, next to Ella, because she was always so happy and bubbly); and mama's cousin Ducky, who had been married to mama's brother Uncle Ernie but who decided she would rather be married to Uncle Vladimir's son Kyril, who she really loved.

There were more relatives than I could count or name, most of them with round faces and fat necks like Great-grandma Victoria. There were also some American ladies, Mrs. Yerkes and Mrs. Martin and Mrs. Astor and several others.

Grandma Minnie arrived on the arm of a grey-haired, respectable looking gentleman whom she introduced as Mr. Schmidt, and who apologized to mama for coming uninvited to her tea party for ladies.

"I have no wish to intrude," he said in German-accented English, the accent different from cousin Willy's and Adalbert's.

"He is here as my escort," Grandma Minnie said. "I felt a bit shaky this afternoon, and took some of my Quiet Drops, and then needed a man's arm to hold onto when I came over in the launch. Nicky was out on the *Meteor* with Willy, so I asked Mr. Schmidt if he would accompany me."

Mama had a chair brought for Grandma Minnie and welcomed Mr. Schmidt, urging him to be at his ease. He went to sit in a corner of the salon and smiled and nodded at the ladies. He said little, I noticed, but observed all that went on around him.

Mama, who was usually very elegantly but simply dressed, had decided on that afternoon to wear, over a plain ivory gown, a colorful Japanese kimono.

"How very singular," I heard one of the American ladies say when she arrived. Another whispered "odd, very odd" to her companion—but I heard her despite her whispering.

"And is this the way they dress in Russia now, Alix," said mama's Aunt Helena with some asperity. "I don't think dear mama would have approved."

Only Queen Alexandra was charitable in her reaction, praising the lovely kimono for its fine silk and beautiful embroidery and adding how lovely mama looked in it.

The room was filling with cigarette smoke as mama, made tense by the frowning looks and disparaging remarks her kimono attracted, lit one cigarette after another.

"I know my mother would have liked my kimono," she said to no one in particular. "She probably would have worn one too. She went her own way, made her own choices."

I had often heard mama say this about her mother, my grandmother Alice, praising her as the most outspoken and the most intelligent of Queen Victoria's nine children. I had also heard mama say that her mother and Helena had often quarreled.

"She was a freethinker, my sister Alice was," Helena remarked, not making the least effort to hide her disdain. "An atheist. She questioned all the truths of the Bible."

"She was a student of the Bible, yes. As of many different religious texts. She had a brilliant mind. A mind made to probe into the truth of things."

"I'd like to probe into that delicious-looking plate of cakes," piped up one of the American ladies, moving toward the tea table where silver trays of finger sandwiches, scones, breads and cheese and shrimp pâté were displayed, along with a large red velvet cake and lots of different kinds of pastries. "Serious talk makes me hungry."

Several others got up quickly and joined the American lady. But the interruption did not prevent mama from continuing to talk about her mother.

"She was the best mother anyone could have. She died for her children. Maud, Louise," she went on, addressing the princesses, "you remember my mother don't you, your Aunt Alice?" The young women nodded. "How loving she was, and how intelligent? You must remember."

"I remember something about Providence," Maud remarked timidly. "I think she said it didn't exist."

"There! What did I tell you!" exclaimed Helena. "She was an atheist."

A thought struck me.

"Where do atheists go when they die?" I asked. "For them there is no heaven or hell."

"They are eternally damned, of course," said Helena with a snort. "They deny God. Where else should they go but hell?"

"My mother is not in hell," mama said with feeling. "Her spirit is still among us. I see her often."

The murmur of conversation in the room ceased, and all eyes were turned on mama, who nervously lit another cigarette and stood where she was, her kimono awry, staring at Helena and smoking.

At this point Mr. Schmidt slowly rose from his seat and came over to mama, looking down into her frowning face and saying, very quietly, "It is no wonder this talk of your late mother has distressed you. Won't you come and sit with me for a moment, just until you feel calmer?"

She looked up at him, suspiciously at first, then questioningly, and finally with a look that I rarely saw on her face, a look of submission.

Who is this man? I wondered.

"Mama? Are you all right? Can I come with you?"

"Of course Tania. Come and sit beside me. Let the ladies have their tea."

"I find that a quiet talk often calms me," Mr. Schmidt said, seating himself and patting the cushion next to him. Mama sat down, loosening the waist belt of her kimono and sighing.

"Ah, that's better. Do you know, I believe this obi has been making me uncomfortable. It's just like a Japanese corset."

Mr. Schmidt nodded. "I wondered whether that might be the case. How are you feeling now?"

"Perhaps I have a migraine coming on. Upsetting things affect my health."

"Do you have these migraines often?"

"They are the bane of my life. My, how easy you are to talk to, Mr. Schmidt."

He smiled. "I enjoy the conversation of beautiful ladies. And their daughters," he added, looking over at me.

"I have been admiring your kimono," he said presently. "Have you been to Japan?"

"No, but I should like to go. I often wish—"

"What is it that you often wish?"

"That I could escape to someplace like Japan, where no one would hate me."

I was startled. I wanted to say, "But mama, no one hates you," but something stopped me. Perhaps it was Mr. Schmidt's kindly, interested manner. Then too I was thinking, was she right?

"Japan is the country that attacked Russia, is it not?" Mr. Schmidt was saying. "And destroyed many ships of the Russian navy? I find it illuminating that you should dress in a Japanese kimono here in Cowes, where the prowess of the British and German sailing vessels are celebrated—and aboard your own Russian yacht. You dress in the costume of an enemy, not a friend. Why do you suppose that is?"

Mama looked at him, her eyes wide open in wonder.

"I cannot imagine."

"Perhaps it is no significant thing." He shrugged. "I once spent weeks trying to imagine why a man I know keeps dreaming of a tree full of white wolves."

There was a pause. I looked out across the salon. The ladies were eating and chatting. They seemed not to be paying any attention to our little group in the corner.

"I have many strange dreams," mama said presently, in a sort of faroff voice. "Sometimes I dream of cranberries—or of pins, thousands of steel pins. I'm trying to pick them all up but I can't, they get stuck in the carpet. I step on them. Alexei steps on them. He bleeds."

"It is only natural that you should be concerned in your dreams about your son. The hope of the Romanov dynasty. He carries so much on his small shoulders. And I know that he is ill."

Mama began to cry.

"There, there, my dear. I had no idea I would cause you pain. I mean to offer only sympathy and kindness—and understanding."

"You are kind," I heard mama murmur when her tears stopped flowing and she was wiping her face with her linen handkerchief. "Even kinder than Father Gregory, who sometimes chastises me. He says my faith is too small."

"I have heard something of this Father Gregory. He sounds like a remarkable man. Tell me, do you ever dream of him?"

"Of Father Gregory? No. Only of cranberries, and pins, and—and—"

"Yes?"

"And the grey dove."

"Tell me about the dove."

Mama thought for a moment. "She makes soft sounds. She is delicate and weak. She needs to be protected."

"Does the grey dove remind you of anyone?"

Once again she paused in thought. "When I was a child and visiting my grandmother the queen, for a few weeks I had a governess called Miss Dove."

"Was she delicate and weak?"

Mama laughed. "Hardly. She was fierce and tough-looking, and had iron-grey hair. My sisters and I were afraid of her."

"Tell me, what happens to the dove in your dream?"

"She tries to fly away, but she can't. Her pink feet are caught in sticky mud, and she flaps her wings but she can't free herself."

"Who has trapped her?"

Mama shook her head. "I don't know."

"Ah, then, perhaps it is not time yet for you to understand the meaning of that dream." Mr. Schmidt patted mama on the leg, in a gesture of affection, as one might make to a child. It happened to be her sore leg.

She bristled, and drew her leg away sharply. "That hurts. What are you doing? You have no permission to touch me."

"I assure you, Your Imperial Highness, it was never my intent to give offense. Thank you for this little talk. I wonder if I might excuse myself now and take tea?" He stood, speaking ingratiatingly and with his disarming smile.

"You are excused." The frosty manner mama usually showed with strangers had returned.

"Who was that man, mama?" I asked, watching his retreating back.

"A friend of Grandma Minnie's I suppose. Or maybe a friend of her sister's. How queerly he talked. And yet—"

"I don't like him."

"Nonsense, Tania. You don't know him. He seems perfectly harmless. Rather soothing, in fact."

I brought mama some tea and cakes and sat with her for awhile, as one after another the ladies came up to say a few words to her before taking their leave. After a time Olga joined us.

"They are all gossiping about Uncle Michael," Olga confided to us. "How he married Aunt Dina without papa's permission."

It was the most recent in a series of family "indiscretions," as mama called them. (Grandma Minnie called them "scandals" or "tragedies.") Papa's handsome younger brother Michael, who was next in line for the throne after Alexei, had refused to marry a royal bride Grandma Minnie chose for him and instead had married one of the ladies in waiting of the court, Dina Kossikovsky. Papa was very upset because Uncle Michael had given him his word that he would not marry this Dina, but then he had gone to France or somewhere else wicked and they had gotten married anyway.

"You are not to discuss these things, Olga. If you hear someone gossiping, just turn your head away or say 'I don't believe that is a fit subject to discuss.' You will shame the other person."

"Yes, mama. But it is so interesting—"

"Hush!"

I brought mama some more tea. She seemed to be her old self again. She stood when Grandma Minnie came to say goodbye, leaning on Mr. Schmidt's arm.

"Thank you for the tea, Alix. We will be seeing you at the race trials, I trust?"

"Of course."

"I fear the *Meteor* will have the advantage, as usual."

"I put my faith in the *New Britannia*, mother dear. Especially since we are in British waters."

"Would you care to place a small wager, Your Imperial Highness?" Mr. Schmidt asked. "Say five pounds?"

"I'm afraid I have only rubles, Mr. Schmidt. And I am not a betting woman."

"I am," Grandma Minnie interjected. "Five pounds on the *New Britannia*, on Alix's behalf."

"Done. We can settle up after the race."

They walked out, Mr. Schmidt supporting Grandma Minnie, leaning close to her so that their heads were very near as they talked. I followed them out onto the deck where the ladies were being helped into the waiting launches. I lingered near, pretending to talk with one of the sailors but actually listening to the casual conversations around me.

"She's as beautiful as they say, but she has such a strong under-look, as if she distrusts everyone."

"She seems more English than Russian to me. They say she's obsessed with the occult. I can believe it."

"I hear Nicky adores her. But there's something not quite right about her, if you know what I mean."

I knew they were talking about mama, and I wished I could make them stop. I moved closer to Grandma Minnie and Mr. Schmidt.

"Well, what did you think?" Grandma Minnie was asking.

"An interesting case," Mr. Schmidt responded. "Severe repression, melancholic in the extreme. If she didn't have so many children I would say she was suffering from frigidity. I think she could be helped."

"So she isn't as disturbed as I thought," Grandma Minnie said, sounding, it seemed to me, disappointed.

"Oh she's quite mad all right. Mad as a hatter, to use your English expression. Oh yes, there's no doubt about that."

Fourteen

Papa was very happy as the day of the yacht race approached, riding along with the crews of the *Meteor* and the *New Britannia* on their trials, inviting cousin Willy and Uncle Bertie aboard the *Standart* afterward, visiting the Royal Yacht Squadron and staying there until very late at night. He was happy—but mama was upset, and eager to go back to Russia. I heard them quarreling over when they were going to return.

"We can't stay any longer. Alexei's leg is stiffening up—and I'm nervous about being too far from Father Gregory in case we need him. I've been feeling a bad migraine coming on—you know how your mother upsets me, and I can't escape her here the way I can at home."

"But Alix, it's safe here. I know no one is going to shoot me or blow me up with a bomb. I don't have to watch where I go or what I do."

"There are assassins everywhere, Nicky. Grandma Victoria was shot at several times, right here in England."

"But she lived to be ninety-three, or some such ancient age, and she died in her bed!"

"It was eighty-one, not ninety-three, and she was lucky. Can we go please? It's time."

"We can't very well leave before the yacht race."

"Why not? We're not racing the *Standart*."

"Oh, Alix, please, you know why not. It wouldn't be right. Bertie would never forgive us—or your cousin Willy, much as you dislike him. Besides, what about your sisters? What about young Adalbert? He's taken quite a liking to our Tania, you know. All the sailors on the *Meteor* were talking about it."

I blushed to hear this. I hadn't realized that Adalbert and I were so closely watched while we were on the *Meteor*.

"Nicky, she's only twelve years old!"

"Royal girls have been married at twelve—and younger."

"Not a daughter of mine. And not to a son of that madman Willy!"

Mama continued to say that she wanted to leave, but papa decided to stay. She complained, especially when he went out at night to the Royal Yacht Squadron or to the Villa Violetta, Uncle Bertie's private cottage on the beach, where, it was said, the king entertained actresses and dancers from London and invited his men friends to join him.

Olga claimed to know, from papa's valet Chemodurov, what went on at the Villa Violetta.

"They do the tango," she told me, her eyes agleam. "The new dance from Argentina. I learned it from Felipe on the *Standart*." Felipe was her favorite sailor, the one we called her "flirt." She began to glide across the floor, her angular body contorted and graceless, as she demonstrated the bizarre steps of the dance.

"One, two, one-two-three. One, two, one-two-three." I thought her movements were revolting, though I didn't tell her so, any more than I told her about what Mr. Schmidt—who I had come to realize was really Dr. Freud—had said to Grandma Minnie about mama's being mad as a hatter.

It had not taken me long to guess who the soothing Mr. Schmidt really was. That he was the celebrated Viennese doctor Grandma Minnie had told Monsieur Gilliard about.

She had said she would try to convince this Dr. Freud to treat Alix. Had he been treating her that day aboard the *Standart*, I wondered, or merely getting to know her? All he did was talk to her, ask her questions. Was this all he intended to do? I meant to watch all closely, to make certain mama was not alone with this Mr. Schmidt.

"And that's not all they do," Olga was going on. "They slide down the banisters on tea trays, and bump each other off the sofas when they sit down, and giggle like children, and light the servants' whiskers on fire. And they drink a lot, and go upstairs to the bedrooms with the actresses and don't come down again for a long time."

I was beginning to learn the ways of the world. How men acted when they were away from their wives. How they egged each other on to do things they would not think of doing when they were sober. I did not like imagining that papa was one of those men, but of course he was. He had to be. He was the tsar.

"Did Chemodurov say that Adalbert was at the Villa Violetta?"

"No! The Germans are not invited. Besides, he says the Germans do other things. Worse things. They gather at their own private retreats and bring in young boys dressed up like girls, or the men dress up like women. Then they drink and carry on."

"Cousin Willy too?"

"I don't know."

I did not like to think of handsome blond Adalbert, with his delicate moustaches, dressing like a girl.

Alexei came down with a cough and mama took that as her excuse to leave Cowes aboard her sister Irene's yacht, taking Marie and Anastasia with her but allowing Olga and me to stay on, at papa's insistence, to watch the race and then return to Russia with him on the *Standart*. In truth I was glad to stay, as I was enjoying myself with all the balls and parties to attend and all the freedom we had to come and go without fear. The English seemed to me quaint and stuffy, but trustworthy, and at times very amusing, while the Germans, for all their bluster (the men tended to talk too loudly, I thought—except for Adalbert—and were always shouting orders), were courtly and charming. I felt that when the time came, I would be sorry to leave, and I grew to like fat Uncle Bertie and his son Prince George, who everyone said would be king soon, as Uncle Bertie was old and in failing health.

Race day finally arrived, and the *New Britannia*, the *Meteor*, and the three other yachts—the *Genesta*, with an Italian at the helm, the *Lady Hermione*, with a German crew under the Baron von Buch, and the *Corsair* from New Zealand—prepared to set out along the thirteen-mile course.

At precisely two o'clock in the afternoon the flag was raised over the

Royal Yacht Squadron and the cannon fired a deafening salute. A military band played the British, German and Russian national anthems while the spectators removed their hats and stood at attention.

Then, at a signal, the boats were off.

A warm sun shone down on rough waters as the wind, capricious and changeable, sped the sleek vessels toward the start line. Cheers went up as the *New Britannia* sprinted into the lead, the *Corsair* in pursuit. Olga and I stood at the rail of the *Standart* with papa, watching intently, shading our eyes against the bright sun. By the time they reached the first buoy in the triangular course my attention had begun to wander and I felt sleepy. It was all I could do to keep my eyes open.

Then I heard papa shout. "Foul! It's a foul!" The sailors took up the cry and I could hear shouts from on shore as well.

"Look! He's hoisting illegal canvas! The villain! The wretch!"

It was the *Meteor*, I gathered, putting out more sail than the racing rules allowed. She shot across in front of the *Genesta*, nearly overturning the Italian boat with her wake, and took the lead as the vessels turned downwind.

"She should be disqualified," papa said. "Bertie will be furious."

The *Lady Hermione*, which had fallen behind the others almost from the start, dropped out when her tiller lines broke, but the *New Britannia* soldiered on, through rising winds and more challenging waves, until the final turn into the wind for the tack to the finish line.

By this time the cheering had become loud and raucous, with horns, whistles and bells added to the cacophony of voices. A strident chant of "*Mete-or! Mete-or!*" was all but drowned out by the singing of "Rule Britannia" in which Olga and I joined, singing as lustily as we could though the strengthening wind carried our voices away and I had to hold onto my hat to keep it from blowing off.

The *Meteor* reached the finish line first, but not by many feet, and the German victory was clearly tainted. Papa swore and went ashore to lodge a formal complaint with the judges. Olga and I had our supper in our cabin, feeling somewhat let down, and wondering aloud what the newspapers would say about the race.

It was a good thing we were to leave the following day, because there was an outcry about the extra canvas put aboard the *Meteor* illegally, not only in the newspapers but at the luncheon tables and tea tables in the Royal Squadron.

"They will make it a casus belli," papa said, his own anger having subsided into wry humor. "But then, Bertie ought to know by now that Willy does not play fair. Your mama could have told him that—in fact she probably did, before she left."

We missed mama, and Alexei and Marie and Anastasia, and were glad to be going home. I said my goodbyes to all the relatives, the fat king and his beautiful queen and their plain daughters, Prince George who kissed my hand and said that he would miss me, the Kaiser who looked even more stern in victory than he had before the race began, all the aunts and uncles and cousins—and especially Adalbert, who took me aside and said he hoped I knew that he had had nothing to do with his father's flaunting of the racing rules. I assured him that I believed him.

"May I write to you, Tania?" he asked. His eyes were very blue and very sincere.

"Yes, of course. As a friend."

"Soon you will be old enough to be more than a friend." And he pressed my hand. "One day before long we will see each other again, I'm sure of it. Perhaps sooner than you imagine. Until then, may I give you a cousinly kiss?"

I did not know what to say. I could not look at Adalbert. I looked down.

With gentle warm fingers he lifted my chin and kissed me on the cheek.

"Goodbye, little Tania."

"Goodbye, Adalbert." He stepped into the launch and waved a final goodbye, and I waved back, until all I could see of him was a small white figure against the dark blue water.

And then we were off, as cannons boomed a farewell salute from the shore, the *Standart* cutting into the waves in the Solent, headed outward toward the open sea and home.

Fifteen

Sometimes, when life became too confusing, I would go and talk to the elephant.

The dusty, shaggy old beast was a comfort to me in a way. He was by far the oldest creature at Tsarskoe Selo, and I felt that he had endured many, many years of loneliness and sadness. For how could he not be sad, taken away from the land of his birth and all his relatives? Hardly anyone paid attention to him except his mahout, the Indian servant who spoke very little Russian and occupied himself with caring for the elephant and napping in the little lean-to adjacent to the great beast's cage.

My sisters teased me about my visits to the elephant.

"Maybe you're going to marry him," Anastasia said, smiling impishly and running off.

"You'll be sad when he dies," Marie said solemnly. "You'll be sorry you were his friend."

"Only crazy people have conversations with animals," Olga announced. "It's a sign you're losing your mind."

But of course I was not losing my mind, I was merely growing up. I know it now, looking back. Then, however, I was just attempting to make sense of all the many parts of my life that didn't fit together: the great wealth and magnificence of my father's palaces, the squalor of Smokestack Town, the fear we felt from seen and unseen assassins and the cocoon of protection in which we were forced to live, the strong family bonds that joined us and the hostility of Grandma Minnie toward mama and all of us girls—for as Marie and Anastasia got older it was clear that she disapproved of them almost as much as she disapproved of Olga and me. And then there was the constant worry over my brother: would he die, as everyone but mama expected? And if he did, would one of Uncle Vladimir's sons become the tsarevich, causing further ill feeling within the family? It was understood that papa's younger brother Uncle Michael could not rule, not after he had disgraced himself and the family by marrying Dina the commoner.

The elephant heard it all, and appeared to nod his wrinkled old head from time to time, or to trumpet his disagreement. I took comfort from his company.

But of course I had little time to spend in idle conversation. I was kept busy by Monsieur Gilliard learning the untidy forms of irregular French verbs, and reading about Russian history, and acting in plays, and by my dancing master Professor Leitfelter learning the steps of the Hesitation Waltz (not the tango, the dance of night clubs and low taverns), and by mama, who had taught me to knit and was encouraging me to produce blankets and caps and mittens to be sold at her charity bazaars.

As often as I dared I met Avdokia the milk woman at dawn and went with her to the slums of the Vyborg district, where I was drawn into the circle of those who lived in Daria's crowded apartment and welcomed as one of them, though my exact identity remained a mystery—a mystery they did not seem to care very much to solve.

My thirteenth birthday was approaching, and I was growing out of my clothes. All my skirts were too short. When the couturier Lamanov came to the palace for my fittings he remarked on how tall I was becoming.

"Tall and elegant, just like your mother," he said. "Willowy. Slender. A nymph. A charming blond nymph."

I outgrew the peasant skirt papa had bought me and Niuta made me another, which I wore whenever I went to Smokestack Town. I had a new pair of peasant boots for my lengthening feet and womanly caps to cover my hair. Altogether I looked like a young girl from Pokrovsky, or so Niuta told me, and even Daria reluctantly agreed.

Daria continued to live in the palace, in one corner of Niuta's attic room, her little dog curled in a basket on the floor. She worked in the ironing room, continuing to lift heavy trunks of clothes, wield the metal iron for hours at a time and go up and down many flights of stairs each day despite her very advanced pregnancy.

"What will she do when she goes into labor?" I asked Niuta, feeling very grown-up because I knew, or believed that I knew, so much about how babies were born. "Will you call a midwife? Or Dr. Korovin?" Dr. Korovin was still Alexei's doctor, and the principal court physician.

"Oh no, he would never be summoned to treat a servant. No, there is a Workers' Clinic in Petersburg. We will take her there. They have midwives and doctors there. The workers are treated for free."

I did not think very much about this at the time, as Niuta seemed so certain about what she would do and where she would go when Daria needed help delivering her baby. Besides, something else happened to occupy my thoughts—and even to give me nightmares.

Papa, mama and the five of us children (when Alexei was well enough) went each Sunday, and sometimes during the week, to attend divine service at the church of the Holy Innocents near Tsarskoe Selo. One Sunday morning we got down from our carriage near the church steps, our protective guardsmen making a cordon around us to ensure there were no would-be assassins in the waiting crowd. We paused, as we usually did, to wave to the people gathered there to see us. On this day there were more people than usual, and we soon realized why.

In the center of the small square in front of the church a young woman sat on the ground, her dark skirts spread around her, a shawl draped over her thin shoulders. I stared at her pale face with its downcast eyes but could see no emotion there, and that dismayed me. Who was she and what was she doing there, all alone, with so many others watching her, as if waiting for something to happen?

Then I saw the open tin of kerosene on the ground beside her.

Calmly, her movement slow and her arm steady, she reached for the tin and poured the contents over her head, letting it flow down her back and over her blouse and shawl, then onto her wide skirt. Her hand seemed to tremble as she reached for the box of matches in the pocket of her skirt, and she shook her head once, as if to keep the kerosene from flowing into her eyes. Then before anyone could stop her she lit a match and touched it to her skirt.

"No! Stop her! Someone stop her! Bring water!" came shouts from the onlookers, most of whom could do little but gasp, the women covering their mouths, the men frowning in frustrated anger.

The woman's skirt flared up at once, then her shawl caught fire and soon she was engulfed in a ball of flame. I did not hear her scream, but others said later that they did, or so it was reported in the newspapers, and that she did not die right away but writhed and clawed at herself and even called for help before the flames turned her body into a charred lump of blackened flesh.

I was standing by papa and as soon as the awful thing began to happen he reached for me and held my arms and shielded me and said, "Don't look, Tania. This is nothing for you to see."

The entire incident took only a moment to unfold, and right away our guards hurried us back into our carriage and the driver cracked his whip and we sped back toward the palace grounds, the crowd giving way before us as we went.

My shock and surprise were so great that for several minutes I could not speak. I buried my head against papa's shoulder, feeling the reassuring strength of his arm around me and aware of nothing but the rhythmic jouncing of the carriage and the clopping of the horses' hooves, the jangling of the harness and the sound of the driver's cracking whip.

After a while I withdrew my head.

"Who was that, papa? Why did she burn herself?"

"I don't know, Taniushka. I wish you and your sisters and brother hadn't seen her. I wish I hadn't seen her."

"But that was what she wanted, wasn't it? That we should see her, and watch her burn herself. That's why she waited in the square. She must have known we would be coming."

"Hush, Tania!" It was mama's voice, unusually stern. "Don't say such things! Who knows what an unbalanced woman wants? I don't want to hear you repeat that farfetched idea again."

But I knew that I was right. The woman's terrible act had been meant to shock us. To tell us something. But what? For days I pondered the awful deed, the image of the young woman pouring her kerosene and lighting herself afire replaying itself again and again in my mind. At night I dreamed of her, only in my dreams her eyes were not downcast but looking toward me, and I thought I saw, in their dark depths, the fearful glare of blame.

Sixteen

When Daria's labor pains began it was night and I was awakened by muffled talk in the corridor outside my bedroom. Certain that I was hearing Niuta and Daria's voices, I quickly got out of bed and put on my plainest gown, not bothering with petticoats or stockings. I fumbled with the fastenings on the gown, I was not accustomed to dressing without help. By the time I had finished my hasty toilette I could no longer hear anyone in the corridor, but I guessed that Niuta would take Daria to the stables and so I went there, as rapidly as I could.

My departure was noticed—there were servants in the corridors, sitting or lying on benches, supposedly on watch but mostly asleep—but no one stopped me. I thought that Sedynov might hear me, if he hadn't drunk too much vodka the night before, but he didn't appear.

When I got to the stables Niuta and Daria were already there, along with a Don Cossack guard I had often seen with Niuta, a burly bearded man who was hitching a horse to one of the rubbish carts. As I watched, Niuta and the Cossack helped the complaining Daria get into the back of the cart.

"What is she doing here?" I heard Daria say as she prepared to lie down, her voice weak and scratchy.

Niuta looked over at me. "Go back, Tania," she told me.

"But I want to help."

"We don't need you. Go back."

"No!" It was the Cossack. "She'll wake the grooms. They'll see us. They won't let us have the cart. Let the girl ride in the back with Daria."

I climbed up into the flat bed of the cart, where Daria lay on a blanket, doubled over and clutching her distended abdomen, a grimace of pain distorting her features. The cart stank of the garbage it usually carried. I felt nauseous, but tried to ignore my reaction and sat down next to Daria, putting my hand on her shoulder and hoping my touch would soothe her. She moaned.

The Cossack climbed into the front seat and gathered the reins. We left the stable and made our way to the road to the nearby village. Though the Cossack cracked his whip again and again the cart rattled all too slowly along the rutted road as Daria's moans grew louder and longer. I wished that I had the wonderworking icon of St. Simon Verkhoturie that Father Gregory had given my father to preserve his life. Perhaps there would be icons where we were going. I hoped so.

Suddenly Daria screamed.

"How much farther?" I called out.

"Only a few miles," Niuta responded, her voice anxious. "We'll be at the clinic soon."

"Just a little farther, Daria," I said to the suffering young woman beside me. But she kept herself turned away from me, alternately moaning and crying out.

The Cossack began to sing in a hearty baritone. His rich, resonant voice rang out in a folk song, and Niuta slapped her knee in time with his singing. The sound was so compelling that I began to hum along. My spirits lifted. It seemed as though Daria's contorted body relaxed slightly and I imagined that the Cossack's lusty voice gave her courage.

The music made the last few miles go by faster and presently we came to a small wooden building with a sign in the window that read WORKERS' CLINIC. Though it was barely dawn, far too early for much activity in the streets, lights gleamed from all the windows of the clinic and people were going in and out of the front door.

Niuta and the Cossack managed to lift the sobbing Daria down from the cart and half-carry her inside, where almost at once a serious-looking tall young man with reddish-blond hair came forward to attend to her.

He looked too young to be a doctor, I thought, yet his earnestness more than made up for his youth.

I was struck at once by the intense expression of concern on his face, his high domed forehead creased as he focused on Daria and lifted her onto a table against one wall, drawing a screen around the table for privacy. I could hear him talking reassuringly to Daria and asking her questions.

He soon called for nurses and also beckoned for Niuta to join him behind the screen where, to judge from the sound of Daria's higher and higher-pitched cries and the young doctor's sharply-delivered instructions, her baby was swiftly coming into the world.

I sat in the large room, listening to the activity behind the screen while watching what was going on around me. Old people with canes, middle-aged men with sour expressions, tired-looking women with children holding on to them, people with bandaged limbs and blisters, swollen feet or vacant, lost expressions waited to be helped. Several drunks were lying stretched out on the hard floor, reeking of alcohol and stale sweat. While I sat there a boy was brought in, his arm bleeding, and was attended to right away. I noticed that there were no icons on the walls.

Nearly everyone in the room was alert to Daria's screams and as they reached their climax the tension grew, as if everyone was holding his or her breath.

"Here it comes now," the doctor's voice rang out from behind the screen. "Bear down, Daria. Bear down hard!" Grunts and groans told us she was obeying the order.

Then—silence—and following it, a baby's cry. Not a lusty cry, but the unmistakable thin gasping wail of a newborn.

Those around me who were able stood, and shouted and applauded.

Before long the doctor, with the swaddled baby in his arms, pushed aside the screen and brought the infant out into the room.

"A new little worker! A little girl!"

Blessings were called out, and good wishes for a long life. I went over to the doctor and the baby and he held her toward me so that I could see her small face, the tiny eyes shut, the curved red mouth pursed. I looked up at him and smiled.

"And are you the godmother?" he asked me teasingly.

"I am Tania—Daria's friend." I realized as I said it that Daria would snort in derision to hear me describe us as friends. "And Niuta"—I nodded toward the screen—"is her sister."

The doctor went back to his patient and I sat down once again amid the sick and injured. I was beginning to feel sleepy. Where was the Cossack, I wondered. And what had he done with the cart? How was I going to get back to the palace?

Lately I had begun to make lists of my worst faults and my best virtues. On the list of my faults I wrote, "Has a tendency to act without forethought." I liked that phrase, "without forethought." It sounded so much better than "rashly." I had left the palace that morning without giving any thought to how I was going to get back. Now I would pay the price.

After an hour's uncomfortable wait Niuta came to get me. She took me into the back of the clinic where there were half a dozen small rooms, each with an occupied bed. Daria was in one of the beds, with her little one in her arms. Both looked as sleepy as I felt.

"How are you, Daria?" I asked.

"How do you think? I'm sore. I'm tired."

"And you are a mother," I said, leaning over and kissing the baby on her forehead.

"What is her name?"

"She wants to call her Iskra," Niuta told me. "The spark. So foolish!"

"Why foolish?"

"Because, as you would know if you read the revolutionaries' rubbishy literature, Iskra is the name of a newspaper. A workers' newspaper."

"A progressive newspaper," Daria said, her voice almost a whisper. "The spark is the hope of change."

"I would have thought you had enough of sparks, Daria, with that awful fire you ran away from, that could have killed you and your baby too."

But Daria had fallen asleep.

Niuta sat down on a chair beside Daria's bed. "I'll stay with her."

"Where is the Cossack?" I asked.

"Nikandr went back to the palace. Guard duty."

My spirits fell. "If I don't get back, I'll be missed."

"You can just say you had to go to dancing class, like you always do when you go out with Avdokia."

I shook my head. "There is no dancing class on Wednesdays. This is Wednesday."

Niuta waved me away. "Then go."

"But I—" I began to protest, then saw that it was useless. I went back out into the main room and sat down. What was I to do? Before long I saw the tall, redheaded young doctor come striding by and I called out to him.

"Excuse me sir, could I ask you, is there a way I could get back to Tsarskoe Selo? The Cossack who brought us all in his cart has left, and I have no way—"

He looked down at me searchingly.

"I've seen you before," he said.

"No, I don't think so."

"Your picture. I've seen your picture."

The newspapers often printed pictures of all of us in the imperial family. Our likenesses were not unfamiliar to the literate citizens of Petersburg.

"Your aunt keeps your portrait in her salon. Not only yours, but portraits of your sisters and brother too."

"My aunt?"

"Grand Duchess Olga Alexandrovna, who is married to my mother's distant cousin Petya."

Ah, I thought. So this young doctor, who works in the Workers' Clinic, had an aristocratic mother and was allied with my father's family by marriage.

"I see. Olenka is my favorite aunt."

"And Petya? Is he your favorite uncle?"

"He never talks to me. I barely know him. He and Aunt Olenka haven't been married very long, have they?"

He smiled. "Such candor! I admire it. And you are right, they haven't been married very long. Petya is an odd duck, as the English say."

"Yes! I heard the king say that, at Cowes during the yacht racing. He said, 'That Willy, he's an odd duck.'"

As I spoke the doctor was glancing around the room, taking in the sick and injured people waiting there, the drunks lying on the floor, the crying babies and one snoring grandmother who sat slumped against the wall, her head on her chest.

"I must go home and eat soon. I can take you to Tsarskoe Selo myself. It is out of my way, but—" He shrugged. "Just be good enough to wait and I will be back shortly."

Before long he returned, no longer wearing the black coat of a physician but a workman's loose white shirt and jacket. In the black coat he had looked, to my thirteen-year-old eyes, like a man in his twenties; in his shirt and jacket he looked much more boyish. He led me outside and down the street. Presently we entered a courtyard where an ornate coach waited. My companion helped me up into the coach, calling out to the driver that we wanted to go to Tsarskoe Selo. In a moment we were off.

"Constantin Melnikov, at your service, Your Imperial Highness," he said, reaching for my hand to kiss. I settled myself in the soft padded seat of the coach and regarded Constantin as he went on. "My father is a surgeon at the St. Mary of Mercy hospital. I am a physician in training. Not a real one yet."

"How is it you are not in training at your father's hospital?"

"Because I am needed here, at this clinic. I intend to go on serving the workers when I complete my studies."

I had a sudden frightening thought. "You are not a bomb-thrower, are you?"

He threw back his head and laughed heartily. I liked the way his eyes crinkled at the corners.

"No. But then, if I were, I would hardly confess it, would I?"

"We have had some narrow escapes."

"I know. I don't mean to make light of your danger. But please be assured that not everyone with progressive ideas is a dangerous radical. Some of us believe in equality and fairness, and democratic government. We even believe in votes for women."

"Votes for women! Now, that would astonish my Grandma Minnie."

"You mean the dowager empress?"

I nodded. "Grandma Minnie thinks she ought to rule our family, and dominate everybody, even my father, but she would be horrified at the thought that women might ever vote."

"You mark my words, Tania—I mean Your Highness—"

"Tania is fine," I said, interrupting him.

"Well then, Tania, you mark my words, that little girl I helped to deliver today will one day vote, and maybe even run for office, the way women are doing in Britain."

We talked on, of Constantin's political beliefs and of his ambitions to become a surgeon like his father. I told him about our trip to Cowes and my impressions of mama's Uncle Bertie and cousin Willy, how much I liked England and enjoyed the bracing air off the Solent. He talked with zest and vigor, his shining face with its high forehead alight with intelligence, like our tutor Monsieur Gilliard. The conversation made our trip to Tsarskoe Selo go quickly, and I was sorry when the coach drew up before the tall main gates of the imperial compound.

"Your Aunt Olga is a patroness of our clinic, you know," Constantin told me as he helped me down out of the coach. "She is giving a charity ball soon to raise funds for our work. Perhaps you could persuade your mother to subscribe as well."

"I will ask her."

"Au revoir, Your Highness—Tania." He took my hand and kissed it.

"Au revoir, Constantin."

I went on thinking of our pleasant conversation, and of his crinkly eyes and hearty laughter, long after the clopping of the coach horses died away.

Seventeen

I must now write about something I feel ashamed of, not ashamed for myself, but for my father.

He began drinking more, and staying up all night, so that his eyes were always red-rimmed and bleary, and when Olga or I talked to him he looked as though his thoughts were far away and he didn't answer us.

At first I thought it was because he was having to make more speeches than usual—he always dreaded making speeches, especially before the Duma, the new Russian Parliament, and usually drank a lot to calm his nerves—but I soon realized that it wasn't his dread of speeches that was causing him to get so little sleep.

In fact it was a woman. Mathilde Kchessinsky, the ballerina Professor Leitfelter was always praising for her elegant extensions and her lightning-quick pirouettes. I had seen her dance, we all had, I suppose everyone of consequence in Petersburg had, as she was quite celebrated. She was not only agile, but very pretty, with a small figure and a girlish face and tight brown curls.

The ballet audiences loved Mathilde, but socially she was in disgrace, she belonged to that class of women Grandma Minnie never allowed to be mentioned in her presence and mama grew tight-lipped and flushed when anyone indiscreetly blurted out her name. She was living with Uncle Vladimir's son Andrew, or so my sister Olga told me. But she was going every night to Cubat's, the Cuban restaurant that mama called a den of vice and Grandma Minnie said should be blown up and demolished. And my father was meeting her there.

I did not like to think of my father going with his rowdy highborn friends to a place where they knew they could act as wildly as they liked, for as long as they liked, though I understood such things had been going on ever since papa's grandfather's time. "It is the way of the world," I told myself, echoing an expression Monsieur Gilliard often used. Just as at Cowes Uncle Bertie caroused all night with his wilder companions, so in Petersburg my father did the same. Kings and emperors could not very well bring their mistresses into the palace, or have drunken all-night parties there with naked or half-naked dancers, loud music and an endless supply of drink. So they went to special restaurants and night clubs—everyone knew which ones they were. At that time Cubat's was the most notorious place in Petersburg.

Papa, I knew, was always weak when he had drunk a lot. Anyone could persuade him to do anything. In his youth, Chemodurov told Olga, he had been in love with Mathilde and she had been his mistress for several years. He still had some keepsakes from those times that he kept in a locked metal box. Now he was spending time with her again, and sometimes he did not come home until after breakfast. There were some mornings, Chemodurov said, when his eyes were mere slits and his face was so flushed with vodka and lack of sleep that Chemodurov had to put stage makeup on his flushed cheeks and powder on his red nose just to disguise the effects of his debauchery.

Knowing this, I was embarrassed and ashamed when I saw him in the mornings. I did not like to meet his eyes.

There had been a change in our family, but the change did not come just from papa. Mama changed too.

Her terrible headaches now went on for days at a time, and she shut herself in the mauve room and would not see us. Sometimes she had trouble breathing and when she was upset—which was often—she took pills Dr. Korovin gave her that made her calm but also made her very sleepy. She slept a lot, even during the day, but then she complained of having bad dreams, dreams that made her scream with fear. She often talked about her mother, and confided to me that she saw her and spoke to her. Whenever she said this I was frightened, because I knew Grandma Minnie was hoping for an excuse to have mama confined as a madwoman and when mama talked about seeing her dead mother she did sound a little mad.

I couldn't help remembering what Mr. Schmidt—or should I say Dr. Freud—had said that afternoon at Cowes aboard the *Standart*. The words echoed often in my head: "She's quite mad all right. Mad as a hatter."

But most of the time she seemed more or less like anyone else, though more nervous, and with more illnesses. And added to that, papa's late nights upset her a lot and made her brood. She sent Sedynov to Cubat's to spy on papa and poor Sedynov hated going there, I could tell by the shamefaced look he had, though he tried to hide it. She sent others too, private detectives who gave her written reports telling her what went on in the special upstairs rooms at Cubat's and how long papa spent there with Mathilde.

She was careless with these reports, flinging them on the floor in exasperation and then forgetting to pick them up again to prevent the servants from finding them. I found several and, feeling very furtive and guilty, read them and then put them away in mama's writing desk, hidden under her piles of unanswered letters from her sisters and brother and cousins abroad.

I was worried. What could it all mean? What would happen to our family?

Grandma Minnie criticized papa for smoking too much and even tried to snatch his cigarettes out of his hand as if he were a child. Her comments became very bold. She said quite loudly that papa was no longer able to do his duty as tsar and that Uncle Michael should become tsar in his place. She seemed to forget all about Uncle Michael's grave sin in marrying Dina Kossikovsky. Of course she never mentioned Mathilde Kchessinsky but she didn't have to. It was no secret that Mathilde and papa were seen together at Cubat's, and Aunt Olenka told us that there were murmurs and rumors about them all over the capital. Grandma Minnie could not very well mention Mathilde openly but from the way she glared at papa and the way he shrank from her glare I was sure she was angry at his late nights and at the company he was keeping.

It was all very sad for mama, and I felt sorry for her, though I loved papa no less and I knew that most husbands had mistresses. I continued to use Monsieur Gilliard's sophisticated expression, and to say to myself that it was the way of the world. I said this whenever some painful but seemingly inevitable circumstance arose. I remember I felt very grown up when I said it. But I still felt ashamed about papa.

In the midst of all this I received a letter from Adalbert saying that he was coming to Petersburg with a group called the Young People's Peace Initiative, and that he wanted very much to see me. I was just turning fourteen and Monsieur Gilliard was encouraging Olga and me to read a newspaper every day, so I was well aware that there was much talk of war, even of the End of the World through a great and final war in which mankind would destroy itself.

"It is well to apply moderation when reading of such things," our tutor told us. "Journalists exaggerate, in order to frighten people and make them buy more papers. Still, they are right when they say that the great powers of the world are preparing for warfare. Europe has known no war for more than a generation. If history is any guide, this interlude of peace cannot last."

"What about the fight between our navy and the Japanese?" I asked.

"That was a mere skirmish," Monsieur Gilliard said. "A matter of a few ships and a few months of unequal combat. The warfare that is being talked of now would involve many nations and tens of thousands of troops."

"But Cousin Willy and Cousin George would not actually go to war against each other, surely. I saw them playing skittles together at the Royal Yacht Squadron at Cowes." Mama's Cousin George had become King George V, the fat King Edward having died not long before, somewhat to my regret.

"I imagine the members of the Young People's Peace Initiative agree with you, Tania. That is why they are coming to Petersburg."

"Tania thinks Prince Adalbert is coming because he's in love with her," Olga said in a mocking tone.

"I do not."

"You do. I heard you tell Niuta and Elizaveta."

I was about to slap my sister but Monsieur Gilliard stepped between us and reminded us that young ladies did not resort to violence.

The truth was, Olga was envious. The Crown Prince of Romania never did come to Tsarskoe Selo to meet her, as had been expected, and there were no other princes eager to marry her, though she was old enough to marry. I, on the other hand, had an admirer in Adalbert, and I had grown taller and prettier than Olga (I am not being boastful, everyone said I was prettier) and that winter I began receiving my monthly flow so Olga could no longer say I was a child and behind in everything.

On the afternoon that Adalbert arrived I stood before the mirror examining how I looked in the grey satin gown Lamanov had made for me. The effect, I decided, was very flattering. I had bought some light pink lip rouge at Druce's in the Nevsky Arcade, and I applied it to my lips and cheeks. The effect was dazzling. My eyes sparkled, my face seemed to glow. I was indeed pretty, I told myself. Was I vain? Perhaps, just a little.

But then I quickly wiped the pink tint from my mouth and cheeks. Lip rouge was for low women, women like Mathilde. Not for a young grand duchess, who was expecting a visit from a prince.

The Hall of the Nobility was full of visitors coming and going, ushered in and out of the immense room by the dignified doorman in his old-fashioned wig and wide purple doublet trimmed in gold braid. Music played, lights gleamed brightly, then dimmed, then brightened again as the flow of illuminating gas widened and narrowed. The gas jets were newly installed, and rarely worked properly—plus the gas smelled terrible and the guests could not help wrinkling their noses at the odor every now and then.

I sat with papa and mama on the raised dais at the far end of the long room, waiting for Adalbert. I was excited but also nervous, because papa wore his faraway look and was stroking his beard absentmindedly instead of paying attention to what was going on in the room, and mama, who said the smell of the gas gave her a headache, was impatient and cross. She disliked having to greet unimportant visitors, and she considered the prince to be very unimportant, because he was Cousin Willy's son.

But when Adalbert appeared in the wide doorway, looking so tall and straight and handsome in his white uniform, his long golden sword at his side, flashing in the glare of the lights, I held my breath and felt my cheeks grow hot.

The doorman called out his name and titles and he walked toward us, smiling, his step confident. I was so happy at that moment that I forgot to be nervous and worried and when Adalbert reached for my hand to kiss I held my breath with the pleasure of it.

Later on he dined with us, in our private dining room at the palace, and explained the purpose of the Young People's Peace Initiative. There were twenty-five in the delegation, he explained, all highborn young men and women from Germany, France, Italy, Sweden, and even one from England.

"We hope to add some Russians to our group," he said, looking at me as he spoke. "Our purpose is to be a living example of cooperation between countries and nationalities, to show that we can understand one another and not provoke each other to conflict. I am hoping that Tania might like to join us, at least while we are here in Russia." He smiled at me. "Can we count on you?"

I nodded eagerly but stopped when I heard mama's voice.

"And what does your father think of this peace initiative of yours? Does he really want cooperation, or does he prefer competition? Competition that he can win, that is."

Adalbert's composure was unruffled. "I am here with my father's blessing," he replied. "And I bring you all his good wishes."

After dinner I took Adalbert out to the Children's Island and we walked among the trees, wrapped in our warm coats and hats. There had been a snowfall the night before and every so often clumps of wet snow fell from the lower branches of the trees, narrowly missing us. I felt that we were in a dreamlike state. After a time conversation faltered, and Adalbert took my gloved hand in his as we continued to walk.

"This is where my father comes when he needs to be alone," I said at length. "He is always happiest when he is on his own, tramping through a wood or bicycling or stalking ravens or elk. He was born to be a countryman."

"We could be compatible that way, in the future. Your father and I, I mean."

I looked at him, unsure what to do or say.

"Of course, you would come to live at Potsdam. But we could visit your family here, as often as was practical." We stopped walking. He looked down at me fondly, and kissed my forehead.

"Yes, little Tania. I have come here to Russia not only to lead the Young People's Peace Initiative, but to ask your father for your hand in marriage."

My lip trembled. My knees felt weak, and at the same time I wanted to run. A jumble of thoughts tripped over one another in my mind: won't Olga be jealous, won't Niuta be happy, would I like Germany? I don't want Cousin Willy for a father-in-law. And then there was the main, central thought. The only thought that mattered. Adalbert. Adalbert wanted to be my husband.

I tried to speak, but all I could do was look up at him. I could not find any words.

"Of course, we wouldn't be married for some time yet. Not for another year, at least. But I intend to ask your father for your hand, as a promise for the future." He paused. "You do love me a little, don't you, Tania?"

"I—I—of course I do. You are my second cousin." As soon as I spoke the words I thought, why am I saying this? This isn't the way a girl is supposed to respond when a man proposes to her. In my mind's eye I saw, not Adalbert, tall and handsome in his white uniform, but Constantin Melnikov, the young doctor from the Workers' Clinic, looking rather rumpled, watching me searchingly.

I shook my head. "We shouldn't be speaking of these things until you have talked to my father."

"I have to know whether or not you will say yes, when the moment comes."

He bent down and kissed me then, and he tasted of wine and smelled faintly of cologne. His lips were soft, I could feel the tickle of his thin moustache. It was a pleasant sensation, but hardly an overwhelming one.

"My parents are eager for me to marry, you see, Tania. They have presented me with several princesses but I did not like any of them. You are the one I like."

"Why? What is it that you like about me?"

"You are lovely. You will grow up to be a beautiful woman. And you are intelligent, and kind, and you have a gentle manner. You would never try to dominate me, or make me miserable."

"I may be quite different in a few years, when I am grown up." Thinking back, I cannot remember why I said that, but I'm glad I did.

I felt Adalbert stiffen. "What are you trying to tell me, Tania? That you want to wait? Or that you do not want to be my wife?"

"I don't know! Don't make me decide!" And with that I lost my courage, and ran back toward the palace, feeling impatient and befuddled, wishing I had not drunk any wine at dinner and aware that my cheeks were burning in the chill night air.

Eighteen

Artipo was getting old, and could barely drag himself across the floor. His sore paw refused to heal, and his left foreleg was so swollen and red where the grey fur had worn away that he could hardly bear to let me touch him there or try to pet him.

"Ah! Taniushka," papa said when I brought him into my room to look at the old dog, lying on my bed, wagging his tail weakly as we came up to him. "How sad! He looks so poorly." He reached down and petted the soft grey head.

"He must be at least ten years old now, maybe twelve. I remember when the litter was born. We gave you the best of them. I know how you love him, but dogs can't live forever." He bent down and looked into Artipo's red-rimmed old eyes. "He must be in a lot of pain, with that infected leg. Maybe you should let Sedynov take him out to the burying ground and be merciful to him."

I burst into tears, and papa hugged me, trying to comfort me. I couldn't bear the thought of Artipo's being shot and buried, which was what "being merciful" meant.

"No, papa, there must be something the kennel master can do for him."

Papa assured me that he would have a word with the kennel master, who kept a locked cupboard full of medicinal compounds for curing puppy rash and worms, coughing and the wobbles. But I didn't think he had a medicine to cure old age, and I spent a wakeful night, with Artipo nestled against me, dreading the moment when I would have no choice but to call Sedynov and let him take my beloved dog out to the burying ground.

I took him for a walk the next day as usual, though he walked very slowly because of his limp and I often let him stop and rest. We were walking along the shore of the small lake by the Chinese Pavilion when I saw Father Gregory coming toward us.

I was always startled to see him, he had an almost feral look about him, like a creature from the forest. Bits of bark and dried leaves clung to his coat, as if he had been sleeping on the ground, and his greying beard was stringy and matted. His sandals were muddy. He carried no satchel or knapsack.

As he came closer I felt myself relax, and the sweetness of his presence poured over me like a balm. His face shone, his deep-set eyes, when he turned them on me, were alight with purpose and a dark vitality that seemed to penetrate to my very core. He came up to me, then looked down at Artipo, shambling along with his head down, sniffing the ground.

"No sorrow!" he called out, lifting his hand, as he always did, in blessing. "All sorrow forgotten! Only the joy of the afternoon!"

He knelt down and put his hand on Artipo's head. At once I saw Artipo straighten his back and raise his neck and head.

"There, there now, strong young pup!"

Artipo pricked up his ears, licked Father Gregory's hand and barked. Father Gregory ran his hand lightly down the swollen leg and paw, and murmured something under his breath. Then he stood and looked at me, nodding.

"He will be well."

Humming, he stood and looked around the garden. He went over to a bed of shrubbery and took a stone from the ornamental edging, then, showing it to Artipo, flung it as far as he could across the brittle grass.

With another bark Artipo took off at a run, chasing the stone, his tongue hanging out and his ears flattened against his head. He retrieved the stone and brought it back to Father Gregory, dropping it at his feet and looking up at him.

I was beside myself with astonishment and delight. I flung my arms around my dear Artipo and buried my head in his fur. I heard Father Gregory murmur, as if from a distance, "Yes! All love!" but when I looked up a moment later he had gone.

Nineteen

When *Aunt Olenka* gave her charity ball for the Workers' Clinic mama agreed to subscribe, donating five hundred rubles and offering to supply a table of attractive goods to be sold for the benefit of the clinic so that even more money could be raised. She agreed to donate, but she did not agree to attend the ball; her headaches were plaguing her, she said, and besides, she did not want to encounter Grandma Minnie or Auntie Miechen or any of the other haughty nobles and society women who ridiculed her and spread ugly gossip about her.

Olga and I were sent in mama's place.

I had been knitting what mama called "woolies," warm hats and scarves and vests (I couldn't seem to learn to knit entire sweaters, the sleeves always came out wrong), and my knitted goods plus many more that mama herself had made plus some brocade pillows Aunt Xenia had brought from Paris and some lovely Alençon lace that had once trimmed one of mama's gowns (she never allowed the same lace to be used on two different gowns, but gave it away) were spread out attractively on the long table and Olga and I took our places behind it. We were to sit there until all the goods were sold—then and only then could we dance.

Dancing made me think of Adalbert, but he was not invited to the ball. He had gone to Moscow with the members of his peace delegation and was not expected to return for a month or more, which gave me plenty of time to mull over what he had told me at our last meeting.

I kept asking myself, why did I behave as I had during that dreamlike evening on the Children's Island? Why did I run away? Was I simply too young to think about marriage, even to a man I liked so much? Girls of royal blood were not, as a rule, expected to ponder men's proposals; they were expected to obey their fathers and marry the men chosen for them. Adalbert was honoring me in speaking to me first, before he approached papa. But I wished he hadn't. Oh, how I wished he hadn't!

It was hot in the grand, high-ceilinged room where the charity ball was under way. A crowd of guests milled among the many tables piled with goods for sale, chatting and flirting, some flinging down coins in careless abandon, as if to say, what do I care for a knitted vest or a silken rose to pin on my gown? I can't be concerned with such trifles! But I will donate money all the same. There was a good deal of variety in the crowd. Handsomely dressed courtiers mingled with military officers, teachers and professors in black coats stood next to bureaucrats wearing stars of commendation on their gold-trimmed jackets. A good many of the donors, having made their contributions, stood tapping their toes to the music and looking bored.

Aunt Olenka, brisk and cheery as she nearly always was, her buck teeth showing prominently when she smiled, came to our table and said how pleased she was that our goods were selling well. And in truth Olga and I were having a good deal of success, for many in the crowd, wanting an excuse to say they had met the grand duchesses, had made purchases.

"Better you are here tonight than your mother," Olenka confided to me in a loud whisper. "So many have turned against her. Such things the newspapers are saying! That Father Gregory is her lover! And that she has not only one, but many paramours, some of them women!"

"I don't want to hear it," I said as firmly as I could. "Such things should not be repeated within the family, especially since we know they are untrue, and hurtful to mama."

"They are hurtful to your father, and his government. That's what matters. Everyone agrees."

I said nothing. I was well aware of the rumors and newspaper reports, the slanderous posters and graffiti picturing mama and Father Gregory loving each other. It was preposterous. Yet the public craved the sensational images, and wanted more.

Just then Constantin came striding energetically through the crowd and up to our table, bringing two saucers of ice cream and handing one to me and one to my sister.

"Good evening ladies," he said. "I hope you like raspberry." He winked at me as he handed me my saucer.

"Ah, Constantin," Aunt Olenka said, "I'm glad you are here at last. I need help with Baroness Essen's table. The baroness has had to retire for the evening, will you please fill in?"

"Glad to oblige. Will you join me later, Tania, when all your goods have been sold? I'm sure I'm going to need some help."

"Yes, of course."

Aunt Olenka and Constantin moved off through the crowd, watched closely by my sister.

"Am I imagining things, Tania, or has Aunt Olenka been getting fatter? You don't suppose she's pregnant, do you? They say her husband never sleeps with her."

"No, she isn't pregnant." In a lowered voice I added, "Niuta heard from Aunt Olenka's dresser that she's been taking Oriental Pills."

"Those pills that enlarge the breasts?"

"Shh!" I nodded.

Olga and I giggled. "What she needs are pills to improve the face!"

"Don't be unkind. Aunt Olenka has been good to us." And she had been. Ever since mama's headaches worsened, and she began shutting herself away from the world more and more, Aunt Olenka had been inviting us to her Petersburg house for tea on Sunday afternoons, taking us on excursions to Druce's, buying us ices and trinkets and generally taking us under her wing. I liked her more and more. She was not like the other women in my father's family; she spoke her mind frankly and was not afraid to show her feelings. She even discussed politics, which almost no one else in the family did, at least not in front of us. And she could be jokey and funny, she made us laugh.

At last our table was nearly bare. Only mama's length of beautiful Alençon lace was waiting for a buyer. Olga and I unrolled it and spread it out across the length of the table to show it to full advantage.

Uncle Vladimir's son Andrew came toward us from out of the crowd, and with him was a petite, curly-headed brunette, holding his arm and smiling amiably. Her movements were lithe, her face animated and attractive.

I realized, with a shock, that it had to be Mathilde Kchessinsky!

Olga too recognized her, and fumed. She looked our cousin in the eye and said, loudly enough for others to overhear, "I can't believe you have brought that woman here tonight. She doesn't belong here. She belongs in a brothel!"

"Olga! Don't lower yourself to her level!" I said in a measured tone, taking hold of my sister's arm and pulling her toward me. With a flash of anger she yanked her arm out of my grasp.

"I'll say what I please! All the world knows she's a whore!"

I heard a few gasps from the people around us. Mathilde, seemingly unconcerned, was fingering the beautiful lace.

"This table is closed," I said, beginning to roll up the lace.

"Ah, but Tania, I think my companion may want to buy your lace," Cousin Andrew drawled, taking a purse of coins from his pocket and spilling them out onto the table.

"This is my mother's table, and that is her lace, and if she were here, she would certainly not sell it to—to—anyone unworthy." My heart was thumping, I could feel my cheeks growing hot. I was doing my best to keep my composure.

"But this lace is just what I need for the gown Lamanov is making for me to wear to the English ambassador's ball, Andrew," Mathilde said in a light, trilling voice. A voice that I had to admit was sweet and charming. "Please, won't you buy it for me?" She looked up at him.

Andrew emptied his purse of coins. They lay, a gleaming pile of gold, amid the lace.

"We will take the lace, Tania. I think you will find our contribution generous. There must be several hundred rubles there."

"We don't want your money," Olga said firmly, sweeping the coins onto the floor and walking off into the crowd, leaving me standing by the table, exasperated.

I struggled to summon my dignity. I remembered the lessons Monsieur Gilliard had given Olga and me in how grand duchesses ought to deport themselves. With politeness and dignity, he said. Always politeness and dignity.

There was a commotion as people in the crowd, with shrieks of excitement, bent down to scramble for Andrew's coins.

"I'm sorry," I said, "but as I told you, this table is closed. Perhaps you can find some lace elsewhere." And I continued to roll the lace as rapidly as I could into a fat ball. It slipped through Mathilde's fingers; to her credit, she did not grasp onto it but let it go.

Andrew reacted with amusement. "Come, dear. There are other tables, and I have other purses of coins." And with a wave of his hand to me he steered Mathilde through the knot of scavengers while I, having stuffed the lace into my carpet bag, went off in search of Constantin.

Twenty

Constantin was puzzled. The lines on his high forehead deepened, the look in his light blue eyes was one of disbelief.

"How old did you say it is?"

"I didn't say it, the patriarch Makarios said it. He said the earth is exactly six thousand, seven hundred and fifty years, ten months and seven days old. As of last Wednesday."

Constantin burst out laughing—a laugh loud enough for the others in the adjacent salon to hear. We had been having tea at Aunt Olenka's Petersburg mansion, and a lively discussion had begun over the exact age of our planet. Constantin and I had retired to an adjoining room to discuss this issue more fully. We sat on a comfortable sofa, side by side, having had our fill of frosted orange cake and biscuits and strong Indian tea that sharpened our wits and quickened our senses.

"But that's absurd."

"It is what the Bible says."

"I see. And how much older is the earth likely to get? Does the Bible tell us that too?"

"Only God knows that. But Monsieur Gilliard has told me that there are many scientists who say the earth must be millions of years old, and as to its end, my father has read that it almost ended a few years ago when there was a huge explosion in Siberia."

Now Constantin looked serious. "What explosion?"

"He read about it in a scientific journal. There was a flash of light in the sky, a thousand times brighter than the sun."

"Really, Tania, you do exaggerate!" He cuffed me lightly on the shoulder.

"I exaggerate! You're the one who says the earth is a billion years old!" I cuffed him back.

"You can't even count to a billion!" He grasped me playfully and began to shake me, laughing at the same time.

"I know you have a billion germs on your hands, from the clinic! Don't touch me!" I was laughing too.

But he only held onto me harder, and I liked it, and I smiled, and then he kissed me.

Our arguments often ended in kisses, and both the arguments and the kisses excited me. We met more and more often, at the clinic, where I went to visit Daria and baby Iskra, and at Aunt Olenka's house, and several times at Constantin's parents' house, where I met his gentle, friendly mother and his self-important father. I joined in many a discussion about political reform, scientific discoveries, medical advances—a whole host of topics. I was encouraged to read more widely, to inform myself about what was going on in the world of thought and to ponder the meaning of what was called "modern," by which people seemed to indicate what was new and therefore superior. All too often we discussed the most vital question of the day, whether or not Europe would soon find itself embroiled in war.

I was intrigued by nearly everything we talked about in those heady days. Constantin and I were both intensely curious, and even though he, being older, knew a lot more than I did he was always learning, always aware of how much more there was to learn and to know.

However serious our discussions, they always had one outcome: the deepening of our infatuation with each other.

Can one love at fourteen? Yes. An emphatic yes. I was eager for love, he was ardent and we quickly became so wrapped up in one another that we neglected other things. He got behind in his studies. I was so distracted by thoughts of him that I daydreamed for hours, ignoring mama's delicate state and papa's escapades, Olga's quizzical looks and Niuta's warning glances. (Nothing fooled Niuta; she knew I was quite infatuated.)

One thing I could not ignore, however, and that was Father Gregory's increasingly frequent visits to the nursery wing, where my sisters and I had our bedrooms. I told Constantin about this, and he became alarmed.

"You mean to say, Tania, that he just visits the nursery whenever he likes, with no one stopping him?"

"He always comes and goes as he chooses. Papa told the servants long ago never to hinder him. Mama calls him Our Friend and says he must always be allowed entrance, day or night. You see, she believes that he knows when he is needed, without being summoned, and he comes every time."

"And what does he do, when he comes into your room or Olga's?"

"He sings to us, and prays with us. He sits on our bed, and tells stories about his home in Pokrovsky while he rubs our feet or massages our sore necks."

I saw the muscles in Constantin's face constrict. His jaw was set, his eyes filled with a cold anger I had never before seen there.

"Tania, I must ask you a very serious question now, and you must tell me the truth. Has he ever touched you anywhere besides your neck or your feet?"

I thought a moment. "He pats me on the head sometimes."

"Has he ever kissed you?"

"Only on the cheek, like my uncles and aunts do. But I have sometimes thought—"

"Yes?"

"I have sometimes had a feeling that—he wanted to kiss me, the way you do." I winced as I said it, the thought was repulsive to me.

I could tell that Constantin was upset by that conversation, and soon afterward he came to me and told me he wanted to meet Father Gregory.

"Where does this self-proclaimed starets live?"

"Number Four Roszdestvenskaya Street. He lives with a priest, Yaroslav Medved."

Shortly after that conversation Constantin and I were riding along Nevsky Prospekt in his carriage, going toward Father Gregory's apartment.

I had confided to him Father Gregory's remarkable healing of Artipo, a healing which appeared to be absolute and without flaw, for my old dog continued to run and leap like a puppy, and I also confided the amazement I felt when my brother Alexei's suffering was ended by the touch of Father Gregory's hand or by the few words he spoke. This had happened many times, I told him. The sick had been made well, pain taken away, suffering eased. I was firmly convinced that without Father Gregory's healing presence, my brother would be dead.

"Hypnosis is not healing, Tania," was Constantin's response. "And if this man truly has the powers you attribute to him, your brother would be cured. He would never again need healing from the starets or anyone else, save God Almighty."

"But Artipo was not hypnotized," I persisted in arguing. "Artipo is just a dog. An old, sick dog who is now young and healthy."

Constantin shrugged. "Who knows what tricks of the mind can be played, even on an old dog?"

The street Father Gregory lived on was near the Haymarket, Petersburg's huge square where vegetables and flowers and old clothes were sold, and where pickpockets and thieves flourished. Prostitutes strolled among the booths, displaying the yellow tickets the police required them to carry. Pigeons rose from out of the mass of bodies and stalls, flying upward in flocks into the overcast sky and toward the river.

"Your Father Gregory lives in an unsavory part of the city," Constantin remarked as we passed the vast square.

"Mama says it is because he chooses to be poor. To be more like Christ and the saints. They did not live grandly."

"I doubt whether Christ or his saints would have wanted to live on Roszdestvenskaya Street," came the wry response.

We arrived at the address and found a dingy brick building, six stories high, the entrance partially blocked by uncollected rubbish. Constantin told the carriage driver to wait and helped me down onto the muddy roadway. No doorman was standing in the dirty entryway to admit us, no servant stood by the stairwell to caution us about the broken handrail as we began to climb the stairs.

"Niuta has been here," I told Constantin. "She brings him messages sometimes. She says he lives right up under the roof. With the pigeons."

It was a wearying climb, up many flights of stairs, and I had to stop and rest several times, Constantin waiting patiently for me to catch my breath. We passed no one else on the stairs, but when at last we arrived at the top floor we found it crowded with people. The door to the single apartment on that floor was wide open, and we walked through it into a fairly large room full of the treble murmuring of women's voices.

No one looked at us as we entered. The women were seated in chairs arranged around the walls of the room, and we found two chairs and sat down. Presently a grey-haired woman in peasant dress brought us some tea.

"You are welcome," she said. "The father is in his inner room, occupied as usual. He regrets that he cannot see everyone, but if you will wait, you may at least receive a blessing."

We thanked her and drank our tea, watching all that was going on around us. It had been agreed between us that when we saw Father Gregory I would introduce Constantin as my friend who had a terrible pain.

We waited. An hour passed, then two hours.

"This is worse than the Workers' Clinic," Constantin whispered to me. "Why are there only rich old women here?"

The room was indeed filled with aging women—at least they seemed aging to us, young as we were—in furs and beautiful clothes, with gold earrings and bracelets. There was no one from Smokestack Town there, no one from the Haymarket, none of the beggars that crowded the steps of St. Isaac's Cathedral only a few minutes' walk from the building we sat in. From time to time one of the women would come out of a little door at one end of the room, and another would go in. Through the dirty windows we watched the waning of the afternoon light. As Niuta had said, Father Gregory lived among the pigeons, which perched on the windowsills, cooing and clucking.

The servant brought out some plates of fish and rolls and a bowl of pickled cabbage, along with some iced buns, and we helped ourselves.

"Try and look ill," I whispered to Constantin. "Maybe you will get to see Father Gregory more quickly."

Eventually the door to the inner room opened and Father Gregory came out, looking much as he always did, his stained, shabby peasant tunic and trousers rumpled and neglected, his beard and hair in need of combing. I thought I detected the smell of alcohol on his breath, but I couldn't be sure. He raised his hand in blessing as he came into the room, and said "Peace be to you, wayfarers."

To my astonishment all the well-dressed women knelt, and remained kneeling as Father Gregory sat down and began eating, carelessly and greedily.

"We had better kneel too," I whispered to Constantin. "We don't want to stand out." He raised his eyebrows but did as I suggested, murmuring "A grand duchess kneeling to a peasant. Now, that's something I never heard of."

For a long time we remained kneeling there, our knees on the cold bare floor, listening to the slurping and other digestive noises Father Gregory made. No one spoke or moved. Finally he was finished. He wiped his hands on the stained tablecloth and stood. He took off his tunic, pulling it over his head, and handed it to the servant. Then he went back into his inner room.

At once a clamor arose. The kneeling women got to their feet and began calling out. "Fifty rubles!" "Seventy-five!" "It's mine, I tell you!" "No, mine!"

We watched the undignified auction of Father Gregory's torn, sweat-stained tunic, conducted by the grey-haired servant. When it was over Father Gregory opened his inner door once again and beckoned to me.

I went in, with Constantin.

"Close the door, Tania," Father Gregory said gravely. There was no hint of the rapturous joy, the lovely innocence he had projected on our previous encounters. Instead he seemed subdued, matter-of-fact. A shrewd peasant about to conduct business. On the table in front of his chair was a large bowl full of money—contributions, I assumed, from the people who came for healing and blessing.

"Father Gregory, I have brought my friend Constantin—"

"He is a skeptic, he does not want to believe. He mistrusts me. He listens to the dirty gossip about me. You love him. All this I can see. Also I can see that he suffers. His left eye—yes—it gives you pain, does it not?" he said, addressing Constantin.

Startled, Constantin nodded. "Sometimes, yes."

"You do not need me. You need new glasses."

"Father Gregory, I am a medical student. Also I serve at the Workers'

Clinic in the Vyborg. I see much suffering, and there is little enough I can do to help. If you have something to teach me, I will gladly learn."

I looked at Constantin, no longer certain whether he was trying to maneuver Father Gregory into revealing his secrets—possibly his frauds— or making a sincere request.

"What I do cannot be taught. You must be born with the grace to ease pain and bewitch the blood."

"Can you knit together broken bones?"

"I can cause them to knit themselves together very quickly. All is done through faith."

"But how then can you heal animals, who have no faith?"

"Animals know love, loyalty, faithfulness. Why not faith?"

There was a long moment while Constantin and the starets looked at one another. I felt quite left out.

"I must ask you one thing more. What happens to all the money I see here on your table? All the gifts that are given to you?"

He responded with a gesture that indicated indifference. "I send most of it to my village, to Pokrovsky. The money I send fed nearly two hundred families there last winter, praise God. But make no mistake. I have no wish to be thanked. This money is not for me, but for the grace that comes through me. If it comes to me, it must flow out again, where it is needed."

"Are you always so generous?"

For the first time Father Gregory smiled. "I am a man. A flawed man, like any other. I have wants, needs, urges—"

Constantin, who had been sitting, now stood up, his height and his physical strength intimidating, or so I assumed, to Father Gregory, who was much older, and not nearly as big or strong.

"As to your urges, I am here to tell you that you are never to enter Tania's bedroom again. Or the bedrooms of her sisters."

"Papa and mama allow me to go where I will." Father Gregory always called my father papa and my mother mama.

"But I do not. And if I hear that you have bothered the grand duchesses again, I will seek you out and bring the tsar's police with me."

There was a long silence, during which Father Gregory looked into Constantin's eyes, and I felt afraid for him. Father Gregory had great power. Could he use it to hurt Constantin?

"Perhaps you are aware of Captain Golenishchev?"

"The chief of police, yes."

"Several years ago Captain Golenishchev's favorite daughter was dying of typhoid, and he sent for me. I healed her. Since then Captain Golenishchev has protected me from all manner of false prosecutions."

"I think we should go, Tania," Constantin said, holding out his hand to me. "I'm sure this peasant from Pokrovsky will remember what I have said, and will not imagine that he can evade me, if I learn that he has been bothering you or your sisters."

We left then, making our way out through the roomful of women and down the many flights of stairs to the street. I felt shaken by the experience, confused by the change in Father Gregory's manner, put off by the reverence paid to him by the worshipful women and upset by the thought that my mother could well have been one of them, had her rank not prevented it. I had never seen anyone stand up to him the way Constantin had; on the other hand, I had never seen Father Gregory meet another man face to face and talk with him frankly, and I liked that.

"I still think he is a hypnotist," Constantin said to me as we were leaving. "And I don't trust him. But what intrigues me is, how did he know about the pain in my left eye? And how did he know that when I read, I wear glasses?"

Twenty-one

$\mathcal{H}$*ow very nice* to encounter you again, Your Highness."

As soon as I heard the soothing voice I recognized it. It was the voice of the doctor who called himself Mr. Schmidt.

"And your lovely daughter," he added, with a grave smile at me.

Mama looked at him, at first with wariness, then her gaze softened. Mama and I were sitting in a swing on the terrace of Grandma Minnie's town house, waiting for a concert to begin. The evening was mild, and through the open doors we could hear the musicians tuning up and the audience arriving.

Mama had not wanted to come to the concert, even though she knew Grandma Minnie would not be there, as she was in Stockholm visiting relatives. But papa had urged her to attend. The Italian singer was very fine, he said, and there would be very few guests, and those congenial ones.

"You must go, dushki," I heard him say, using the name mama once told me he had called her during their courtship. Dushki in Russian means "my soul."

"Take Tania with you," he said. "If anyone should say an unkind word to you, just ignore it. Pretend you can't hear it. You are losing your hearing, after all. Dr. Korovin says so."

Mama could not hear as well as she once had, and I had to make an effort to speak more loudly to her.

"A deaf woman going to a concert!" she said, laughing. "Imagine that!"

But she decided to go, and I went along though I missed Constantin and thought of him for much of the evening. He and I had gotten into the habit of writing a letter to each other every night.

"Do you mind if I sit here in the fresh air with you and your daughter?" Mr. Schmidt was asking. I was on guard, determined to be protective of mama. But I could tell that her initial wariness had disappeared; the doctor had a soothing effect on her, she trusted him at once.

"Please join us, if you like. What brings you to Russia?"

"I have colleagues here. I like to stay in contact with them from time to time. And besides, St. Petersburg is a very beautiful city."

"Very beautiful, yes—but full of worms."

"Worms?"

"Earthworms, ear worms, ice worms—"

"Tell me about these worms. I would like to know more."

"My daughter is trying to breed them. They escape. They crawl all over her bedroom. They crawl into her bed, onto her skin—" She grimaced and shut her eyes and hugged herself, shivering.

"Tania, are you breeding worms?" Mr. Schmidt asked me with a gleam of humor in his eyes.

"No. My sister Anastasia is. She's only ten. She doesn't know any better."

"I know a man who is very worried about rats. He says that he believes rats are eating his flesh. Tell me, Your Highness, are you worried that these worms may crawl on you the way they do on Anastasia?"

Mama's eyes opened suddenly and she blinked. She looked at Mr. Schmidt, and frowned.

"Of course not. What an absurd idea. No, it isn't the worms that are attacking me. Not at all." She spoke crisply, then her voice changed. "It's just that I've been having such bad dreams."

"The cranberries again? The pins?"

"It's that awful smell. I dream of that awful smell."

"Tell me what it smells like."

"Like—eggs gone bad."

"In your dream, are you in the kitchen, with the rotten eggs?"

Mama shook her head, frowning, looking as if she were in pain. "No, no!"

"Where are you? Don't be afraid to tell me. You are safe here with us."

She continued to shake her head, as if unwilling to confront what was in her mind. I wondered what was happening to her.

"No! It was—out in front of the church." Tears came from her eyes. "It was terrible. A terrible thing to see." She spoke in gasps, her tears falling.

"What terrible thing did you see?"

"She died. She died. She burned up. We all saw it."

I looked at Mr. Schmidt. "I know what she is thinking of. It was the girl who killed herself," I told him, surprised at how calmly I was able to say the words. "It was the most dreadful thing I have ever seen. She poured kerosene all over herself and lit it on fire."

"Why?"

"I don't know," I said. "I wish I did."

Mama dried her eyes with her fists. "I know," she said after a time, her voice low, almost a growl. "I found out. How could anyone see that and not try to find out? How could anyone smell that stinking kerosene and not try to find out?" She peered at us accusingly, her eyes large and round and fierce, as if daring us to answer her. Mr. Schmidt and I were silent.

"She was a student. Only eighteen years old. Her name was Raissa Lieven. From a noble family, if you can imagine it." Mama's voice was low and even, it was almost as if she were repeating words she had memorized, words from a play or script, words whose meaning she did not want to know.

"She was put in prison for criticizing the government. One of the guards raped her, again and again. She couldn't bear it. When she was released from prison, she decided to kill herself. She told others that she wanted to make certain my husband and our entire family was there to see her die. So she waited for a day when she knew we would be coming to church, and when we got there, she—she—"

"Yes. You have told us now. No wonder you have bad dreams. You smell the odor of the kerosene because it brings back the ghastly image of the burning girl. I wonder, do you believe yourself to be somehow at fault?"

Mama suddenly stood up. "I think we should go in now, Tania. I am getting chilly." She spoke brightly, with no shadow of her former anguish or of the unnatural calm I had discerned in her tone. She did not look at Mr. Schmidt. "Do you know, Tania, they say that suicide has become quite fashionable in Petersburg. There is something called the Suicide Club where people go at night to drink themselves to death—or almost to death." She laughed. "I saw a newspaper that said papa went there. Can you imagine? The things people write!"

With a charming smile she held out her hand to me, and I took it and got up out of the swing.

"Your Highness," Mr. Schmidt said as we prepared to go inside, "what of the things they are writing about your Father Gregory? About you and him together?"

Mama stopped. "Father Gregory? Why, he can do no wrong. Yes. He can do no wrong, whether we are together or not."

"And you? Would you say you can do no wrong?"

Mama did not answer, but turned her face away.

"Good evening, Your Highness. Good evening, Tania," came the pleasant, soothing voice.

"Good night, Mr. Schmidt," mama replied over her shoulder. "Pleasant dreams."

Twenty-two

It should not have taken long, after Adalbert asked papa for my hand in marriage, for his proposal to be politely rejected.

But it did. It took far, far too long—and the reason was that Grandma Minnie had decided that the time had come for her to intervene in our family's affairs and insist on things being done her way.

She had just returned from Stockholm where she had spent a month or more with her Swedish and Danish relations, all of whom, mama told me, were very European in their outlook and thought all Russians were barbarians.

"They always influence her," mama said. "They make her believe she must save Russia from self-destruction. I have no doubt she will be insufferable for a while."

Grandma Minnie arranged a family dinner at her Petersburg house and invited most of the family, including Auntie Miechen (who was by then a widow), Uncle Bembo, Aunt Olenka and Petya, KR, and even Aunt Ella, who was no longer called Aunt Ella but Mother Superior, for she had founded her own order of nuns, the Sisters of Mercy, and always dressed all in white with a white wimple and veil. Papa's sister Xenia was not at the dinner, I remember, because she and her husband Sandro had become separated and were staying away from the rest of the family just then.

As soon as the last course was taken away, Grandma Minnie ordered us all into her salon and began talking to us. It was late in the evening, and everyone there had drunk a good deal of wine, and some were enjoying their second or third postprandial cognac. Her words fell on numbed brains—which, no doubt, was part of her plan.

"I wonder whether any of you realize the seriousness of our situation," she began.

"I do," came Petya's annoying voice. "We are almost out of cognac." There were one or two guffaws. Grandma Minnie glared at Petya and then went on.

"Russia is in peril. If my late husband were alive he would be leading his regiments to guard the borders. He would be expelling every German from this land—"

"Every German?" asked Auntie Miechen, looking pointedly at mama. I thought at once, I am German, because mama is. Was Grandma Minnie hoping to expel me?

"Now, mother," said papa, speaking slowly and with a drawl of inebriation, "you go too far."

"German arms threaten us all. But family bonds may yet save us. I am told that the Kaiser's son, Prince Adalbert, intends to offer marriage to Grand Duchess Tania."

Papa interrupted her. "Yes, he came to me the other day and said he had his father's permission to propose to Tania—if I agreed. The wedding would not be for another year."

"And did you agree?"

"Of course he didn't!" Uncle Bembo put in, his voice gruff. "He has to consult his ministers! This is a matter of state!"

"I think it is first a family matter," was Grandma Minnie's response. "An alliance between Hohenzollern and Romanov will benefit both families—and both countries. The prince is pleasant and well spoken. He is a naval officer. Tania's marriage can do much good."

I felt many eyes on me. Was I expected to say something? Surely I was not expected to express my true feelings, which were that though I felt fondness for Adalbert I much preferred Constantin and wished very much that I could marry him.

Olga, who was sitting next to me, elbowed me in the ribs, making me cry out.

"Yes, Tania?"

"Nothing, grandma."

Then mama spoke up, enunciating very clearly and distinctly though her German accent had never been more conspicuous.

"No! There will be no wedding! No daughter of mine will marry a Hohenzollern! Not while Cousin Willy is Kaiser! The man is a bully and a braggart. He has no humanity, none!"

"It is not his humanity that is at issue," remarked KR, who tended to mumble his words.

"What was that?" Mama sat up in her chair, looking around for the speaker, but KR did not repeat what he had said.

"I know someone said something! It was something about me, wasn't it! Something spiteful!"

"Dear, no one said anything against you," papa said, looking anxious and attempting to reach for mama's hand. But she was incensed, and would not be stilled. We had grown accustomed to seeing her this way. We never knew whether her irritation would build into a full-scale tantrum, or would subside into seething, thinly-disguised anger.

I thought I saw the faintest glimmer of a smile hover on Grandma Minnie's lips. I hated her then.

"Mama," papa was saying to Grandma Minnie, "Willy is a bore and an exhibitionist, but he would never start a war. I have said so many times. It continues to be my view. To say otherwise is to make the situation worse. The more we fear him, the happier he is, and the happier he is, the more ships he builds."

"He cheated, you know, during the yacht races," mama was saying, her tone now seeming detached, speaking to no one in particular. "He put out more sail than he was allowed. Nicky had to make a formal complaint to the judges." She looked around the room. Everyone was staring at her.

"Well, he did. You all don't know! You weren't there!"

Before mama could become angry and vehement again Grandma Minnie interrupted her.

"Is that what your drunken monk told you? The filthy one who calls himself Rasputin? The one you worship?"

Mama got to her feet and, with a scream of anger, rushed toward

Grandma Minnie, but before she could reach her Ella stepped between them and caught mama by the shoulders.

"Ah, Sunshine, don't let her goad you. You know better. Here, come with me. We'll say a prayer to St. John of the Battles, shall we? His icon is nearby, I think. We can find it." Ella led mama, who had begun to weep, her shoulders shaking, out of the room.

Papa got up to follow them.

"Stay with us awhile, Nicholas. I have more to say. Necessary things. Things everyone in the family knows must be said, yet no one but myself is brave enough to say."

There was a stir of unease in the room. I had an impulse to get up and follow mama and Aunt Ella, yet I felt I needed to hear whatever it was that Grandma Minnie was about to tell everyone. There was still the question of Adalbert's proposal—had papa agreed to it? But at that moment Adalbert no longer seemed very important.

I looked at Olga, who appeared vexed, as she often did when she was bored.

"Nicholas, I have found out the truth about this Rasputin, this man your wife relies on so greatly, and worships, and probably loves. Yes, loves. Carnally."

"Mother!"

"I will be heard!" Grandma Minnie drew from the pocket of her gown several sheets of paper, and held them up so that everyone in the room could see them. They were stamped with a large red official seal.

"I have here police reports on this criminal, Gregory Yefimovich Novy, called Rasputin, a convicted thief and rapist from the village of Pokrovsky, a fraudulent so-called healer." She read from the papers. "He has abandoned his wife and three children. Two of the children have come to Petersburg looking for him. While living on Roszdestvenskaya Street with the priest Yaroslav Medved he has been seen hiring prostitutes on Morskaya Street and taking them to bathhouses. Sometimes he hires two or three in one night. He cheats rich women out of their fortunes in the afternoons, then goes out into the street at night and urinates against the walls of churches."

"And he has kept our son alive, through his prayers," papa added.

"And I do not know how I could have survived all these last weary years without him." He hung his head.

But Grandma Minnie ignored his heartfelt words, and went on.

"Did he tell you he had gone to Jerusalem as a pilgrim, walking all the way, dragging heavy chains?"

"Yes."

"It was a lie. Did he claim that he could raise the dead?"

"No. He never told us that."

"Well, he has said it to others. And he has cheated them out of thousands of rubles."

"No! I don't want to hear it. Any of it."

"He healed my Artipo," I said loudly. "And I have seen him heal Alexei many times."

"All lies! Delusions! Imaginings of the superstitious Russian soul!" I had never seen Grandma Minnie so agitated.

"Enough!" papa suddenly shouted in his loudest voice, a voice I had rarely heard during my entire life because he was usually the mildest of men. "I will not hear any more! Away, all of you!"

The others in the family hastened to obey, and soon the room was almost empty. But Olga and I stayed where we were, sitting on the sofa, and Grandma Minnie hesitated to leave. She opened her mouth as if to say more, but at a glare from papa, she shut it again, folding her papers and putting them back in her pocket. With dignity she walked to the double doors leading to the corridor beyond. When she reached the doors she turned back.

"This is my house, Nicholas. You would do well to show me courtesy here. And as to your precious Father Gregory, and your precious German wife—who, by the way, may soon be certified as mad by a respected doctor—you can be sure I have more to say, and that more action will be taken."

"What about Adalbert?" I asked, but Grandma Minnie had already swept out and papa sank back into his chair, his head in his hands, so my question went unanswered.

Twenty-three

I had a lot to talk over with the elephant in those days. I went to his enclosure often and he came slowly up to the fence and extended his withered grey trunk toward me, hoping I would give him some tender leaves. I confided everything to him—my feelings for Constantin, the troubles in our family, my worries about mama and, deepest of all, my hopes that I would grow up to be a good and honorable woman and my fears that I might not.

The elephant trumpeted now and then, and shook his shaggy head when the flies gathered around his eyes, but he never listened to me for very long and soon he was ambling off toward the opposite end of his paddock where the mahout slept in his hut.

One reason I sought the company of the elephant was that I wanted to avoid seeing Adalbert. I knew he would be returning to Petersburg with his Young People's Peace Initiative soon, and that he would want an answer to his proposal. What would papa tell him? If the answer was no, would I have to see him again? What would I say?

But in the end all was well. Adalbert sent me a note asking if he could see me, and I had to say yes—how could I not? He came alone, and as soon as he was shown into the small sitting room I felt all my old affection for him return. He was so handsome, his eyes full of a gentle tenderness and with a hint of wistfulness.

"I only wanted to say goodbye, dear Tania," he began after kissing my cheek. "Your father explained to me that after consulting with his ministers, it was decided that a marriage between us would not benefit Russia. I had hoped very much that the answer would be different."

I felt great relief.

"Dear Adalbert, can we be friends?" It was all I could think of to say.

"Of course. Warm friends—for life, if you will have me."

"You know I will. I value you so much. Will you promise to write often?"

"As often as I can. My father is eager for me to go to sea again, and long voyages make correspondence difficult."

I was aware that there was a strain between us.

"Adalbert, I—"

"No need to say more, Tania. All has been said and decided. We will go on as we were." He hesitated, then added, "Or perhaps not quite as we were."

"Oh?"

"You see, I have met a lovely young woman, one of the delegates on our Peace Initiative. She is of noble blood, and she has a sweet nature and shares my hope for greater understanding between peoples. Her name is Adalheid."

"Adalbert and Adalheid! You were fated to be together!" We both laughed, and the strain was eased.

We said our goodbyes, and assured each other that we would write. Then I set off to meet Constantin at the Workers' Clinic, taking a wagonload of food.

I had begun distributing the food I brought from the palace at the clinic instead of at Daria's old lodgings. A room was set aside for my use, and Avdokia and I, sometimes aided by volunteers at the clinic, handed out loaves of bread and plates of meat and fowl, vegetables and pastry to all who stood in line patiently waiting to receive them. There was always a crowd at the clinic, and Constantin, overworked and tired, struggled valiantly to see as many patients as he could. He had great reserves of vitality, but he was not made of iron, and I often saw him trying to snatch a few moments of rest between patients, only to give up because the demand was too great.

With the clinic drawing more and more people from the surrounding

Vyborg district, not only for medical aid but for food as well, it became a gathering place where political speakers—rabble-rousers, as my father called them—addressed the factory laborers from the ironworks and mills. Under the greenish-yellow fog that never seemed to disperse but hung like a shroud over Smokestack Town, representatives of Petersburg's radical organizations harangued the crowd.

That day, the day Adalbert came to say goodbye, the number of workers assembled in front of the clinic was so large that Avdokia could not urge her spavined old horse through to reach the front door. We were stuck, enmired in bodies.

A speaker was holding forth, drawing much interest in the gathering. Shouts of agreement, occasional applause, whistles greeted her words. She was a tall woman with a red jacket and scarf over her head. She had a strong voice that carried well, and she spoke with force and verve.

"Workers!" she was saying, "I bring you word this afternoon of a bright dawn that is arising—coming closer and closer with each passing day. A bright dawn, I tell you, when tyranny will be no more! When exploitation will be no more! When we will own all the factories, and we will run the government, and we will share the wealth of Russia and not let the exploiters take it all away!

"Just imagine, my friends, waking up to the dawn of freedom!"

A huge cheer went up at these words, and I felt a surge of emotion in the crowd around me. It seemed as though more people were gathering, more bodies pressing in all around the cart. Avdokia didn't mind, in fact she was shouting and clapping at the speaker's words like everyone else.

"Now I bring you the best news of all. We, yes, all of us, have the power to bring the bright dawn of a new day of freedom to Russia! We have only to reach for it: it is within our grasp. Ours is the force, ours are the numbers, ours is the will!

"Nothing can stop us, when we all work together. When our minds are set on one goal, and our will is directed in one way!

"And our goal is: freedom!"

Once again a huge roar went up from many throats, until voices all around me were strained, some breaking from the strain as they shouted again and again.

I could not help remembering, at that moment, the immense roaring from the crowd on that long-ago day when I stood with my family on the balcony of the palace, listening to the shouts of "Batiushka, Little Father, may you live forever!" Back then, when I was a little girl, my father had been loved—we all had—and Russia had been at war with Japan. Now, all these years later, the workers wanted everything to change. My father was an obstacle in their way. They wanted to rule all. It was both thrilling and terrifying: the speaker's words ignited a powerful vision of improvement and betterment, yet every word was a menace to our way of life, and especially to my family.

Something was happening. The woman in the red jacket and scarf was being muscled aside by a large baldheaded man. I heard angry words, a slap, laughter. Soon the baldheaded man began to speak.

"Enough of this talk of bright dawns and new beginnings!" he roared. "These are fairy tales for babies! What we want are actions, not words. Guns, not dreams. I say, to arms! Take out your knives, your clubs, your old rusty spears! Leave your machines and your looms and march on the palace! March on the garrisons! Seize the police stations!

"Let the cannon roar against us, and the bullets fly and the long sabers slash at us! We are stronger. We can fight on, to take what is ours, until all the enemies of the people are dead and Russia belongs to us!"

And to emphasize his words he held up a long knife, the blade gleaming in the thin sunlight that filtered through the yellow fog.

Through the roaring of the increasingly agitated crowd I could hear him cry, "Blood! Revenge! Death to the exploiters!"

The cart began to rock from side to side as the agitation increased. Avdokia tried to stand, shouting for the people around us to stop their restless pushing and shoving, but she could not keep her balance and was thrown to the floor of the cart, dropping the horse's reins.

I picked them up and tried in vain to hold the cart steady.

"Blood! Revenge! Death to the exploiters!" All around me the cries went up. Fists were shaken near me—at me, as it seemed.

"Quick! Avdokia! The food! Throw the food out into the crowd!"

We began lightening the cart of our baskets and bags of food, handing out what we could—many hands were thrust forward to snatch it from us—and tossing the rest out into the sea of moving bodies, waving fists, scowling, angry faces.

The poor horse neighed in fear and stamped his feet. I was afraid the cart would tip over but the horse's weight and ours kept it barely stable.

Over the heads of the crowd I could see the door of the clinic open. Constantin stood in the doorway, waving his arms, apparently shouting to the people nearest him (though I could not hear his words for all the din). I waved to him. As I watched, I saw the woman in the red jacket and scarf detach herself from the angry, clustered knot of workers and run to Constantin, pressing against him for protection. He put one arm around her while with the other he returned my wave.

I wanted to go to him, but we were separated by so many people, so much noise and tumult.

The baldheaded man was speaking again.

"Workers! There is not a moment to lose! I say we seize the Putilov factory!" And he set off in the direction of the nearby plant, walking briskly, the crowd parting to give him room, then falling in behind him.

But just as the baldheaded man began his march, I could see, at the opposite edge of the crowd, that the first of the police had begun to arrive.

Now there was a renewed upsurge of emotion from the gathered workers, a volatile mix of anger and fear. Women screamed as the police approached the crowd. People began running in panic. It was as if our cart was the still point at the center of a maelstrom. Avdokia and I crouched on the floor of the cart, our eyes shut, clutching each other, while around us boots pounded on the cobblestones, voices rang out, more shots were fired.

But the knot of workers was dispersing, running in all directions, and the cart no longer rocked and heaved. Cautiously I lifted my head and looked out over the side. A pathway was clearing before us, a pathway to the clinic's door.

"Avdokia!" I called out and she too raised her head.

"We can get to the clinic now. We can get Constantin away."

Nimbly for such a large woman, Avdokia climbed onto the driver's seat and flicked the horse with her whip. Old and tired as he was, he sprang forward and in a moment we were with Constantin, who lifted the slender woman in the red jacket into the back of the cart and climbed in behind her.

"Tania! Avdokia! Thank heavens you are here!"

Avdokia drove into the dingy alley at the back of the clinic and down along narrow streets that took us away from the sounds of the rioting.

"The police will protect the clinic," I heard Constantin say from the cart bed. "I'm not worried about that. We've had demonstrations here before and they have always guarded the building. To safeguard the patients."

We said little on the long ride back to Tsarskoe Selo. Once we reached the outskirts of the city and knew we would be safe from any more disturbances, I could hear Constantin snoring in the back of the cart. From his companion there was only silence.

Was she a bomb-thrower, I wondered. She was certainly a radical, but was she a violent one? Her inspiring words had not spoken of violent acts, only of a vision of a happier future. Yet there was violence in the air in those days, when I was in my fifteenth year. The chief minister of my father's government, Stolypin, was assassinated and other ministers were attacked. The secret police were out in force, Constantin had told me. They had eyes and ears on every street corner, hoping to prevent more attacks. Even so, the radicals continued to shoot at governors in the provinces and burn down the mansions of the wealthy and issue manifestos proclaiming the advent of a new nation of workers arising out of the ashes of the old order.

Who was this courageous woman, I wondered, who had delivered a strong speech before hundreds of people, only to be thrust aside by a cruder, more incendiary voice?

I turned to look over my shoulder into the back of the cart. There, sprawled on the bare boards, was the snoring Constantin. And next to him, leaning against the side rails, her eyes shut, was the woman, her red jacket open, her red scarf fallen back off her face, no longer veiling her features.

It was Daria!

Twenty-four

"Are you going to have me arrested?"

Daria confronted me as soon as we arrived at Tsarskoe Selo and were admitted through the high iron gates (for Avdokia the milk woman was a familiar figure to the guards and servants, the Cossack Nikandr among them, and they never stopped her cart) into the courtyard and stables beyond. Daria stood before me, slight, small, but with a fierceness in her expression that belied her size and a new determination in the tone of her voice.

"Should I? Are you dangerous?"

"Only if it is dangerous to raise people's hopes, and spur their ambitions."

"My father and Monsieur Gilliard say that some radicals are only ambitious to destroy."

"I am not one of those."

We regarded one another for a moment.

"Have you ever thrown a bomb?" I asked.

"No."

I believed her, I decided to trust her, but then immediately doubted my belief.

"Because I love your sister Niuta, who as you know, has served my family all my life, and for the sake of your little daughter Iskra, I will not have you arrested. Not tonight. You must give me your word, however, that you will never do anything to cause my family harm."

She nodded. "I give you my word. I swear on my daughter's head."

"Very well."

Her expression softened. "Thank you." And greatly to my surprise she dropped briefly on one knee, making the traditional gesture of reverence from peasant to master or mistress. I reminded myself that she was a peasant girl from Pokrovsky, after all. The time-honored patterns of social obligation that had prevailed in her village were still at work in her. Yet the gesture continued to amaze me. Was she putting me off guard? I would have to watch her closely.

It was too much to hope that there would be no repercussions from the rioting by the Workers' Clinic. Papa called me into his study and told me to sit down. He began rubbing his beard absentmindedly, as he did when unsure what to say.

"Your grandmother tells me," he began, "that you were seen in a mob of radical workers. That you were listening to radical speeches. That you have been visiting a certain workers' clinic instead of attending your dancing classes. And that you have, shall we say, formed an attachment to a young medical student, a man not of royal blood."

"Constantin is related to Uncle Petya, father."

Papa raised his eyebrows in surprise. "Is he? No one told me that."

"Has Grandma Minnie been spying on me?"

"She was concerned to know where you were and what you were doing. She asked the imperial secret police to watch you—to watch out for you."

"She wants to get rid of me. She wanted me to marry Adalbert so that I would go and live in Germany. She wants to get rid of Olga too."

"Don't talk absurdities. Now, as to this Workers' Clinic, I have decided to close it and I forbid you to go there again."

"But papa—"

"Your mother and your Aunt Olga have many charities. Devote yourself and your good works to them. Meanwhile I will ask Monsieur Gilliard to give you extra lessons, to fill your idle hours. And I don't ever want to hear that you have been seen listening to speeches by rabble-rousers! Don't you know that they are enemies of all decency and humanity? Don't you remember what happened to Uncle Gega? And to my own dear grandfather who was blown up by a bomb, all those years ago?"

His voice broke, and tears came into his eyes. Until this moment he had done his best to be firm, but now all his pretense of firmness fell away. I couldn't help wondering whether he wept while conferring with his ministers. It was no wonder mama was always telling him to be stronger and more forceful.

"Off you go, Tania," he said, his voice shaky, when he had wiped his eyes. "Be a good girl, won't you." And he lit a cigarette and gazed off into the distance.

My father was weak—and growing weaker, as it seemed to me. But the dynasty he represented, the proud Romanov legacy, was still held in reverence by many Russians—by nearly all Russians, he would have said, since he assumed that those who wanted to rid themselves of a tsar and rule on their own were only a small minority in the population. As the three-hundred-year anniversary of Romanov rule came closer, great preparations were made for official celebrations.

"The year 1913 will be a proud year," papa said to us all one evening. "A year to remember. In 1613 the first Romanov came to the throne. Here we are, three centuries later, still revered by our people. Our family symbolizes this grand continuity. Three hundred years from now there will still be a Romanov on the throne of Russia. Alexei will rule after I am gone, and his sons and grandsons will succeed him, and so on and on through many generations."

Despite papa's optimistic words it was hard for me to believe that my fragile, charming brother would indeed live to succeed to the imperial throne. Only a month earlier he had fallen off a chair and hurt his right knee, and his entire leg swelled with blood that would not clot. He could not move, the leg was so distended; he lay on his bed, moaning and screaming, unable to sleep, the pain was so acute and his fever so very high. With each new attack quiet preparations were made for his death. His golden shroud was brought from its oaken chest and got ready to receive his body, the imperial casket that would hold his corpse (a new one was made each year, as he grew) was brought into an anteroom and fitted out with velvet lining and a velvet pillow bordered with wide gold lace. This attack was no exception. All the funeral accoutrements were laid out, though kept out of his sight, naturally.

Father Gregory had been summoned but he was thousands of miles away in Pokrovsky, in faroff Siberia. He could not be expected to arrive in Petersburg any time soon. And besides, he had been heard to say that his healing powers, once so strong, were losing their force. Mama and papa, who relied on him so heavily and drew such comfort from his presence, refused to believe that he could ever fail to heal Alexei, but this time I was not so sure. Week after week my brother continued to grow more feeble, his face a sickly white and his eyes rimmed with dark shadows, and still Father Gregory did not come, nor was there any message from him. We all worried. This had never happened before.

Meanwhile Petersburg was decorated for the coming tercentenary celebrations. It was midwinter, the river ice was thick and the streets clogged wth newfallen snow that turned to slippery ice. Bunting was draped from windows, flags flew from atop all the tall buildings. Along the banks of the Neva signs were put up reading GOD SAVE THE TSAR in red letters thirty feet high. There were commemorative hats and mugs and medals for sale in all the shops; rich people could buy diamond-studded jewelry with my father's face engraved on it. For the poor, there were gifts of food and warm clothes, accompanied by notes reading "From the Bounty of the Tsar."

For a few weeks the newspapers were filled with pictures of papa and mama and stories about the coming ceremonies and social events. News of the ever-expanding armies and navies of Austria and France, Germany and England was crowded out by announcements of fetes and banquets to come, and of a triumphal tour our family was to make of historic towns and sites important in the history of the Romanovs.

All this would soon be upon us—yet my brother, the hope of the Romanov dynasty, grew weaker and more ill by the day. What if he were to die, I wondered, just when Russia was celebrating the long continuity of the Romanov line? What a terrible omen that would be! I had heard Grandma Minnie say, with asperity, that mama was too old to have another child, and that even if she did have another son, he would be cursed with the English disease just like Alexei.

My worried musings were cut short by the arrival of a telegram for papa—from Pokrovsky.

Joy to everyone! All fear dispelled! A blessing on sweet Alexei. I will be with you soon. Gregory Novy.

Mama, who had been praying before all the icons in the palace for Father Gregory's return, was greatly relieved. Yet when he finally arrived, it was as if he had become a different man.

Gone were his moth-eaten black tunic and coarse peasant trousers, his shaggy long hair and uncombed beard. Now he wore the silken shirt, embroidered vest and velvet breeches of a prosperous townsman, a full purse of coins that jingled as he walked hanging from his belt, a gold chain around his neck and a large gold ring on one finger. His hair and beard were combed and trimmed. No longer gaunt and ascetic-looking he had grown fat, his cheeks puffy and jowly, his eyes cold. Most important, I thought, was the feeling he brought into the room with him. Gone was the subtle, unmistakable ripple of calm and sweetness, the air of still, serene healing, the radiance of face and eyes. He had become another man entirely.

Still, he raised his hand in benediction as he approached Alexei's bed and I saw Alexei smile happily at him, just as if he was the Father Gregory of old.

"Be thou whole, little wayfarer!" the starets said, and began to hum. We all watched Alexei eagerly, looking for signs that his pain was growing less, hoping to see a healthy pink glow return to his cheeks. But nothing happened. Father Gregory stayed beside his bed for a long time, praying and humming, but poor Alexei, far from improving, wept and screamed just as before, and mama, deeply upset, got up and left the room in tears.

I followed her into her mauve sitting room, her sanctuary, talking to her and trying to soothe her. She patted my arm appreciatively but I could tell that my words had no effect. She poured a little water into a glass and then, taking her vial of Veronal and her eyedropper, measured out six drops into the water—twice her usual dose. She drank it and lay back on her chaise longue. I covered her with her lavender knitted shawl. Soon she was asleep.

It was unlike mama to leave Alexei's bedside when he was in the midst of one of his bad attacks. The shock of Father Gregory's failure to heal Alexei must have been very great. I went back into the nursery and sat with my brother for awhile, holding his hand. No one else was with him but the medical orderly and one of the nursery maids. Papa, I was told, had had to meet with the members of the tercentenary committee. Father Gregory had gone.

That night, as Niuta brushed out my hair with the silver hairbrush my sisters had given me for my fifteenth birthday, I asked her about the change in Father Gregory.

"What happened to him there in Pokrovsky, Niuta? Something must have happened. You have relatives there, you must know. He is so different. And Alexei is no better. His blessings are having no effect."

Niuta sighed, and went on brushing. I could not get her to talk for a long time. I was insistent, then I pleaded, then I threatened to tell mama that Niuta sometimes put on her White Rose perfume. Still Niuta shook her head and went on brushing, more vigorously than before. I did not give up.

"I'll tell Nikandr that I saw you flirting with Gennady." Gennady was one of the guardsmen, a handsome Uzbek.

"Tania! You wouldn't!"

"Tell me about Father Gregory and I won't."

At last, exasperated by my persistence, she threw up her hands.

"All right! I'll tell you what I know—if you promise not to tell anybody else."

"There are far too many secrets in this household!" I burst out, jumping to my feet, sending the hairbrush flying off into a corner. "Too much that cannot be brought to light. Who Daria really is. Little Iskra. Mama's illness—her mind is ill, Niuta, and we all know it. Don't try to deny it. Papa's drinking too much. Grandma Minnie's hateful spying on everybody. Aunt Olenka's love affair—"

"What love affair?" Niuta looked genuinely surprised.

"You truly don't know?" She shook her head.

"Well then, she's taken up with another man and is going to divorce Petya."

I gave her a moment to digest this news.

"Now—one more secret. Tell me about Father Gregory."

"If you reveal this," Niuta said, "the beast may come after me." Niuta called Father Gregory "the beast" because, she said, he was untamed, uncivilized. He was like a wild thing in the forest.

"Then I won't reveal it."

She bent down and whispered to me that during his months in Pokrovsky Father Gregory had been arrested and put in jail for raping a young girl.

I remembered the police report Grandma Minnie had read to us about Father Gregory. The prostitutes, the drinking, the shameless brawling and time spent in bathhouses, "dens of immorality," as mama called them. Niuta's revelation fitted in with all the police had discovered. Though I was sure that mama would claim every bad thing said about Father Gregory was mere slander, not the truth.

"In the past," Niuta was saying, her voice low, "the priests protected him. His healing brought great donations to the village church. He had a great following, as he has here in Petersburg. Pilgrims came from villages twenty and thirty and even fifty versts away just to see him and touch his filthy robes. But he always had a wild, beastly side. He drank, and started fights, and ran after women.

"When he began seducing young girls, the good Lord punished him. He started to take away the healing power from his hands. The priests abandoned him. Now he is no longer a starets, but just a peasant farmer from Pokrovsky—with a small fortune he has made over the years from the donations of those he has healed."

"Perhaps his powers will return. Perhaps he will reform," I heard myself say—yet even as I said the words I felt deep misgivings. People rarely reformed. Bad people became worse, not better. It is the way of the world, I told myself, feeling very grown up at the thought. But if Father Gregory became worse, who would mama and papa turn to for comfort, for hope? Who would heal Alexei?

I looked at Niuta, who knew me so well, and saw the same questions and worries in her eyes. Servants know everything, I had often heard Aunt Olenka say, and of course she was right. I sat down at my dressing table and let Niuta resume her brushing out of my hair, using an old hairbrush with a tortoiseshell back. Usually I found the brushing soothing, a relaxing preparation for sleep. But that night I only found it irritating, every tug of the brush a rough, jarring reminder of the snags and tangles that always seemed to rise up before me, just when things began to go well. In the end I dismissed Niuta before she had finished and went to bed with snarls in my hair and troubling thoughts on my mind.

Twenty-five

A *week before* the grand tercentenary celebration began, Captain Teraev of the security police gave us each our own revolver and taught us how to shoot. Everyone in the family received one except Alexei, who was only eight, and Anastasia, who was not yet twelve. We were taken out to a shooting range and shown how to load, aim and fire at practice targets.

"A prudent family takes precautions," the captain told us. "You will be out amid large crowds in the coming weeks, and it is possible that an emergency may arise. Of course you will be guarded. Soldiers, police, men dressed as spectators will all be keeping a close watch to make sure no one in the crowd tries to cause you harm."

Papa had his own nickel-plated revolver, beside his large collection of firearms and hunting weapons. He needed no instruction. But mama, until that day, had never wanted to own a weapon of any kind.

"The Lord will watch over me," she had always said, "and Father Gregory will as well." But now she accepted her revolver from Captain Teraev without demur, and listened carefully to his instructions. When she practiced shooting at the target she took calm, precise aim and shot true.

A bright March sun shone over the snowy streets on the day of the grand parade, the day we rode in an open carriage amid vast throngs of clapping, chanting people. Alexei rode beside papa, waving and smiling, his stiff, swollen leg hidden under the warm woolen blankets covering our laps as we rode. He had improved, and was improving—but not because of any aid provided by Father Gregory. Somehow he found the strength not to succumb, amazing us all. He did not succumb, but he did not thrive either, and the next attack, we all knew, might prove to be his last.

Bands played and soldiers marched and cheers of "God Save the Tsar" followed our carriage as we rode slowly along the broad avenues. The singing and shouting rose above us into the frosty air as all the guns in the Peter and Paul fortress boomed out their prolonged salute.

I looked out into the sea of faces and saw, among them, a few scowls and dark looks directed toward us. There were even cries of "German bitch!" directed at mama, who turned her head away when she heard them and tried to ignore the insult. As the menace from Germany grew, so did the accusations that mama, who had been raised in Darmstadt and whose father was a German nobleman, was a German spy. A traitor to Russia.

I reached into my pocket and felt the reassuring metallic hardness of my loaded revolver. If an assassin should burst out of the crowd and run toward our carriage, I wondered, would I have the courage to shoot him?

Most of the faces were smiling and enthusiastic. Hands were held out toward us, blessings were called down on our heads. Every now and then people fell on their knees to kiss the shadow of our carriage as we passed—an old custom that I found very touching and beautiful.

At the tercentenary ball held that evening Olga and I were much admired. We had new gowns with overskirts of a shimmering silvery lace and when we danced the lace seemed to float through the air around us in a very becoming way. It felt odd to have to conceal my revolver in a pocket of the beautiful gown, but Captain Teraev had been insistent: we were to take the weapons everywhere with us during the celebrations. I did as he bade us.

I remember dancing with one good-looking young officer or nobleman after another, enjoying the knowledge that I was much in demand, feeling buoyant and lighthearted—though wishing that Constantin were there. Duty prevented him from enjoying the ball; earlier in the day, at the parade, there had been a stampede when souvenirs were distributed, and hundreds of people had been injured. Constantin volunteered to stay on at St. Mary of Mercy hospital into the evening, missing the festivities, in order to ensure that all those who were hurt were treated.

I was so wrapped up in my own pleasures that for hours I failed to notice how the long day and evening were weighing on mama and making her uncomfortable. Public functions always wearied her. She sat now beside papa, both of them in tall thronelike chairs, mama wearing her heavy diamond-and-pearl tiara, her hands folded in her lap, her whole posture stiff and a look of fatigue and strain on her lovely face. I suppose that to those who did not know her she looked bored, even impatient. But I knew better. The redness in her cheeks and hands, the faint tremor in her hands when she reached back to rub her neck, the occasional panic I saw in her eyes when she gazed around the room, looking (I knew) for a way to escape told me that she needed to leave.

I went up to her. When she saw me she seemed relieved.

"Oh, Tania, there you are. How very pretty you look! Dear, would you please ask one of the valets to call Dr. Korovin? I am feeling quite dizzy."

"Why not let me call Constantin? His hospital is nearby. Dr. Korovin would take an hour to get here."

She was too tired to protest. She nodded and I went out to find a telephone. But when I called the hospital, I found that Constantin had gone out with an ambulance to the site of the stampede earlier in the day and was not expected back for a long time. I was disappointed. I had hoped to see him.

Dr. Korovin was summoned and I stayed near mama until he arrived. It took quite a long time, and as we waited, mama became more nervous. She could not sit still, but squirmed in her chair, fingering the religious medal she wore around her neck, adjusting her tiara, finally taking it off and doing her best to stuff it into the elegant jeweled bag that hung suspended from her beet-red wrist. I tried to distract her with conversation but she answered only "yes" or "no" or "oh" and would not be drawn in on any topic other than her health. She was short of breath, she told me; her teeth hurt, she had a pain in her leg. She was exhausted.

Nor did her distress abate when at last we were told that the doctor had arrived and we made our exit from the ballroom. After examining her briefly in a private chamber Dr. Korovin said that mama should return to Tsarskoe Selo at once and lie down.

"But none of the servants are there tonight," I said. "They have all been allowed to attend the parade and the evening's celebrations." There were street fairs and bonfires, parties and dinners all over Petersburg that night, and papa had wanted everyone in the imperial household to enjoy the fireworks and other entertainments.

"Is there no one at all?" the doctor asked, incredulous. "No guards, no sweepers, no stable boys?"

"I suppose there may be a few." I was doubtful, however. Papa had insisted that on this one special day everyone should be free to come to Petersburg for the rejoicings.

"Then you and I will look after her."

We helped mama into the carriage and began the long drive to Tsarskoe Selo. She produced her smelling salts from her bag—dropping the priceless tiara on the floor in the process—and inhaled deeply. The carriage windows were rolled up against the wintry air and a light snow had begun to fall. Despite the cold people were still in the streets in large numbers, warming their hands at huge bonfires, standing under sheltering eaves, swaying to the music of balalaikas and impromptu choruses. Jars and jugs were being passed from hand to hand and I thought, they are enjoying their Little Father's free vodka tonight.

When we arrived at Tsarskoe Selo mama was dozing. It was a shame to wake her, I thought, but of course she had to go inside. She was irritable when I shook her shoulder gently. Dr. Korovin and I helped her out of the carriage and into the spacious front hallway of the palace, then up the grand staircase and along several corridors to the hallway outside her suite. It was eerie, seeing no one, not even Sedynov, who usually hovered near our innermost family rooms, either the nursery or mama and papa's apartments, which included a salon, papa's study and mama's mauve sitting room in addition to the large bedroom and dressing rooms they shared. But there was no sign of Sedynov, or of Niuta or Elizaveta, or of any of mama's maids or dressers. They had all gone to Petersburg.

As we walked along I wondered idly who had lit the gaslights that illumined the long corridors. There had to be someone still here, I thought. Not everyone has left.

Then, from the far end of the long dim hallway came a shambling figure, more stumbling than walking. Frightened, I held tightly to mama's arm and with my free hand reached into the pocket of my gown for the revolver. Feeling it, I felt my fear recede, but only a little.

"Who is it?" Dr. Korovin called out. I felt mama stiffen, then relax as she recognized who it was.

"No sorrow! All sorrow forgotten! Only the joy of the day!"

"It's night, not day," I called out as Father Gregory came up to us. "And what are you doing here?" His puffy face was red, his nose bulbous and pockmarked, his eyes more bleary than piercing, as they usually were. He had a furtive look, and he smelled strongly of drink.

"I thought I might be needed," he said, speaking slowly, trying not to slur his words.

"Yes, yes," mama said. "You always know when I am weak and faint and in need of your blessing. Bless me now, please bless me."

"But he has lost his powers, mama. You heard him say so. His blessings fail."

She glared at me, and dropped my supporting arm. "God never fails," she said, and opened the door into her suite, beckoning Father Gregory to follow her in and indicating that he should shut the door behind him. Dr. Korovin and I were left standing in the corridor.

"Not proper," the doctor muttered. "Not proper at all. For an empress to be alone in a room with such a man. And what is he doing prowling through these halls? He doesn't belong here."

Father Gregory had always been given permission to come and go in and out of the palace as he pleased. The servants resented his special privilege, and glowered at him when they encountered him—when mama or papa were not watching, that is.

"I was going to give her a sleeping draft," Dr. Korovin said. "Otherwise she will not sleep the night through. Now I suppose I'll have to wait until that drunken creature comes out." He looked at me searchingly. "What if he stays in there with her all night?"

"No," I said firmly. "That doesn't happen."

The doctor looked at me for a moment. "Are you certain?"

"Yes."

"Well then, I suppose we had better make ourselves comfortable while we wait."

There were benches in the corridor for servants to sit on during the long night hours when they were on guard, or awaiting a summons to do some service for a member of my family. We sat on one of these, side by side, I in my lovely lace-skirted ball gown and Dr. Korovin in his black coat and trousers. We must have looked very odd, like a grandfather and granddaughter sitting rather incongruously together at a party, not conversing, both alternately nodding off and then jerking back to wakefulness.

At length Dr. Korovin took out his pocket watch.

"It is nearly three o'clock. I don't think your Father Gregory is going to come out of that room tonight. I don't want to know whether he does or not. I want to believe the best about your mother. I'm going to bed."

He got up from the bench and went off down the corridor.

More and more uneasy, I went to the door of the suite and, feeling a little guilty, put my ear to the thick, highly polished wood.

I could hear the rise and fall of voices, a susurration, a silence, then Father Gregory's voice raised in drunken anger. Concerned for mama, I tried to turn the door handle but it was locked.

"Get away! Get away, whoever you are!" came Father Gregory's snarl. I heard him kick savagely at the door with his boot. Instinctively I backed away.

A string of harsh curses followed the kicks. "Stay away, I have a knife!"

I ran along the corridor and hid behind a carved pillar.

In a moment the door burst open and Father Gregory came out, a large knife in his hand, his long shaggy hair loosed from its restraining band and hanging around his face—looking for all the world like a thief or highwayman.

I held my breath and pressed back against the wall, hoping my full skirt was hidden. I felt for the revolver. If he hurts mama, or comes after me, I'll shoot him, I vowed silently. I'll shoot him and I'll kill him.

But he did not come after me. Instead he went off down the corridor in the opposite direction, away from me, the sound of his boots on the floorboards gradually growing fainter with each step.

Twenty-six

It was when his footsteps had at last died away completely that I heard the dog begin to bark.

It was a high-pitched, yapping sort of bark, the bark of a lapdog, not a wolfhound like Artipo.

Then I heard a small child crying.

And in a moment I knew: it was Daria's dog that was barking, and little Iskra that was crying. It had to be. I remembered in that moment that Niuta had told me Daria didn't intend to go to Petersburg with the other servants to attend the celebrations of the Romanov dynasty's three hundredth year. Daria was no monarchist, she was a revolutionary. She worked at the palace, but she despised everything about it, and my father too, and all of us in the imperial family. She made no secret of it. Niuta said she intended to work all that day, while the rest of us were celebrating, and to complete her ironing, as if this day was just another ordinary workday.

She had to be in the ironing room, I reasoned, with her dog and little Iskra sleeping in their basket nearby as they always were. But why was her dog barking and her child crying? Was it possible? Could Father Gregory have disturbed them? Or could there be others in the palace? Could thieves have broken in?

I tiptoed in through the open door of mama's sitting room and saw her lying on her favorite white chaise longue, with her crocheted blanket covering her legs. She had fallen asleep. I left her there and went down the corridor toward the wing where the ironing room was. Something told me to hurry. The dog was barking more loudly now, and the child was wailing without interruption.

I mounted the old, rickety stairs that led to the servants' quarters and saw that the door to the ironing room was open. I stepped inside.

There, against the far wall of the large room, was Daria, behind her long ironing board, the heavy iron in her hand. And on the other side of Daria's ironing board was Father Gregory, his back to me, reaching out clumsily toward Daria and laughing when she lunged at him with the iron, missing him. Save for the two of them, and the wailing Iskra, the room was deserted.

It was a grotesque scene. Father Gregory was twice Daria's size. He loomed over her, massive, hulking, menacing. I remembered the police reports Grandma Minnie had read to us all, about the prostitutes, the midnight wanderings, the accusations of rape . . .

Staying where I was, at the opposite end of the room from where Father Gregory and Daria were now struggling, the little dog growling and biting at Father Gregory's heels, I took the revolver out and shouted, "Stop! Stay there!" as loudly as I could.

He turned to face me, with a look, in that moment, more wolf than man.

I pointed the gun toward the ceiling—and fired.

The noise startled Father Gregory, who released Daria and, blinking hard, stared at me.

With a sharp scream Daria reached down and grabbed the basket with Iskra inside and ran around the end of the wide ironing board, evading Father Gregory's snatching hands, and on toward me.

"Tania!" she called out. "Help me!"

"Run down to the surgery," I told her. "Dr. Korovin is there. Lock the surgery door."

She ran past me and out into the corridor, her little dog, still yapping, running along behind her. I stood where I was, determined not to let Father Gregory pursue her.

"Fool! Little bitch! Crazy daughter of an even crazier mother!" Father Gregory lowered his head and charged toward me.

I shot again, this time at the floor in front of him, barely missing his feet.

"Come closer and I'll kill you. I swear it!"

I was shaking all over, more violently and uncontrollably than when I had the ague when I was eight years old. But my will was strong. I did not retreat from him. I did not waver.

"By all the saints, I order you to stop!"

He appeared to stumble, swearing loudly and incoherently, and then swayed and dropped to his knees, the way a drunken man will do when his legs cease to support him.

I heard doors opening, voices, cries of alarm. There were others in the palace after all. The sound of the shots was bringing them out to see what was going on. Without waiting to see who might come to my aid I ran out of the room and back down the rickety stairs, then along several hallways to the wing where Dr. Korovin's surgery was. Before I reached it I encountered half a dozen police who, as it turned out, had come in response to Dr. Korovin's telephone call to report hearing gunshots in the palace.

"Rasputin tried to rape a woman," I told them, using the name by which Father Gregory was known to the public at large. "She shot at him."

"I hope she killed the bastard," one of the men said. "Where is he?"

"Either in the servants' quarters or in the empress's private rooms. He might try to take refuge there." They rushed off and I went on into Dr. Korovin's surgery, where I found Daria hiding in a cupboard, her little girl whimpering.

"The police are here. They will find Father Gregory and keep him from attacking anyone."

As soon as I said the word police I saw fear in Daria's eyes, and remembered that her fiancé, Iskra's father, had been killed by my father's police.

"Don't let them take me," she begged. I had never seen her this way. Always before she had been tough, defiant. Now there was pleading in her voice. Was it the stark fear she felt at Father Gregory's attack that had brought out this terror, or something more? Had motherhood changed her?

"Of course I will do all I can to protect you from anyone who might harm you, or your child. Wasn't I there when she was born? Didn't I help you then? I'll stay here with you until we can be sure Father Gregory has been taken away."

But he was not taken away. He was not even jailed. Mama protected him from the police and would not let them arrest him, or even question him. And no doubt the chief of police Captain Golenishchev, whose daughter Father Gregory had healed, sheltered him also.

"But mama, he attacked one of your servants in the ironing room," I insisted when I learned he had not been arrested or detained. "I saw him do it. He would have raped her if I hadn't frightened him by firing my revolver."

"Tania! You were given that weapon to use only in an extreme emergency, against a bomb-thrower."

"I used it to frighten a criminal. Grandma Minnie is right about Father Gregory. He is a dangerous criminal."

"Hush! I don't want to hear any more!" She put her hands up to cover her ears.

"Mama! He came after me too! He threatened me!"

She took her hands down from her ears and a fixed look came over her face. Her mouth was shut very tightly, the lips compressed together.

"You must be mistaken," was all she said, but it was clear to me from her tone that the real meaning of her words was that she could not bear to hear or even consider any more of the truth about Father Gregory. The unbearable truth that the man she depended on so completely was capable of wickedness.

"Now then, Tania, I know how you love stories," papa said the following day when I tried to tell him what I had seen and experienced. "You have a strong imagination. You are like me in that way. Your mind is full of fancies. You say you were all by yourself in the palace in the middle of the night. It was dark. You were very tired. You heard noises. You went up to the servants' quarters. And then—well, then, I believe, your imagination simply took over."

"But papa, a woman was attacked!"

"What woman? Where is this woman now? Why hasn't she come forward to tell her own story?"

On that point I was at a loss, for I had promised Daria I would not reveal her name to anyone as the victim of Father Gregory's attack.

"I don't know," I said. "Perhaps she is frightened that if she does reveal what happened, he will come after her again."

"If she is an honest woman, she will have nothing to fear."

But Daria, as I well knew, was not an "honest woman," of the kind my father envisioned. She was a woman who made inflammatory speeches, and who refused to acknowledge or attend the anniversary celebrations in Petersburg. A woman who feared to encounter anyone in authority, lest she be questioned and investigated and arrested.

I was angry—at my family, for not believing me, and at Daria, for not adding her voice to mine in what I revealed, though I understood why she couldn't. Most of all I was angry at the two-faced, black-hearted Father Gregory, for being what he was: a fissured soul, his healing gift tarnished and corrupted by his untamed desires, his innocence shrouded in a darkness I had now seen face to face.

Twenty-seven

Constantin was more important to me than ever in the months following my frightening encounter with Father Gregory. Unlike the others (except for Niuta and Sedynov and a few of the other servants), he listened to me and believed me when I told him what had happened in the ironing room, clenching and unclenching his jaw in anger and smashing his large round fist into his palm. He even went to Father Gregory's apartment on Roszdestvenskaya Street, taking a thick cudgel with him, only to be told by the housekeeper that the starets had gone to Pokrovsky in Siberia and would not be back for many months.

"I'd follow him there if only it wasn't so many thousands of versts away, and I wasn't needed at the hospital," Constantin said when he returned. "That villain needs a good thrashing."

There was an outbreak of typhoid in the city just then and all the hospitals were full and had to turn many typhoid victims away. Constantin was kept very busy at the St. Mary of Mercy hospital, though he came to see me as often as he could, or we arranged to meet at Aunt Olenka's house on Sunday afternoons—Sunday being his one day off.

Aunt Olenka liked Constantin very much and was sympathetic to our need for privacy. Her own love affair with Nicholas Kulikovsky was her all-consuming focus at that time, and she was divorcing Petya, much to the dismay of the family. As Constantin had once remarked, Petya was an odd duck, and something of an embarrassment to all his relatives and in-laws—but divorce was a scandal, and Aunt Olenka was the tsar's sister. It was a shocking fact that at that time, my Uncle Michael was in disgrace and married to a commoner, Aunt Xenia was contemplating divorce from Sandro—though they ultimately stayed together—and Aunt Olenka was going through her divorce proceedings to rid herself of Petya. What next, I thought: was it possible that mama might divorce papa, because of his carousing and his visits to Mathilde Kchessinsky?

It didn't seem possible—yet the impossible was happening all around me, all the time. I told myself it was the way of the world and did my best to put the more sordid aspects of it all out of my mind.

Constantin and I had been becoming more passionate with each other as the months went by. When riding in his carriage with the shades pulled down over the windows, or whenever we could find a dark alcove in the interior of a house we hid there, kissing, exploring each other's bodies tentatively, then more and more eagerly. Knowing that we might be seen by others only made us more excited.

We were both virgins. Constantin confided to me that he had not yet been with a woman, though his father, impatient and embarrassed by his son's lack of experience, had tried taking him to expensive brothels, expecting that he would lose his virginity with a sophisticated older woman.

I dreamed of surrendering myself body and soul to Constantin, my heart was eager to join with him in the most intimate way possible, but in truth I knew so little about sex that my fantasies were very vague. All I knew about the male body I had learned from my attempts to draw the classical statues in the garden at Tsarskoe Selo. I had seen animals coupling, but I did not associate that rough, brief and rather mechanical act with love, merely with a physical urge like the urge to eat or sleep or urinate. Besides, animals did not choose their partners, they mated with whichever of their kind was nearest them.

When Constantin and I were together I was aroused yet modest, shy about revealing my nakedness to him. I felt myself drawing back from him in what I supposed was a perfectly natural response—the response of a girl in love, but a well-brought-up girl who kept her self-respect.

In truth I was nervous about displaying my young body, my small breasts, slender waist and hips. I was not voluptuous like Niuta or the curvaceous Countess Orlov, whom all the men of the court gawked at when they thought their wives and mistresses were not looking. I did not have a full bosom like Aunt Olenka, who thrust herself forward as she walked, proud of the deep curves her Oriental Pills had given her. I did not have the round, full bottom of a mature woman. I did not fully appreciate then—I could hardly appreciate it, given my age and inexperience—the allure the slim body of a young girl can have for a man, her very freshness and budding curves a magnet for his lust.

I was nervous, and Constantin knew that I was. I didn't dare say what I was nervous about. If he saw me naked, I wondered, would he like what he saw? Would I be able to please him? How did wives please their husbands? I had heard whispers, rumors, I had seen the salacious posters depicting Father Gregory and my mother doing unspeakable things. Yet I felt ignorant, and as time went on my inexperience was creating a barrier between us.

"My dearest Tania," he said on one of our afternoons together, his voice kind as he took my hand in both of his, "we have reached an awkward point. You know how very, deeply fond I am of you, and I believe you feel the same way."

"Oh yes, dear Constantin, I do. You are all I think about." Which wasn't quite true, but there were times when it was, and besides, I didn't know the right words to convey my strong feelings.

"The last thing I would ever want to do would be to hurt you or take advantage of you, especially since you have never been with a man. If you tell me you want to stay a virgin until you marry, I will not touch you or kiss you again."

"But I want you to, you know I do."

He looked at me fondly, knowingly.

"Some men try to trick young girls into sleeping with them. They try to convince them that they are being cruel in withholding themselves. 'Ah, my dear, you are causing me pain,' they say, or 'you are cruel to tease me, to torment me.' I would never do that. I leave it to you to decide what you want—for both of us."

"I want to follow my heart," I said. "I want to be like Aunt Olenka, and be modern." To be modern, in my aunt's progressive social circles, meant sleeping with a lover, ignoring old sexual taboos and looking on marital fidelity as something of a nuisance or even a joke. My promiscuous family did not offer me examples of fidelity or purity, except mama, and she was accused (wrongly, I felt sure) of sleeping with Father Gregory. Aunt Ella was the only relative I had who was not promiscuous, and she was the head of a religious order!

"Well then, Tania," Constantin said, kissing me lightly on the ear, on my cheek, and down my neck, making me catch my breath with excitement, "I think you ought to have a talk with your Aunt Olga. There are things you need to know before we go any further, things I imagine your mother hasn't confided to you, because she expects you to be pure until you marry. Will you talk to your aunt?"

I nodded, my eyes closed, my pulse racing—and then I kissed him back, with more abandon than before, and wishing more than ever that I could be fully, finally his.

With her usual wide toothy grin Aunt Olenka brought me into her rose-tinted boudoir the following day and sat me down on a soft sofa covered in ivory silk striped with gold. I had never before been in this room of her mansion, and felt both shy and privileged. It was as though I were entering an elite circle, the circle, as I thought of it afterward, of experienced women, women of the world.

When we had eaten our fill of tea cakes and drunk a glass of sherry Aunt Olenka told me that Constantin had spoken to her and that she understood where things stood between us.

"I like your Constantin so much," she told me. "Such a serious young man, so eager to do good. You know he has helped me out with my charity bazaars. I think if I were to be sick, he is the one I'd call.

"You don't know how fortunate you are to have such a considerate young man as Constantin," she went on. "He really cares about you. He wants you to take no risks. There must be no unfortunate consequences of the love you share."

Patiently and thoroughly, she told me what I needed to do to avoid becoming pregnant—and much more. She described the varieties of lovemaking, she spoke with no embarrassment of the male and female anatomy, helping to satisfy my curiosity and calm my fears. She told me about her own initiation into the act of love—with one of our coachmen, when she was younger than I was—and prepared me for the joy and beauty of sexual union.

"All will be well, if you are gentle and loving with each other," she concluded. "Your first affair will be a lovely memory for the rest of your life."

I understood, by that time, that there could be no question of my marrying Constantin, that papa would never permit me to marry a commoner. But deep in my romantic heart marriage was what I wanted, not an affair. An affair sounded too French ("affaire de coeur" was the current expression), too much like something to be taken lightly.

"I do love him, Aunt Olenka."

"Of course you do, and a part of you always will."

I began to cry then, though I could not have said why, and she hugged me.

"Say goodbye to your innocence, sweet Tania. With Constantin you will enter a new world."

And enter it we did, shortly afterward, with Aunt Olenka's help.

There was a small apartment above the garage at her town mansion. It was meant for a chauffeur, but ever since her accident Aunt Olenka had not employed a chauffeur—indeed she preferred not to ride in an auto at all, though she owned several. She gave us the key to this secluded place and assured us it was ours to use.

Constantin grinned. "I have a passion for autos," he said. "Shall we go and have a look?"

The apartment, warmed by a large tiled stove, had a sitting room, kitchen and bedroom with a wide, somewhat lumpy bed and frayed green bedspread. Aunt Olenka had provided champagne, blinis, strawberries and rum cake in the well-stocked icebox.

I remember how excited I was to actually be sharing a bedroom with Constantin. It was almost like being married, I thought to myself. A pretend marriage, not an affair. My heart leapt at the thought. I took off my gown and slipped beneath the blanket in my underclothes, letting myself luxuriate in its warm softness.

But nothing had prepared me for the sight of Constantin's naked body. I watched eagerly as he removed his clothes, taking in his strong, muscular arms and legs, his fleshy, thick torso, his hairless chest and the rest of him—all of it, I was dismayed to see, very far from the male perfection of the garden statues of the Greek gods.

I think I knew then, even before he got into bed with me, that our tepid kisses—always before, when shared in stolen moments, so thrilling—and his fumbling efforts to give me pleasure were not to excite me or lead to the rapturous delight I had hoped for. Despite all that Aunt Olenka had told me, I found myself shy about revealing my nakedness to him and he, considerate as ever, let me keep myself covered with the green bedspread.

He did manage to make love to me, after a fashion, but we were both embarrassed and let down afterward.

"I have disappointed you, Tania," he said as I lay in his arms. "I'm so sorry! I am becoming a good doctor, I know, but that is probably the only thing I am good at. As a lover I fear I have no talent at all."

"Could it just be because it is our first time?"

He kissed my cheek. "Let's hope so."

We lay there, both of us uncomfortable, until he finally spoke again.

"You had better wash yourself thoroughly, inside and out," he told me, urging me toward the bathroom. "Take a douche."

I stood under the tepid water and cried.

When I had dried myself and put my clothes back on Constantin was sitting at the small dingy table in the kitchen, eating a cold blini and drinking champagne. He blew me a kiss and smiled wanly, holding out the bottle to me.

"No, thank you," I replied. And as I said the words, I realized that I was saying no to more than the champagne. I was saying no to Constantin, high forehead, hairless chest, disappointing sex and all.

Twenty-eight

$\mathcal{M}$*ama had become* convinced that Cousin Willy would soon declare war against everyone, including Russia, and she was determined that when that time came, we all would have to do our part for the war effort. She arranged for Olga and me to go to nursing school, in order to be ready.

"My mother advises it," mama told us. "She came to me just as I was going to sleep, she sat down on my bed and talked to me for a long time about the coming war, and how we must prepare for it."

"Surely it was a dream, mama," Olga said. Olga was disturbed by how often mama said she saw the ghost of her mother Alice. Like me, Olga was aware of the many emotional crosscurrents in our family, as she was of mama's erratic behavior, but while I took these things to heart Olga tended to deny them or grow angry about them. It also angered her that she was nearly eighteen years old and yet no betrothal had been arranged for her. She was pretty enough (though I was a lot prettier, everyone said so, a fact I enjoy repeating), but her temperament was harsh and she lacked empathy. She certainly had no empathy for mama's delusions, and tended to speak up unsparingly when mama mentioned seeing her mother.

"A visitation from the other world is not the same as a dream. Mother comes and visits me."

"And is she going to take nursing training too?" Olga asked. I thought her sarcasm cruel.

"No, but I am," was mama's reply. "I want to do my part. I have enrolled myself along with you girls."

It was settled; Olga and I and mama took classes every morning and spent several hours in the wards of St. Mary of Mercy—Constantin's sole hospital, since the closing of the Workers' Clinic—every afternoon.

Our Red Cross training was very thorough, beginning with instruction in basic hygiene. We learned how important it was to keep ourselves and everything we touched and used scrupulously clean, including our uniforms and aprons and the uncomfortable wimple-like caps that shrouded our heads, leaving only our eyes, noses and mouths visible. We learned how diseases spread, how infection occurs and how it may be arrested. We learned how to bandage wounds and make tourniquets and bind up broken limbs with splints.

There was a great deal to learn, and Olga and I and mama were all told that we were apt pupils—except that mama had to miss class quite often because of her headaches and the pains in her leg. We studied diligently, learning the names of medicines and what each was prescribed for. Finally, after three months, we were ready for our final examinations.

"But Your Imperial Highness," the chief Red Cross instructor said to mama, "there is no need for you or your daughters to sit for any examinations."

"Why ever not?"

The instructor looked nonplussed. "Why—why—because you do not need to trouble yourselves—" she stammered.

"Nonsense. Unless we take the examinations, we cannot receive our diplomas and make ourselves useful when the war comes."

The instructor crossed herself. "I pray there will be no war, Your Imperial Highness."

"It will come," mama replied calmly. "Now, when are we to be examined?"

We took our examinations, Olga passed with distinction, mama and I merely passed. But we all stood proudly, along with about thirty other women and girls, to receive our official diplomas. And we volunteered at the hospital three afternoons a week. I often encountered Constantin there, and was friendly—even affectionate—with him. But clearly our feelings had changed. There was a tacit understanding between us that we were not destined to be a loving, intimate couple. We were fond of each other, and good, trusting friends—friends who made each other laugh and relied on each other—and that was all.

It was not long after we completed our training that a letter came from Cousin Willy, inviting us to come to Berlin to attend the wedding of his daughter Sissy, Adalbert's sister, to a Prussian nobleman. Mama did not want to go, but papa insisted. Delicate diplomatic negotiations were under way between our two countries and it was essential that the family appear to be on the best of terms.

I had never been to Germany, but I had read about the great city of Berlin with its imposing architectural monuments, theaters, broad boulevards and parks. Adalbert had told me about his family's splendid palaces though he had to admit that ours in Russia were larger and finer. The Germans, I had always heard, were large, stout people who drank a lot of wine and beer and were fond of their "Gemütlichkeit"—a word, Adalbert assured me, for which there was no equivalent in Russian or English. The closest he could come to translating it for me was to use the English words "comfort" and "coziness."

But Berlin, when the family gathered there in the late fall of 1913, was anything but comfortable or cozy. The city was filled with marching men. It seemed as if military parades were being held every day. Along the broad main thoroughfares there were more men in uniform to be seen than men in civilian clothes, and soldiers crowded the restaurants and café bars and night clubs.

"All our efforts to promote peace among the young people of Europe have come to nothing," Adalbert told me after the banquet Cousin Willy gave for Sissy and her fiancé. Adalbert looked older, harder, the gentle boyishness that had so attracted me all but gone from his handsome face.

"My father is determined to use the might of our armies to intimidate the rest of Europe. I see it clearly now."

I told him about my Red Cross course and how I was volunteering in the hospital.

"Mama wants us to be ready when war comes."

"Ah, Tania, you should be dancing, shopping, laughing with friends, falling in love—not thinking of disasters and injuries. You should be becoming engaged, like me."

He introduced me to his fiancée Adi, a charming, fresh-faced young woman with bright blue eyes and curling blond hair.

"We are going to be married next summer," Adi told me. "In August. You must come to the wedding. By then it may be your turn to announce your engagement." She smiled and slipped her arm through Adalbert's. "I only hope you will be as happy as we are."

I thought of Constantin, ruefully. "There was someone for a while, but— I decided that we would not be happy together, so now we are just friends."

Thinking back to those days we spent in Berlin, I am struck by how much we felt like one large, sprawling, somewhat inharmonious family. The ties of blood were strong, the family resemblances striking, especially the uncanny resemblance between papa and King George, who almost looked like twins. There were so many of us: mama's cousin King George and Queen Mary and the dowager Queen Alexandra, who was of course my Grandma Minnie's sister, and all the many many English cousins whose names I could barely remember, and mama's sisters Irene and Victoria and their husbands and children and mama's dear brother Ernie, who lived the life of a bachelor though he had a male companion, and all Cousin Willy's large family and Sissy's friends and her fiancé's friends— in short, a mob of relatives, all of whom seemed to talk at once and none of whom seemed to have anything very interesting to say.

Perhaps the vapid conversation was the result of our trying very hard to say nothing about the one thing that was on everyone's mind: the overwhelming presence of the military.

Berlin is an armed camp, I thought to myself. Yet no one wants to acknowledge it openly; that would be impolite, and contrary to family feeling. Everyone knew that England and France and Russia were joined in an alliance whose purpose was to defeat the aggression of the German Empire. While the diplomats endeavored to preserve peace, the armies were preparing to wage war, as Monsieur Gilliard had explained to my sisters and me before we left to travel to Berlin. Each country was rushing to increase its armaments and to recruit more men to increase the size of its armies.

I noticed that mama avoided Cousin Willy, though he sent her a handsome gift on our arrival in Berlin, together with a note wishing her well and expressing a hope for greater understanding and harmony between Germany and Russia in the future. It seems he had very much wanted Adalbert to marry me, as a token of good will between our two imperial families. He had been disappointed when papa refused Adalbert's request, and he blamed mama—rightly—for the decision.

Grandma Minnie, who had been spending time with her sister in England before coming to Berlin, gave a tea for Sissy and mama agreed to attend, provided Cousin Willy would not be there.

"My father does not attend ladies' teas," Sissy announced to us in a rather arch tone. "He has more important things on his mind."

"We all know what is on his mind," was mama's tart reply.

I felt a stir of uneasiness sitting at the large table where several dozen of us were gathered, handing around plates of cake and sandwiches.

"Oh? And what is that?"

"There is no need to say what we all know."

"Don't be cryptic, Alix," Grandma Minnie said. "Tell us what you mean."

"Some subjects are better left undiscussed," spoke up Queen Alexandra, who, I remembered from our happy days at Cowes, had a way of smoothing over awkwardness with her kind and emollient manner. "Ah! That pound cake reminds me so of my dear Edward. He used to love pound cake with his tea."

Mama drank her tea in nervous silence, as Sissy went on about her future husband, who was an officer in command of the Fourth Prussian Fusiliers.

"We are to be billeted in Königsberg," she said. "The society is not so good there, only officers' wives and the provincial nobility of course. But I'm told there is a very fine chamber music society, and my fiancé is quite musical. He plays the flute."

"I doubt whether the sound of the flute will be heard above the pounding of the guns," mama remarked in a low voice.

"Did you say something, Alix?" Grandma Minnie asked.

"Not to you."

I sensed that mama was about to have one of her outbursts. All the signs were there, her red cheeks and hands, her restlessness.

"Shall we go, mama?" I whispered. "I am ready if you are."

"My daughter thinks it is time I left," mama announced, standing up so abruptly that she nearly overturned her plate. "Perhaps she is right."

As we were gathering our things and saying our goodbyes I glimpsed a figure entering the room, a man in a dark grey suit. He stood by the door. I was sure he was waiting for us. Looking more closely I recognized him. It was Mr. Schmidt.

Twenty-nine

May I escort you and your daughter, Your Imperial Highness?"

Mr. Schmidt spoke with a kindly gravity, and mama, as she had in the past, responded gratefully, her tense body relaxing in his soothing presence.

He took us in his carriage to an imposing house which, he said, belonged to a colleague of his. The house was in a parklike setting, carefully tended and tastefully landscaped, surrounded by a high stone wall.

"My friend, who is a doctor, opens his home to visitors," Mr. Schmidt explained as we went in the broad, thick front door and were shown into a comfortable salon with deep soft rugs and inviting sofas and chairs. A restful room, I thought.

"Please, have a seat and we can talk, if you like."

"I always enjoy talking with you," mama began.

"My patients—I mean my acquaintances—frequently tell me that. The cares of the world press in upon them so heavily, but while we talk, those cares fall away for a time, and they enjoy relief."

"Yes. That's it exactly." Mama's voice grew lower and her shoulders dropped, the muscles in her face relaxed and she allowed herself to sink back into the cushions on the sofa.

We all sat for awhile in silence. Then mama spoke.

"War," she said. Just the one word, war.

"Many fear its coming."

"Death."

"For many, yes."

"The end of all our hopes, all our aspirations. No future for my children."

"You speak a profound and sorrowful truth. But never forget—out of wars have come beneficial changes."

"I see no benefit in death—except relief, that all is over at last."

"And do you ever think of bringing on that relief for yourself, through your own efforts?"

"Yes."

"Mama!" I gripped her arm. "No, mama!"

"It is the truth, Tania. With Mr. Schmidt I speak the truth."

"What are you doing to her? Stop doing this to her!" I stood up. "If my father were here, he would put a stop to this."

"I believe, Tania, that your father would want to help your mother. The kind of talk we are having helps her. It unburdens her."

"Yes, Tania," mama said softly. "It is good to talk openly, like this, even of painful things."

"I understand that you take Veronal to calm yourself," Mr. Schmidt went on. "Three drops at a time. Am I right?"

"I sometimes take six drops now."

"Are you ever tempted to take more? So many that all your troubles will end for good?"

"Yes."

"No, mama no!" I held her arm tightly, my tears flowing. I wanted to run, I wanted to pull mama with me, to take her as far away as possible. Yet at the same time I knew that there was nowhere to run from the wrenching, terrible truth she was revealing. So I stayed where I was, and wept.

"And what is the reason you choose not to end your life? Is it because you know what suffering it would cause your daughter, who I can see loves you so much, and your other children?"

"Yes. That and—"

"And what?"

"I do not give up easily."

"No. I suspect you are a fighter."

Through my tears I could see that mama was smiling. "Yes. I am a fighter."

Mr. Schmidt smiled too. "That is very good to hear."

He reached around behind his chair and picked up a small golden bell that stood on a nearby table. He lifted the bell and rang it. In a moment there was a knock at the door of the salon and a man came in, carrying some papers, which he handed to Mr. Schmidt.

While this was going on mama turned her attention to me, putting her arm around me and hugging me. "Dear Tania," she said. "You mustn't worry. Whatever comes, all will be well. Don't you remember my ring, with the symbol of well being? I always wear it."

"Your Imperial Highness," Mr. Schmidt was saying, "this house we are in is a very special place. Troubled people, people who are thinking of ending their lives, or who are in anguish over unbearable thoughts or nightmares, come here to be helped and healed. There are many who have come in desperate trouble, and who have left feeling themselves to be whole and at peace."

"Is it a monastery then? It doesn't look like a monastery."

"In a way, yes. Only there are no icons and no altars. This is a cathedral of the mind. Sanity, balance, a healthy outlook on the world: these are the iconic treasures to be found in this place. And now I am privileged to be able to offer you a respite here, among us."

"A respite?"

"Would you like to stay here for awhile, and have unburdening talks like this one, and find relief from all that perturbs you?"

Mama sighed and hung her head. "Yes," she said, very softly, in a voice so high and so trusting it might have come from a child and not a middle-aged woman.

"Good. Then all you have to do is sign these papers"—he spread out three sheets on a table in front of the sofa—"and you will be made welcome."

I felt a sharp prickle of unease.

"Mama, don't you think you ought to talk this over with papa?"

"You can talk to him all you like, once you have moved in here with us."

Mama took the pen Mr. Schmidt held out to her.

"I want peace, Tania. Above all, I want peace."

At that moment a piercing scream came from outside the room. Mama grew tense and rigid.

"What was that?"

"At times our guests feel a return of their old disturbances. They have to be subdued."

"Subdued?" I said loudly, suddenly remembering the horrible device Grandma Minnie had forced me to wear when I was a child, the heavy steel brace that trapped and imprisoned me. What put that into my mind at that moment I couldn't have said. "Subdued how?"

"Restrained. Kept from hurting themselves."

"Is this—" I could hardly force myself to say the words. "Is this—a madhouse?"

"No, Tania. We don't use that old outworn term any more. It is a sanatorium. A healing house for the mind."

"Come, mama. Come at once. We must not stay here a minute longer."

"But Tania—" She looked confused.

"No, mama. No. This is no place for you." With all my strength I pulled her up from the sofa and toward the door. Mr. Schmidt, I noticed, made no effort to stop us. We reached the door, mama protesting all the while, and I managed to fling it open.

There stood two tall, strong-looking Cossacks, both with long sabers hanging from their belts.

I cried out in surprise and terror. Then I saw—blessed sight!—that one of the Cossacks was Nikandr, Niuta's lover. The man who had helped us convey Daria to the Workers' Clinic when she was about to have her baby.

"Nikandr!" I called out. "Help us! Don't let them keep mama here in this terrible place!" He frowned.

"You know me, Nikandr! You can trust me. Niuta trusts me. I helped Daria on the day her baby was born. I helped her when Father Gregory attacked her!"

He nodded.

"Take the empress upstairs," the doctor said quietly. The other Cossack moved to seize mama, but Nikandr stopped him, holding out one muscular arm and barring him from reaching out for mama.

"No," he said in his loud ringing voice. "Wait. Let the emperor decide. He is not far away. He has gone to shoot ravens in the hunting park."

And with that he swept mama up into his strong arms and took her out into the wintry garden, the other Cossack by his side, and with me running along behind, my blood pounding so loudly in my ears that Mr. Schmidt's angry shouts were no more than thin wails in the cold wind.

Thirty

As I hoped and expected, papa did not allow mama to be confined in the sanatorium, and in fact we left Berlin soon after the incident. Immediately after Sissy's wedding we left for Petersburg, saying a hurried goodbye to our English and German relatives and receiving assurances that whatever happened between our various countries, we would all love and help one another in any way we could.

Adalbert kissed my cheek and looked at me soulfully. "I am at your service, Tania, whenever you may need me. I will always be your loving friend." I assured him that I felt the same and that I hoped to see him at his wedding.

As we boarded our train I noticed that Grandma Minnie was not with us.

"We will not be seeing her for awhile," papa confided to me. "I have sent her away, to Kiev. She has friends there. She will not be making trouble in our family again."

I felt as if a huge weight had been lifted from my young shoulders.

"Oh, thank you, papa! Now she won't always be plotting behind our backs, and criticizing us."

"And always snatching cigarettes out of my mouth when I'm about to light them." We laughed.

During the long train journey I talked to papa again, this time much more seriously. We were in a comfortable, secluded section of the imperial train, a car whose walls were paneled with old oak and whose furnishings were upholstered in red plush embroidered with gold threads in patterns of crowns and eagles. We sat beside a large window, looking out on the snowy landscape of dense forests and quaint small towns and villages.

"What should be done about mama?" I asked him. "A sanatorium is not the answer, even an enlightened one—if such a thing exists. But what other answer is there? She says she has thoughts of doing away with herself."

Papa patted my hand. "She has been saying that ever since I first met her, as a girl. It is a sort of Wagnerian fantasy, the wish for a glorious romantic ending to an otherwise rather conventional life, even though it is a life of exalted status and privilege. I don't think she really means to do it." He sighed. "Besides, if the worst should happen—and I have lived with that possibility for decades now—then I know that all is in God's hands."

"I don't believe God wants mama to die."

"Then He will make sure she does not die." He smiled. "We cannot prevent from happening all the sad things we imagine might happen. I learned that years ago, when my dear grandfather was blown up."

"I wish I had your resignation."

"Faith, Tania. Not resignation. Faith." He turned to gaze out the window, and I realized that there was nothing more to be said.

Thirty-one

𝒯*he warm, wet* summer of 1914 brought mold to the dripping, south-facing walls of the palace infirmary, and another outbreak of typhoid to Smokestack Town, and, inevitably, a series of crippling strikes.

Half the laborers in Petersburg were on strike, it was said, and their refusal to work meant that in the idle factories, the guns and shells and rifles for the army were not being made, the railroad cars needed to bring food into the city were not being assembled and the large, dissatisfied crowds in the streets were becoming more vocal and more unruly by the day.

I began volunteering four afternoons a week in the hospital because of the number of typhoid victims and my sisters Marie and Anastasia helped out too by carrying trays and scrubbing floors ("It's good for them!" mama said, and she was right), delivering meals to the patients who were recovering and able to eat and carrying messages between the wards.

Marie had grown into a beautiful, dark-haired girl, buxom and strong—so strong she helped out by moving heavy iron bedsteads in the wards—but she was troubled and kept her distance from the rest of us. She called herself a changeling, a child from another family deposited in our nest by mistake. Mama brushed off this absurd suggestion and papa was faintly amused by it. Neither took the time to either comfort or confront the prickly Marie, who spent a great deal of time with Aunt Xenia's family where she felt more at home.

Anastasia was a will-o'-the-wisp, always in motion, hard to keep track of and even harder to discipline. She slipped in and out of rooms with the same quicksilver ease that she showed in slipping in and out of obligations, particularly unpleasant ones. She came to the hospital with us, and did some of her assigned chores, but ignored others, exasperating us all. She ran errands for mama, who called her "my legs" and was grateful for her help—until she looked around and discovered that her "legs" were nowhere to be found.

I loved my sisters, yet I found them trying, each in her own way; I'm afraid that at times I lectured them, the way older sisters do, and I must have irritated them a good deal.

As the summer wore on the slow drizzling rain continued to fall, but the rain did not prevent the growing number of strikers from coming together at street corners and glaring at the police and mounted guards who kept an eye on them, and sometimes beat them with truncheons or slashed at them with their sabers when they spilled out into the streets and became disruptive. Peasants, looking very odd and out of place in their sheepskin coats which were far too warm for the summer season, joined the strikers and helped them erect barricades in the broad avenues, walling off whole neighborhoods from police interference and singing and chanting provocative songs and slogans.

I watched all this, going back and forth most afternoons between the hospital and Tsarskoe Selo in its protected suburb. I was aware, too, of the unease that spread following the latest act of bomb-throwing. In June a revolutionary had thrown a bomb at the heir to the Austrian throne, Archduke Franz Ferdinand and, when the bomb missed its target and blew up others in the archduke's retinue, another assassin came forward and shot and killed Franz Ferdinand and his wife Sophie as well.

Once again Tsarskoe Selo was full of police searching for people with hidden bombs. And the hospital where we all volunteered was searched several times a day for hidden weapons and "agitators," as papa continued to call them.

I was looking forward to returning to Germany for Adalbert and Adi's wedding, which was to take place early in August, but as the time came nearer I realized it would probably not be possible for me to go. I sent a wedding gift, a beautiful silver samovar on a handsome tray, and with it a letter wishing the couple all good fortune, and saying how sorry I was that I would not be able to attend the ceremony after all, I knew they would understand why.

Private concerns were giving way before the larger events that were rapidly encompassing us all. Just as I had seen German soldiers in great numbers in the streets of Berlin, so now our Russian armies were assembling, and the Petersburg streets, once full of strikers, were now filling with troops and guns, gathering in the capital before being sent westward to the borderlands between Germany and the Austro-Hungarian Empire.

Everyone, even the most peace-loving among us, now conceded that war was coming; it was only a matter of time. Finally, in August, we learned that Germany had declared war on Russia. Cousin Willy had turned against us at last, just as mama said he would. It was up to us, to Russia, along with our allies France and England, to defeat him.

A patriotic mood gripped the city as flags waved, troops marched, guns boomed in salutes to the motherland and to papa. The icon of the Holy Virgin of Kazan was carried in procession through the streets of Petersburg to spread her protection over us, and priests with religious banners paraded past the troops and guns, blessing them and leading the crowds in singing hymns and odes to the motherland.

I had never before seen such an effusion of feeling, not even when I was a child and I watched the crowds from the balcony of the Winter Palace at the time of the war against the Japanese.

"You see, Tania, how my people love me. They long to do their part to defend our land. There are so many recruits, so many volunteers, that there aren't enough uniforms to clothe them or guns to arm them."

Feelings ran so high, in those rainy autumn days, that some of the peasants crowding in to the recruiting stations in hopes of joining the army were trampled and killed, becoming the first casualties of the war. Constantin and his ambulance crew brought in one man who had been caught up in the rush to enlist and accidentally pushed under a cart, his legs crushed by its weight. Accident victims were often brought to the ward I volunteered in and this man was no exception. He was put on an examining table where Constantin looked him over and shook his head.

"We'll be lucky to save his life," he said. "His legs have got to come off." I had never before assisted at an operation but I did so now, for the ward was understaffed and more hands were needed. Constantin began giving orders loudly and with assurance, just as if he had been a trained surgeon instead of a surgical student. I cut the cloth of the injured man's trousers away from his bleeding legs and swabbed the blood as best I could with towels while a nurse put a mask over his face and dripped ether onto it—the sharp smell of the ether making me nauseous and then sleepy.

After passing his knife through a candle flame (antiseptic being in short supply just then, and kept in a cupboard at the opposite end of the building), Constantin cut the flesh—slimy and green in places—and sawed the bones of the man's legs, ignoring his piteous half-delirious screams and the repulsive smells that issued from his tormented body.

I nearly passed out, brought back to consciousness by Constantin's loud, sharp orders directed at me.

"More towels! More pressure!"

I did my best, knowing without having to be told that the man would die if he lost more blood. My apron was soaked in blood, my shoes squelched when I took a step, they were so drenched in blood. My arms and hands were red. I must look like some horrible butcher, I thought to myself. I fought the confusion and disorientation that threatened to engulf my consciousness. I felt myself sway. Yet I held on, pressing with all my strength against the raw flesh and flinging aside each of the towels as it became saturated.

His hasty cutting and sawing complete, Constantin tied tourniquets to the man's thighs and paused for breath.

"The bleeding's stopped for now," he said. "Take the legs away."

The words were so strange to my ears that I almost asked Constantin to repeat them. Take the legs away? Take them where? I had never before handled amputated body parts; how was it done? Surely severed legs were not to be casually deposited in the refuse bins, along with used bandages and swabs and filth swept from the floors?

I found an old torn pillowcase and, lifting the legs gingerly one at a time, placed them inside it. Then I carried the pillowcase into the herb garden adjacent to the hospital and, finding a shovel, began to dig a sort of grave. For if we bury the bodies of the dead in the earth, reverently and with prayers, I reasoned, then it had to follow that we ought to bury parts of bodies with the same attention to their spiritual value.

"What are you doing there!" came a harsh croaking voice—the voice of the matron, a hardbitten, flinty-faced woman who, I had observed over the past few months, was skeptical of upper-class and aristocratic volunteer nurses, much preferring trained and seasoned professionals like herself.

"I'm burying some remains, matron."

"Where do you think you are, a churchyard? Take your remains and put them in the incinerator, as we always do."

"I didn't realize that was what was expected."

She glared at me, her look and her tone of voice unsparing.

"If you are ignorant, girl, then ask. Don't invent. What have you got there anyway?" She grabbed the bloody, stinking pillowcase from me and peered inside it.

"Humph! Legs again! We've been having too many legs come off this autumn. Now, here's a lesson for you, one that the Red Cross didn't teach you. Amputated limbs are full of pus and germs. They reek of gangrene, as a rule. Gangrene is horrible stuff, perhaps you've heard of it? The moist, slimy green kind, the kind you can see on your legs there, spreads very rapidly, simply by touch."

I gasped, and looked down at my bloody hands, the hands that had reached for the sawed-off limbs and lifted them. Was I infected? I wiped my hands on my apron, making the matron laugh.

"Do you really think you can wipe away germs?"

"No, of course not. We were taught about hygiene, and antisepsis, and—"

"It is one thing to be taught in a class, and quite another to learn about sickness and death inside a hospital, where there are real germs and real blood!"

She snatched the pillowcase out of my hands. "Give that germridden thing to me! Now, before we both get sick, follow me to the incinerator and watch me burn these remains to bloody ashes!"

Thirty-two

The first of the wounded soldiers to reach our hospital from the killing fields of East Prussia were the gallant Red Hussars and the elite Chevaliers Gardes, the proudest and finest of my father's many regiments. They straggled in, some limping, supported on the arms of servants or orderlies, some on stretchers, many simply crowded into wagons or carts, feverish and half mad with pain, lying side by side in their own filth, and left at the entrance to the admitting rooms.

The doctors did what they could, saved as many as they could, but every day the death carts came to the back door of the hospital—the door used for food deliveries and waste removal—and more corpses were piled in and taken away.

They named it the Battle of Tannenberg, that monumental struggle in August of 1914, and with every fresh wave of wounded and dying men the horror of the terrible battle revealed itself to us.

"We were surrounded," an officer in the Red Hussars gasped to all who would listen as he was being examined. "We couldn't escape them, there were so many. The ground was all marsh, it gave way beneath our feet, beneath the weight of the great guns. We sank into the quicksand. The guns were lost." He looked up at the doctor who was pressing on his chest and stomach, making him wince, then around at the nurses.

"So many died. So many were taken prisoner by the Germans. The dirty Germans! The shame of it! The dishonor!"

We all felt it—the dishonor of great Russia being humiliated, her brave soldiers slaughtered by the arrogant, soulless wicked demonic Germans and their Austrian allies.

We hated all Germans and everything they were associated with in those early days of the war: we hated Wagner and his operas, German chocolates, German books and the German language—a language my mother, raised in Darmstadt, spoke far more fluently than Russian.

(I did not hate Adalbert, of course, or any other German I actually knew, except for Cousin Willy. It was only the Germans I did not know that I loathed.)

Papa changed the name of our capital from the Germanic St. Petersburg to the Russian Petrograd. Olga's little dog Fritzie became Ivanka. Mama no longer called papa "Liebchen" but "dorogoi," which is darling in Russian.

With a new demon to despise and fear, there was a sudden decline in speechmaking against papa and his ministers. The workers' newspaper *Pravda* was outlawed and many of those papa called "agitators" were exiled to Siberia. Even Daria, with her great animosity toward my family and toward Romanov rule, turned all her passion into volunteer nursing and support for our soldiers.

Ever since the night Father Gregory attacked her and I came to her rescue, Daria had stayed close to me, along with little Iskra, volunteering at the hospital and staying near me at Tsarskoe Selo wherever I went. She never went back to the ironing room and Niuta got permission from mama to let Daria become a maidservant in the nursery.

As the Russian war losses mounted there were more and more bereaved families clamoring for someone to blame. Mama, who for years had been called the German Bitch, was at the top of the list. Oh! The dreadful things that were said about her! That she was a German spy, that she made money from the Russian losses, that she was collaborating with the enemy and weakening papa with her hectoring and badgering.

To my amazement, all the slander and pamphlets and speeches directed against her only served to make mama stronger. There was none of the constant illness or weakness I was used to seeing in her, none of the awful air of surrender and wan desire for oblivion I had witnessed in the sanatorium in Berlin. Instead, mama threw herself energetically into war work, not only nursing in the wards (where the men sometimes spat on her and swore at her, so great was their contempt for all Germans and for mama in particular) but turning parts of the great palace at Tsarskoe Selo into a new hospital and organizing her own hospital train to bring men there from the front.

In order to raise money to equip her new palace hospital and pay for the operation of the train she made speeches before women's groups, met with wealthy donors and exhorted her aristocratic friends and relatives to donate.

"See, Tania," she said to me one morning, taking me aside so that others would not overhear us, "I have a letter from brother Ernie, with a bank draft, to support my hospital! Ernie has such a good heart, he isn't like Cousin Willy at all. He writes that he is appalled at the losses on the German side and wishes the war would come to a swift end."

"If only Cousin Willy would listen to him."

Mama shook her head. "No, not Cousin Willy. But Ernie is a natural diplomat. I would not be surprised if he had the ear of some of the imperial ministers."

Her face fell. "Oh, Tania, I just had the most terrible thought. What if Cousin Willy sends Ernie to fight, and on the Russian front! What pain that would give me!"

She was concerned, not only for Ernie, who was a civilian, but for her sister Irene's husband Henry who was an admiral in the German navy, and her sister Victoria's husband Louis who held a parallel position in the British navy. Our family, divided against itself; it was a fearsome thought, and it preyed on mama's mind, as she continued to work tirelessly to increase the number of wards in the palace and to equip them with beds and blankets and medicines and—yes—more incinerators for the ghoulish work of disposing of mutilated body parts.

The awful Battle of Tannenberg was over by September, and long before Christmas we had to admit, privately, to ourselves and one another, that Russia was losing the war. Despite some gains on the Austrian front in Galicia and the Carpathians—gains the Austrians quickly reversed—our armies were in retreat, and the wounded soldiers we encountered daily were full of complaints about shortages of guns and shells and shrapnel, shortages of rifles and cartridges, shortages of oats and hay for the horses and nourishing food for the soldiers themselves. The striking workers in what I must now call Petrograd had gone back to the factories and were laboring extra hours to provide war materiel, but the demand was far greater than they could fill.

Shortly after Christmas papa met with his principal officers and ministers and emerged shaking his head.

"We simply were not prepared," I heard him say to himself. "We did not realize what it would be like, all that would be needed." He retreated to his isolated spot on the Children's Island and walked there, in the snow, for hours.

A rumor spread through the capital that the Austrian army, which was advancing eastward, would soon be in Petrograd. There was an exodus of sorts. People crowded into the train stations hoping to ride the trains to Kiev or Moscow or even Siberia, away from the oncoming enemy. But the trains were filled with soldiers, and what space there was, after the soldiers were loaded on and off, was allotted to food and necessary supplies. There was no room for ordinary passengers.

The cry of "The Austrians are coming" became more clamorous. Servants hurried through the halls of the palaces removing statues and paintings and valuable tapestries, packing them in crates and hiding them in hastily dug earthen cellars, hoping to keep them from the enemy.

Amid it all, my sisters and I, and mama at times, went on with the exhausting, dirty, disheartening, endless work of nursing, for more and more soldiers were delivered to our wards daily, until there were no beds to hold them all and makeshift clinics had to be set up in haste, without proper staff or equipment. Many nights Olga and I worked on, long past the end of our shifts, until exhaustion overcame us, and we simply fell asleep on mattresses in the nurses' anterooms without even taking off our uniforms.

Marie too worked long hours some evenings, though as she was only fifteen in that first year of the war I thought three days a week quite enough time for her to take from her studies. I could not really keep track of Anastasia; sometimes she was there with us, helping out, sometimes not. She still bred worms in the palace attic, and occasionally, to our disgust, brought her best wriggling specimens into my bedroom or Olga's to show them off. Mama could not abide them and said they gave her nightmares.

No one who has not been a nurse in wartime can possibly know what it was like for us, called upon as we were to confront and try to assuage so much human damage. The sight of suppurating wounds, covered by stinking bandages that had to be changed hourly, the wounds growing slowly septic because they could not be kept clean. The vomit and urine and blood, torrents of blood it seemed, that poured out during operations. The crazy patients with head wounds who babbled and shrieked and knocked the food out of my hand when I tried to feed them. The thankless labor of changing blood-soaked sheets. The stench of the bedpans. The haunting look of a man with shell-shock, a grey-faced look, the eyes vacant, the features ravaged. The screams and moans. And most of all, the sight of grown men, strong men, men in uniform, crying piteously like children and calling for their mothers.

Oh, how I welcomed the occasional feel of Constantin's kind hand on my shoulder and his voice in my ear, saying, "Rest, Tania dear. Rest now."

Blessed rest, how I needed it. For the sheer drudgery of the long days exhausted me, my feet were sore, and always wet (how I longed for clean, dry warm feet!) and my back ached terribly, since matron, in addition to demanding that we always wear clean, starched aprons, refused to let us sit down in the wards lest we appear idle.

My hands swelled, my face was chapped, my ankles were constantly swollen—but at least I never came down with a serious illness, though I was hourly exposed to dangerous germs. That, at least, was something to be thankful for.

Yet I confess that sometimes, at the end of a long day, my compassion spent, my overworked body in full rebellion, all I could feel was revulsion. Revulsion at the waste of life—for many men died before my eyes simply because there were not enough doctors or nurses to care for them, or medicines to give them. Revulsion for the cadaverous, delirious dying men, revulsion for war and the men who make war, and, in my worst hours, revulsion for everything and everyone, even my beloved father, who had brought this horror of war upon us all.

Thirty-three

They brought him in on a stretcher, a dark-haired, dark-eyed boy with a wound in his chest and another in his forehead. He was pale and weak, but conscious. He reached out his hand to me and said, in the accent of the south, "Please, give me water."

I took his hand and squeezed it, to give him comfort, and I saw then that he was beautiful.

"Chest wound!" the doctor called out. "No water."

"I'm sorry," I said to the boy, still holding his hand.

"Please," he said again, more weakly this time, and then he lost consciousness.

Oh Lord, don't let this one die, I prayed, and for the next hour I stayed by his bedside, while his wounds were cleaned and tended and the doctor probed and prodded for the bullet that had lodged under his breastbone.

"Is he going to live?" I asked when the hasty, unhygienic operation was over.

The doctor shrugged. "If he is strong, and has good nursing. Make sure he has clean bandages."

"Can I give him water when he wakes up?"

"You can give him vodka for all I care," the doctor said wearily, and went on to the next emergency.

It was spring, 1915 and I would soon turn eighteen years old. The river ice was groaning and cracking and the air held a faint warmth. Amid the bleakness of war the earth was awakening, and would soon flower.

The Germans were coming closer and closer and our Russian losses were mounting ever higher. Petrograd was filling with thousands of refugees, fleeing the fighting and taking shelter where they could, beneath bridges, in the porticos of shopping arcades, in the parks, anywhere they could huddle together for warmth against the cold wind and sleet, anywhere they could try to stay dry.

The newspapers did not print the worst news—that a large part of Russian territory was now in German hands, and that, in the west, our allies the British and French had lost five million men to German assaults, with some seven million wounded—but we knew. Constantin, who had been appointed to a position in the war ministry, was well informed, and so were many of the doctors that worked in mama's hospital at Tsarskoe Selo. Through them we received much unwelcome news, augmented by the rumors that flew from street to street and mouth to mouth in the capital.

I stayed by the boy's bedside all that afternoon and long into the night, feeling his bandaged forehead to see if he had a fever, listening for any obstruction in his breathing, still holding his clammy hand. He bled from his chest wound and I changed his bandages. In the night I had an impulse to talk to him, hoping that the presence of a caring person and encouraging words would help to prevent him from sinking into a terminal state as so many patients did following an operation. I had seen it so often: the still living bodies that seemed to shrivel as I watched, the skin yellowing, the eyes half open, half closed, only the whites showing. The fretful hands plucking at the bedclothes. Then only stillness, and presently the stench of rot . . .

I wanted this boy to live.

So I talked to him, about anything that floated into my mind in those late-night hours: about how strong he looked and how I was sure he would recover, about how I wondered where his home was and how old he was and how many were in his family, about how I would be happy to write to his parents for him if he liked and tell them how he was doing as soon as he began to recover.

When I ran out of thoughts about the boy, whose forehead, I was glad to notice, was not getting hot and whose breath came and went evenly, I began to talk about myself. I told him about Adalbert, how he was at sea on a battle cruiser and how he had gotten word to me, through a diplomat friend, that his ship had foundered in an engagement with the British off Dogger Bank. How Adalbert had wanted to marry me but my father had said no. (I did not reveal, even to a sleeping patient, who my father was.) Yawning, I told him about the elephant and how I rarely got to see him just then, because of my spending so much time at the hospital. Running out of things to say, and becoming increasingly tired, I told him about my sister Olga and her tiresome search for the man whose name started with a "V," the man she had been expecting to marry ever since the night she had thrown her slippers over her shoulder and they had formed a "V."

In the end my eyelids grew very heavy and I began rambling about how spring was coming, spring was just over the horizon, and perhaps with the greening of the earth, peace would come.

Toward morning I dropped off to sleep, sitting on a chair beside the boy's bed (hoping matron would not catch me and chastise me for sitting down), my head resting on the bedclothes.

I was awakened by a voice.

"Do you have any chocolate?"

I sat up, my eyes bleary.

The voice came again, a warm, resonant voice, from the bed. "Do you have any chocolate? Nut chocolate, the kind in the blue wrappers."

"So you're awake then," I managed to respond. "How do you feel?"

"Hungry. And thirsty."

He was pale, but his eyes were clear and his voice steady. He didn't look at all like someone about to die. His smile, ah, his smile! I cannot describe it, but in that moment, as I smiled back, and took his outstretched hand, I was changed.

"Tania," I said.

"Michael."

So simple, so sudden, was the exchange between us—and yet, it held everything. It held our future.

"I know the kind of chocolate you mean. Swiss chocolate."

"Yes."

"I haven't seen any Swiss chocolate since the war began. But I can bring you water, and soup."

He drank the cool water I offered and let me feed him nearly an entire bowl of vegetable soup with a few bits of meat floating in it. Meat was a rarity for us in those lean war times; even at Tsarskoe Selo we had only small portions of ham and chicken and mama said it was important that we not have luxuries (meat being then a great luxury) that were denied to others.

After he ate, he slept again, and I left his bedside, going through the ward and doing what was necessary, changing bandages and cleaning bedpans and helping with the men brought in that day from the hospital trains. Between tasks, however, I found myself returning to Michael, to see that he was all right. And when my shift ended, I went into the nurses' room and washed my face and pinched my cheeks to give them color and dampened the hair around my face to make it curl more tightly. I straightened and smoothed my apron, regretting the stains that darkened it and wishing I had a clean one.

Just then Olga came into the room and sank down on the sofa, putting her feet on a stool.

"Ooh, my feet," she groaned. "I don't think my ankles will ever be normal again."

"Olga, do you have a clean apron I can borrow?"

"Why? It's time to go home."

"I'm going to stay a little longer tonight. I would feel better in a clean apron."

She looked suspicious.

"All right, what is it? What's going on? Is it that Constantin again? Are you meeting him?"

"I've told you, Constantin and I are friends. Nothing more."

"That's not what Aunt Olenka says."

"She's mistaken."

Olga continued to look at me quizzically from under her blond brows. "There's one in my basket. You can borrow it. But you have to give it back to me tomorrow, washed and ironed."

"Daria will do it for me."

"Your worshipping shadow. Your slave."

Olga was sarcastic about Daria, and, I thought, jealous, for she had no devoted servant of her own to follow her everywhere. At the mention of Daria I realized, for the first time that day, that she had not been at my side or within easy reach ever since the previous afternoon's operation. I had not heard her dog bark or little five-year-old Iskra prattle on for some hours. It was unlike Daria to stay away like that.

I found the crisp white apron and changed into it. Then, thanking Olga, I went back into the ward, to the boy's bedside. To Michael's bedside.

I leaned over him.

"Pretty girl," he murmured in Russian, then added some words in a language I didn't understand. Then he winced, and I felt his forehead. He was hot.

I fretted over him for the next three hours, while he tossed uneasily in the narrow bed and I kept trying to find a doctor who was free to examine him.

There were fewer and fewer doctors available. Not only in our hospital, but in all the hospitals in or near the capital. Many had volunteered to go into the field with the regiments when the war began, and a number of those had been killed along with the men they tended. According to Constantin, whose work at the ministry involved training and recruiting physicians for the army, it was becoming harder and harder to find qualified men—and a sprinkling of women—who had both the skill and the stamina to treat the wounded, to work long hours in overcrowded wards where the screams of men in pain clashed jarringly with the scratchy sound of gramophone records.

Finally a harried-looking doctor responded to my pleas and came over to Michael's bedside. He felt his forehead, then turned down the blanket and peeled away the bandages from his chest. There was inflammation, and a yellowish liquid oozing from the wound that I had not noticed before.

"Purulence," was all the doctor said. "He'll not last the night."

Purulence was a terrible word, a death sentence. It meant infection.

"Oh no, you must be wrong. He had a good night last night, following his operation. He had no fever and no trouble breathing."

The doctor shrugged. "You can see for yourself. You can smell for yourself. There's rot in the wound."

"Then we must treat it."

"We have nothing to treat it with, except iodine." (We kept iodine for the treatment of gonorrhea, which many of our patients had.)

"Then we will use iodine."

He shrugged. "If you must. But I would save it for the men who have a chance. This one doesn't. You might as well pull the blanket up over his head now."

Anger welled up in me as I watched the doctor walk away. How dare he consign this lovely boy to death?

Just then I caught sight of a patient who had died being laid on a stretcher, a shroud over his body, a candle being lit and placed beside his head. Those caring for the corpse paused to cross themselves and bow their heads, then lifted the stretcher and went out to where the death carts waited.

No, I said aloud. No, this boy, this Michael that I care about—he will not die. Not if I can prevent it. And I went out to fetch the iodine.

Thirty-four

Returning with the iodine, I swabbed it over Michael's chest wound and on his forehead, the strong scent of the brown liquid overpowering the stink of his infected wounds.

"Now then," I said as I finished, doing my best to sound as confident as possible. "That ought to help a lot."

I kept him as comfortable as I could, straightening the sheet beneath his body and turning his pillow over so that it would be cool under his head.

It was when I lifted his pillow that I saw the dagger.

It was a long, straight sharp-pointed steel dagger, the handle carved with silver and set with two gleaming blue jewels. There was writing carved into the handle in a script I couldn't read.

I turned the pillow and put it back under Michael's head, covering the sharp blade.

I heard the matron's quick, efficient step and tried to look busy as she passed Michael's bed.

"Wash that one," she said in passing, sniffing the air. "Now."

After many months of nursing I had become used to washing men's naked bodies, or parts of their bodies. At first I had been embarrassed, having only seen Constantin naked and my brother when he was ill and the physicians were packing him in ice in an effort to bring down his fever. I tried to look on this task of body-washing as another in a series of necessary chores, like washing the drinking glasses or disinfecting a bed after a man had died in it.

But as I gathered the towels, soap and bowl of warm water I needed to wash Michael, I felt a tingle of excitement. My breath came faster, and as I ran my soapy hands over his shoulders and broad chest with its curling dark hair (avoiding the wound) I could feel my heart beating faster as well. He was slim, muscular, lithe of limb and well proportioned. His body, I saw, was as beautiful as his face, the skin smooth and unlined, and of a ripe golden-brown color.

I allowed my eyes to wander down his torso, to his navel, and below to where his strong loins began. I tried to avert my eyes, but could not help but admire what I saw. He looked like the statue of Apollo in the gardens at Tsarskoe Selo, his male organs virile and well formed, his legs lean and as shapely as any athlete's. My hands trembling, I went on washing him—neglecting no part. It was the most sensuous experience I had yet known, and I confess that I lingered over his belly and taut buttocks. When I finished, and began dressing him again, I was intensely embarrassed to discover Daria standing behind me, watching me.

"I saw you with him yesterday," she said. "When they first brought him in. And later on, when you were tending to him. I knew. I could tell."

"Tell what?" I asked, but my tone betrayed me. For of course I knew what it was that she could tell.

"That the two of you have—started to join."

"I don't even know him."

"You know his body. And I believe you have begun to see into one another's hearts." It was the first time I had ever heard her speak that way. I remembered that she had been in love, that her fiancé had been killed by my father's Cossacks. There was a depth of feeling behind her previously flinty exterior.

"You see a great deal."

"I came for your apron. I know you need me to wash and iron it."

I took off my dirty apron and handed it to Daria. She was rummaging in a pocket of her skirt.

"I've brought a plaster for his chest. My grandmother taught me how to make it. It is mostly herbs—some catnip, some hyssop, some herbs grown only in Siberia. It is an old remedy for healing wounds."

"Thank you Daria."

She smiled—another rarity!—and went away.

I applied iodine and Daria's plaster to Michael's chest wound, calculating that two helpful remedies had to be better than one. Then I covered him with the blanket, touched his face lightly with my fingertips and went about my other duties.

In going from bed to bed I crossed paths with Olga, who looked me up and down.

"Hmm," she said. "You don't really look any different."

"And why should I?"

"Because of your romance."

"There is no romance. Only a patient I care about."

"Care for."

"Care about."

"Dear me," she said in her most syrupy voice, "what will Constantin say?"

I didn't reply.

"Oh, and Niuta wants to know where you have been. Why you weren't with us for supper last night. Or has it been two nights?"

"One of the patients who had an operation had to be watched. I volunteered."

"Daria says he is very handsome."

"He is very ill."

"He doesn't have the typhus, does he? I've been seeing more and more cases in the past two days. If he gets the rash, you'll know he has it. Don't go near him. You don't want to die because of one handsome boy." She started to walk on past me, then turned. "By the way, I met a handsome boy too. And his name is Victor." She emphasized the "V."

I started to say something tart but stopped myself. I was feeling expansive, generous.

"Good luck with him, Oliushka."

The day wore on, and every time I returned to Michael's bedside he looked worse. His cheeks were flushed and hot, he tossed uneasily, and when I changed his bandage, the skin around his wound was swollen and very red, with pus leaking from it. I saw no signs of the dreaded red rash that was the mark of typhus, however and that, at least, was positive.

I wrapped him in cold towels and reapplied the iodine and Daria's herbal plaster. On an impulse I took the dagger and put the handle into his open hand. At once his fingers closed over it, and a faint sound came from his lips.

"What did you say?"

"They fear us," he murmured in a hoarse whisper. "Russians fear us." Then he opened his hand, letting the dagger fall onto the blanket. I put it back under his pillow.

When midnight came and Michael was no better I sent a messenger to the palace to ask for the icon of St. Simon Verkhoturie, the powerful icon Father Gregory had sent to my father years earlier. If Michael was beyond human help, as the doctor thought, at least he was not beyond divine help. The icon could work its wonders.

After waiting an hour or more I was surprised to see mama come into the ward, dressed all in black as she always was in those wartime days, her hair arranged very simply, a clear sign that she had come in haste on learning of my request for the icon.

I was surprised to see her, because she had once again become withdrawn and was living the life of a semi-invalid.

In the first months of the war, from August 1914 when it began until Christmastime, mama had been volunteering in the wards just as Olga and I and Marie were doing and we had often worked together, or at least near one another. But then, with the coming of winter, her energy faltered and she suffered with her migraines and with pains in her leg that worsened her limp. The demanding care of the wounded was not possible for her, even occasionally, nor were her other pursuits of money-raising and the organization of clinics. She mourned the war dead in the solitude of her mauve sitting room—to excess, I thought—and her one concern became to support papa and convince him to take over the command of the Russian army, which he did, despite his dislike of all public duties and his lack of experience of command.

But here she was, limping on her sore leg and looking as if she hadn't been sleeping well.

"Where is the icon, mama? This patient is dying."

"I sent the icon to your father at his command post in Mogilev. But I brought you a stick Our Friend brought from the Holy Land."

She held out an ordinary-looking piece of wood, about two feet long, with a few small twigs branching out from it. It was quite dead.

"An old stick? What good is that?"

"It carries his blessing."

"It may carry his blessing, but he certainly did not find it in the Holy Land. He was never anywhere near the Holy Land. The police know that for certain."

"Many lies are told about him. You will see that this is no ordinary stick. Touch the patient where the pain is, and observe the stick. It carries Our Friend's power." And having delivered her holy object, she left.

I didn't want anything to do with Father Gregory or his stick. I threw it on the floor, resisting an urge to stomp on it and smash it. But later, hearing Michael's increasingly labored breathing, all my instincts telling me that he could not last much longer, I remembered how Father Gregory cured my Artipo, how he knew in some uncanny fashion that Constantin's eye hurt him and that he needed new glasses, how he had stopped my brother's bleeding many times and eased my parents' anxieties again and again. What was it that he had said to me and Constantin the day we visited his apartment? That he was flawed but that the power that flowed through him was of great force nonetheless?

I bent down and picked up the stick and placed it on Michael's chest.

Right away I thought I saw some color come into his pale face. He fluttered his eyelids a little. At first I assumed I must be mistaken, that the slight changes I thought I detected in him were only tricks of the dim light—or illusions, the wished-for result of my fervent hope for his recovery. But the longer I watched, the more I was convinced that there was indeed a change, that Michael's forehead was not as hot as it had been and that his rasping breaths were coming more easily.

Keeping the stick in place on his chest, I lay down beside Michael and, yielding to my weariness, went to sleep.

When I awoke at dawn, something remarkable had happened. On one of the twigs a white bud had appeared. By midmorning the bud had opened. It was a small white flower that gave forth a heavy sweet scent, a scent so strong that it overcame the reek of the iodine and the stink of the infection, indeed it seemed to fill the entire ward with its perfume.

And a few hours later, when I changed Michael's bandage, I saw that the wound on his chest was no longer inflamed, or weeping the awful yellowish ichor. There was no stench of inflammation—only the delicious scent from the white flower, and with it, a growing certainty in my heart that this boy I cared about so much would soon be well.

Thirty-five

Two weeks later Michael was well enough to get out of bed, and a month later, around the time of my birthday, he was fit enough to go with me out into the small hospital garden and sit on a bench beside me in the spring sunshine.

He turned his face to the sun and shut his eyes, breathing deeply, a smile on his face. Then he kissed me, a long, lingering kiss that left me dizzy and all but breathless. He had kissed me before, in the ward, but never with such passion. This was the first time we had ever been alone together, without the constant near presence of other patients, doctors, nurses, and orderlies. Without the incessant drama of pain and illness, agony and death.

"I could never do that with the matron always around," he said.

"She doesn't come out here," I answered, and pulled him toward me again.

The feel of his mouth on mine, the smell of him, his familiar touch, the look in his dear dark eyes when at last our mouths parted and we caught our breath—a breath that had almost become one single breath—was far beyond my power to describe. I was completely enraptured. Had I found out, in that heady, enchanted afternoon, that he didn't love me I think I would have died. So completely open was I to all that he could give me, all that I felt for him.

Is there anything sweeter than first love? Not honey, not a ripe peach, not even the Swiss nut chocolate that the clever Sedynov was able to buy for me through his contacts in the ministry of defense.

I had been infatuated with Adalbert, I had known excitement with Constantin, but I loved Michael. Loved him, body, heart and soul. Loved him, as I then thought, as no woman had ever loved before, or ever would again. Such are the precious dreams of early youth, dreams that deny all common sense and refuse to see the dross of life in all its murk and ugliness. Having spent so many months amid the stark, cruel human wreckage of war, I was eager to enter a realm of unalloyed joy, a realm Michael opened to me with his kisses and his passion.

There was a lull in the war in that summer of 1915, a lull in the flow of wounded men. I found my duties growing lighter, which allowed me to spend parts of many afternoons with Michael, sitting in the hospital garden and, as he healed, walking on the palace grounds or along the riverbank. As we walked, hand in hand, we talked.

He told me of his life in Daghestan, high in the Caucasus Mountains, where the constant winds shriek along the cliff faces and villages cling to the jagged peaks, their stone houses centuries old.

"My father's house had been lived in by his clan for nine generations. Since long before the Russians came and conquered us. One of my ancestors invaded the neighboring kingdom of Imeretia in the seventh century and became king there.

"Warmaking was all we knew in my village. I was born in the saddle, my father liked to say, with a dagger in my hand."

"What are the words written on your dagger?"

"They mean, 'I am thy everpresent strength.' That dagger belonged to my great-grandmother Lalako. She was a renowned warrior who took many heads. She wore them hanging from her waist-belt, to frighten her enemies.

"My father and my uncles were brave warriors too, but my father took pity on my mother because so many of her babies died and we moved to Tiflis, and changed our name from Gamkrelidze to Gradov, to sound more Russian. My great-grandmother was dead by then. If she had known, she would have turned over in her grave."

"So you are a Georgian."

"My grandmother would say we were of the Ghalghaaj people. But yes, living in Tiflis, my family is Georgian." He smiled and took my cheeks between his two hands and kissed me.

"Now, my Tania, what of you, and your family? I have seen people bow to you, and call you grand duchess. But you are not like the proud, heartless highborn Russians I have seen in the spas of Georgia, in Kisslovodsk and Piatigorsk. Haughty women who look on us southerners as if we were vermin."

"I am the daughter of the tsar."

"So we are both descended from kings." He laughed. "Only your family is a little richer and more powerful."

I confided in him. He listened patiently while I talked on about papa and his difficulties as commander of our army and about mama and her disordered state of mind, and her many troubles.

"And you, sweet Tania. What are your troubles?"

"I have none—since I met you."

One afternoon I took Michael to the stables at Tsarskoe Selo to show him our horses. As always, Nikandr was there, the burly Cossack who had married Niuta soon after the war began and looked on his sister-in-law Daria and his niece Iskra with special tenderness.

The first thing Nikandr noticed, when Michael approached him, was the dagger hanging from Michael's belt.

"Ah! A khinjal! So you're a Georgian, are you?"

"From Daghestan, originally—though my family has lived in Tiflis for nine years now, and we are settled there."

"Watch out for Georgians, Tania," Nikandr teased. "They're all wild murderers. They fought us Cossacks for a hundred years." Then turning to Michael, he asked his name.

"Michael Gradov."

"But Gradov is a Russian name, not Georgian."

"My father's clan name was Gamkrelidze, but he had it changed to Gradov."

"Very wise. Russians are frightened of Georgians."

"That's what you said, Michael, when you were in the hospital. When you were delirious. You said, 'Russians fear Georgians.'"

He grinned. "I wonder what else I said."

"Michael was wounded in a battle outside of Riga," I told Nikandr. "He has been at our hospital for many weeks. Now he's nearly well."

"And he wants to make himself useful," Michael added, interrupting me. "Tania tells me you are shorthanded in the stables."

Nikandr sighed. "We are shorthanded everywhere. All the strong men have gone off to the war, and"—here he crossed himself—"hardly any of them have come back. Even my youngest stable lads, may the Lord preserve them, left last fall and only one of them came home, and that one had only one leg."

"I have two legs, and two good arms besides. I was born in the saddle, my father likes to say. Tania has heard me repeat this many times. I know horses, and I love them. I'm a fair carpenter as well. I can hammer and saw and wrench out a nail. What do you say, can you use me?"

"Why don't we ask the master? Our Imperial Majesty has summoned me to Mogilev, where the army headquarters are. Come along with me. I can use your help with the horses on the journey."

Thirty-six

I had not seen papa or Alexei in months, and had no difficulty convincing mama to let me go to the military command headquarters at Mogilev to visit them. Marie and Anastasia wanted to come too, as they missed papa and our brother as much as I did, but mama said no. Olga professed to miss papa and Alexei but it was obvious that she preferred to stay near Victor, the officer she flirted with and who she thought might marry her. (I could have told her she was wrong about Victor, but it would have been pointless; she would not have listened to me.)

"There is fighting near the staff headquarters," mama said when Marie and Anastasia pleaded with her to let them go with me. "I do not want my girls to get hurt."

"If Tania goes, she might get hurt," Anastasia said, "so why do you let her go?"

"Because she is old enough now to take such risks. Besides, Nikandr will protect her."

"And Michael," Marie added before I could stop her.

"Michael? Who is Michael?" Mama was suddenly on alert.

"My patient," I said before Marie could call him "my love." "The one Father Gregory's stick healed. He is one of our stable lads now, and will be going with us to visit papa and Alexei."

Niuta, who was folding mama's handkerchiefs in a corner of the room, cleared her throat noisily at this.

"Yes, Niuta?" mama said. "You have something to say?"

"No, nothing." Her tone indicated the opposite.

"Were you hoping I would send you to Mogilev with Tania?"

"I will do as Your Imperial Highness commands."

Niuta knew all about Michael and me. She had heard about him from Daria, and as soon as she found out from Nikandr that I had brought a handsome young Georgian to see him, she insisted on meeting Michael and judging him for herself. He told me about their conversation afterward, laughing and shaking his head over how she had interrogated him.

"Your Niuta is worse than the matchmakers in Tiflis," he said. "She demanded to know if I had a wife, if I had ever been in jail, how I met you, and what my intentions are in trifling with your affections, as she put it. She was not at all happy when I pointed out to her—in a teasing way, of course—that if I were a villain I would hardly answer her questions honestly."

In the end all was settled and preparations were made for the journey. Niuta was to accompany me as my maid. Nikandr would gather supplies and fresh horses to be taken to the officers' camp. It was arranged that a troop of Cuirassier guards would accompany us, as we would be passing through a dangerous stretch of territory where the Russian army was in retreat and a large force of Germans and Austrians was advancing in pursuit of them.

A warm autumn rain was falling the day we left Tsarskoe Selo, and mists rose before us as we traveled southwestward through marshy country and along the banks of slow moving streams. I rode in a closed carriage with Niuta sitting opposite me, and Michael rode along beside the carriage, a dashing figure in his high boots, tall fur hat and long tunic, his khinjal hanging from his waist. The muddy, unpaved roads were crowded with soldiers and equipment, entire families of villagers with carts high-piled with furnishings, chickens in cages and small children clinging to the swaying loads.

"Poor wretches," Niuta remarked, echoing my thoughts. "I know how it is for them. My family had to leave Pokrovsky with everything we owned twice when I was a girl. Once in a terrible winter when the wolves came, and once when your grandfather's tax collectors were after us."

"But you went back."

"After much hardship, yes. Both times. In the end we had nowhere else to go. My mother's cousins took us in and protected us from the wolves and the tax collectors."

We were on the roads many days, our progress hindered by the other travelers, their vehicles, their cows and goats—all of them, human and animal, going the opposite way from us. They were all going away from the fighting, we were going toward it.

The farther we went, the more the countryside showed evidence of war—entire settlements burned to the ground, crops withered and dying in the untended fields, new graves hastily dug and unmarked save for a stark wooden cross.

"German swine," I heard the Cuirassiers swear as we passed these horrors, and I thought I detected more than hatred in their outcries, I thought I detected fear.

As we neared Mogilev we heard, in the far distance, the rumbling and booming of artillery and saw companies of our soldiers on the march. Their ranks were thin, the men were gaunt-faced, dirty and haggard and many had bandaged limbs. They did not look like an army fit to defend a country, much less defeat an enemy army. They looked like refugees from catastrophe.

Once, when our traveling group had stopped beside a stream to fill the water casks, Michael and I were standing side by side at the edge of the road, watching the ongoing parade of soldiers in ragged uniforms.

"That could be you," I said. "Thank heavens you are out of danger."

"That was me. And you know better than anyone how close I came to dying. It happened in an open field like that one over there." He pointed to a wheat field not far from where we stood, the crop trampled into the muddy earth. "We knew the Austrians were close. We sent out scouts but they hadn't come back to give us the enemy's position. We were just beginning to set up camp for the night, the men were pitching our tents and starting to dig a makeshift rampart. A few cooking fires had been lit.

"Then they came. The guns began to boom, and the shells to burst over our heads like fireworks—only these fireworks were deadly. We hardly had time to mount a defense when we heard the rat-tat-tat of their machine guns. Our men began to fall. I heard the whistling of the bullets all around me and all I could think was, I'll never see my father again.

"Then they were running toward us, yelling, their cries inhuman. I know I shot some of them, I saw them fall. I had killed Austrians and Germans before but never when they were so close I could see the spikes on their helmets, the mud on their uniforms. I could hear their cries, even though the noise all around me was so loud—the guns, the shouting, the terrified yelling of some of our men—cowards!—who tried to run away, the screams of the horses—oh Tania, it was all I could do to stand where I was, with nothing but an old cart between me and the enemy, and take aim between the slats of the cart, and shoot. My eyes were filling with sweat and tears from all the smoke in the air.

"Then I felt a thud, as if a huge stone had hit my chest. Only it wasn't a stone, it was enemy fire. I put my hand up to my forehead—and that's all I remember."

"Oh, my dear, precious Michael!" I clung to him, sobbing and trembling. "My dear, pray God you never have to face another assault."

"And mercy on those who must. Mercy on those who die even as we are speaking."

He held me for a long moment before we resumed our journey.

The camp at Mogilev was more rustic than I had imagined, and just the sort of place papa loved. There was an official headquarters building in the town but papa and Alexei had their large tent pitched in a leafy forest several miles from any populated area. There were a dozen or so tents nearby for the staff officers, and others for the cooks and servants, papa's personal corps of guardsmen and all the laborers—carpenters, blacksmiths, armorers, and so forth—needed to keep a fortified position functioning.

Papa and Alexei came out to meet us, Alexei eager and happy, papa gratified but obviously weary, and I hugged them both at once, which was not easy. Alexei was getting to be a big boy—I think he was about eleven years old then—and I could hardly get my arms around him and papa too. I heard a gramophone record playing inside the tent, a sultry tango, and all of a sudden I thought, I hope Mathilde Kchessinsky isn't here.

"Tania! Come and see Joy!" Alexei cried.

"Wait! Let me admire you!"

Father and son were dressed alike in raspberry-colored peasant shirts and wide pantaloons, held up by cords. Papa's expression was sweet and soulful as always, though his face was grey and more lined than when I had last seen him. Alexei's cheeks were flushed with excitement.

"Don't you both look fine!" I said. "Like fat, prosperous peasants from Belarus."

"These clothes were a gift from my townspeople here," papa remarked. "They have been very respectful, and hospitable to us."

Alexei, impatient, grabbed my hand and took me into the tent where a tawny spaniel was curled up asleep on his small camp bed.

"This is Joy. Isn't she wonderful?"

I petted the dog's soft fur and she licked my hand.

"Papa, there is someone I want you to meet."

He smiled. "He sounds important. Bring him to me."

I introduced Michael, who bowed low and addressed papa as "Little Father."

"Your daughter is a very skilled nurse, Little Father. Without her care I would not be here."

"I understand from one of my wife's letters that a certain stick of wood blessed by Father Gregory had something to do with your survival." Papa looked at me, expecting me to confirm what he had said. He had not forgotten my claim that Father Gregory had attacked one of the servants and threatened me—accusations he still preferred to think were the products of my imagination. Now he wanted me to acknowledge Father Gregory's healing powers.

"We have all seen evidence of his remarkable healings," was all I would say.

A telephone rang, its jarring sound clashing with the tinny tango music.

Papa swore. "Damn thing! Keeps interrupting me!"

An orderly joined us.

"Begging your pardon, Your Imperial Highness. His Excellency the Minister of War needs to speak with you."

"Let him wait. Can't you see I have visitors?"

"Forgive me, Your Imperial Highness, but His Excellency says it is most urgent that he confer with you."

Papa swore again, under his breath this time, and nodded to the orderly.

"Very well then, if he must." Uncomfortable and restive, he lit a cigarette.

"Why do they keep at me?" he said, not really speaking to us. "I've already given out several medals today, and I read the report they sent me this morning—at least I tried to. Why must they insist on coming to see me?"

I started for the open flap of the large tent. "We'll leave you to carry on with your business, papa."

"No! Stay! Please stay. It will be easier for me with you here."

Michael brought a chair for papa, and was rewarded with a grateful look.

Soon the War Minister Ignatiev came in, followed by several secretaries and—to my surprise—Constantin. All bowed to papa.

"Sire, may I present my new deputy, Constantin Melnikov? He has been with the ministry for nearly a year, and I value his services highly."

Papa acknowledged Constantin with a smile and a nod, puffing at his cigarette so that his head was wreathed in smoke, which made him cough.

The war minister, a short, balding man of fifty, bristling with purpose, began talking rapidly. Knowing Constantin as I did, I could tell that it was all he could do to be patient and listen. He was clearly very perturbed, his high forehead was creased with worry lines.

"Your Imperial Highness, it is past time that immediate action be taken if Russia is to be preserved. I have sent telegrams, I have telephoned, I have done everything I can to alert you to the most urgent needs of the army and the civilian population of the capital. Yet I have not had any response. So I have come here to speak with you, in person, in hopes of gaining your attention. I respectfully ask for that attention now."

"I am listening."

But I could tell that he was not listening, not really, and with his free hand he drummed his fingers on the table in front of him while the war minister went on.

"Sire, here is what needs to be ordered." He drew a paper from his jacket pocket and read from it.

"First, we must have six more trains to run between the front and Petrograd. One will travel between Mogilev and Petrograd exclusively.

"Second, we must have more provisions, or the army will never survive the winter. The men have begun to eat the oats for the horses because they have nothing else."

Papa smiled at this, and murmured, "Imagine!" I saw Constantin stiffen as he observed this response.

"Reserves must be called up at once, sire. The First Army has been weakened beyond fighting strength, and the Siberian Rifle Regiment lost half its effective men in the last gas attack. The Keksholm Regiment simply is no more. There is talk in the ranks of a coup d'état, sire, and desertions are increasing."

Papa turned pale.

"Shall I get you a glass of brandy, Your Imperial Majesty?" It was Michael's deep, soothing voice.

"Yes. Please." Michael went out and found Chemodurov, who I had seen earlier, dozing under a tree. Before long Michael returned with a snifter and a bottle of brandy on a tray. He set it down on the table in front of papa and poured it out for him, as if he had been serving him for a long time instead of just having met him.

Meanwhile the war minister was going on with his list of urgent matters, citing high casualties in the ranks, the resignation of many ministers, the social anarchy in Petrograd—a long and frightening list.

Papa, drinking his brandy and lighting one cigarette after another, was increasingly nervous.

"I really don't see what more I can do," he finally said. "I help out as best I can, I read the reports you send me, I listen to you. Haven't I donated my newest Rolls-Royce to the medical corps to serve as an ambulance? I really don't see how you can fault me."

He turned his face away. "I really do feel like Job, in the Bible, the all-suffering Job who was visited with all the plagues and sorrows and evils of the world. Do you know that my birthday, May sixth, is the festival of Job the patriarch?"

When his remark met with silence he turned his head slightly back toward us, and looked at me.

"Tania," he murmured. "Tania, would you be so good as to take my setter for a walk? I usually take her out at this hour. She must be getting restless."

"Of course, papa."

But as I rose to go I heard a resounding thud. Constantin had pounded on the table with his fist.

"Tania!" Constantin's naturally loud voice was even louder than usual. "Tell your father that he must not only listen, he must act! And act now! Before it is too late!"

Thirty-seven

Constantin's forceful words rang in the air. Without thinking, I rushed to him and tried to pull him away from the table.

"Stop!" I shouted. "You are only making things worse! Bullying papa won't do any good. You ought to know that."

Constantin was a large and heavy man, and I was far too slight to move him.

"Ah! Dear Tania, you are good to defend me. But truly, I need no defense. All is in the will of God." Papa spoke gently, he had not let Constantin's outburst provoke him. He refilled his brandy snifter and held it under his nose for a moment before he drank, savoring its aroma.

"This is preposterous!" Constantin spat out. "A country falls, because one man is weak and foolish! What better argument could there be for putting an end to monarchy?" Exasperated and disgusted, he began backing away from the table, while the war minister, open-mouthed, his eyes wide with astonishment, watched helplessly.

Michael moved so swiftly, and so soundlessly, that Constantin did not hear him until he had come up behind Constantin and pinned his arms behind his back.

"Sire, shall I call your guardsmen to take this traitor away?"

Papa sighed wearily and set down his glass.

"No," he said at length. "Just sit him down, and I will hear what he has to say. He is an old friend of Tania's, after all."

Michael looked at me. "Is this the man you told me about? The doctor? The one who worked in the clinic?"

I nodded. I saw a new firmness come into Michael's eyes. Constantin and I had once been in love. Therefore Constantin was a rival.

"If I release you," Michael said to Constantin, his tone harsher than before, "do you give me your word that you will sit down and keep your temper, and behave as a man of honor should when speaking to the tsar of all the Russias?"

"I will attempt to."

"Your Imperial Highness—" the war minister began, having found his voice at last.

"Never mind, Ignatiev. I will hear your deputy, provided he does not go on for too long."

I watched the seated Constantin struggle for self-mastery. When next he spoke he was calmer.

"Your Imperial Highness, I apologize for my outburst. I speak bluntly because of my love for Russia and her people—"

"And her ruler, let us hope," Ignatiev put in.

"And her ruler, and his family. Let me tell you what I believe must happen."

"Very well."

"I believe that you need to look beyond the army and its losses and needs, beyond the likelihood that Russia will lose this war."

The war minister gasped, but papa held up his hand. "Let him go on."

"I believe you must pay close attention to the situation in Petrograd."

"Petrograd? What situation in Petrograd? When I left it the city was fairly peaceful—as peaceful as it ever is."

"Things have worsened since you left. The workers are striking, the city is filled with refugees who have nothing to eat and nowhere to go and who are listening in greater and greater numbers to the speeches of the revolutionaries."

"Agitators!" papa cried. "They are only agitators—and criminals at that! Let the soldiers deal with them just as they always have."

I could tell what effort it was costing papa to speak up in this way, to listen to dire news, to argue with Constantin. His voice was becoming hoarse, his breath came in shorter and shorter gasps.

"Sire, there are not enough soldiers to fight the enemy and subdue the revolutionaries. They cannot keep order. They cannot prevent chaos. Day after day, Russia is being destroyed, not by foreign enemies but from within, by her own people. People who want change, who demand power for themselves, since those in power cannot seem to govern effectively."

Papa set down his empty snifter. I noticed that his hand was shaking.

"If things in Petrograd have gone as far as you say, then there is nothing I can do to stop what is happening."

"With Your Imperial Highness's permission, I have drawn up a brief memorandum listing all the immediate steps that are required." Constantin took a folded paper from his pocket and handed it to papa, who did not read it but tucked it into the cord wrapped around his waist.

The war minister got to his feet. "We will await your orders in Mogilev, Your Imperial Highness," he said with a bow. With a glance at Michael, Constantin stood, bowed, and, murmuring "Your Imperial Highness" one more time, followed the minister out of the tent.

"What a relief!" papa said when they had gone. "I thought they would never leave. Now, Tania, let me offer you and Michael a good dinner. You have come a long way and you must be hungry and tired."

We were indeed very hungry and very tired, but when we had eaten and drunk our fill (there seemed to be no shortage of food in Mogilev) and retired to the tents prepared for us I could not get to sleep. I was alone in my tent, having urged Niuta to join her husband in a tent of their own rather than stay with me as she usually did. Wrapping a blanket around me I lifted the tent flap and went outside.

The air was cool and moist, but there were no overhanging clouds, and the sky was brilliant with stars. I found my favorites: the great red star called Betelgeuse in the constellation of the hunter and fiery Aldebaran in the constellation of his prey, Taurus the bull, and the bright white dog star that always followed the hunter in his progression across the dark bowl of sky.

Enjoying the quiet, I stood and mused on the immensity of the spangled worlds above me, trying not to let my worries about papa intrude. I stayed where I was until I smelled the rich, sweet, fragrant aroma of pipe tobacco. I looked around and saw the glow of a pipe. It was Michael, sitting not far from me, looking up at the night sky just as I was.

"Come and look at the stars with me," I called out.

He got up and came over to join me, knocking out his pipe on the ground and stomping on the burning ashes.

His face gleamed in the starlight, his dark eyes soft, his full lips warm and inviting, his caress thrilling yet at the same time soothing, making me feel safe and protected.

"No guns pounding tonight," he said. "No war."

"Only the stars. Monsieur Gilliard says the universe has no edges and no center—how can that be?"

"Perhaps it is like love—immense and unending."

He kissed me then, and our kisses went on and on, until we found ourselves inside my tent and under the blankets of my camp bed.

"So beautiful—so very beautiful," he murmured as he kissed my throat, my shoulders, my breasts, my nightgown tossed aside. Lovingly I helped him undress, though the sight of his strong, lean body was already very familiar to me—nearly as familiar as my own. He lifted me so that I lay on top of him, kissing and nipping at him playfully, feeling him growing hard against my groin, my own desire increasing to match his.

No words of mine can tell of the splendor of those moments, the first time our bodies joined and we reached love's most rapturous heights together. Nothing could have prepared me for the boundless joy I experienced again and again that first night with Michael, our first night as lovers in the deepest sense. I told him that I loved him, but the words fell so far short of my feelings that they sounded hollow.

"My own dear Tania, my very own at last," he said, holding me close. "Promise me you will never love anyone else."

"I promise."

"Swear on the stars."

"I swear on the bright dog star, and the hunter and the bull. I swear on the universe that has no end, like our love."

"Then we are pledged."

"Yes."

"Come what may."

"Come what may, Michael, I am yours."

Thirty-eight

We were blissfully joined, and pledged—and then we were separated.

The longer papa spent with Michael, the more he felt he could trust him, as servant, companion and protector. Chemodurov had served papa faithfully since his boyhood, but now Chemodurov was aging; a younger man was needed to replace him. Papa offered the position to Michael, who thought it his duty to accept. He retained his military rank but was assigned to papa's personal staff instead of serving in his regiment.

And since papa was in Mogilev, Michael was to be there too, for the foreseeable future.

I wept when I left papa and Alexei and Michael to return to Tsarskoe Selo, as I did not know when I would see any of them again, and I could not know when or if the Austrians and Germans might overrun the camp, putting all their lives at risk.

There was another danger too, a more private one. Papa took me aside before I left, and we talked frankly about it.

"I want to keep your brother here with me, Tania, even though I am aware of the risks to his health. If he should fall, or cut himself, or bump his head, there would be nothing the local doctors could do for him. He is alive by the grace of God and because of the prayers of Father Gregory, we all know that. It is nothing short of a miracle that he is still alive, when nearly everyone in the family expects him to die."

"I expect him to live. He looks stronger than I thought he would, and he is happy being here with you."

"He is my great comfort. But we both know that this may be the last time you see him."

"Cousin Waldemar has the bleeding disease, and he is still alive. He is much older than Alexei."

"Your cousin is remarkable, yes. But remember, his brother Henry died."

"I will continue to believe that Alexei will survive."

"You are a good girl, Tania. Always remember that I love you."

"I love you too papa. So very much." And we hugged each other tearfully.

It was a terrible leavetaking, my departure from Mogilev on a wet morning, with Alexei in tears and Niuta trying to hurry me along and Michael trying his best to delay me.

How soon would Michael and I be together again? How would I bear not knowing?

Finally I ran out of excuses, and with a last embrace I broke away from Michael and got into the carriage beside Niuta. Our military escort in place, and all the luggage and supplies for the journey loaded, the driver cracked his whip and we were off.

Once we reached Petrograd, I saw all too clearly that what Constantin had tried to warn my father about was true. An angry mood prevailed throughout the city. Our carriage was pelted with stones and pieces of filth as we made our way along the broad avenues. Peasants, striking workers and ragged people I took to be refugees were gathered at street corners, talking together, reading newspapers—most of those in Petrograd could read—or, in some cases, listening to fiery speechmakers standing on benches or stone walls and haranguing the crowds.

Some of the people we passed held up big signs. "The land belongs to God, not to the landlords," was one that I remembered long afterward. "Little Father, Feed your People" read another, crudely scrawled in red paint—or could it have been blood?—on an old board. I felt a chill when I read several signs saying "Kill the German Bitch," for I knew only too well who the "German Bitch" was. Niuta tried to distract me when we passed the worst of the ugly signs—those that had no words, but only crude filthy pictures of my mother, a crown on her head, embracing her bearded lover, meant to be Father Gregory.

Such hatred, such venom—and such hardship. Even as the sights I saw frightened me and made me want to protect my family, they also aroused my compassion, for winter was coming and I knew that many of the people we encountered in the streets would have no way to survive it. I remembered what Daria's apartment had been like the first time Avdokia took me to see it, the single crowded filthy room, the crying babies and the stinking water on the floor, the hunger on the faces of the people living there that I had done so little to assuage. I had been in peasant cottages before, and though they were small and cramped, at least they were warm and had charm, with an old stove in the corner and icons gleaming on the walls. Daria's squalid apartment provided shelter but nothing more—not even decency.

When we reached Tsarskoe Selo and the immense ornamental metal gates closed behind us I took a deep breath and thought, now we are safe. At least here, on the palace grounds, with so many soldiers and guardsmen to protect us, we will be safe. The first thing I did when we arrived was to find mama and my sisters and hug each one, and I did not even mind when Olga chattered on endlessly and annoyingly about Victor. I did not share with her all that had happened between Michael and me, that was far too private and too precious—and besides, I didn't want mama to find out how much he meant to me or how I had risked my reputation by letting him share my bed.

With Michael constantly in my thoughts, I did my best to settle back into a routine of family life. Olga, Marie, Anastasia and I all continued to volunteer at the hospital, and also helped out with the new charity mama founded, the Mothers and Babies fund, meant to provide warm clothing and food for the many destitute soldiers' widows in the capital. In the evenings we gathered in the mauve salon and I read aloud from some old novel (I avoided War and Peace) or Olga played the piano for us. While mama knitted wool mittens and sweaters for her charity we sat at a table doing jigsaw puzzles or playing cards, though Marie sulked if she lost and Anastasia could never keep her mind on the game, which made Olga irritated with her.

There was very little time for lessons, but sometimes Monsieur Gilliard read to us from books of Russian history or listened to us practice our French conversation. He also brought us the latest war news from France (he had a cousin in the French embassy who provided him with newspapers), where month after month the English and French were fighting the Germans at Verdun and it seemed as if the terrible battle would never end.

I wrote to Michael every day and sent my letters along with mama's letters to papa by courier to Mogilev. He wrote me letters too, as often as he could, though his duties kept him busy from sunup until late in the evening, as papa liked to spend his evenings watching the American movies he had sent to the camp and wanted Michael beside him for company while he watched.

Month after month our life went on in this fashion, until one day in the summer of 1916 I was shocked to see Father Gregory entering mama's mauve salon. He was just turning the handle of the door as I was coming along the corridor. He saw me but did not acknowledge me, his face remained expressionless as he continued turning the handle, went inside and shut the door. He was bearded and his long stringy hair—almost entirely gray by then—hung down over the satin collar of his expensive tailored shirt. Even from a distance I could see the flash of jewels on his rings.

I went to the door and tried the handle. The door was locked.

"Mama," I called out. "Mama, are you all right?"

"Perfectly all right, dear," came her response.

"What is that man doing here? I thought papa sent him to Siberia."

"He has come back from Pokrovsky to help us dear. You know how I rely on him."

I heard laughter on the other side of the door at this remark, the low-pitched laughter of the villainous Father Gregory.

"Send him away, mama! Don't listen to him!"

"You are being foolish, Tania. We are fine. I need Father Gregory's advice."

I pounded on the door. "No, mama, no. Send him away!"

But I knew, even as I was protesting, that nothing I said would do any good. Finally I went away and put my fears and worries in a letter to Michael.

Constantin came to the palace one evening, with the recently dismissed war minister Polivanov (Ignatiev having been dismissed soon after my visit to Mogilev, and Polivanov appointed in his place), and asked to speak to mama.

"It is very important, Tania. Can you please ask her if she will see us?"

I shook my head. "No, Constantin, I don't want you yelling at her the way you yelled at papa. Besides, she never sees anyone in the evening. She takes her Veronal, and then after awhile she complains that her stomach is hurting—the Veronal always makes it hurt—and then she takes her opium to relieve her stomach pain and soon she is asleep."

Constantin shook his head sadly. "You know she is injuring herself by doing that, don't you." It was a statement, not a question. "You know how serious addiction can be."

"I can't stop her. I've tried to explain how bad the drugs are for her body, but she only says her poor legs hurt and her poor heart hurts and her poor nerves are always on edge and what else can she do? I have no answer for that."

"I urge you to find one. Meanwhile, Polivanov and I have some news about this new war minister of hers, Boris Stürmer."

"What about him? I will tell her in the morning."

"We want her to know that when the next Duma convenes—I am going to be a member, Tania, did you know that? For the Cadet party—we will reveal that this corrupt Sturmer, who is now prime minister, war minister and interior minister all in one, has been taking bribes and selling army contracts. He is also selling military secrets to the highest bidder."

"I will tell her."

"This Stürmer is in league with your corrupt Father Gregory. They are making a fortune together."

"He was here just last week. I thought he was in Siberia, but he has come back. Father Gregory has come back."

Constantin's expression hardened.

"Where is your Michael? He should be with you now."

"He is still with papa in Mogilev. He has become a member of the imperial household."

"I see. Well then, keep your pistol with you, Tania, and stay away from Father Gregory. Don't let him near your bedroom, or your sisters' bedrooms."

"I think he only comes to see mama now."

"He's at the root of it all, you know," Constantin went on, taking out his handkerchief and mopping his troubled brow. "All this corruption. All this rot at the heart of government. He must be gotten rid of somehow."

"Twice people have shot at him, and twice he's survived. The last time was in Pokrovsky. A woman he raped tried to kill him, or so I have heard."

Constantin took me gently by the arm and led me from the sofa we sat on to a curtained alcove at the far end of the room. He stood very close to me and spoke in a whisper.

"What I am going to tell you now is never to be repeated. There are people in the imperial family that are planning to eliminate him. It will happen soon. Make sure your mother does not hear of this or she will try to prevent it."

Something in Constantin's tone and expression made me fearful for him.

"Are you a part of this, Constantin?"

"Not directly, no. But I will help in any way I can."

"But why murder? Why not just have him arrested?"

"You know how your parents protect him. And he has allies among the police. People hate him—but they fear him too. No, the only way is to treat him like a mad dog and kill him."

I thought for a moment. "He says he is immortal. No one can kill him."

"I will enjoy putting that myth to rest!"

Before he and Polivanov left I murmured, "Be careful, Constantin. Don't put yourself too much at risk."

"What must be done, must be done," he said darkly. "And it must be done soon."

Thirty-nine

A *loud shriek* woke me one snowy night not long before the Christmas season began. I listened, and the shrieking came again.

It's mama, I thought, and hurried to put on my dressing gown. "She must be having nightmares again." Niuta was faster than I was and was already out the bedroom door, going down the corridor toward mama's bedroom.

When we entered the room we saw mama, sitting upright in bed, her nightgown askew and her hair in a flyaway state, her eyes large and round and her face pale.

"Someone has trapped the grey dove!" she screamed. "They are sticking him with pins . . . he is bleeding . . . his blood is red as cranberries. . . . He can't escape. . . . Oh! Oh! Someone has trapped the grey dove!"

Niuta tried to comfort mama but she waved her away, repeating again and again that someone had trapped the grey dove. She was awake—yet not awake. She looked as if she herself had been trapped, inside her own terrifying dream, and was unable to find her way back to wakefulness.

I sat down beside the bed.

"Light some candles," I said to Niuta. "The darkness is frightening her."

Remembering the soothing effect of Mr. Schmidt's voice and the gentle way he had of finding the meaning that underlay images, I began to talk to mama about the grey dove.

"He wore grey," she said when we had talked for a minute or two. "He had grey hair. He was so innocent, so helpless, so dovelike."

"Who was, mama?"

"Why, you know who." She looked directly at me for the first time. "You used to love him. Now you hate him. Why have you trapped him?"

"Tell me who I used to love. Tell me his name."

"No. You hate him. You think he is evil."

There was only one person who, in my childhood at least, wore dingy-looking grey tunics and trousers and had greying hair, and who affected an air of innocence. Only one person I could think of who I used to love and now hated. Father Gregory.

It was as if a cold hand had run down my spine. The images—of entrapment, piercing, bleeding—could it be that mama was seeing, in her dream, what Constantin had been telling me about? The elimination of the Dark One, Rasputin?

Forty

*I*t was *Sedynov* who brought us the first rumors.

"It's all over the Narva district," he said, out of breath from climbing the stairs to Olga's bedroom where my sisters and I were gathered. "They talk of nothing else in the workers' taverns. They toast the liberators who have killed Rasputin!"

"He's dead for sure," Niuta chimed in. "I heard it yesterday in the Schlüsselburg Road. Nikandr heard it too."

Was it true, I wondered, or only a rumor, one of the dozens of rumors that spread like typhus through the crowded Petrograd streets? Had mama's terrible nightmares been an omen after all?

Then Captain Golenishchev, a guards officer who had formed part of our escort at the time of the tercentenary celebration, arrived at the palace and asked to see mama. She was helping me with a sweater I was knitting when he was ushered in.

Mama swallowed hard.

"Yes, Captain Golenishchev?"

He was agitated, unsure of himself. "Your Imperial Highness, bloodstains have been found on the Great Petrovsky Bridge."

"Indeed? There have been many suicides this winter. Perhaps this is one more."

"If only I could agree, Your Imperial Highness. But—you see—there was a boot found there also."

"Blood and a boot—and you bring this news to the palace?"

The captain looked shamefaced.

"I would never dream of disturbing Your Imperial Highness with an unimportant matter. But in this case, as the boot belonged to Gregory Novy, known as Rasputin—I believe you call him Father Gregory—"

Mama sat up very straight in her chair.

"Are you certain the boot is his?"

"Our investigators are certain, yes."

Red blotches appeared on mama's cheeks.

"I ordered him guarded! Why was he not guarded!"

"Efforts were made, Your Imperial Highness, I assure you. Like you, I have wanted Novy protected for a long time. I have done my best.

"But it is not only about the boot and the bloodstains that I have come. We believe that your family may be in danger."

Mama made a dismissive noise. "We have been in danger for years. Perhaps you remember the bomb-throwers, the would-be assassins—"

"This threat may come—from within the imperial family—certain disaffected family members . . ."

Mama reached for me and pulled me to her.

"Tell the guard to surround the palace at once. Warn my husband—"

"He has already been warned, Your Imperial Highness. He has known for some time that this threat exists."

Mama's breath was coming in rapid gasps. The terrible shock of hearing that Father Gregory was dead alternated with dread at Captain Golenishchev's words.

"No," she was repeating. "No, no, no. Not my family. Not my children." She gripped me so tightly that my chest hurt.

"Please, mama. I can't breathe."

Sedynov kept us informed, over the following days, about the massive upsurge of joy that greeted the news of Father Gregory's death. All our servants were delighted—especially Daria—and could hardly keep from smiling though they did their best to hide their delight when in mama's ashen-faced presence. In Petrograd, Sedynov said, one could see shopkeepers, soldiers, peasants stopping in the streets to kiss one another and embrace when exchanging the joyful news.

Rasputin is dead! they cried. The empress's evil lover is dead!

It was as if a dark spell that had hung over the empire for years had been lifted, and the people in thrall to it set free. Political oratory flared up as never before, for if Rasputin could fall to assassins then the monarchy too could be brought down, or so the most radical of papa's subjects declared. And so the noisy rejoicing went on.

Poisonous threatening letters arrived for mama.

"Unless you stop ruining the country with your meddling, murders will continue," one of them read. She was convinced that the letters came from within the family, just as she believed Father Gregory's murder was a family plot. The killers—who were soon identified as Aunt Xenia's son-in-law Felix Yusupov and papa's cousin Dimitri—were never punished, and in mama's mind the entire Romanov clan was behind the assassination, as if each of them had plunged a dagger into Father Gregory's side.

"They will come after me next," she confided to me.

"No—don't say that mama!"

"Just you watch. See if they don't."

For awhile I began sleeping in her room at night, my loaded revolver under my pillow. Guardsmen were on duty outside the bedroom door, but this gave none of us comfort as we knew it was rumored in Petrograd that many of the imperial soldiers were no longer loyal to papa or his family. The men outside the door might well be assassins, we told one another in confidence. There were said to be traitors everywhere—and spies, and enemy agents. Hardly anyone could be trusted; we had to rely on each other as never before.

How I wished, in those tense days, that papa and Michael were with us at Tsarskoe Selo and not far away in Mogilev. I told Michael everything that was happening in my letters, and received loving and concerned but infrequent replies. I missed him so very much, and longed for the day of his return.

A deep hole was dug in the frozen earth to receive the broken body of Father Gregory. I didn't want to see the body but mama insisted that each of us glance into the oak coffin to say our goodbyes, and place a keepsake inside. I forced myself to look at the swollen, disfigured face, framed by scraggly grey hair, one more time, and put a jar of wormwood oil (falsely labeled "Honey") into the coffin before the lid was closed and nailed in place.

We stood silent around the newly dug hole, snow falling in soft flakes on our coats and hats and warm woolen scarves. No choir sang, no procession circled the grave with icons and incense. For Father Gregory was being buried in unconsecrated ground, and the priest who spoke the briefest of words over his body was not sent there by the bishop, but summoned, and paid, by mama.

I disliked being there. I felt forced to honor a man I could not help but despise, even in death. I cringed when I saw mama reverently handling Father Gregory's bloodstained shirt—the last shirt he ever wore—and placing it inside a large hollow wooden cross that she hung on the wall. Aunt Ella had done the same thing with the bloody shirt Uncle Gega had died in, I remembered. Did mama think of Father Gregory as a sort of second husband? I couldn't bring myself to imagine that she had slept with him, though there were many in Petrograd who believed precisely that; the idea seemed too preposterous—and too painful.

"Don't frown like that, Tania," mama said to me as I stared down at the cold ground. "It's disrespectful to the dead."

In the pocket of my coat was a crumpled note I had found on the floor in mama's mauve salon, a note she or someone else had torn and meant to discard. It was still readable. I recognized Father Gregory's distinctive large, spiky handwriting.

"God is love," the note read. "I love, God forgives. Gregory."

I took out the note and glanced at it, then crushed it and threw it into the grave. The priest finished reciting the last prayers, as mama sobbed into her handkerchief. Fog was descending and swirling around us, its cold breath making me shiver. I was relieved when the gravediggers came and began shoveling the dark earth in on top of the coffin, and after crossing ourselves one last time we all went silently home.

Forty-one

No one had ever seen such snow! The winter of 1917, the bitterly cold January, the icy February, the frigid March stung and seared and battered the tens of thousands in the Petrograd streets cruelly, until it hurt to breathe and the air was like frozen fog, opaque and menacing. Blizzard after blizzard broke with fury over the city, leaving deep high drifts of snow, twelve feet high, fifteen feet high, so high they might have been the ice mounds at a winter carnival.

Only there was no carnival atmosphere: there was nothing but suffering and starvation, and the incessant inchoate urge for change. For a transfer of power to the people. For revolution.

There were fires at every crossroads, every street corner had its small blaze where men in torn dirty coats held their hands out to warm them—hands in which fingers had been lost to frostbite. Everywhere one heard the crunch of boots on ice, the thick black ice that was so slippery the horses could not make their way across it without falling.

I saw the high-piled drifts, the ice and the angry, frozen people when we went into Petrograd to visit Aunt Olenka to quietly congratulate her on her recent marriage to her longtime lover Nicholas Kulikovsky. I saw it again when mama, against all sound advice, took me to Ouchinnikov, the goldsmith's shop on Bolshaia Morskaia Street to buy me a gold bracelet like the one she wore, and the crowd in the street nearly overturned our carriage. I heard about conditions in Petrograd from

Sedynov, who went into the capital at least once a week, and from Daria, who was overjoyed to think that at last her dream of a Russia where the people governed themselves was about to come true.

We sat one morning by the window in my bedroom, the crust of ice so thick on the glass that we could barely make out shapes on the other side. Daria's little dog was in its basket, Artipo sleeping beside my chair. Iskra sat on a cushion on the floor, reading from an English book mama had given her. Monsieur Gilliard gave her lessons from time to time. He told me she was a precocious child with a gift for learning. She had Daria's light hair and blue eyes, but her face had a more exotic shape than Daria's, almost Asiatic, and her skin was golden. Her father, Daria had told me, had come from Mongolia. How he had found his way to our Russian capital I never learned.

We were sitting quietly, talking, when Niuta came in.

"Tania," she said, "your mother needs you in her salon immediately."

I went at once and found my sisters and brother standing in the room, along with mama's dressers and Monsieur Gilliard.

"I have had some very distressing news," she began, struggling for self-possession. "From the military headquarters where your father is."

And where Michael is, I thought to myself.

"I have been told—" she broke off and swallowed, then continued.

"I have been told—" once again she paused, her hands trembling. She clasped them and held them tightly at her waist.

"Children, I need to tell you that your father has decided that it is best for Russia if he steps down as tsar in favor of your Uncle Michael."

We were speechless. Then Olga began to cry, quietly, and soon we all had tears running down our cheeks. But we were all grand duchesses, and we had been trained well. We continued to stand, our backs straight and our heads up, watching mama. If she could be strong, then so could we. But poor papa!

"So he has abdicated," Monsieur Gilliard said. "He has been forced to sign the instrument of abdication."

It hurt to hear these words.

"Yes," mama said quietly, obviously short of breath, her hands still held tightly at her waist.

"Will he be allowed to return here, to Tsarskoe Selo?"

Mama shook her head, and began to speak, but could not. Then her eyes closed, her knees seemed to buckle and she sank to the floor.

It may seem odd—it seems odd to me, looking back—but the thing I remember most clearly about the first confusing weeks and months after my father's abdication was the sound of scraping, constant scraping. It was the workers on the roof, scraping off the snow and ice. They never stopped, except for a few hours at night when I suppose they must have slept.

There had been a great deal of snow, after all, and no doubt there was an unusually large concentration of ice on the roof. All I know is that the scraping sound persisted, and the laborers continued to work, even though many of the household servants ran off without so much as a word and the troops that had been guarding the palace also began to desert in large numbers.

The changes that came over the palace were sudden and severe. First our electricity was cut off, leaving us with only candles to light the rooms and only firewood to cook our food. Then we discovered we had no water flowing from our taps; we could only get fresh water by breaking the ice on the lake in the palace park and scooping up the freezing water in buckets. For a few days Niuta did her best to provide warm baths for my sisters and me, heating the lake water over the stove and pouring it into our silver tub which was brought into the kitchen to make her task easier. But it took too long for each bucket to heat up, and the air was so cold that the heated water cooled down once it was poured over us. We soon gave up the thought of bathing in the tub. Instead we gritted our teeth and washed with cold water, soaping ourselves and then rinsing under an improvised shower, our teeth chattering.

We were worried about papa—all the more so when we heard that Uncle Michael, unwilling to take on the hated role of tsar, had abdicated. Romanov rule was over—though mama continued to insist that papa's forced abdication was invalid and to insist even more strongly that an anointed tsar could never renounce the authority given him by God.

We watched for a message, listened for a phone call, but none came. Why hadn't papa come back to us? Was he in jail? Surely the new Provisional Government we were told of would not order his execution.

Surely they had a vestige of feeling, a vestige of pity left for the Little Father who had always ruled over them.

Then Constantin came to the palace—officially, as a deputy in the new Provisional Government. His task was to report on the effectiveness of palace security, meaning how loyal to the new government were the guardsmen who were our jailers, keeping us from escaping, and how safe would we be in the event of a mutiny by the guards or an attempt on our lives by the real rulers in Petrograd: the newly formed Soviet of Workers and Soldiers Deputies.

"What you all must understand," Constantin told mama and the rest of us in the few private moments we had together, "is that there is chaos in the capital. We delegates are attempting to rule—that is, to keep chaos at bay—but we disagree on so many things. We fight, we argue. We cannot seem to find a common will. We have so many issues to face—the war, the shortages, the dissatisfied workers who see us as no better than the old monarchy, and want more radical change."

He paced back and forth, his brow furrowed. Deep worry lines had dug themselves in his forehead since I saw him last.

"You can't imagine how bad things are. There is no meat, no bread, no salt in the marketplace. For the homeless, there is not even a closet to rent. Looters are raiding the mansions on the Fontanka, breaking into the wine cellars, getting drunk. No one is working—"

"The workers have been bribed to go on strike!" mama burst out. "Enemies of the state are undermining all authority. Dark forces are loosed, murderous instincts—"

"Don't you understand? There is no state! There is no authority! While we argue and debate, the Soviet is raising the red flag of the Bolsheviks over every public building. They have seized the railroads and the telegraph. The people turn to them for help, not to us."

"Why doesn't papa come home?" Anastasia asked. There was silence, and in the silence the incessant scraping of the roof continued.

Constantin stopped his pacing and looked down into my sister's face.

"I don't know, dear," he said. "I'm sure he will be with you as soon as he can."

Then he had to leave, and after pressing my hand and giving me the briefest of worried smiles he was gone.

One dark, cloudy afternoon the guards admitted a familiar burly figure to the palace, as tall as a man but with a grimy yellow skirt and small gold earrings.

"Avdokia!" I cried when I saw her. "Oh, how glad I am to see you!" And indeed I was glad to see anyone who was not a guardsman or a visitor from the Provisional Government in those isolated, difficult days.

"I have brought this for your mother," she said gruffly. She held out an icon to me, an image of the Virgin Mary, her head veiled in gold and her garments gleaming in the candlelight. "It is from his grave."

I knew at once whose grave she meant.

"The guards have dug up the body of my cousin Gregory Novy. I saw them when I came to deliver the milk. They put the body in a truck. It stank. They said they were going to burn it, and everything else in the grave. I asked for the icon. They gave it to me."

"You did this—for my mother?"

"No. For myself. That icon would bring a hundred rubles in the marketplace. I was going to sell it. But I knew my cousin. He would want your mother to have it."

She turned to leave, stumping off on her thick legs before I had a chance to thank her.

"Avdokia!" I called out after her. "Why do you still come here? Most of the servants have left us."

She shrugged. "Everybody needs milk," she said, and left.

Mama hung the icon on the wall of her mauve salon—a wall already covered with icons—and prayed before it every night.

"It is a miraculous icon," she confided to me. "The virgin weeps. She is weeping for Russia, and she cannot be consoled."

Forty-two

Michael! At last, after so many long weary months, he came back to me, riding through the gates of Tsarskoe Selo beside papa, both of them surrounded by an escort of stern-faced soldiers.

How we hugged and kissed each other and cried, shamelessly, in front of my family and the rough guards who sniggered at the sight of us and Niuta and Nikandr who smiled and reached for each other's hands and Daria, who nodded in satisfaction. Our joy was only a part of the greater joy the entire family felt at papa's return—a bittersweet joy, to be sure, because the man we were welcoming home was a man stripped of his proud uniform, his sword and his many medals, stripped of his rank and titles and called plain Nicholas Romanov, a man, in short, robbed of his dignity.

And not only robbed of his dignity, but subjected to abuse and humiliation.

It gave our captors pleasure to harass him, to push him from behind as he walked along, to bark orders at him that he knew he dared not disobey. In the days following his return we saw him being mistreated again and again, and subjected to petty acts of meanness. We all felt an angry urge to intervene, but papa wouldn't let us. He just held up one hand and said quietly, "It's of no consequence. Let it pass."

On the first warm, overcast day after he came back to the palace, as the long harsh winter began to give way to early spring, we were allowed to take a picnic lunch out into the palace grounds. It was a new privilege for us; we wondered whether it might mean that there was a thaw in the attitude of our jailers to parallel the thawing of the snow and ice on the palace roof.

The entire family was herded through the gardens—much overgrown and neglected since papa's abdication—to the very edge of the lawn, and there the guards ordered us to spread our thin picnic cloth on the brittle grass beside the tall iron railings that ringed the park. To our surprise, there were people standing on the other side of the railings, shouting to us, calling us rude names. One or two spat on papa and called mama "German bitch."

"Look at the little German bitches!" they yelled at me and my sisters while our guards laughed. "All little whores, like their whore mother!"

"And there's the sick one!" they shouted at Alexei. "The one with the English disease! He looks like he's about to drop dead!"

Papa raised his hand and gave us all such a look that we did not respond to the taunts, though I felt myself growing hotter and hotter and it was all I could do to stop myself from shouting back at the cruel voices.

"Go ahead, eat your picnic, Romanov!" the head guard ordered papa. "Eat, I say!"

"I think it is going to rain," papa answered gravely and quietly. "May we take our picnic inside?"

"Later! Eat now!"

At a signal from papa we sat on the picnic cloth, hastily unwrapped the food in our hamper and tried to eat it as quickly as we could. But it was hard to force ourselves even to take a single bite, with the constant yelling and jeering. To chew was torment, to swallow all but impossible, though I managed to force down a few small bites. The food was tasteless and stuck in my throat, making me cough.

Anastasia spat out her food. Marie managed to spill her plate, though whether she did this intentionally or not I couldn't have said. Mama sat on the cloth, unmoving, stony-faced. Papa ate, slowly and methodically, until the first raindrops began to fall.

We all looked up at the sky gratefully, hoping that we would be allowed to go back to the palace now that the weather had changed.

But we were wrong. We were forced to stay where we were, while the tormenting, taunting crowd grew, heedless of the rain, and the guards, enjoying our humiliation, stood by and watched the scene, making rude remarks to us and to each other and elbowing one another in the ribs and laughing.

The rainwater ran down our faces and into our mouths, mingling with the tasteless food, until in the end the plates were washed clean, the food having run off into the grass, and we were completely bedraggled.

"All right, Romanov," the head guard spat out. "Back to your jail now. The picnic's over."

My stomach hurt. I was nauseous. But I was afraid that if I threw up in front of our jailers there would be more punishment for us all. As we walked back to the palace I did my best to fight my nausea, holding on to Olga—who, I could tell, was feeling ill too—and concentrating on taking one step at a time.

With great effort I managed to hold back until I reached my room. Once inside, however, I rushed to my washbowl and threw up every bit of food I had eaten, heaving and heaving until nothing more would come up and feeling as if I never wanted to eat anything, ever again.

None of the servants had been allowed to come with us on our mortifying picnic, but had Michael been there I am certain he would have lashed out in anger—and been punished for it. When we were alone together on the following day in the room he was given in the palace servants' quarters he showed me the fresh scars he bore on his chest and arms from fighting with papa's captors during the initial days after his abdication.

"I seem to collect these souvenirs," he said, smiling his wry smile as he looked down at the red welts and gashes. Neither of us spoke of the older scar he bore, his scar from the battlefield that was now well on its way to being completely healed. We lay in each other's arms, the balm of our lovemaking soothing the daily chafing of our tormentors. When I was with Michael I was aware of nothing but him: his breath, his smell, his hard strength pressed against me, the safety I felt when near him. He was all to me, and when we lay together in his narrow bed, his face above me soft in the warm candlelight, I could not help thinking, there is no greater joy in life than this.

I felt guilty, wrapped in the protective cocoon of my love for Michael and his for me, while my family was suffering. I was suffering along with them, to be sure, but deep down, where love lay curled at the center of my being, no suffering could touch me.

Forty-three

They wouldn't let us eat fruit. They wouldn't let us wash ourselves more often than once a week. They forced us to do our own laundry. (I thought of Grandma Minnie, who had always sent her clothes and linens to Paris to be laundered.) They wouldn't let us make tea before ten o'clock in the morning, or after four o'clock in the afternoon.

They wouldn't let us have flowers in our rooms. They wouldn't let us make telephone calls, except from the telephone in the guardroom, where they could overhear everything we said. They took away Anastasia's worms and buried them in the garden, where immediately they all died. They read mama's diary, and took down all the icons on the walls in her mauve salon, smudging them with their dirty fingers, before reluctantly letting her have them back.

They tore everything apart, looking for any evidence that might be used against us as enemies of the revolution. Antique chairs and sofas were ripped open, antique trunks overturned, paintings slashed and wardrobes gutted. Every ironing board in the vast ironing room was destroyed, nearly every book in papa's fine library shredded, the leather bindings torn and the gold leaf lettering on the spines carved away and tossed into a basket.

And over the shambles of a palace that remained, they mounted a red flag, and renamed the building the People's House.

What more would they do? We dreaded what was to come, and

speculated endlessly about it. We heard from Constantin—who continued to come to the palace, observe us, and report back to his colleagues in the government on our condition and on the security under which we lived—that the political situation in Petrograd was fluid and unstable. The members of the Provisional Government seemed to change every few weeks, he said, with little continuity of membership or purpose from one change to the next. People were saying that a coup d'état was coming, that everything the revolutionaries had done would be swept away and a new authority would come to power—some said it would be Grandma Minnie, ruling from Kiev, others that it would be papa's cousin Nikolasha, the former commander of the army.

Still others predicted that the Soviet of Workers and Soldiers Deputies would before long become the ruling power, and that papa and the rest of us would all be treated mercilessly, probably even executed. It was this chilling thought that made me realize that we would be foolish to stay a moment longer in the new People's House. We had to find a way to leave—and soon.

Lying on my bed, pretending to read, I drew up a list of those I felt we could turn to for help. First was papa's cousin King George of England, who was of course mama's cousin too. Beyond the close family ties, England was Russia's ally. Surely the king was obligated to rescue his relatives. Maybe, I thought, King George was already preparing, at that very moment, to rescue us. Maybe we would not have to wait long.

Then I wrote down Adalbert's name. I had not heard from him very often since the first year of the war when his ship, the SMS *Derfflinger*, was crippled off Dogger Bank in a battle with the British navy. He wrote to me after the battle to tell me that he had survived and that he was being reassigned. But since then I had had only two very brief letters, assuring me of his affection and concern and telling me that he hoped all was well with our family. I wondered whether he might have written more letters that I never received, letters that our guards had intercepted and destroyed.

Who else was there? Mama's sisters Victoria and Irene, both of whom had husbands who were high-ranking naval officers and who might be able to send a rescue party by sea. Mama's brother Ernie? Aunt Olga?

I pondered each one, but apart from King George and possibly

Adalbert, with his yacht *Mercury*, it didn't seem very likely that anyone would be able to come to our aid. Unless help arrived soon, we would have to look to ourselves to escape.

Michael and I went to talk to papa about it.

We found him walking on the Children's Island, with two guards, lolling against a tree and smoking, watching him. Our own guards, who had escorted us from the palace, joined papa's—which meant that we were some twenty feet from the little cluster of soldiers who occasionally glowered at us but were mostly preoccupied with smoking and talking among themselves.

Papa embraced us both. He was becoming increasingly fond of Michael, and always beamed at the sight of him.

"Do you see, Michael," he said, pointing to his own left shoulder, "they have refused to let me wear my epaulets. They have taken them away somewhere, I suppose. What do you imagine they've done with them? I don't mind telling you, I don't feel dressed without my epaulets."

"I miss my uniform sometimes too, sir. The Fifth Circassian, you know."

"A fine outfit, the Fifth Circassian." Papa nodded, a dreamy look coming into his eyes.

"I was proud to be a part of it."

Papa looked startled. "You are still a part of it."

"No—that is, in the army's view, there is no more Fifth Circassian."

"What? I was told nothing about this."

"Papa," I interjected, "remember, you have given up your throne—and you are not commander of the army any more. You are not informed of—of anything that is going on."

He bristled at my words, but said nothing.

"When the men of the Fifth Circassian learned that you had been forced to abdicate, they refused to accept any other command than yours. They denounced the Provisional Government as a fraud. Some were imprisoned for what they did, the rest remain rebels. I have heard from my friend Archile that a large group of them have gone south, back to the Caucasus, and only about two dozen are still in Petrograd. For what it is worth, they are still loyal to you, sir, and will obey any orders you give."

I could tell that papa was moved to hear of this small pocket of loyal men. But when he spoke again it was of other things entirely.

"Tania, did you know that Michael and I went hunting in the woods by Mogilev?" he asked as we resumed our slow walk around the island, our guards trailing behind.

"Yes, papa. Michael wrote to me about your hunts."

"Did you know that we shot two elks in one day? Did you write her about that, Michael?"

"Yes sir, I did."

"And we trapped a bear too, didn't we?" Papa was suddenly full of energy as he talked. "He was young, he became tame. We called him Dobrinya. Kind Bear. He made a good pet, didn't he?"

"He did."

Papa gazed at us both, and in his gaze, I felt his love.

"We had some good times together at Mogilev, didn't we?"

"We did our best, sir. If only the war had not been so terrible, and so much in our thoughts all the time—"

But I could tell, even as Michael spoke, that for papa, the war—the real war, the war of bullets and corpses and helpless suffering—had been only a sort of distant sorrow. A regret, but not an acute pain. He knew, but his mind refused to know, the truth of his life, which was that all he had been, all he had ever tried to be, now lay in ruins around him, and that unless he took drastic action soon to prevent it, even the ruins would be swept away.

Forty-four

He *won't accept* us. He won't take us in. Can you imagine?"

Angrily mama snapped the pen she was writing with in two and snatched up a new one.

"I'm just writing to him now, to tell him what I think of him!"

"Hush, mama! The guard!" Olga warned.

"The guards can go to hell. I've had my fill of them!"

Olga and I looked at each other, each of us knowing what the other was thinking. We were wondering whether mama's anger would grow until she began to yell, and we would be forced to try to calm her before the guards became impatient and locked her in her room and deprived her of food for a day.

They had done this twice before, despite papa's severe protests.

But she went on talking, in a loud and aggravated tone, about her mother, whose spirit she believed she saw and conversed with, and about the unnamed man who wouldn't accept us.

"Mama warned me he might say no. She says he's a coward. Grandma Victoria never thought much of him."

"Hush! You know your mother is dead," Olga chided. "She has been dead for many years, ever since you were a little girl! You can't see her or hear her. And just who is it who won't accept us?"

"Why, cousin George of course."

Cousin George was, as we well knew, King George, the rather stiff, ill-at-ease young man I had met when mama and I went to Cowes years earlier. He had been Prince George then. I remembered how he had kissed my hand when we left England for home and said that he would miss me.

"How do you know?"

Mama reached into her desk and pulled out a much folded piece of paper.

"From your Uncle Ernie," she whispered. "Written in a baby-language only he and I know. We haven't used it since we were children." She raised her voice for the benefit of the guards. "My laundry list," she said. "Niuta will have to get busy on it. I am told that no more laundry can be taken in in London. All the laundresses are on strike!"

"You will wash your own clothes, Alexandra Romanov!" one of the guards spoke up.

"Why are they on strike?" I asked, my eyes fixed on mama.

"Because they fear that bringing in outside laundry will contaminate their own with foreign germs." Mama's metaphor was strained but adequately clear. Evidently King George feared to import revolutionary ideas along with our family, if he offered us shelter in England. Even though we were about as far from being revolutionaries as it was possible to be.

"Perhaps your mama can tell you where else to send your laundry," I suggested, prompting Olga to frown at me. "Where are the laundresses not on strike?"

"I will ask her."

If Uncle Ernie's letter to mama was to be trusted (and how, I wondered, did Uncle Ernie, who was in Germany, know what Cousin George was saying?) then England would not be offering us a refuge. I wrote to Adalbert and sent my letter via Monsieur Gilliard's friend in the Swiss embassy in Petrograd. But I had no idea whether the letter would actually reach Adalbert or not. Or whether, if it did reach him, he would be able to offer any real help.

Meanwhile Michael had been pondering our situation just as I had, and he told me there would be a surprise at the People's House in the near future.

"Your father's mention of the tame bear at Mogilev gave me a thought," he told me. "I have an idea how we might all find a way out of this People's House before long."

"How?"

"You will see." Michael smiled—and told me nothing further. "It will be better if you do not know in advance, Tania. Just trust me. You will see."

It was the season of the White Nights, that time of the summer when dusk meets dawn and even at midnight the sky is as bright as day. Petrograd is so far north that the seasons meet their extremes there; in the depth of winter one hardly sees the sun, and in the summer, during the end of June, there is no night.

It is a season of heightened emotions, when people like to stay up all night singing and drinking with friends, when lovers take to the woods and do not return until morning, when the pious seek revelations and desperate romantics, feeling cheated of the transcendent which they have sought so long in vain, drink vials of laudanum and end their lives under the lucent sky.

Our guards were restless, wanting a respite from their duties (which were, I'm sure, very grim and dull and even unpleasant, much as they laughed and joked and played cruel tricks on us for their amusement). So when, one bright evening, a swarthy, curly-headed gypsy with black eyes and a thick uncombed black beard wandered up to the main gate of Tsarskoe Selo and asked to be admitted, the guards jeered at him and swore and poked their rifles through the bars to threaten him.

Until they saw the bear.

Lavoritya, the great honey-brown dancing bear, twice as tall as a man and with small flat ears and a long snout and tiny eyes almost lost in her thick crust of fur.

"Friends!" the gypsy called out, "Let Lavoritya come in and dance for you. I promise you, you will not be sorry! And if you should dislike what you see, we will ask for no payment, the bear and I!"

The jeering stopped. Grinning, the guards opened the gates.

The bear and her master came in, but before they had gone far the latter made another request.

"She dances best with music. There is a band—" he indicated a clutch of men carrying musical instruments and wearing matching silver and gold tunics, rather bulky at the waist as if amateurishly tailored but gaudily trimmed at the neck and hem.

"No bands!" It was the voice of the guard commander.

"We dance too!" came a voice from out of the band, and as if on cue all the men put down their instruments, folded their arms and began alternately kicking and squatting in a folk-dance, while at the same time singing and shouting together to punctuate their movements.

"Let them in!" came the clamor from the guards, and after watching the dancing for a moment their chief relented.

All the guards came out into the palace courtyard to watch the show. The gypsy, a skilled entertainer, paced the great bear's antics so that each dance was wilder and more fanciful than the one before. Lavoritya wore many costumes; first she was dressed as a ballet dancer, then as a nun, then a soldier. She stood on her two hind legs, on one hind leg, she rolled, she jumped, she clapped her immense paws together, she tossed her huge head and opened her savage mouth when the gypsy offered her honey from a red pot.

Between dances Lavoritya rested, and the gypsy changed her costume, and the musicians sang and danced in their turn. The evening was warm and the music inviting, and eventually my sisters, mama and papa, and all the servants came out to see the performance, even Alexei, who had been in bed for days with a swollen arm, complaining of pain. He sat in a little chair at the front of our family group, absorbed in watching the show, laughing and swaying to the music.

I felt a hand on my shoulder and heard Michael's voice in my ear.

"Tania, keep your eyes on me. If there should be a commotion, and you see me nod, take your sisters back inside at once. Go to the kitchens and stay there."

"Yes," I whispered. "All right."

"Good girl."

The gypsy had called for a bucket of water and Lavoritya was dunking her snout in it, drinking noisily and sloppily. The soldiers, impatient for her to resume her dancing, began a rhythmic clapping. They were unruly, they had been handing around flasks and bottles for some time and were becoming rowdy with drink. They began shoving one another, egging each other on to dance with Lavoritya, and the gypsy encouraged them.

I kept my eye on Michael, who joined enthusiastically in the clapping as he made his way unobtrusively to where a group of guardsmen had formed a circle and were doing something—I could not see what.

The gypsy shouted above the noise.

"And now for our final presentation. Prepare yourselves to be amazed! In a few moments you will see—your former tsar!"

Loud laughter greeted this announcement. Two men detached themselves from the circle near Michael and dashed into the palace, returning shortly afterward carrying a bundle. I could not see what it was.

I was beginning to be nervous. I felt a need to warn my sisters about what Michael had told me, yet I didn't want to alarm them or to cause the unpredictable Anastasia to blurt out some question that would draw attention to what Michael was about to do.

I moved nearer to Olga and whispered, "Please help me lead Marie and Anastasia into the kitchens if we need to."

She gave me a sharp look. "What?"

"Just help me. Be prepared to help me."

"Not unless I know why."

"Don't be difficult now, Olga. This is for our own good, believe me."

"Who put you up to this?"

"Never mind."

At that moment I felt no love for my sister at all. Why couldn't she be cooperative, just once?

I could feel a stir of restlessness flow through the crowd of men, amid the general enthusiasm. The gypsy was taking too long preparing the bear for the final part of the show. I thought, in a minute the head guard will order everyone back into the palace and whatever Michael has planned will be thwarted.

Then suddenly there was a renewed burst of laughter as a ludicrous figure emerged from among the guards near Michael. One of the guards stepped out from the group. A woman's long white lace veil cascaded from his head down to his knees, covering his drab brown uniform. He carried a bouquet of lilies—where had they come from? We were never allowed to have flowers in the palace—and there was a crude paper tiara perched on top of his veil. As he walked he swayed to and fro in the manner of a young girl twirling her skirts, evoking guffaws from the men, and he batted his eyelashes and pouted.

As if on cue the gypsy led Lavoritya forward, now wearing a gaudy replica of an imperial crown on her head and with a short red jacket and sash that were not unlike what papa had worn as tsar on ceremonial occasions.

The musicians began playing wedding music. The guardsman and the bear drew closer together, and the gypsy, as if presiding at a wedding, made the sign of the cross before the couple. Amid the crescendo of laughter that accompanied this pantomime Lavoritya farted—a loud, prolonged fart that was like a cannon shot.

Now the guards were convulsed with laughter and one of them accidentally—drunkenly—leaned too far over and tipped Alexei's chair onto the ground. Alexei fell. Mama screamed. And Michael, at last, nodded to me—the signal I had been waiting for.

"Quickly! Olga! Marie! Anastasia! Follow me! Don't ask why! Just follow me!" I grabbed the two younger girls by the hand and ran to the palace, trusting that Olga would follow. Behind me I could hear sounds of confusion, shouts and cries, a cacophony of music, mama's anguished screaming, the voice of the gypsy calling his bear, and above it all, Michael's strong voice ringing out.

"The boy is hurt! Get the doctor! Get a stretcher! He must be taken to Petrograd at once, or he will surely die!"

Forty-five

We ran. I dragged the girls behind me and Olga too followed, though somewhat unwillingly. I think she was frightened by all the commotion and didn't know what else to do.

We went into the palace by a side door and down several long corridors until we came to the uncarpeted stairs leading into the kitchens, whose vast cooking rooms and storerooms would have been quite dark had it not been June with its luminous white night. We encountered no servants in the kitchens. It was long past the hour when any cooking would have been done and in any case, our household had grown quite small.

Panting from our exertions, we chose a place to hide, inside a pantry closet, and shut the door.

"Michael has a plan to free us from this place," I told my sisters.

"What is it?" Anastasia asked.

"I don't know. We have to wait here. That's all I know."

"Should I find Niuta and tell her to pack a bag?" asked Marie.

"No time."

"But there's no one here. We are just waiting. She could pack quickly while we wait."

"No, Marie. We must stay here."

I expected at any moment to hear footsteps, voices. I expected activity. The walls of the kitchen were thick, I could not hear any noise from outside. Nothing from the courtyard where Lavoritya and the others had been performing.

"I'm hungry," Olga said presently. "I'm going to find some food."

"Stay near us."

"Do you think Alexei will be all right?" Anastasia asked in a low voice after a time. "I couldn't see if he was bleeding."

"He's always bleeding," Marie replied. "You know that. He never stops. The question is, will he die of his bleeding? Or will he just hurt, and scream, like he always does?"

"Marie!" I had never heard her speak so callously before.

"Well, he does. We all know it. He's all mama and papa care about anyway. Not us."

I could have slapped her then, but controlled my reaction. I reminded myself that, deep down, she was probably worried about Alexei—and that like the rest of us, she had been under great strain for months. I knew that she felt neglected and, to an extent, rejected by our parents. Her worst side was showing itself.

Olga returned with some black bread and a few wilted cabbage leaves, which she proceeded to eat without offering any of the food to the rest of us. I could not have eaten it if she had offered it, and besides, it did not look at all appetizing.

We sat down on the stone floor of the pantry, our backs against the wall, saying nothing. Marie started kicking Anastasia's leg irritably. Anastasia protested. As their bickering went on, I thought to myself, Michael planned the entire evening. The distracting presence of the bear, the freely flowing liquor, the comedy, the uproar, and, at the climax of it all, the emergency involving Alexei. All a grand diversion—though how could he have known that Alexei would have a fall? Was that too prearranged? And if so, did that mean that my brother was in fact unhurt? I hoped so.

After what seemed like several hours, we heard the sound of a door bursting open and men's voices. I opened the pantry door a crack and saw—the musicians! I took a chance that Michael had sent them and stepped out from behind the door.

"Your Highness!" one of the men addressed me, with a bow. A real bow! No one had bowed to me for months!

"Your Highness, we have come to take you and your sisters to safety. Permit me to introduce myself and my fellow officers. I am Sergeant Major Archile Dartchia, of the Fifth Circassian regiment, at your service." He introduced the others, at the same time deftly discarding the shiny loose tunic he had been wearing to reveal a dark green officer's jacket and a thick black belt—with a long jeweled khinjal fastened to it. A khinjal such as Michael wore. Such as all the Georgian officers wore.

His companions also transformed themselves from gaudy musicians to officers, fearsomely armed and formidable.

"We of the Fifth Circassian are loyal to Tsar Nicholas II. We believe that he was wrongfully deprived of his command and his throne."

"I'm sure that if my father were here, he would thank you for your loyalty—but urge you not to take any undue risks."

"The life of a soldier is risk, Your Highness. Risk for the sake of a great cause—and for glory."

All the men assented to this, nodding.

"Can you tell us what is going on?" Olga asked the men as she came out of the pantry, with Marie and Anastasia following her. "Are we leaving soon? Where are you going to take us?"

"We will do as Captain Gamkrelidze orders. We have put ourselves under his command." I realized that they were talking about Michael, who had once explained to me that his family had changed their name from Gamkrelidze to Gradov when they moved to Tiflis. With these men from the Caucasus, it seemed, he had chosen to use his original family name. "Please, Your Highnesses, do not distress yourselves," the sergeant major added.

But we could not help but be anxious. Michael was so long in coming. What if he never appeared at all? What were we to do?

Fortunately Michael came through the door not long after this, but I could tell right away that he was worried. Even so, the sight of him comforted my fears.

"Everything is ready," he said. "There are carts waiting to take you into the countryside. All should go smoothly. There is only one problem."

"What is that?"

"Your father and mother are refusing to go."

"What?"

"They will not come with us. They say there is no need."

I thought quickly. "Where are they?"

"On the Children's Island. I couldn't think of anywhere else to take them after they refused to leave with the men of the regiment. Alexei is with them. Apart from his swollen arm, which has been troubling him for weeks, he appears to be unharmed."

What could we do? The loyal men of the Fifth Circassian were ready to take me and my sisters to safety. But if we left, and our parents refused to leave with us, what would that mean for our future as a family? Would we find ourselves orphans in some foreign place, amid sympathetic people but bereft of family? Or would we be captured and killed, leaving papa and mama and Alexei to mourn us?

"I must speak to them," I said at length. "We cannot go alone." And telling my sisters to wait for me, protected by the loyal soldiers, I set off with Michael for the Children's Island, under the pale and luminous sky.

Forty-six

There was bedlam on the palace grounds. The revolutionary guards ran here and there, searching frantically for us (who else?), calling out to one another, now and then shooting off their rifles into the air. Michael threw a long green army cape over my shoulders and tucked my hair under a green soldier's cap, pulling off his own thick boots and telling me to put them on over my shoes.

"I'll go barefoot," he said. "Another barefoot Georgian will not cause any comment."

Thus attired, and summoning my courage, I walked rapidly beside Michael in the direction of the Children's Island, both of us attempting to look as though we too were joining in the general search.

There was a small summer cottage on the island—hardly more than a one-room enclosure—and it was in this little structure that we found mama, pacing up and down, jittery and on edge, and papa, watching her uneasily and smoking, and Alexei, stretched out on a wicker sofa, his swollen arm jutting stiffly out from his slender side.

We reached the cottage unhindered and went inside. I took off the soldier's cap and returned Michael's boots to him but left the cape on.

"Tania! Tania, are you all right? Where are your sisters?" Mama came up to me and looked into my face, half concerned, half accusing.

"I left them with some of the loyal soldiers, safe in one of the kitchen pantries."

"Tania, why all this sudden hubbub? We are in no danger. Our situation here is only temporary. I've tried to tell Michael this, but he doesn't believe me. Perhaps you can persuade him—"

"Papa, we must get away now. Tonight. You and mama and Alexei must come with us."

"But that's absurd!" mama insisted. "We have no need to leave our home. I have been told—my mama's spirit has told me—that there is a great change coming. Your father's illegal abdication is going to be reversed. All these rough soldiers who have held us captive will be court martialed and executed. Justice will be done!" She grasped her velvety lilac rosary and began repeating her prayers, her lips moving silently.

I avoided looking at Michael. "Papa, you must listen to me. We cannot put our trust in anyone or anything but ourselves. We must decide our own fate. We must act now. Tonight."

"But the Provisional Government has assured me that we will be allowed to settle somewhere outside Russia—perhaps at the Danish court among Grandma Minnie's relatives if Cousin George continues to deny us a refuge."

"The Provisional Government may fall tomorrow!"

"What?"

"Constantin says he fears there may be a sudden change—that the Soviet may take over everything."

"Those hooligans? The people would never stand for that! Constantin is impetuous. He is imagining things."

"There is no time to argue," Michael said with quiet authority. "The hour to leave has come." He started to draw his khinjal. "Sir, madam, I must insist that you accompany me—"

But before he could finish his sentence we heard shouting, and a commotion in the little wood adjacent to the cottage. Men in heavy boots were tramping across the wooden bridge that connected the island to the broad lawn with its statue garden.

I took Michael's arm.

"They are coming. It's no good," he muttered. "Tania, I can't let them take me. I can help you more if I go. God be with you all!" He embraced me tightly, then kissed me on the lips and ran outside.

He had only a moment to get away. Almost at once the cottage was surrounded and some half-dozen guards burst in.

Throwing off the green cape, I confronted them.

"Where have you been all this time?" I asked. "We have been waiting for you here. Don't you know that my brother is ill? He had a terrible fall tonight. He is in pain and can't move. Help us take him back to the palace—I mean the People's House—at once. Find Dr. Korovin. Well, don't just stand there! Help us!"

Forty-seven

Michael was gone. I couldn't be sure he had gotten away safely, for I heard nothing from him. The men of the Fifth Circassian who had helped him on the night of our failed escape attempt had melted away as well. My worst fear was that all of them, including Michael, had been captured and executed by the revolutionary guards. But I simply didn't know.

In the palace, it was as if the events of that night—the dancing bear, the commotion, the tumult, and finally the restoration of our captivity—had never happened. The guards never mentioned them and neither did we, though my sisters and my parents saw that I was worried about Michael and knew very well what the cause was.

Papa missed Michael. He had grown accustomed to his companionship and service, and no one could take his place, as old Chemodurov had been pensioned off. My sisters and Alexei—especially Alexei—missed Michael too. He played games with them and gave Alexei rides on his strong back and his presence always lifted everyone's spirits.

Only mama was, I suspect, relieved that he was gone, for it meant that she did not have to pretend not to know that Michael and I were lovers. I had always thought her to be exceptionally open and natural about sex and love, just as she said her mother and Grandma Victoria had always been. But when it came to my love for Michael and his for me, she had never said a word about the physical side of our relationship.

In this she was the opposite of Aunt Olenka, who was happy for us and had often told me how glad she was that I had found a lover who pleased me so completely.

Aunt Olenka! Where was she now, I wondered. We had heard that she had gone to the Crimea with Aunt Xenia and Uncle Sandro and Grandma Minnie. We had had several affectionate, concerned letters from Aunt Xenia—proof that not all our mail was confiscated or destroyed by our jailers—but as the summer wore on we heard nothing more, and we wondered whether they were all still safe.

One very important letter did arrive, not long after Michael left (somehow I dated everything from that last glimpse of Michael, running off into the woods on the Children's Island). It came via Monsieur Gilliard's friend in the Swiss embassy. It was from Adalbert.

"My dear Tania," he wrote, "how glad I was to get your letter. We have all been concerned about you and your family. We hope that everyone is well, especially your brother. I will sail the *Mercury* into the Baltic as soon as the ice breaks. Send word where I should wait for you. Trust me. Remember the Peace Initiative. Ever your loving friend, Adalbert."

Overjoyed, I started to take the letter to Michael—and then remembered that he was gone. How glad he would be, I thought, to know that someone in my family was concerned about us, and was coming to help us.

Being careful to hide my excitement from the ever watchful guards, I folded Adalbert's letter again and again until it was just a small square of white paper and slipped it into one of papa's books—not all of which had been destroyed by the guards. I put the book beside his plate at our midday meal.

"Monsieur Gilliard has been reading Gibbon to us," I commented to papa as we ate. "I marked some passages that we thought were especially eloquent."

"I don't remember us reading any Gibbon," Olga countered. I kicked her under the table.

"You must have been dozing. You are too old for lessons anyway."

"I should think Gibbon would be depressingly apt reading," mama said wearily. "The decline and fall of Rome. We are taking part in the decline and fall of Russia—at least for now. And like the Romans, we are drawing strength from a new spiritual force rising in our midst."

"If you don't mind, Tania, I'd much rather go on reading *The Girl with the Diamond Bracelet,* the crime novel I brought from Mogilev."

I moved over and whispered in his ear.

"This is important, papa. There is something in the book."

"Are you whispering about me again?" Mama spoke sharply.

"No, mama. It's nothing. It's not about you."

"I'm sure it's not about me. Nobody cares about me." It was Marie's familiar complaint, which we all heard far too often.

"I don't like Gibbon," Anastasia remarked. "Too many long words. Too many long sentences."

"What a dolt you are," Olga snapped. "I don't know what you are doing in this family anyway."

"Be quiet, Olga. You know I don't like it when you criticize your sisters." Papa spoke wearily. He got up from the table.

"I'm going to ask you all to excuse me. I've been told to expect a visit from the new prime minister of the Provisional Government, Kerensky. I must prepare to meet him. Tania, come up to my study. I can look at your Gibbon there."

"Now then, what is so important, Tania?" papa asked once we were seated in his study. He opened the volume of Gibbon and the small white square of folded paper fell out. He unfolded it and read it.

"Ah, I see. Your faithful Adalbert. A good boy. Yes, a very good boy."

"He's hardly a boy, papa. He's a married man and a naval officer."

"To me, he will always be the boy who asked for your hand. In the old days, before the horrors came upon us."

"We need to prepare to meet the *Mercury.* We are being given a second chance to escape. We must take it."

"Tania, the German army is practically at our doorstep. The Germans and Austrians have killed a million of our men. More than a million. Do you really imagine that your mother would go aboard a German vessel claiming to offer us rescue?"

"But Adalbert is not some savage murderer, he is my friend. He offers help and friendship to us all."

"Was he not a serving officer in vessels that fired on our navy?"

"Yes—and we sank one of the ships he was serving in. He could well have drowned."

"The point is, Tania, Adalbert is the enemy."

Oh papa, how little you understand! I wanted to cry out. Instead I said, quietly, "What will it take to make you understand?"

He said nothing. He reached for his pipe and began to fill it from the tobacco jar on the table beside his chair.

I shook my head in despair and was about to get up and leave when one of the guards opened the study door and announced, "Prime Minister Kerensky."

He was a very short, nervous man, with darting black eyes that took in at a glance my father's unhurried filling of his pipe, my look of evident frustration and dissatisfaction, the elegance of the high-ceilinged room with its thick, richly patterned Persian carpet and its ornate plaster moldings. He strode rapidly toward my father, extending his hand. Papa rose and grasped the proffered hand.

"Romanov!"

"Prime Minister. May I present my daughter Tatiana."

Kerensky bowed politely—not deferentially—and turned his attention back to papa, who offered him a chair.

"Tatiana," papa said to me, "we must congratulate the prime minister on his recent appointment—I mean election."

"Congratulations sir," I said.

"Thank you but my tenure may be brief. Elections will be held very soon and no one can predict their outcome. I need hardly tell you, sir"—he turned all his attention back to papa—"that it is becoming more and more difficult to control the Soviet."

"That's the radical group, Tania. The rabble-rousers."

"I know, papa. Constantin keeps me well informed."

And I have heard the radicals speak with my own ears, I might have added, but didn't.

The thin, wiry prime minister, unable to keep still, got up from his chair and went to stand by the marble fireplace. There was no fire, as the afternoon was very warm.

"I have had to arm the workers," he confided to papa. "Otherwise the radicals would create chaos—"

"But if you arm the workers they will take over the city!" I burst out.

"I must gamble on their loyalty. Meanwhile, I must not gamble on your safety, Romanov. I understand you had some trouble here not long ago."

"Nothing of any significance," papa said, drawing on his pipe. "Some of the guards got excited when a gypsy came, with a dancing bear."

"Then it isn't true that an escape was foiled?"

"An escape? No one escaped. As you see, Tania and I are here, and the rest of my family is also here in the palace, as always."

The prime minister looked at me.

"Was there an escape, miss?"

"No," I said simply. Which was true. Had he asked whether an escape was attempted, I might have had to answer differently.

Papa continued to smoke his pipe; he appeared to be serenely indifferent to the short little man's piercing eyes and sharp inquiries.

"Be aware that, should you attempt to escape, you would most certainly be executed. The Soviet—the rabble-rousers, as you call them—are eager to eliminate your family. They fear—quite correctly—that many Russians do not welcome either your abdication or the authority of the Provisional Government. Many Russians reject the revolution and want a return to monarchy."

"I appreciate their loyalty," papa said softly.

"But not the danger to you—and to the country—that they represent. A counter-revolution would mean civil war. Your family would be the first casualties—but far from the last."

"Yes. I see. If only the British would let us in."

"As you know, that is what I have wanted from the start. And King George continues to hope that a refuge will be found for you. Just not in his country."

"We have an of—" I began, before papa interrupted me.

"There is no point in bringing up what can never be, Tania."

Kerensky turned his piercing eyes on me. "What were you going to say?"

I hesitated. "Perhaps papa is right. No need to raise false hopes." I regretted nearly blurting out what Adalbert had written, about sending his yacht to rescue us. So papa did not trust the prime minister, even though they had discussed our possible departure for Britain.

"Tania has a friend who would like to help us."

"Private help would be inadequate. There must be a sponsoring government. And as long as this war continues, grave difficulties remain."

The prime minister sat down again, on the edge of the chair.

"Meanwhile, we are formulating a plan. We want to send you far from Petrograd. To Siberia, in fact."

Papa opened his mouth and his pipe fell on the rug.

"Siberia! That frozen icebox!"

"Frozen in time. The town where you will be going has not changed in decades. Your grandfather, if he were alive today, would be right at home there. There are no disgruntled, radical factory workers—no factories at all—and no bomb-throwers. Only small town folk who go to church and revere the saints and the tsar, not necessarily in that order."

"It sounds very safe," I offered.

"It is."

"But Siberia!" papa repeated, bending down to retrieve his pipe, which had gone out.

"You needn't be so shocked," the prime minister was saying, having gotten up from the chair again and begun pacing around the room. "It seems a perfectly natural and sensible choice. You need not be there long. In time we will be able to negotiate a permanent refuge for you."

He bowed to us both. "I will take my leave. You will be sent instructions about your departure." And he was gone.

Papa and I sat in silence for a few moments, each lost in our thoughts. I was wondering how Michael would be able to find me if we went so far away. How could I get word to him? What if he never found me? What if I never saw him again?

Papa seemed dazed. He looked out unseeing into the opulent room, his dead pipe lying forgotten on the table beside him.

"Siberia!" he said again. "Surely, Siberia is the end of the world."

Forty-eight

For four hot, dusty days in August of 1917 we traveled on a lice-infested train into the bleak wasteland of Siberia.

I had not known that Russia possessed such empty lands—empty of towns, empty of vegetation, above all, empty of people. We traveled for hours without seeing so much as a tiny village, through barren steppe country and swampy lowlands glistening with small lakes and over mountain passes where the train, huffing and puffing slowly, seemed to strain to its utmost to pull its heavy load.

We were a large party, the seven in our family plus our three dogs plus Niuta and Nikandr, Daria and Iskra, who had come to seem, at least to me, like a second family, plus mama's maids and Sedynov and Monsieur Gilliard and Dr. Botkin, Alexei's most recent doctor and a better one than Dr. Korovin, and our greatly reduced household staff of cooks and valets and the several hundred guardsmen who had been our jailers ever since the outbreak of the revolution five months earlier.

Our family baggage filled an entire car of the train, as mama would not leave anything behind and had packed trunk after trunk with her precious icons and family heirlooms and photographs, not to mention her many gowns and hats and pairs of gloves and yards and yards of handmade lace. My sisters and I each had several trunks and papa brought his remaining books and some treasures that had belonged to his father and grandfather.

Our most valuable possessions, needless to say, were mama's jewels. Extravagant, magnificent diamonds and emeralds and pearls, tiaras and necklaces each worth a fortune and many beautiful rings papa had bought her over the years from his great personal wealth. Had my parents been willing to admit to themselves that the revolution was inevitable, they would surely have sold some of these jewels and deposited the profits in Swiss banks or placed them with discreet agents in London or Paris. When we took our trip to Cowes, Mama could have left some of her pearls and diamonds with kindly Queen Alexandra to be hidden away with the royal jewels in the Tower of London, or so I imagined.

But of course they had not foreseen that our family would be all but dispossessed, and the vast Romanov fortune confiscated. So all we could do, as we prepared to move out of Tsarskoe Selo, was to take the beautiful, costly jewels out of their settings and conceal them. Some we hid in our corsets, others we wrapped tightly in silk and made into buttons to be sewn onto our gowns. We each carried thousands of rubles' worth of gems on our persons and in our clothing, and we were aware that they might represent the difference between poverty and wealth in our unknown future.

Before we left the palace I made one last trip to see the elephant. He was still there, in his sadly run-down enclosure, looking as dusty and shaggy as ever. His pond was muddy and he shuffled through piles of dirt and leaves as he made his slow, undulating way from one side of the barred enclosure to the other.

"Goodbye, dear old thing," I said to him as I put my hand through the bars and he lifted his trunk to smell it, searching for treats. "I have nothing to bring you. I'm sorry.

"We're going away," I went on after we had looked each other in the eye. "I don't know for how long. I hope you will be well. I hope you've had a good life."

He lifted his trunk and as I watched it rise I saw, on the brick wall that formed the rear of his pen, a row of freshly made holes. Bullet holes. The soldiers had been shooting at him, or near him, in order to frighten him. No doubt they enjoyed tormenting him as much as they did tormenting us.

I longed to be able to protect the old elephant from whatever fate awaited him when we left. Would he starve? (There was no sign of his mahout.) Would he be executed as an enemy of the revolution? Or would he just be overlooked, one more victim of the chaotic state into which Russia was falling?

I leaned my head against the iron bars and once again he came up to me and put out his trunk to smell my hair.

"You know I love you, don't you," was all I could say before I had to go. I hoped he understood.

As we traveled eastward the air became hotter and whenever we had to stop for coal or to pass a village we had to pull down the blinds to avoid being recognized, which made the air inside hotter still. We had brought along clean drinking water and we helped ourselves to the champagne from the restaurant car, which made us all tipsy and helped to pass the time.

Trying our best to forget the biting of the lice and the jolting and swaying of the train—which made it very difficult to sleep in our narrow beds—we joked about our situation. There we were, jammed into an ailing elderly train, on our way to the ends of the earth (as papa put it), our journey itself disguised as a Red Cross mission for our onetime enemy, the Japanese! Our train flew a Japanese flag, and two Japanese guards had been hired to patrol the tracks with guns every time the train stopped to take on coal and water.

Once our uncomfortable train journey was finally over we went aboard the steamer *Russia* at Tiumen for the trip upriver to our ultimate destination, the small town of Tobolsk. There were far too many of us to ride on the steamer, and my sisters and I all had to share one tiny room with beds that were hardly more than planks and hardly big enough for our dogs to sleep on. I will say nothing about the toilet and washing arrangements because, quite simply, there were none. Whoever had traveled in this steamer before, they had not been very clean and I could not wait to get out onto dry land and into our new palace.

But there were no palaces in Tobolsk, as we soon found out.

Indeed there was only one large house, known as the Governor's Mansion, and the rest were log houses barely large enough for one family, let alone an entire aristocratic household with servants and a tutor and a doctor and, in our case, our many jailers.

The Governor's Mansion was all boarded up and abandoned, yet we were expected to move in and just make the best of things. Sedynov and Nikandr tore some of the boards off the windows and went inside to have a look around.

"You can't possibly move in there," Sedynov told us gruffly when we returned to the steamer. "There is hardly any furniture, the walls and floors are filthy and the gas has not been turned on. There is no water and the pipes are clogged. The boat is better."

"I can't possibly stay another night on this horrid steamer!" mama complained. But we had no choice. We stayed aboard the *Russia*, kept awake by boat whistles and bugs and by the discomfort of the cramped plank beds, for another week, while the house was made ready.

"I can't believe a governor ever lived in this house," papa remarked when we finally came ashore and moved in, and our trunks were being unpacked. "Everything is so old and shabby. The smell is terrible. And the attic! I'm ashamed to have the servants living there."

Niuta and Nikandr, Daria and Iskra moved into rooms elsewhere in the town and many of our servants lived in a house across the street from ours. We spread out, and did our best to make ourselves at home. Olga and I sewed curtains to cover the dirty windows. Friendly neighbors brought us lamps and tables and, quietly, wished us well when they thought our guards were not listening. All the rooms needed painting and the old wallpaper was peeling off the walls, but papa insisted that it didn't matter, as our quarters were only temporary.

"Any day now we will hear that we have been offered a home abroad," he said. "It is everyone's wish. I have Prime Minister Kerensky's word on it."

We tried our best to keep his encouraging words in mind as we coped with the mess and stench of overflowing drains and toilets that refused to work.

"We might as well be living in a cave," Marie complained. "We live like animals here!" When a kind neighbor delivered a piano to the mansion, Olga fairly screamed.

"What do we need a piano for, when we don't even have a toilet that works! If these people really want to help us, let them clean out our septic pits!"

But of course no one wanted to do that, and the donor of the piano was thanked and our plumbing continued to be broken.

Still, for all its backwardness, the town and its people were genuinely welcoming to us. There were no jeering, gaping crowds here, no angry marching workers. Instead the townspeople of Tobolsk took off their hats and crossed themselves when they walked past our house. Some knelt on the ground. Some bowed in reverence. I never saw anyone kiss the earth when papa's shadow fell across it, but it would not have surprised me if someone had.

Most striking of all, no one called mama a German bitch or whispered the ugly gossip that had been told and retold in Petrograd so often.

"None of that nonsense here in Tobolsk about me being a German spy or being Father Gregory's lover!" she told us with a wide grin of satisfaction. "They know who I really am, they bow to me. Perhaps they know that their Babiushka's abdication is about to be reversed!"

Mama had her daily moments of satisfaction, when she went to sit in the window of her upstairs room and the passers-by outside paid her respect. Papa, however, was in very low spirits for he learned that the advancing Germans had taken Riga and that his beloved Russian soldiers were in what everyone knew would be their final retreat.

We knew the worst; we were allowed to read the local newspapers and also to receive telegrams from Petrograd and elsewhere, though our guards read them first and edited out anything they did not want us to see or know. None of the news, it seemed, was positive. Though Tobolsk retained its traditional values and continued to revere the (now dissolved) monarchy, elsewhere in Russia—especially in the industrial cities—the revolution was careening farther and farther into radicalism. In the increasingly dominant soviets or committees of workers and soldiers, those who called themselves Bolsheviks were growing stronger and stronger, and were calling for "Peace, Land and Bread" while the Provisional Government was losing support.

We read of these things, and whispered to one another about them, while doing our best to maintain an orderly life of outward calm in our run-down mansion, and waiting for the first signs of the dreaded Siberian winter to arrive.

Forty-nine

The nuns of the nearby Ivanovsky convent came and went from the side door of our mansion at all hours of the day, soft-footed, soft-voiced, bringing us vegetables from their root cellar, fresh-baked loaves, even fish, always with a greeting and a blessing and making the sign of the cross with their gnarled hands.

At first they all looked alike to me, elderly ladies with lined faces under their black wimples, but as the days passed I began to learn some of their names and, whenever I was allowed, I passed the time of day with them before they left. Sometimes they came for the evening prayer service which a local priest was allowed to hold in our sitting room. At other times they came when someone in our household was sick, or when special prayers were needed.

Our guards tolerated the nuns, tripped them occasionally, sending them sprawling, their thin white legs poking out from under their long black skirts, but on the whole the nuns and the guards appeared to ignore each other. Both became familiar parts of our new environment, the nuns welcome, the guards an everpresent source of annoyance, a tormenting nuisance.

It was the nuns who brought us the newspapers, week-old newspapers with carefully worded descriptions of the worsening situation in Petrograd. We read them—or rather, papa and I read them, the others preferring to remain in ignorance—and tried to imagine the truth behind the guarded, brief accounts of riots and vigilantism, strikes and food shortages.

"How much more can the city take?" papa asked in despair as he skimmed one of the papers following our scant noon meal. Our own food ration had been cut, by order of the Provisional Government; we were given peasant fare, cabbage soup and black bread and turnips, and no second helpings were allowed to anyone, not even Anastasia who at sixteen was growing quite fat and was always hungry.

"Things were certainly very bad last winter," papa went on, "but it appears they will be even worse when the cold weather sets in this year."

One of the nuns came with a basket of fresh loaves and as I took them from her she whispered, "There is one among us who wishes to speak to your father."

"Tell him to come out into the yard," I answered. "Papa will be chopping wood as usual this afternoon and he can always use help. My sister Marie and I do our best but our piles of firewood are always small. Tell him to say to the guards that he is here to help papa chop wood."

It was Papa's one true pleasure: swinging his axe and chopping the stumps that were brought for him by the guards into sticks of wood to be burned in our stoves. The weather was growing noticeably colder now that November had arrived, and we knew we would need a great deal of wood to heat the house throughout the long winter.

A short, energetic man in a thick fur coat and tall fur hat was admitted into the yard shortly afterward and, picking up an axe, set to work reducing the stubborn stumps to firewood. I thought he looked familiar but couldn't remember where I might have seen him before. As soon as I overheard him speaking to papa, however, I knew him at once. It was the Prime Minister, Kerensky!

I went over to him, but before I could speak he put a finger to his lips.

"Please, Miss Tatiana, I beg you not to address me. I am not who you think I am."

"Then who are you?"

"A traveler passing through Tobolsk on my way to Murmansk."

"As far away as that!" papa said. "Tell me, traveler, where did you begin your journey?"

"Petrograd."

"And how is my old haunt?"

Kerensky shook his head.

"As bad as I have ever seen it. When I left—I left in a hurry, I can tell you, I was very lucky to get out of the city alive—" he stopped talking, aware that one of the sentries was strolling closer to us. When the man strolled away again, he resumed, his voice anxious. "When I left, the streets were full of looters. Every house was being sacked, every wine cellar raided. No one was doing any work. The trains were not running. There was no food in the marketplaces. The soldiers were refusing to restore order. Imagine! The men of the Preobrazhensky regiment refusing our command to go out into the streets and shoot the looters!"

For a time the prime minister and papa and I continued our work in silence.

"Who is in charge now?" papa asked at length.

"No one—legally. The Bolsheviks rule by terror. They call themselves the Military Revolutionary Committee."

"But what about the Provisional Government?" I asked in low tones. "What about my friend Constantin?"

Kerensky shook his head.

"The Provisional Government doesn't exist any more. The Bolsheviks drove us all out of the palace where we were holding our meetings. Then they made their great announcement: all private property has been abolished."

"What?" Papa, astounded, sank his axe into a stump with a resounding *whack*.

"It is the Bolshevik leader's dream, the evil one they call Lenin. He says everything is the property of everyone. No one can keep anything for himself."

Papa sat down on a stump and gazed into the distance.

"Don't they know that can only lead to anarchy? To a jungle state, where the powerful take all, and the weak are butchered?" He raised his gaze to Kerensky's face but Kerensky merely rolled his eyes and shook his head.

Two of the guards, who had been wrestling with each other and paying little attention to us, now remembered their duty and came closer. Papa immediately got up and resumed his chopping, while changing the subject, his voice taking on a matter-of-fact tone.

"I'm told the winter is even harsher in Murmansk than it is here. Tell me, what will you be doing there?"

"I am a scientist. I research the walrus herds. Did you know that a walrus can grow tusks that are four feet long?"

"My sister has a necklace made from walrus ivory," I put in. "But she never wears it."

The guards began to move off again. When they were far enough away, Kerensky resumed his serious message.

"I came here to warn you. You are in more danger than ever now. And you are on your own. No foreign government is going to take you in, now that the Bolsheviks are in control. They imagine that the Germans will conquer Petrograd and restore you as tsar. That the Germans will force you to order all the radicals killed."

"They would not have to use much persuasion to make me do that!" papa said through gritted teeth.

"Before that can happen, the Bolsheviks will order your death. You must find a way to escape."

Papa's shoulders sank. "As to that, all is in the will of God."

"The Bolsheviks have outlawed God."

For another few moments we worked in silence. I could tell that papa was growing tired. The terrible news Kerensky had brought was weighing on him. He was far from being an old man—he was only forty-nine in the year that we moved to Tobolsk—but he was beginning to have the worn, frail look of age, and much as he enjoyed physical exertion, it fatigued him more than in the past, and he had to take cocaine to revive himself.

"You there!" one of the guards called out. "You're slow! Look at that pitiful pile of wood! You're going to freeze all winter!" The others laughed, then started to sing. They often sang revolutionary songs in their rough voices, slapping their thighs in time to the music. The songs were always about liberty and the triumph of the workers.

"Is there no one to stand up against these Bolsheviks?" papa asked Kerensky at length. "Here in Tobolsk God is still in his churches, and people still own their houses and their fields. Nothing has changed."

"That is why we arranged to have you moved here, because the revolution has not yet reached Tobolsk. But it is coming—and soon—and in a more violent form than ever. There is a bloodbath in Petrograd. The Bolsheviks are murdering everyone who opposes them, even the union members and the soldiers who refuse to obey their orders."

"They are murdering soldiers?"

"By the hundreds."

Papa turned his head away. I had no doubt he was in tears.

My one thought was, Michael is still a soldier. Was he safe?

"Do you know anything of the Fifth Circassian regiment, and of an officer named Michael Gradov?"

"No. But if he is not a Bolshevik then he is in danger—or more likely, he is already past danger. He has already met his fate."

My heart stopped.

"But you can't be certain. He may have escaped."

"One can always hope—even against all the odds," Kerensky admitted, with a faint smile. "Was this Gradov a radical?"

"No. In fact he was a member of my household," papa said.

"Ah! Well then, the Committee would be sure to show him no mercy."

Hearing Kerensky's words I could not suppress my own tears. My dearest Michael, killed by the Bolsheviks! The ugly, hateful Bolsheviks! In my fury I spat in the direction of the guards, who once again came over to where we were standing.

One of them kicked our carefully stacked pile of wood, scattering the sticks in all directions.

"Pick that up, Romanov! You've made a mess! And you"—he indicated Kerensky—"get going."

After the briefest hesitation, Kerensky saluted my father, nodded to me, and left.

Papa bent down and began picking up the wood and re-stacking it.

"Help me, Tania," he said. "Just help me, and ignore the men."

"But papa—"

"This is what we must do, right now. Don't think about anything else. Just help me."

I did as he asked, despite the anger, sorrow and fear that churned within me. Despite my urge to fling the wood at the guards, to kill them all, to take as terrible a revenge as I could against those who, I dreaded, had killed my Michael and were bent on destroying everything and everyone I loved.

Fifty

What is this doing here!!"

He burst into the yard where we were chopping wood one frigid afternoon, a thin, scruffy man in dirty clothes with long red hair and wire-rimmed glasses. He ran toward Iskra, who was playing with a sled on a small mound of snow near us, and grabbed her roughly, frightening her and making her scream.

The lounging guards came to attention at once.

"Put her down!" I cried.

"Get rid of this at once!" the redheaded man shouted to the nearest soldier, tossing the writhing Iskra to him so carelessly that I was amazed she did not fall onto the snow-covered ground. "Take it inside. Find the mother. Shoot her."

Now it was my turn to scream.

"Don't you know that any outsider can be used to carry arms, or messages? No one can be admitted to this compound. No one, do you hear!" He harangued the guards, his long red hair flying around his sharp-featured face as he spoke, the menace in his voice clear and terrifying. The guards cringed.

Papa put down his axe and approached the crazy man—for that is how I thought of him at that moment. He held out his hand.

"Romanov," he said.

"Do you think I don't know who you are, exploiter? Tyrant! Monster!"

He turned his back on papa and walked up and down slowly in front of the guards, who stood stiffly in formation, hands at their sides, unmoving.

"Rabble!" he hissed. "We must get some real guards in this place. Red Guards. Dedicated revolutionaries. Not you slipshod amateurs, who allow anyone and everyone to enter what should be a sealed prison!"

The head guard stepped forward. "Sir, I—"

The redheaded man slapped him so hard that he staggered. He stepped back in line.

I had stood frozen in place while this went on, shocked by what I was seeing. But then my wave of paralysis passed.

"You can't shoot that child's mother," I said. "She has done nothing wrong."

He looked me up and down, then went back into the house, leaving us alone. I began to follow him but papa restrained me.

"No, Tania. Confronting them is not the way."

"But papa, he's insane, whoever he is."

"Remember what our visitor told us, the one who is on his way to Murmansk. A new group of revolutionaries have come to power. He must be one of them."

We soon learned from our guards who the redheaded man was. They seemed eager to share what they were hearing.

"They call him the Bayonet. No one knows how many he killed in the bloody days after the Bolsheviks took over in Petrograd. Dozens. Maybe hundreds. He has the blood lust."

"They say he went insane while he was in prison. He was confined for fifteen years. Fifteen years alone, starving, craving food and light and heat. It's enough to make any man insane. Now he sits on the new Commission, the one they call the Cheka."

"I had not heard of that," papa remarked. "What is the Cheka?"

"The All-Russian Extraordinary Commission to Combat Counter-Revolution and Sabotage. The Cheka is deadly. They kill people, then they find excuses for what they did. That's what we hear."

"They kill anybody they dislike. The Bayonet does not spare anyone."

But he did, in the end, spare Daria and Iskra—only to order them locked in the basement of our house, in a sort of prison-within-a-prison, bitterly cold and damp and with only a single small stove to warm themselves by. A stove that worked badly and was poorly ventilated.

I thought of them there, night after night, huddled together in the cold and dark, and the thought weighed on me like lead, lowering my spirits still further. For I was already very low indeed. After what Kerensky had told us I dreaded that Michael had been killed in Petrograd, and I thought, once I am certain that he is dead, once I hear that terrible, final news, I won't want to live.

How can I describe the cold of that severe winter? I am Russian; I know cold. But the deep, penetrating, numbing cold of Siberia was new to me. It swept down upon us in a vengeful tide of ice, wind and darkness. It held us in its painful grip. It overwhelmed and weakened us, in body, mind and spirit.

Though we were indoors we felt the cold as if we had been caught shelterless in an unending storm. The cold came in right through the walls, coating every surface with a rime of frost. Whatever we put on the floor froze solid. Our feet turned blue inside their double coating of thick wool socks and felt boots.

The pipes froze and we had no water except meltwater from the ice. We boiled ice in a pan on top of our one stove, which we kept choked with firewood. The ice grew tepid, and melted, but the water never boiled—the air was too cold. So we had water to drink but no hot water to bathe in; we were both cold and dirty, and this added to our misery.

Worst of all was the wind that shrieked and howled like a live thing, as if all the furies of hell had been loosed and were bent on destroying us. Sometimes at night when we gathered around the stove, attempting to talk, mama trying to knit with her gloves on, Monsieur Gilliard trying to play chess with Olga or Anastasia, papa in his overcoat reading his thick volume of *Universal History* though the pages kept ruffling up and annoying him, the wind shrieked so loudly that talk was impossible and we clutched our ears with our hands.

The freezing blast came through every unsealed window, under every ill-fitting double door. It burned our lungs and made us cough. It burned our eyes and made them water. We tried to sing—singing always made us feel better—but the wind snatched the very breath from our mouths and we soon gave up.

The worst time of all was late at night, when we could no longer delay going to sleep. We shivered in our damp, comfortless beds, our fingers blue with frostbite and sore from chilblains. We swore, we prayed, we swore again, and in the end we sank into a chill slumber, dreaming of steambaths and blazing fireplaces and hot, sunlit beaches. Of anywhere that was not haunted by the merciless wind.

So much snow accumulated on the roof that papa was afraid it would cave in on us. Wrapped in his greatcoat, his head covered in layers of wool and fur, thick gloves on his hands that were already raw from chopping firewood—he went up on the roof and tried to scrape off the snow. But his efforts were wasted. The snow had turned to ice. We heard him trying in vain to smash the ice with his shovel, and we knew, though none of us said it aloud, that in his own way he was fighting, and fighting hard, not only against the ice but against all that assailed us: the cruel weather, the cruel soldiers and the murderous Bayonet, the unknown hardships that lay ahead. I felt so much pity for him in those moments that I can hardly convey it—a world of pity, just then, for the father I loved so much.

It was in those grey, despairing days that I began to fall ill.

I caught a chill, then began to burn with fever—a fever that rose, day by day, until Dr. Botkin became very concerned about me and asked our guards to allow me to be moved to the nearest large city where there was a well-equipped hospital. But of course this request was denied.

I was having a lot of trouble breathing and my heart was racing even though I was lying in bed, resting. Mama, the doctor and some of the nuns hovered over me, watching me. I was aware that I was watching them back, or trying to, but my concentration kept slipping, and soon I couldn't remember whether it was day or night, and my thoughts were confused.

I reached down and felt ice on my blankets, yet I was burning up. I felt hands rubbing my arms and legs to try to keep me warm—but whose hands? I heard voices, but could no longer tell whose they were.

I remember seeing the icon of St. Simon Verkhoturie, and hearing mama say, "He weeps for her."

I coughed, my teeth chattered with the cold and my chest hurt when I breathed. I reached out my hand, but Michael was not there to take it.

I tried to say his name. I knew that my lips moved, but I couldn't hear any sound other than the keening of the wind.

I closed my eyes. Someone was sobbing. Was it mama? I smelled papa's tobacco.

Then I seemed to slip downward, as if I were on a sled going down the side of an immense snow mountain, going faster and faster, wanting to stop but not being able to.

All was whiteness around me, and the only sound I heard was the muffled plop of snow falling in clumps from the branches of trees onto the frozen earth. Then silence.

Fifty-one

*I*s she dead?"

"No. But she hasn't moved in two days."

I felt a hand clasp mine, and I tried my best to squeeze the fingers. Strong, warm fingers. A man's fingers.

I continued to feel the touch of the warm hand, and to draw strength from its heat in the freezing cold room.

Then I felt something placed in my hand. It felt like a frozen stick.

"Hold this," a voice said. A comforting, loving voice. "Hold this, and it will help you get better."

"Is it Father Gregory's stick?" I managed to whisper.

"What do you think?"

I tried to put all my concentration into that stick. My thoughts began to cohere. And gradually, hour by hour, I began to feel a little better.

Grasping the stick, I remembered the time, long before, when I had put it onto Michael's damaged chest, when I was his nurse and he was near death in the crowded hospital. I remembered how the stick had put forth a bud, and then a sweet-smelling white flower. And Michael had come back to life and health.

Eventually I was able to open my eyes. The first thing I saw was—Michael! Alive and well, and grinning down at me. He took me in his arms and I could feel life and strength surging within me.

Everyone gathered around my bedside was smiling: mama, papa, my sisters and brother, the nuns, Monsieur Gilliard—and Daria and Iskra. Weak though I was, I did my best to smile back.

"Daria," I whispered. "You and Iskra were let out of the basement!"

"Only while the Bayonet is away. He has gone to the Regional Soviet Meeting in Ekaterinburg. He won't be back for days."

I clung to Michael, who hardly left my bedside. He insisted on taking care of me himself, as I had once cared for him. He fed me on black bread and soup, raw cabbage and radishes and very weak tea, and he sang to me and told me stories about Daghestan and Georgia, and his fellow soldiers, the men of the Fifth Circassian regiment.

"They are here, you know. In Tobolsk. Waiting for the time when they can be of use to your family. Some money has been raised. Weapons are being gathered. There are many groups here in Siberia eager to oppose the new Bolshevik government. It will be overthrown in time. I am confident of it. Petrograd will be retaken. Extremists like the Bayonet will be executed for their crimes."

Dr. Botkin came and put his stethoscope to my chest and listened to my heart and lungs.

"You are recovering, Tania, but you must not try to recover too quickly, especially in this icy house. You have had double pneumonia, and you could have a relapse." On his orders my bed was moved as close as possible to our one stove, and Michael built some makeshift screens to try to shield me from the constant drafts.

In a few days I was able to sit up, and my appetite improved—unfortunately, the food did not.

"Michael," I asked when we were alone, "however did you escape from Tsarskoe Selo? And how did you find me?"

"The worst time was right after I left you and your family there in the little cottage on the Children's Island. I ran into the woods, but the guards were everywhere on the island and I was sure they would find me. I couldn't see anywhere to hide. But I was lucky. They had been drinking all evening. I stumbled over one who had passed out. I put on his uniform. If only the night had been dark! Still, I managed to blend in with the others until I found my way to the elephant's enclosure. I went inside, and bribed the mahout to let me hide in his hut all night, under the pile of rags where he slept, until it was safe to leave the grounds.

"I don't mind telling you, Tania, I was terrified. In the morning I took a load of elephant dung in a wheelbarrow to the shed where the night soil man comes with his wagon to collect the waste to be dumped into the Stavyanka. No one questioned me—or wanted to get near me. Oh how I stank! I hid on the underside of the wagon until it went out to the river through one of the side gates. From there I was able to find my way to the garrison of the Semyonovsky regiment which I knew had many officers who were still loyal to your father and were opposed to the growing power of the Soviet.

"I was welcomed as a brother officer and given clothes and a little money. I said that I was in the personal service of the tsar (I did not call him the 'former tsar') and they applauded me and wished me well and told me of a special military train that was due to travel eastward in a day or two. Before I left I went in search of Constantin, who was in hiding. He was lucky to be alive. He was able to tell me where your family was to be taken.

"I got on the train and rode for four days but we were attacked near Perm by a force of Red Guards and the train was stopped. I stayed in a village on the edge of the Urals for a time, but had to move on when someone informed the local soviet of my presence there. I was nearly shot. Many others were not so lucky.

"I was told there were monarchist bandits in the foothills so I went in search of an outlaw band, hoping I might join them. They took me in because I was a soldier, and they needed training. I can tell you, Tania, the life of an outlaw is like the life I knew when I was a boy in the mountains of Daghestan. Completely free, with no one telling us how to live or what to do. My great-grandmother Lalako would have been right at home among those outlaws of the Urals. She would have wound up as their leader!

"I knew I had to get to Tiumen and hoped that I might be able to take the river steamer from there to Tobolsk. But by the time I finally reached Tiumen the river was frozen. I thought I might have to spend the winter there, in Tiumen, but there were wolf hunters setting out from the town in sledges and I managed to ride along with them. In time I found my way to the Ivanovsky convent and the nuns took me in. They told me all that had happened with your family—and that you were very sick and were not expected to live.

"I knew that the nuns came here to your compound every day with food and the newspapers. I decided to disguise myself as a farmer bringing butter and eggs and coffee. I became very popular with the guards—and your mama, who loves coffee. Even the Bayonet likes coffee, though he sometimes throws it in people's faces when he is displeased."

I held out my hands and Michael took them in his.

"What a lot you have gone through for me—and my family."

"I would do it again—a thousand times."

We embraced then, as if we would never let each other go, and I thanked heaven for bringing my Michael back to me.

"I must ask you one thing more," I said at length. "Why did you keep Father Gregory's stick with you all the way from Tsarskoe Selo?"

"What?" He laughed.

"The healing stick. The one that brought you back to life when you were wounded, and saved me from my pneumonia."

"Oh, that. That was just some stick I picked up in the yard. It was nothing special."

"But I thought—"

"I know what you thought. I knew you would think that. You needed to put your faith in something, so I found you a stick. The truth is, it was your own strength that saved you."

"No. It was my faith—and you. Promise me you won't leave me again, Michael. I couldn't bear it."

He leaned down and kissed me. "I couldn't either," he whispered. "Now, eat your soup."

Fifty-two

As I recovered, I noticed that the nuns who often came to sit at my bedside were sewing. They stitched so rapidly that their hands seemed almost to flow over the cloth, the tiny needle flashing as it went in and out of the woven fabric almost too quickly for the eye to follow. Sometimes they did embroidery, sometimes they made lace. But quite often, it seemed, they were stitching garments: their own black habits and white wimples, lavish vestments for the priests, and most often, clothing for the poor.

"Would you be so kind as to make us some new underwear?" I asked one day. "We have had none in almost a year. Ours have been patched and darned so many times there is almost nothing left of them."

I was assured that supplying new underwear for me and mama and my sisters would be no trouble at all, and in a matter of days a basket of petticoats and corsets and intimate undergarments was delivered to us, each garment very skillfully made though rather loose-fitting and without ornament.

"This is practical underwear," Olga said, holding up a petticoat. "Not stylish silk undergarments from Paris. Besides, what can nuns be expected to know about costly lingerie for fine ladies?"

"What impresses me," I said, "is how very quickly all this was sewn. I imagine these nuns could make a ball gown overnight if they were shown one to copy, and given all the materials."

"In the old days, before the war, Lamanov would take two or three weeks to make a ball gown for mama or Grandma Minnie."

"Yes, that's just what I mean. These nuns are so very quick!"

The Bayonet returned from his faraway meeting of the Regional Soviet and spread fear throughout the house. Daria and Iskra were shut in their cellar once again and Michael was forced to return to his refuge in the Ivanovsky convent, though he did visit every day with the nuns, bringing us his gifts of food and never forgetting the Bayonet's coffee.

The guards had begun to build a snow mountain in our small yard, but the Bayonet ordered it destroyed.

"Don't you know that the exploiter and his family could climb to the top of the mountain and see over the fence? Don't you realize they are conspiring with the Whites to destroy the revolution?"

The Whites was a term the Bolsheviks used to refer to anyone who opposed them.

"But the carnival is coming," I heard one of the guards protest. "We always have snow mountains at carnival season."

"What carnival?" barked the Bayonet. "Superstition, God-worship! That is all over and done with. There will be no carnival!"

But the townspeople of Tobolsk thought otherwise, and we could see, from our fog-shrouded window, that preparations for the pre-Lenten carnival were under way, whether the Bayonet and his Bolshevik superiors approved or not.

There had always been a week of celebration before the beginning of the Lenten season, Lent in Russia being the eight weeks preceding Easter Sunday. It was a tradition centuries old. It was called the Maslenitsa, or Butter Week, because of the butter we smothered over our sweet pancakes called blinis, butter that dripped deliciously down the chin and into the beard or onto the bosom. Butter that symbolized fat, and plenty, and looked forward to the end of the long hungry winter when food would be abundant again.

In Butter Week there were contests to see who could consume the most succulent blinis, filled with sweet fruit or jam or caviar, salmon or smelts from the White Sea. Michael joked that in this year of 1918 there would be only Bolshevik Blinis, filled with nothing, but unlike Petrograd, where there was mass starvation, Tobolsk had fresh game and fresh fish in the marketplace and stores of food from the farms and market gardens just outside the town, so I thought that the blinis would be filled to overflowing.

How I daydreamed of rich, good food in those days of thin cabbage soup and black bread and turnips! As I recovered my health my appetite returned, and even the smell of the Bayonet's coffee was enough to send my stomach churning and my thoughts racing. Try as I might to suppress the memories, I could not help but remember the banquets we had at the Winter Palace and at Tsarskoe Selo, the heaping platters of marinated mushrooms and anchovies, smoked salmon and herring, stuffed goose and puree of ham and broiled hare garnished with truffles. The pâtés, the escargots, the delicate sauces and tarts and éclairs. I have never been a gourmand but in those lean days my thoughts ran wild. I envisioned suckling pigs and grouse roasted in sour cream, reindeer steaks and Volga sterlet, tender white asparagus and iced puddings and cloudberries with sugar. My mouth watered and my poor stomach hurt.

I could not help remembering mama's Cousin Bertie at Cowes with his jars of Bar-le-Duc jam. How he ate! I wondered what he would think if he could see our family now, thin from deprivation, shivering in our icebox of a house, and humiliated in a way he could never have imagined royalty being humiliated. But then, Cousin Bertie would never have allowed this to happen to us. He would not have been cautious, as his son King George was, fearful of intervening in Russian affairs to rescue us even though he knew our lives were at risk. No! Cousin Bertie would have sent his army and his navy and all the forces at his command to rescue us, and would not have been satisfied until we were sitting at his table again, enjoying the bounty from his kitchens.

The English were not at hand, but we were learning that there were others who had our best interests at heart and who were busy making plans to aid us.

There was a kitchen accident and one of our cooks was badly burned. An old man was brought in to replace him—at least he seemed old to me, young as I was then. Probably he was no older than my father. He had been working in the nuns' kitchen, but I heard one of the nuns tell our head guard that they could spare him since our kitchen was understaffed.

I noticed that the old man, who was bald and slightly bent, but still spry, was making himself useful not only as a cook but outside the kitchen as well, sweeping the rooms, cleaning the windows (a hopeless task, since as soon as the frost was cleared away new frost accumulated), and even helping papa chop wood.

Our wood supply was running low. Our family's one stove, the kitchen fires, and the stove in the basement that kept Daria and Iskra alive were consuming more wood than we could chop. The Bayonet ordered thick beech trunks brought into the yard and papa worked for hours every day reducing them to sticks of firewood that would fit in the stoves. Despite Dr. Botkin's cautions about the state of my lungs I went outside and did my best to help papa, small though my contribution to the woodpile was. It was too cold for my sisters; they stayed inside.

One afternoon the old bald servant came out as usual to offer his assistance. He bent down to pick up his axe—but instead of bringing the axe down on the chunk of wood before him I saw him look toward the house. It was a frigid day, the guards had gone inside to avoid the wind. No one was observing us. The old man turned to papa, with a look on his face of such benign reverence that it went to my heart.

Then he knelt in the snow at papa's feet.

"Babiushka," he murmured. "Babiushka, Little Father, we are here to help you."

I saw tears in my father's eyes.

"Who are you?"

The old man got to his feet again.

"I am Georgy Kochetkov," he whispered, "leader of the Brotherhood of St. John."

"A religious order?"

"No—but we are inspired by the patron saint of Tobolsk, St. John, and the Cathedral of St. John is our headquarters." He looked around, and saw that three of the guards had come out into the yard but were staying in a cluster near the door to the house, as if eager to go back in and get warm again.

"We have a cache of weapons in the basement," Georgy confided. "The cathedral is our rallying point—for when we retake the town."

Papa's eyebrows rose in surprise.

"How many of you are there in this brotherhood?"

"More every day."

"You there!" It was the harsh voice of the Bayonet. "What are you talking about? I demand to know!"

He had come out of the house and was striding across the snow toward us, bareheaded despite the cold, his long red hair flying, his nose turning red as well.

Georgy bowed deeply. "Your worship, I was saying I had never seen a winter as harsh as this one, not in all my seventy years."

So I had been wrong about his age. He was not of my father's generation, he was an exceptionally fit old man.

The Bayonet frowned.

"Seventy years in Siberia! It's a wonder you're not dead! You will be soon enough if you keep talking to the exploiter!"

"Yes, your worship."

His posture submissive, Georgy moved off, toward the far corner of the yard where he began chopping at a log. We resumed our work. The Bayonet stood watching the old man for a time, then shrugged and went back into the house.

After about fifteen minutes Georgy brought an armload of wood to add to our accumulation. He dropped it in the snow, then began stacking it carefully alongside our pile. As he did so he whispered to papa once again.

"Little Father, there are many in Tobolsk who hate the revolution. We hate these new men, these brutal, cruel men who claim to speak for the people. Who are they really? Criminals! Traitors to the true Russia!

"We are growing strong in numbers. Some of us are landowners like myself who fear that the peasants will seize our estates and murder us. Some are soldiers. There are three hundred officers of the Tiumen garrison who are pledged to support us when the time comes for our rising."

He took another quick look around the yard, then went on, keeping his voice very low.

"Money is being raised. Contributions are pouring in to our banker in Tiumen. There is another banker in Petrograd who is secretly collecting funds from all over Russia. I hear he has already raised two hundred thousand rubles. We want our tsar back!"

I watched papa's face as he heard these remarkable words. It seemed alight from within.

"Is it possible!" he whispered, shaking his head in disbelief. "Is it really possible!"

"Our aim is to seize Tobolsk when the thaw comes," Georgy said. "Tobolsk will become the new capital of Russia, with you, Little Father, restored to your throne and your rights.

"Meanwhile we are recruiting more aid, and our numbers are growing. Your wife's oculist and dentist carry messages for us, and your laundress too."

"And does the Bayonet suspect how strong you are?"

"He suspects everyone. He knows that as long as you are alive, there will be opposition to the Bolsheviks and their aims. But he cannot convince his superiors in Moscow to order your execution. They think you may be more useful to them alive than dead."

"If only we could be sure of that!"

"Certainty is the one thing we cannot be certain of," Georgy whispered, with a wry smile.

We had read in the newspaper that the Bolshevik government had declared Moscow to be the new capital of Russia, and that all their orders now came from there. They had, it seemed, abandoned poor Petrograd to its fate. Beautiful, sad Petrograd! I could hardly bear to think of it.

Georgy went back to his far corner of the yard and we continued to hear the sound of his axe biting into the stubborn wood, though the daylight was beginning to fail and the wind was growing colder.

Eventually papa and I each took an armful of firewood into the house and left him there. But all that evening papa's thin face glowed with happiness, and he could not seem to stop smiling, at us, at the guards, at the weeping icon that hung near the stove.

It was the icon of St. John.

Fifty-three

I collected all our dirty laundry in a large basket and waited by the door for the laundress to arrive, as she did each Wednesday. I tried to avoid reacting to the snickering of the guards, who rummaged through the basket, making off-color jokes and tossing our underwear back and forth to each other. It was an old routine by then, it had become tiresome.

Several nuns arrived along with the laundress, who brought with her a basket of clean clothes and linens.

"Be sure to hang out the blue petticoat," one of the nuns remarked to me. "It is not quite dry. Hang it by the stove."

I took the basket to the bedroom I shared with my sisters, as I always did, and began to sort and fold the clothes, looking eagerly for the blue petticoat. I had no doubt the nun had mentioned it for a reason. When I found it I hung it on a hanger and took it into the sitting room and draped it over a chair, smoothing out the wrinkles but actually feeling in the folds and creases of the fabric for any irregularity. In a pocket of the bodice I felt the hard edge of a folded paper. I managed to slip the small paper out and conceal it in my sleeve.

I took it into the bathroom and quickly unfolded it—aware that even in the bathroom I had no privacy, as the guards liked to burst in on us at our most intimate moments.

"Come down to the basement when everyone else has gone to bed," the note read, in Michael's small spiky handwriting.

I tore it into tiny pieces and flushed the pieces away, worrying that they might not disappear but be spewed up again by the faulty toilet. When I had flushed three times I felt confident enough to leave the bathroom and go and sit with mama, who was knitting a sweater. She had dark circles under her eyes. She greeted me with a wan smile. I noticed the vial of Veronal on the table beside her, and a glass half full of cloudy water—she continued to increase the amount of Veronal she took each day, sipping from a water glass with ten or twelve drops of the sedative in it—and several letters.

"Did you know, Tania, that this is the feast day of St. Euthymius? No—wait—I believe it is St. Alexis, or perhaps the Feast of the Most Holy Mother—" She broke off in confusion, worry lines deepening on her white brow. "I have it written here somewhere." She put down her knitting and searched in the blanket covering her legs for something. "Never mind, I can't find it."

"Your calendar?"

"Yes. My calendar of saints' days and feasts."

"I would have thought you knew them all by heart."

She shook her head, a rueful half-smile on her pale lips. "My memory—so poor these days—"

She took up her knitting again, and I noticed that the pattern of white stripes running through the grey wool was askew; mama, whose knitting was always so precise, the stitches uniform and flawless, the colors in perfect alignment, was becoming sloppy and careless.

"It must be hard, knitting with your gloves on."

"I have gotten used to it. But my fingers hurt." She yawned.

"Shall we have a game of bezique later?"

"If you like dear. I have some letters to write." She trailed off, as if her thoughts had wandered. "Do you know, Tania, that there is some lady in this town who is writing me letters in Old Church Slavonic?"

"Can you read them?"

"A little. But it tires my brain."

"They could be important, you know. They could help us."

She looked befuddled. "I don't see how." Her face brightened. "At first I thought they might be coming from mama. But I don't think mama ever learned Old Church Slavonic."

I knew that there was no point in trying to explain to her that the letters might be from the Brotherhood of St. John (of which she knew nothing), and that they might contain instructions or encouraging information. I wondered, did the nuns read the obscure old church language? Did Georgy Kochetkov know it, or was he in contact with someone who did?

I was excited and anxious all that day, waiting for the hour when the family went to bed—usually about ten o'clock—and most of the guards too retired, leaving only two or three men who dozed beside the stove all night and sentries who watched the outer doors to the basement and main house.

It was not thought necessary to post guards outside during the night; were anyone so foolhardy as to venture into the extreme cold of a Siberian midnight unprepared, so we were told, their skin would freeze in less than a minute and in another minute, when the cold had penetrated their forehead, they would be unconscious.

Come down to the basement, Michael had written. Putting on every garment I possessed, my woolen socks and felt boots, I took a lantern and crept down the stairs into the basement. I stepped out onto the floor of frozen earth and waited.

It was a dirty, damp basement that smelled of mold, empty save for an ancient coffin-sized chest, its lid torn away, its metal hinges rusty. Daria and Iskra, I knew, were in a locked pantry at the far end of the room. I heard no sound and thought they must be asleep. I shone my lantern around the walls. Like the floor, they were of frozen earth. Nothing in the room offered a scrap of comfort or character. It was dark, bleak and empty with the dispiriting emptiness of extreme cold.

Before long I heard a very faint sound.

At first I thought it might be coming from the pantry, but then I realized it was closer than that. It seemed to be coming from the dilapidated chest.

I walked closer to the chest, shone the lantern down into it, and peered in.

I almost shrieked when the sound came again and the wooden bottom of the chest began to move. It rose slowly upward, as if on hinges.

"Tania?"

"Michael? Please say that it's you, Michael!"

With a creak the wooden slab rose higher still, and now I could see a fur-clad arm, and then a head—Michael's head, encased in hat and scarf—and finally the thick slab was upended and the lantern shone down on another staircase.

"Come," he said, and reached out for me. I took his hand and followed him down the wide set of stairs, pausing while he closed the false bottom of the chest over our heads.

"You'll never guess where this leads," he said as we went on, my lantern showing the way, along a narrow passage that led into darkness.

Fifty-four

It really did seem, for awhile at least, as though our liberation was at hand. The passage Michael led me along on the night I met him in the basement of the Governor's Mansion went all the way to the basement of the Ivanovsky convent.

An escape route for us all!

He explained that the nuns had revealed to him the existence of the passage, which had been built by the former governor of Tobolsk in case he and his family needed to leave their house quickly in an emergency. No one besides Michael and the dozen or so of his fellow-soldiers in the Fifth Circassian regiment who had followed him to Tobolsk knew about it. Neither the Bayonet nor our tormenting guards suspected its existence.

"So this way out has been here all along, ever since we were first brought here, only we didn't know it!" I exclaimed as we made our way along, Michael walking ahead of me, the passage so narrow that my shoulders brushed against the cold walls with every step.

"We only learned of it a few weeks ago," Michael said. "The nuns didn't tell us right away. They had to make sure they could trust us with your lives."

But the question remained, if my entire family went along the passage to temporary safety among the nuns, where were we to go after reaching the convent?

The river was frozen; we could not leave the town by boat. To attempt to travel overland by sleigh was treacherous in winter, even if enough changes of horses could be provided. To hide our family in the convent basement would be futile, as there was a price on papa's head— a high price of five thousand rubles, Michael heard in the marketplace— and beyond that, we felt certain that if we were to try to hide among the nuns, somehow our presence would become known and someone in the town would betray us.

The Brotherhood of St. John had a ready answer to the question of where we would go: we would not go anywhere! Georgy Kochetkov advised us to stay where we were, freezing in the Governor's Mansion, until the spring thaw began. Then the Brotherhood would seize the town and expel the Bolsheviks. Once the Bolsheviks were gone, the Brotherhood, acting for the Russian people as a whole, would crown papa tsar once again (they had elaborate plans for the coronation) and make Tobolsk the center of a glorious new Romanov realm.

So for the time being we stayed.

Meanwhile Butter Week was approaching. Already the bakers were beginning to sell the little cakes called larks, in the shape of birds with thin pastry legs and currants for eyes, that were the herald of the Maslenitsa. In the warmer corners of farmhouses and town kitchens, milk was being churned into butter, cheese was being made, and in the town square, carpenters were constructing booths where nuts and gingerbread and bonbons would be offered for sale. Tobolsk was filling with people arriving for the holiday; we heard the jingling of sleigh bells in the street below more frequently than in the past, and knew that traffic was increasing. We also heard, though more faintly, the music of the merry-go-round that was being hauled out from its storage in the basement of the town hall and put together, piece by painted piece, on the snowy swath of land in the main square.

The Bayonet found two of the guards drunk on red currant vodka (a variety always supplied in abundance during Butter Week) and angrily ordered them to be shut in the cellar next to Daria and Iskra. We heard their raucous singing as we sat eating our meager dinner on the upper floor.

"We'll hear no more singing when they have gone without food for a few days," the Bayonet snapped. But they continued to sing, hour after hour, despite his orders, and Georgy whispered to us when he collected our plates that the other guards were secretly ignoring the Bayonet's commands and giving their imprisoned colleagues food and more vodka.

Whether it was because of the approach of the festival or because of a growing rift between the guards and their Cheka commander it was evident to us all that the guards were growing more lax, and even disobedient. They did not watch us as closely as before, and they seemed not to care nearly as much as in the past what we did or said.

"Do you suppose it is a trick?" I asked Michael. "Are they trying to entrap us, to fool us into thinking we can do whatever we like, and then, when we do something wrong, arrest us and send us to Moscow?"

"I can't tell, but I do know this: the guards complain that they haven't been paid in three months, and the Bayonet is trying to replace them with Red Guards brought from Ekaterinburg, and they know it."

"Starving people right before the Maslenitsa is not right," I overheard one of the guards say to another, referring to their drunken colleagues. "Nobody deserves that. Not after what we've had to deal with this winter."

"You mean who we've had to deal with," his companion muttered, with a wry smile.

The two imprisoned soldiers continued to receive their clandestine meals, and after a week they were back among us, looking no thinner than before their drunken binge. I wondered why the Bayonet did nothing to punish those who had disobeyed him.

"Perhaps he is getting into the spirit of the season," Georgy remarked as he was cleaning our rooms, referring to the Bayonet. "We have a splendid carnival here in Tobolsk every winter. Not only plenty of good food but lots of entertainment. Plays and shows, jugglers and clowns, all sorts of performers in costume. Everybody dresses up, even the tea vendors and the candy sellers. It wouldn't be Butter Week without all the play-acting and disguises. I myself will be dressing up as Tsar Peter the Great."

"If only they would let us join in and have fun," Anastasia said wistfully. "I want to slide down the ice mountain."

"And I want to ride in a sleigh," Alexei added. "I haven't ridden in a sleigh in so long." He rubbed his knee as he spoke, and I noticed that it was slightly swollen.

"Did you bump your knee, Alexei?" I asked him.

"Only a little. It only hurts a little."

"You'd better have Dr. Botkin look at it."

But despite the concern and very limited ministrations of Dr. Botkin—for there was really nothing any physician could do for his illness—Alexei's knee continued to swell, and within a few hours his entire leg was growing stiff and sore and the next day it was completely engorged with blood and he was moaning with pain.

The nuns came to pray over him, and mama sent Sedynov to hold the icon of St. Simon Verkhoturie above his chilly bed. Michael told him funny stories and made him laugh, even as he winced with the pain and shivered in the cold. We all took turns sitting by his bedside. He was brave, and endured much. As usual when he had a severe attack, he had no appetite and he looked alarmingly pale.

Although I tried to drive morbid thoughts from my mind, I couldn't help remembering how, when he was much younger, a coffin was kept ready in his nursery at all times, lined with purple velvet and decorated with gold leaf. Then he had been heir to the throne of Russia, now he was just a prisoner of the Military Revolutionary Committee, a thin thirteen-year-old boy in pain, a boy whose life or death was no longer of much consequence outside of his family and who, if he died, would lie unregarded in a shallow pauper's grave.

Fifty-five

"*Wake up! Get* up! Get dressed!*"

The Bayonet had a voice that was an assault; his raw screech attacked us very early one dark cold morning and I could tell at once that something important had happened.

"What is it? Why do we have to get up?"

As usual he ignored all questions and concentrated his energy on yelling at us and at the guards, who were also crudely roused from their slumbers and lined up, ready to receive his orders.

I looked at the clock. It was not yet six in the morning.

When we had washed, as quickly as we could, from the bucket of meltwater on top of the stove and put on our clean but rumpled clothes he looked us over.

"Coats! Hats! Boots!"

Olga and I looked at each other in astonishment. We were going outside! And not just into the yard, it seemed, but into the town. A first, in all those months! But why? Were we going to be put on public trial?

There was a squabble, first over Alexei, who was far too ill to be moved, and then over mama's wheeled chair, which she insisted she needed, because she could not walk very well on her bad leg. The Bayonet was insulting, mama was insistent—though her querulous tone was much more feeble than in the past—and in the end the long-unused chair was found and one of the guards assigned to push her.

When we went outside the cold assaulted us far more cruelly than the voice of the Bayonet. We were driven, sleigh bells jingling, in a closed carriage along Freedom Street to a large two-story building and taken inside. It was the town hall.

As soon as we went inside a blast of hot air shocked us with its very welcome embrace. We were in a spacious candlelit wood-paneled room with not one but three stoves, and we sat down gratefully next to the nearest of them, luxuriating in the unaccustomed warmth. The room was full of benches crudely made from split logs, evidently more people were expected.

For several hours we waited there, as the room slowly filled with townspeople who nodded and bowed to us, some kneeling briefly to papa. There was a raised stage at the front of the hall with several long tables and a dozen chairs arranged around them. Men I assumed to be town officials took their seats on the stage. None of the men, I noticed, had the keen-eyed, lean and hungry look of dedicated revolutionaries, nor the brusque, nervous energy of the former prime minister Kerensky. Instead they looked like prosperous country folk, unaffected as yet by the unsettling events in Petrograd and more recently in Moscow, men and women who had not yet begun to appreciate the extent of the political upheaval going on in their midst.

I was aware of a stirring in the room, a ripple of excitement. Two men entered, walking side by side in a companionable way, nodding to those in the audience as they approached the stage. One of the men was dark-haired, burly and bearded, wearing the rough shirt of a laborer and trousers held up by a rope belt. The other, tall, blond and handsome in his white naval uniform and long golden sword—was Adalbert!

I blinked. I looked more closely. But I was not mistaken. It was indeed Adalbert, confident, smiling, looking every inch the prince he was, and looking benign as well, despite his naval uniform. I hardly had time to grasp the improbable sight of Adalbert when I realized that he and his companion were coming toward us.

"Sir," Adalbert said, bowing to papa and also to mama, who very pointedly avoided meeting his eyes.

"And Tania." Smiling broadly, he reached for my hand and raised it to his lips, which led to an audible murmur of surprised approval from the onlookers. "What a beautiful woman you have become!"

Oh no, I was thinking. I am too thin, my clothes are shamefully plain, my hair needs arranging, and my poor hand—the hand you kiss—is scarred from chilblains.

"This beautiful woman," Adalbert was saying to his bearded companion, "once did me the honor of considering becoming my wife. But we were kept apart by—political circumstances."

"How very unfortunate," the bearded man responded, looking at me so intently that I was in no doubt he meant to convey something of vital importance. His wordless message could only mean one thing: that Adalbert's presence in Tobolsk was for the benefit of our family.

"I'm so very glad to see you Adalbert," I said, kissing his cheek in what I hoped was a familial way, "so very glad."

"Dear Tania, we must talk after this meeting concludes. Promise me you will."

"If the guards permit."

"I think we can persuade them," the burly man assured me with a slight smile.

Adalbert and his companion climbed the steps onto the stage and the audience rose. The burly man began to sing the "Internationale," the anthem of the revolution, and a number of voices joined in. My family kept silent, though I'm sorry to say we did know the song well, having heard it sung and whistled and hummed so many times by the soldiers. Even the Bayonet bawled it out stridently on occasion.

When the song was ended everyone sat down again, but the burly man kept standing.

"Comrades," he began, "some of you know me but many of you don't. Let me introduce myself. I am Commissar Yuri Pyatakov. I am sent here by the Military Revolutionary Committee in Moscow, of which I am a member. I bring with me my friend Prince Adalbert who comes to us, not as our adversary from the German Empire, but as an emissary of future peace and good will. But I will let him enlighten you further. Comrades, I give you Prince Adalbert. I will translate his words."

Mild applause greeted this announcement as Adalbert stood and began to speak. I heard mama whisper loudly, "What's he doing here?

What does he want?" Because her own hearing was failing, she spoke more loudly than she should have, and her words were overheard. I saw some of those sitting near us look at her with puzzled expressions.

"My new Russian friends," Adalbert began, his warmth and sincerity apparent, "I bring good news. A peace agreement is being reached between the Military Revolutionary Committee and the Central Powers. Your commissar Pyatakov and I, along with many others, are privileged to serve as negotiators of this most welcome peace." There was a pause while the commissar turned Adalbert's German sentiments into Russian.

At first there was no response from the listeners, only silence, but then, gradually, there came a trickle of applause that broadened into a resounding, then a thunderous ovation. People around us, as they realized the full implications of what was being said, wept openly, hugged one another and shouted approval. Some even went forward toward the stage and reached out toward the commissar and Adalbert in gestures of thanks and good will.

But papa, who not only had worn his old soldier's shirt, khaki trousers and scuffed officer's boots but had added his officer's epaulets that day in defiance of the Bayonet and our guards, sat silent, his head in his hands.

"I too rejoice," Adalbert said as he resumed speaking once the hubbub in the room died down. "More than you can know. When I was young, before this terrible war swept across Europe, I was a man of peace. I came to Russia with the Young People's Peace Initiative, a group drawn from many countries—France, Sweden, Italy, even England. We were joined in a common purpose: to be a living example of cooperation between countries and nationalities, to show that we can understand one another and not provoke each other to conflict. I believed in that mission. Despite all that has happened to me and to my country and yours, I still believe in it."

Once again there was a delay while the commissar translated, then more applause.

"And my friend Yuri, who was also a member of the Peace Initiative, and whom I met here in Russia all those years ago, believes in it with me."

Yuri translated, then bowed to Adalbert, and the two men embraced. It was such an emotional moment that I was quite overcome. All the ideals I wanted to believe in but had put out of my heart and mind for so long—goodness, hope, trust, the tight human bonds that develop and flourish when unselfishness prevails—seemed alive in that overheated room, and I allowed myself to believe in them again.

"Much has changed in the years since I first came to Russia," Adalbert was saying. "I served my country in the war. I was wounded. My ship was hit by a British shell and sank under me, and I lost many dear friends and fine officers and sailors on that horrible day. I almost drowned. Throughout the war I did my duty—and I was lucky. I survived. Many of those who served alongside me did not.

"And I am only too aware, looking around this room, that many of you here lost sons and brothers and fathers in the war. Much courageous Russian blood was spilled. May it never, ever, happen again!"

"Never again, never again," I heard many in the audience murmur, as they crossed themselves.

"Never again!" came a rough-voiced shout from the back of the room. "Never again! What nonsense! Wake up, comrades! Right now, today, this very day, Russians are fighting! Not the Germans but each other! The armies of the Whites are attacking, good revolutionaries are dying!! This man—this German in his fancy uniform—he wants to weaken you, to turn you into old women, gutless, spineless babies!"

"Who is that!" barked Pyatakov. "Arrest him at once!"

It was the Bayonet, roused to fury by all the talk of peace.

"You can't arrest me! I am sent here from the Ekaterinburg Soviet to fight for the revolution!"

"And I," thundered Pyatakov, "am sent from Moscow, to speak of peace, and I order your immediate arrest!" Cursing and protesting, the Bayonet was seized by soldiers standing near him who had been guarding the doorway, and thrust outside into the cold.

"Now," the commissar went on, "we can conclude our meeting." He composed himself, looked at Adalbert, and spoke again. "Once when I was a boy," he said in a confiding tone, "I studied to be a priest. I enrolled in a distinguished seminary, and I worked very hard at my studies for years, hoping to be worthy of my calling. I no longer profess the Christianity of my youth, instead I have put my faith in you, the Russian people, and in others of like minds who hope to build a better future for us all. But I still pray—not to the Christian God, but to humanity. To the best in all of us. In that spirit, let us join together in solemn supplication."

Those around me bowed their heads. The room grew very still— except for the faint yelling of the Bayonet, who was evidently continuing his protests outside in the street.

"Great spirit of hope that unites us all," the commissar began, "give us courage to look beyond what divides us. Bring us together. Give us peace. Let us join hands, friend to friend. Let those hands reach throughout the world, until all conflict ends, even such conflict as may arise in our midst. We ask this in the name of humanity, amen."

As he spoke, there was shuffling sound as hands reached out, clasped, and held. I reached for Olga's hand on one side, and Marie's on the other. It was a moment I will never forget, as long as I live.

Fifty-six

I stayed behind as the people in the Tobolsk town hall filed out of the meeting, their faces, as it seemed to me, alight with hope and uplift. I was waiting to talk to Adalbert, and I said as much to papa, whose spirits seemed to me as low as those of the people of Tobolsk were high.

"Do what you like, Tania. This is a sorry day for Russia. A day of dishonor and loss."

"But at least there will be an honorable peace."

Papa shook his head, a wry smile on his thin lips. "I wouldn't be so sure of that. Come girls," he said to my sisters. He began slowly walking toward the exit, pushing mama's wheeled chair in front of him.

"It's an outrage," I heard her mutter to no one in particular. "Imagine that boy coming here. An outrage!"

"I feel sure Adalbert has come here in order to arrange for our release," I murmured to papa. "Surely that is some comfort."

"A German? Don't you know, Tania, that the Germans have stolen nearly a third of our country? And the richest third at that! You can be sure their theft will be in your precious peace treaty! And as to your friend Adalbert, I suspect he is at best misguided. The Bolsheviks are using him to gain their own ends."

"I'll see when I talk to him."

There was no sign of the Bayonet but our guards came forward to take the family back to the Governor's Mansion.

"The girl stays," Yuri Pyatakov called out to the guards from the stage. I looked up and saw that Adalbert was beckoning me to climb the steps and join him and the commissar.

"That was a beautiful speech you made," I said to him when I had gone up onto the stage.

"It was from my heart."

"But did you see how papa reacted? He has become cynical. He distrusts everyone, even you. And mama wouldn't even look at you. I was ashamed for both of them."

"I can understand how he feels. His pride has been injured by Russia's defeat. No doubt he feels responsible."

"But he was forced to abdicate," I said. "He wasn't the one who lost the war."

"Wasn't he? Admit the truth, Tania. He was a poor commander. He got worse as the war went on. He was the one who allowed Russia to fall into ruin, because he did nothing to prevent it."

Though it pained me to admit it, I knew that Adalbert was right, and I nodded.

"But the responsibility for the war is not his alone. My father has far more to answer for. He was the aggressor. Just as when we met at Cowes, and my father was bullying the other yachtsmen into racing him, so he could win."

"And win by cheating."

"Yes."

We looked at one another, both sorrowful, both filled with regret. "How long ago it all seems!"

"No need to look back now—only forward," said Pyatakov. "Blaming will not help us. Besides, we are here in Tobolsk to talk of something else, are we not?"

Once again I nodded. "I hope so."

"We may speak freely here. I have made certain of that." He paused, then went on. "Tania, the Committee in Moscow is divided over the question of how to deal with your family. It is a grim decision, and must be made soon. Adalbert assures me that I can be frank with you, that you are brave enough to face the truth. Is he right?"

I took a deep breath. "Yes," I said.

"Well, here it is. There are many who want your family eliminated. As quickly as possible. Then there are others, like me, who want you all to be simply removed, out of Russia, with guarantees that you will not cooperate with any individuals or governments who may attempt to restore Romanov rule.

"But the argument always arises that wherever you are living, either in Siberia or London or Denmark—those being the three most likely places—you will attract enormous publicity and sympathy, and all the forces that hate our revolution will rally around your father and your brother as his heir. Even if he gives his word not to meet with them or encourage them, he will inevitably become their champion. They will raise money, buy arms, recruit or hire fighting men. Your father will become a Cause, and we, the Committee in Moscow, will be made to look like devils."

"Surely you look that way already for deposing my father and keeping our family in such miserable captivity."

"My own view is that if we arrange your family's release we will look merciful. And we will save many lives."

For a moment I hesitated, wondering whether I ought to trust the commissar and Adalbert with the information I had about the Brotherhood. I decided to go ahead.

"It is happening already. There is a group—"

Pyatakov laughed. "Oh, so you have heard about the Brotherhood. We know all about them. You mustn't take them seriously. They are just a group of old men, full of fantasies of military glory. Their guns are rusty and they haven't the least idea how to fight against a real army, certainly not our Red Army. Have you heard that they have thousands of members, thousands of supporters?"

"Yes."

He chuckled. "Idle dreams, idle dreams, as your father used to say years ago about the dream of democracy in Russia." But then his expression hardened. "The Brotherhood is no threat to us and never will be. But there are others who are gathering dangerous weapons and recruiting young men, men who do know how to fight. Foreign governments are encouraging them and even supporting them. I'm afraid that hothead who was shouting about warfare in the back of the hall here was quite right. Russia is at war with itself, and the war will be spreading. The revolution is already under assault. A day of reckoning is coming. Before that day arrives, I want very much to ensure that your family has been sent away to safety."

"That is why I am here, Tania," Adalbert broke in. "I came with an escort of soldiers. Not Red Guards. They are waiting in Tiumen. I have troikas to take you to there."

"When can we leave?"

"Ah, that is the difficulty," the commissar said. "I must convince the Ekaterinburg soviet to let you leave. And I have just arrested one of its most vociferous members."

"We call him the Bayonet. He is cruel. Even to his own men. He is always threatening to bring in Red Guards to watch us."

"It may be necessary for you to arrange to leave Tobolsk without his permission, without the Ekaterinburg Soviet's permission. Can you do that?"

"I don't know. I will try."

"It must be done quickly, Tania. I'm not sure how much longer I can keep the soldiers here safely."

"I will do my best. The nuns from the Ivanovsky convent come to the Governor's Mansion every day. They carry messages for us. Where can you be reached?"

"I am staying with the mayor," Pyatakov said. "Adalbert is also a guest in the mayoral lodge. But the mayor must not know of our plan. When you escape, he will be blamed."

"I understand." I looked at the commissar, with his burning eyes and thick beard, and was reminded of what he had said about being a seminarian in his youth.

"Commissar," I said, "you once studied for the priesthood. Tell me, can you read Old Church Slavonic?"

"I have studied it, yes. But I am not really proficient. Why do you ask?"

"My mother has been receiving anonymous notes in a language she believes may be Old Church Slavonic, but she can't read it. Here is one of them."

I took a scrap of paper from my pocket and handed it to Pyatakov.

"It says, 'A message awaits. MM. Ivanovsky.'"

"The Ivanovsky convent. But who or what is MM?"

I had no idea. But I decided to ask the nuns. Adalbert and the commissar took me in their sleigh to the convent and waited while I made my inquiry.

"Have you a message from someone named MM, or some group that might call itself MM?" I asked the sister who came out to greet me.

"The starets?"

"Perhaps. Just MM."

"There is an ancient starets who lives in a small izba on our grounds. She is a hundred and ten years old and she remembers Napoleon. She never leaves her izba. Would you like to meet her?"

"Please."

"Come this evening, after vespers."

Once I was back in the Governor's Mansion I sent a message to Michael to meet me in the convent basement at dusk. Just as it was getting dark I managed to make my way down into the basement of the mansion and then along the cold dark passageway that connected the mansion and the convent.

Michael was waiting for me and I told him, full of excitement, all that had happened that day.

"At last!" he burst out, nearly shouting. "Real help, at last! And a goodhearted commissar. Can it be possible?" He threw his arms around me and I hugged him tight.

"I can't believe that Adalbert would put his trust in a betrayer."

"It seems too good to be true. We must be very sure."

"That is one reason I wanted to come here, to meet this woman who has been sending notes to mama."

We were shown the way to the small log hut where the starets, whose name was Maria Michaelovna, spent her days. The convent grounds were quite large and the little hut was hidden within a wood, out of sight of the church and nuns' quarters. Even though we had wrapped ourselves up as best we could against the cold, we shivered as we made our way along, lanterns swinging, through the snow. Finally we reached the door and knocked.

"Come in, children." The voice we heard was high and shrill.

We went inside and shut the door quickly behind us. A single candle burned in the humble room, its light so dim we could barely make out the small, frail body of the starets, lying on her bed. I had never before seen anyone so old, her face as wrinkled and shriveled as a raisin, surrounded by its aureole of scraggly white hair. Yet when we brought our lanterns close and sat down beside the bed, we could see that it was a sweet face, the eyes young and shining, the smile benign and comforting.

The starets held out her thin hand in blessing.

"Be joyous uncrowned bride and bridegroom," she said. "The war is ending, they are ending it. The good men. You will live, you will marry and have many children. You will not live in Russia."

She pointed to the locket I was wearing on a chain around my neck. I opened it and bent down to show her the two small photographs it contained—photographs of my parents, taken at the time of their engagement many years before.

"The heavy cross is upon them," she said, her voice faltering. "They need not fear it, but meet it with joy. It is their blessed fate."

At the old woman's words my heart turned to stone.

"No. No, you must be wrong. There is no heavy cross any more, no doom. We are going to be rescued, and very soon."

The starets's eyes grew sad. She shook her small head.

"They are the martyrs Nicholas and Alexandra."

I stumbled to the door of the izba and went outside. Michael soon followed me.

"She's just an old woman, Tania. She doesn't know what happened today. How could she?"

But I could only shake my head and repeat no, no again and again, in a vain effort to shake off and deny the force of the starets's words.

"Remember the stick, Tania. You thought it was special, blessed by Father Gregory, and so you got well. But it was only a stick. You cured yourself! Don't give power to this woman's gloomy visions by believing in them. Believe in yourself, and in me, and in your friend Adalbert and the commissar. Believe that you and your family will soon be out of Tobolsk, and on your way to freedom, and it will happen!"

Fifty-seven

I lay awake all that night in the cold, turning over and over in my mind the events of that long day. The hope, the promise of rescue—and the chilling prophecy of the aged starets. I tried to force myself to think in practical, logical terms. How could I manage to smuggle my entire family out of the Governor's Mansion and to some safe place where we could meet Adalbert and his soldiers? How could this be done without awakening our guards' suspicions or alerting the mayor of the town to our plans?

We would have to leave everything behind, I felt certain. But that ought not to matter—all that ought to matter was that our lives would be saved.

I thought and thought, and every time I glimpsed a possible plan I also began to see reasons why it would not work. Finally toward morning I dropped into an exhausted sleep.

I dreamed of freedom, of running through the woods on a warm summer afternoon with no one to stop me or restrict me. I dreamed of the old starets, lying on her bed, shriveled and dying. And then I dreamed of the revelers I had seen as Adalbert and the commissar drove me through the streets on our way to the convent. There were so many of them, people wearing fantastic carnival costumes—birds, fish, cows, mythical monsters, the fearsome witch Baba Yaga and other characters from folk tales. They wore elaborate masks, painted and decorated with feathers, spangles, grinning mouths and long pointed noses.

In my dream these fanciful characters were playful, joyful wild creatures but then the dream turned into a nightmare and the costumed figures became pursuing furies, chasing me along the street, howling.

Terrified, I awoke with a start.

I sat up in bed, shivering, and looked around the room I shared with my sisters, assuring myself that what had frightened me was no more than a dream, and that all was as usual around me. A candle burned beside the bed on a little table where I kept my Bible and the photograph album I had brought with me from Tsarskoe Selo with my favorite pictures of our family.

I picked up the album and leafed through it. There we were as small children, Anastasia on mama's lap, Marie leaning against her chair, me sitting at her feet and Olga standing beside her, all of us looking very solemn. There was Grandma Minnie and Aunt Ella, and a photograph of the *Standart* at Cowes. One picture in particular caught my eye. It was of our entire family in medieval costume, dressed for a masked ball.

All of a sudden I thought of a way we could elude our guards and join our rescuers.

If we could be allowed to join in the festival for a day, or even a few hours, in costume (could the nuns make us costumes, I wondered?), then we might be able to slip away and lose ourselves in the crowd. But of course we would be too closely watched for that; the guards would never lose sight of us.

Or would they? There was one place, I thought, where they would be reluctant to follow us. They would not want to enter the cathedral. Early in our captivity when we had been permitted to go to mass, the guards had walked along beside us to the church but had never gone inside. Was it because all revolutionaries were atheists? Were they showing contempt for the church authorities? I didn't know. But it seemed reasonable to assume that if we entered the cathedral for a service, they would not follow us inside, but would wait by the door or on the steps until we came out again.

Was there a way we could escape once we were in the cathedral?

Georgy would know. I would have to ask him. Meanwhile I would have to think of a way for us to obtain our liberty to attend the Maslenitsa.

I went back to bed and had no more bad dreams. Early the following morning I waited for the nuns to bring us our daily food baskets, expecting that Michael would probably be with them. I gave him a note to carry to the commissar at the mayor's house. Next I sought out Georgy and found a place where we could talk unobserved. I told him that the commissar Yuri Pyatakov and his friend Prince Adalbert were offering our family a way of escape.

"The Brotherhood is against this, Tania. I'm sure your father is as well. A scheme thought up by two young idealists who know little of how cruel and treacherous the real world can be. It will be far better for your family to wait until the ice melts and our forces can seize the town as we have been planning all along."

"There isn't time for that. Most of the ruling Committee in Moscow wants our family killed. Pyatakov is one of the few who wants to save us."

"So he says."

"I am going to follow his advice. And now I need yours. You and the Brotherhood know the cathedral better than anyone. Tell me, is there a hidden way out? A way our guards would not think to watch?"

He thought for a moment. "There is an exit from the bell tower out onto the roof. Only the bellringers know of it, because it is hardly ever needed. There is also the coal cellar, but it would not be big enough for more than one or two people to hide in, and getting out would require help from outside, as the coal chute is steep. Why do you ask?"

I told him what I was thinking, that if our family, in costume, were to be allowed to attend the festival then we might have a chance to conceal ourselves in the cathedral, where we could be sure the guards would not be watching us, and then wait for an opportunity to escape by some obscure exit.

He looked thoughtful.

"I don't think you ought to do this, Tania. I think you ought to keep to the original plan. But if you insist, then why not arrange to have others take your place? Then you could go in and out of the cathedral freely, and the guards would be none the wiser."

"How would that work, exactly?"

"You would go in, wearing your costumes, and then others would put them on and go back out again, and the guards would follow the others, not realizing who it was that they were following."

"But that's perfect!" I almost kissed Georgy, I was so pleased at his suggestion. Why hadn't I thought of it myself?

"However, I can't imagine that you would be given any liberty, so this is only a dream."

Exactly, I wanted to say. This is precisely a dream, my dream of the night before. But I reminded myself that my dream had turned to nightmare.

Despite Georgy's misgivings and pessimism, the outcome I hoped for came about. In the note I sent through Michael to Yuri Pyatakov, I asked the commissar to order our guards to let us celebrate the Maslenitsa with the townspeople for one day. He did as I asked, and the Bayonet, sputtering with anger and much aggrieved by his temporary arrest on the day of the town hall meeting, informed us that our family, plus Daria and Iskra, would be allowed to leave the Governor's Mansion on the morning of the final day of the carnival, with an escort of guards, and that we would have to return that evening by ten o'clock.

"And if you do not return, I will order one hundred of the people of Tobolsk shot! I will shoot them myself!" He took out his pistol and waved it in the air. "Do you hear? Shot!"

I had five days to make my arrangements. I started in at once.

First there was the matter of our costumes. I sat down with my sketchbook and drew pictures of a harlequin, a firebird, an ice princess and so on—a costume for each of us. Then I spoke to our unfailing helpers, the nuns: could they make two sets of the costumes I had drawn, one for us and one for those who would take our places, keeping in mind our heights (they knew us well) and making the garments loose enough not to require any fittings? I was assured that they could, and that the costumes would be finished in time for us to wear them on the last day of the Maslenitsa. We would need masks to go with each costume, and I knew Michael could buy these in the marketplace.

Georgy was both surprised and dismayed when I told him that we had been given one day of liberty; I could tell that he had been hoping my plan would not succeed. Yet he was sincere in his desire to see us free, and to be of use. He and his family would take our places, he said; he even had two grandchildren who were close to the sizes of Alexei and little Iskra.

Alexei! Until that moment I had not really considered what difficulties his recent attack would present when it came to attending the festival. He had begun to recover, he was no longer completely unable to walk at all. But he could not walk far, and would have to be carried most of the time on the festival day.

"Can your grandson imitate the tsarevich's limp?" I asked Georgy. "And will he remember to?"

"He is clever. And he knows how important his role will be."

All seemed to be falling in place, yet as the days passed I felt a nagging worry. The elderly starets had prophesied that my parents would be martyrs. I could not purge that woeful thought from my mind, no matter how hard I tried. I forced myself to remember Michael's rock-solid, comforting rationality. He had been right to remind me that the old holy woman could not possibly know anything about Adalbert or his soldiers, nor of the commissar's sincere desire that we be taken out of Russia to safety. Michael had good common sense, I told myself. I was being frightened by a chimera.

Yet I was my mother's daughter—and my credulous, superstitious mother had always put her trust in messages from the beyond. From birth I had been accustomed to having occult healers and seers around me, and to hearing mama talk of weeping icons and wondrous visions. Some were surely frauds, I had seen that for myself. But not all. And surely the aged Maria Michaelovna, lying in her dim hut, waiting for death, could have no reason to lie about what she saw in the future.

I trembled, I said my prayers, and waited for our day of liberty to dawn.

Fifty-eight

It was the final day of the Maslenitsa, and one by one we emerged from the Governor's Mansion, dressed in our carnival finery and shivering in the chill early morning air. Papa, dressed as a harlequin, came first, followed by mama all in red and gold, a fanciful firebird. I was a silvery snow maiden, Olga a furry Grimalkin, Marie a whimsical spotted dog, Anastasia a frog prince all in green. Little Iskra, dressed as a black kitten with a long tail and silver whiskers, bounded eagerly beside her mother—an ice princess all in white—and I was amazed to see that her weeks of confinement in the basement had not broken her childish high spirits. Alexei, in a brown bear costume with a gold crown on his head, was carried in Michael's strong arms but was eager to get down and walk, and as we made our way along Freedom Street, surrounded by our cordon of uniformed guards, he slipped out of Michael's grasp and stumbled along as best he could on his own, eager to watch the jugglers and buy hazelnuts and gingerbread from the street vendors.

At every street corner, ventriloquists and comedians stood on hastily built wooden stages and entertained the crowd; they made fun of everything, even the revolution and its policy of giving land to the peasants and bread to the hungry. I saw our guards frown at some of these irreverent jokes, but more often they laughed, and ate butter-bathed blinis and washed them down with lemon-pepper vodka, all the while keeping us in view.

In our costumes we blended in well with the hundreds of others strolling among the food booths and stages, the rides and decorated sleighs and crowded arenas set apart for dancing and music. There were many harlequins and firebirds and ice princesses and grotesque animals, many scaramouches like Michael. For disguise, after all, was half the fun of a carnival; hidden behind a mask, one could do what one liked. Inhibitions were laid aside, instinct took over. Except for the everpresent guards, we were free to shout, cavort, overeat, even fight.

Fist-fighting in groups was a hallmark of the Maslenitsa and we stopped to watch young men, stripped of their costumes and sweating in their underwear despite the cold, brawling with one another, hitting, kicking and punching with abandon. Each time a telling blow was landed or a dizzy fighter lurched away bleeding or limping the crowd cheered. After looking on for ten minutes or so, two of our guards tore off their uniforms and joined in. In the free-for-all that followed, both men flailed away and managed to damage some of the other fighters, but in the end they crumpled and left the melee, returning to where we were standing, one clutching his stomach, the other his bleeding head.

The injured guards slapped and punched the others, demanding to know why they hadn't come to their aid.

"How could we? We have to watch these Romanovs."

"The hell with them. The Bayonet isn't here now."

"What if they get away? We'd be blamed. We'd be shot."

"I say if they don't pay us, they don't have the right to shoot us."

"And I say you were brave fellows in there," Michael broke in, handing tall glasses of vodka to the two guards who had been in the fight, "and you deserve to be rewarded."

They took the fiery vodka and drank it down.

Alexei and Iskra clamored to go on the whirligig and we took them to find it, our wounded guards putting their uniforms back on and trailing behind. While we were watching the children gyrate on the fast-spinning mechanism mama complained that her leg hurt.

"Then sit down, firebird!" one of the guards responded roughly. "Or just fly away!" The others sniggered. Papa helped mama to a bench where she sat, arms folded, frowning, until the whirligig stopped turning. Daria went to lift Iskra down from the slowing device. Iskra was holding her head.

"She's dizzy. She needs to lie down. I'll take her to her Aunt Niuta's house." And without waiting for permission from the guards she walked away, holding Iskra by the hand.

"Return in half an hour," one of the men called out after her, but his half-hearted command was lost in the music of the carousel.

We stopped to watch a dancing bear and I thought of Lavoritya and the night we had almost been rescued from Tsarskoe Selo. That night our carefully planned rescue had failed. Would we succeed this time? Was this our freedom day, so long in coming? I hoped so.

Just past the whirligig an enormous ice mountain had been created and Marie and Anastasia climbed to the top and slid down. Alexei wanted to slide down it too.

"No," papa said firmly. "You know how badly you could be hurt."

"But this is the last day of the carnival. I won't get another chance until next year."

"Then it will have to be next year."

Alexei went on complaining and cajoling. Mama continued to grumble about her sore leg. Olga, who suddenly thought she saw her old flirt Victor in the crowd, dashed off to speak to him, and shrieked in complaint when three of the guards went after her and roughly brought her back.

It was all too much for papa, who went up to the nearest booth where many flavors of vodka were for sale and asked for black currant by the yard.

I watched as the row of small shiny glasses was lined up along the front of the booth and the vendor filled each one with the dark fragrant liquid. Drinking flavored vodka "by the yard" was an old custom, calling for a man (I had never seen a woman attempt it) to prove his fortitude by downing an entire yard-long array of liquor-filled glasses. It called for a strong stomach and it nearly always brought forth clapping and chanting from the onlookers.

I looked over at Michael as my father began to drink from the small glasses and those around us began to applaud and cheer him on. Michael and I both sensed trouble coming. We knew only too well that when feeling overwhelmed papa drank—far too much. Then he withdrew into a somnolent silence. We needed him to be alert, not groggy—but we dared not tell him why. We dared not tell him the truth about what was going to happen that night, knowing that his reaction would be negative.

As a distraction I encouraged Marie and Anastasia to join in a contest to see who could eat the most blinis. Anastasia, who was always hungry, joined in eagerly and soon the front of her green frog prince costume was daubed with dripping butter. Marie too began eating blinis, but at a more moderate pace, and less messily. Before long she drifted away and joined in some arm-wrestling. Papa and mama went to sit side by side on a bench and it was then I noticed that Alexei was missing.

I knew at once where he was likely to be: sliding down the ice mountain, in defiance of papa's orders.

"Michael! I think Alexei may have gone back to the ice mountain. We can't let him try to climb it!"

We ran as quickly as we could toward the glistening crystal mound that towered above all the other structures in the town. Children were clambering up the back side of the steep edifice, dragging sleds, holding on to ropes and using stairsteps carved into the ice. When they reached the top they lay down on their sleds and careened down the slippery face of the mountain, gathering speed and shrieking with excitement and fear until they bumped to a stop in the snow.

We did not see Alexei at first, and for a moment I thought I might be wrong about his disobedience; maybe, I hoped, he has just gone to buy some gingerbread or to look for Olga, who had left the rest of us once again to try to find Victor. But then, going around the back side of the mountain, I saw the furry brown of his bear costume and the gleaming golden crown. It had to be Alexei. He was limping badly, he could hardly drag himself to the top. Evidently he had borrowed a sled, and was doing his best to pull it along as he climbed.

With an agility that never failed to amaze me Michael was on the mountain in a moment and managing to weave his way in and out of the crowd of climbing children, doing his best to reach the top in time to stop Alexei before he got on his sled. He very nearly succeeded. But then— I was horrified to see Alexei standing on top of the mound, then lying down on the sled, and then disappearing from my sight as he began his descent.

Slipping on the frozen snow beneath my boots, I ran around to the front side of the mound and arrived just in time to see Alexei crumple into a brown heap in the snow, screaming in pain.

Fifty-nine

At a little before six o'clock that evening we went in through the high carved double doors of the cathedral of St. John of Tobolsk, unaccompanied by our guards who remained outside on the broad wooden steps. We were all tired and hungry, for though the day had been an exciting one it had also been very long—and very tense. Our guards had grown increasingly inebriated and belligerent, restricting us more and more as to where we could go and what we could do, and had even refused to allow Michael to go back to the Governor's Mansion to get Dr. Botkin after Alexei hurt himself sliding down the ice mountain.

Olga was irritable, Anastasia sick to her stomach from eating too many blinis, Alexei in pain and mama, I'm sorry to have to say, was badly in need of her Veronal drops (which she had not thought to bring with her) and was nervous and edgy and full of complaints. Yet the carnival was reaching its end, it was the eve of the Lenten observance and all pious believers were obligated to attend the pre-Lenten mass. Not to go to the service was unthinkable.

We had no sooner taken our places than a man in a harlequin costume came up to us.

"Georgy Kochetkov, of the Brotherhood of St. John, here to serve you, Little Father," he whispered to papa. "And my family as well," he added, indicating a cluster of costumed figures standing together in a nearby side chapel.

Papa looked, turned away—and then looked back again. There in the chapel were a red and orange firebird, a grey cat, a silvery ice princess, a brown bear with a gold crown—in short, a duplicate of each of us.

"What's this?" he said aloud. "Why are they—"

"Come with me, papa, and I'll explain," I interjected before he could complete his question. I drew him toward an archway through which I could see a stairwell rising upward. This must be the stairway leading up into the bell tower, I reasoned. The bell tower from which we could exit onto the roof.

"There is something very important I must tell you. I have waited until now because I wanted to make certain all would go according to plan. I'm sorry to have kept the plan from you, but I felt I had to. Please forgive me, papa."

It was hard to tell his reaction, his mask concealed all but the look in his eyes. The slight quaver in his voice betrayed his fatigue and the aftereffects of the yard of vodka he had drunk earlier in the day.

"Go on, Tania."

"Georgy and his family are here to take our places, so that instead of going back to the Governor's Mansion at ten o'clock we can remain here in the church until Adalbert and his men rescue us. It has all been arranged."

"And the Brotherhood's plan to attack Tobolsk in force?"

"Was never more than a hope. Besides, the commissar says we are all in far more danger than we realize. We must go now, if we are to save ourselves."

He seemed to sway slightly on his feet, and I reached out to steady him.

"I must think. I must think," he murmured.

"Papa, you must act. We can talk more later. For now, you must go back to the others and tell them firmly to come to this staircase, quietly and without drawing attention to themselves. Right away. Michael will help you."

He hesitated. "I don't trust them, Tania. Your Adalbert and that commissar."

"As far as I can tell, they are the only ones we can trust now."

"I don't like it," he said, but he went back to where the others were waiting. I stood where I was, watching. The cathedral was filling up, the choir members taking their places. Some of the worshippers were dressed in the warm clothing they would wear to any important mass, but most were in their carnival finery, which made the event surreal, even grotesque. We were real people, trapped in real and very dangerous circumstances. Yet at the same time we were fantastic beings, fairytale creatures occupying a realm of myth and imagination. Dual bodies, dual selves.

I could tell, from my vantage point, that papa was having difficulty persuading the others to leave the sanctuary and come to the alcove where I was waiting. Finally Michael separated himself from the others, carrying Alexei, and shortly afterward papa came, supporting Mama who looked peevish and resistant, like a fractious child. Marie, Anastasia, Olga and Daria trailed along behind, Daria looking around the vast room searchingly. There was no sign of Iskra, I presumed she was still with Niuta and Nikandr.

At last we were all together at the bottom of the staircase and I saw that Georgy and his family had joined the congregation, standing where my family had been.

"Tania! What's going on!" Olga wanted to know.

"We're going up into the bell tower, where we can be safe."

"What? Why?"

"You mean up those steps?" came mama's querulous voice. "You know I can't climb those steps!"

"We'll help you mama."

"What's going on?" asked Marie. "I don't understand."

"When we get where we need to go, I'll explain."

Alexei, who had so far been quiet, now began to moan.

"I'll take him up first," Michael said, beginning to climb upward with Alexei in his arms.

"Follow Michael," I told the others. "I'll come last. I'll help mama." But when papa and I tried to begin the ascent, with mama between us, each of us holding an arm, she angrily wrenched herself free and I was afraid she would start to scream, as she did when feeling nervous and uncomfortable.

"No! I'm staying right here!" And she sat down on the steps and refused to budge.

The service had begun and the voices of the choir, blending in the traditional harmonies of the sung mass, filled the cathedral. The ethereal music seemed to soothe mama a little. She listened, and was still.

But when we tried, shortly afterward, to persuade her to start climbing again she continued to sit where she was, a disheveled, dejected firebird, shorn of her wings (her costume had suffered damage during the day's activities), head bowed, unresponsive. Presently Michael came down and, seeing her limp and listless, spoke gently to her.

"Let me help you up the stairs, madam," he began, but she wriggled out of his grasp.

"The stairs are the way to rescue—to freedom," he whispered.

At this she came alert, and sat upright.

"You mean we are to be taken out of this awful place?"

"Yes. This very night."

"But I have none of my things."

"All will be provided."

"No! My icons! My Veronal! I can't leave without it!"

But before she could protest further, Michael had scooped her up in his arms and was going up the stairs as fast as he could, and papa and I followed.

At the top of the bell tower was a small round room, cold and empty except for seven bells ranging in size from large to enormously large, hanging down from a metal device. Our voices echoed eerily, as from far below us drifted up the sound of the choir.

There was nowhere to sit, other than on the dusty stone floor.

"Now Tania, tell us what is going on," Olga demanded once she had flopped down.

"Yes, tell us," said Marie and Anastasia almost at the same time.

"It is very simple, really. All we need to do is to stay here, right here, until midnight, when Adalbert will come to get us, with an escort of soldiers and three troikas. The town guardsmen go home at midnight. There will be a few men on watch, but they will be sympathetic to us. They will let us go where we like."

"Won't the Bayonet come after us?" Alexei asked.

"He won't know where to find us."

"When the mass is over," Michael added, "it will look to the guards as though we are leaving the church. Only it will be others dressed just like us that leave. The guards will follow them. They will think they are following us."

"By the time they realize their mistake we will be gone," I finished, smiling at the thought.

Anastasia clutched her stomach. "I'm going to be sick," she said.

"Don't be sick all over me!" Olga moved away, pulling at her furry costume. "You're disgusting! You've already got butter all over your vest. Now you're going to have sick on it too."

Marie was nodding off.

"How will Niuta know where to bring Iskra now? I told her I would be in the sanctuary, not in the bell tower." Daria was in distress.

"You can watch for her from the roof." I looked around the circular room for the small door Georgy had told me about, the one he said led out onto the roof. It was not easy to find. It was not a true door at all, but a sort of trap door, painted in the same dull green as the walls, opening from the top, and without a handle. It looked barely wide enough for a single person to squeeze through. When I tried to open it I couldn't.

"It must be frozen shut," Michael said, and came over to help me. He took out his khinjal—which he had been wearing strapped to his waist, under his scaramouche costume—and used the blade to chip away at the ice that had formed around the edges of the door.

"How long do we have to wait?" Marie asked.

"Not long. Only until midnight."

"Do we have any food?"

Daria produced some gingerbread wrapped in a sack. "I bought this for Iskra. You can have it." She handed the gingerbread to Marie, who unwrapped it and ate it.

"I'm sure Niuta and Iskra will be here soon," I told Daria. "Don't lose hope. Maybe Niuta decided to wait until the mass is over before she comes to meet you."

"Why would she do that?"

I had no answer for that question, and in truth I was concerned as well, though I tried not to show it.

Still, up to this point, our plan was working. Papa was distrustful, but he did not resist. I imagined that he was telling himself, as he habitually did, that all was in the hands of God. Mama was napping with her head on Olga's shoulder. Poor Anastasia was lying down, her back against the cold stone wall. Marie was amusing herself playing hopscotch under the big iron bells, avoiding the ropes that hung down from them through holes in the floor and humming softly along with the choir.

There was a snapping sound as Michael managed to cut away the last of the ice around the trap door and pull it down into the room. Immediately Daria squeezed through it and went outside to watch for her sister.

Only a few hours to go, I told myself. Only a few hours, during which the guards would follow Georgy and his family, believing them to be us. Meanwhile we would only have to wait, in safety, for our rescuers to arrive.

Sixty

We were all drowsing when we heard gunshots and the angry shouts of many men and a sudden, ear-splitting crash in the sanctuary below.

"They've broken in the doors!" Michael said, looking at his watch. "It's ten-thirty. They've come looking for us. Quick! Out on the roof! They won't find us out there!"

Without warning the bells began to ring, the sound so deafeningly loud that it hurt our ears and we instinctively began running down the stairs to escape it.

Michael grabbed my arm. "No! No, Tania! Not that way! Out on the roof! It's our only chance!" But his voice was all but lost in the din, and mama was screaming, loudly and continuously. More crashes came from downstairs, but the gunshots had diminished.

"Romanov! Romanov! We know you are up there! Come down at once!" I heard a gruff voice say. It was not the voice of the Bayonet.

Papa was shaking his head, as if to shake the painful vibrations of the horrible clanging bells out of his wounded ears. Mama's screams seemed to get even louder.

"Romanov! Come down or we will come up there and shoot you! We know your family is there with you!"

"Give yourself up," came another harsh voice, "or we will burn Tobolsk to the ground, and kill every soul in it!"

"Oh no! Oh no!" mama cried out again and again.

Michael was tugging at my arm, Alexei struggling to get up off the floor, and my sisters seemed frozen in fear, looking in papa's direction, no doubt expecting him to tell them what to do.

"Stop that ringing!" papa shouted. "Stop it at once!"

Surprisingly, the ropes grew slack. The bells stopped their urgent pealing.

Slowly papa began descending the stairs.

"Take off your mask, Romanov," came the gruff voice.

"But you are not our guards!" I heard papa reply. "Who are you!" It was more an accusation than a question.

"Who we are is none of your concern, exploiter!"

"Are you the ones they call the Red Guards?"

"We are sent by the Ekaterinburg soviet, to arrest you all!"

"Are you sent by the commissar, Yuri Pyatakov?" papa was asking.

"The traitor Pyatakov has been shot. We are sent by the new soviet. Where are the others in your family?"

"They are of no importance to you. Take me. Let the others go."

"My orders are to arrest every one of you. Husband, wife, one son and four daughters."

So they don't know that Michael or Daria or Iskra are with us, I thought. What has happened to Georgy and his family? Where are the guards from the Governor's Mansion?

"Unless you all come at once we will burn the town. Beginning with this place of superstition. Torches!"

I heard a susurration of footfalls. I thought I smelled smoke, but it may have been my imagination, born of dread.

"Savages!" papa shouted.

"It is you, exploiter, who are the savage! I tell you for the last time, all of you, come at once or Tobolsk will be destroyed."

"Tania!" Michael whispered urgently. "You must come now!"

Daria came through the trap door, shivering. "So many people out there in the street," she said. "They came when the bells started ringing. I can't see Niuta. What will become of my Iskra?" She wept.

"Quiet!" I said. "Papa is giving himself up. They don't know you are here, or Michael. Go back outside!"

"But what is happening? Where are the others?" For mama, Alexei and my sisters had begun to go down the stairs, following papa. I felt a strong urge to go with them, but Michael held me in his strong grip.

"Quiet!" he whispered to Daria and me. "Don't talk! Don't move!"

"All of you!" came the gruff voice. "Take off your masks at once!" He paused, then said, "Where is the fourth daughter?"

I gasped.

"She is ill," I heard papa say. "She is not here."

"Liar! Produce her, or you will all be shot!"

I pulled my arm free but Michael quickly grabbed me again. "No! You must not! You must wait for Adalbert, on the roof, with me and Daria!"

In the long, suspenseful moment that followed—it may have been the longest of my life—I saw Daria take off her mask. Her face was surprisingly composed. She began descending the stairs.

"I am here," she said. "I am coming down."

"Daria?" I whispered, but Michael put his hand over my mouth. "No! Let her go! Let her go!"

Daria turned to me. "I know Iskra will not come now," she said, her voice low. "But I can't leave here without her. I will go in your place. God be with you Tania. Thank you."

I cannot describe the anguish I felt, hearing her footsteps as she went down the stairs. Too much had happened, too quickly. I let Michael lead me noiselessly to the trap door and out onto the roof. The bitter wind tore at my face, and I buried it in Michael's chest as he guided me to the lee side of the tower and we took refuge together from the wind and the unfolding horror inside the church. Gradually I went numb, until I could no longer feel anything at all. I could not bear to let myself react to what was happening. I could not bear even to weep as I watched, from the roof, while the Red Guards tied the hands of their new prisoners—my beloved family—and led them away into the night.

Sixty-one

I never saw my family again.

Michael and I took shelter with the nuns, in the tiny izba where the starets Maria Michaelovna was living out her extraordinarily long life. But we did not dare to stay there long. Within a few days we were taken by Georgy Kochetkov to a barn in a small village beside the Irtysh where we stayed, hidden in the hayloft, through the Lenten season.

It was in that village, on a sunlit day in early spring, that we were married.

We had no ring, I had no wedding dress, but Michael made me a bridal wreath out of hay from the manger and I wove some snowdrops into it—the first flowers of that fateful spring. We knelt before the village priest—who had no idea he was joining in marriage Michael Gamkrelidze of Daghestan, whose distant ancestor was the King of Imeretia, and Tatiana Romanov, daughter of the former Tsar Nicholas II.

On our wedding night, spent amid the lowing cows and snuffling horses, Michael and I embraced with a passion I had not known I possessed. I had often enjoyed blissful nights in Michael's embrace, but there was something new in the fire that awoke between us after we became husband and wife.

Having been a captive for so long, I was suddenly free; having been forced to hide and suppress my emotions while living amid guards and soldiers, I now unleashed them, indulging my desire for Michael, my joy in our lovemaking, as never before. He felt the same abandon, and when after many pleasurable hours we lay side by side, watching the first faint colors of dawn light the sky, we turned to each other, flushed and exultant, laughing and embracing for sheer delight.

How could I feel such pleasure knowing that my family was in the brutal hands of the Red Guards, their future uncertain but their present danger very real? I have no answer for that, though I have searched my heart again and again. All I can say is that I was a young, happily wedded woman in love, and that when I lay in my husband's arms, lip to fervent lip, heart to fast-beating heart, limb to searching limb, I found balm for my wounded self, and we both found hope.

It was a hope we were to need in coming days.

By the end of the Lenten season we knew that my father and mother, my sisters and brother had been taken to Ekaterinburg and handed over to the Ural Regional Soviet.

The story was making its way throughout eastern Russia, for it was a sensational tale: the escape of the former tsar and his family and the dramatic recapture of these so-called traitors by the heroic Red Guards.

But it was an incomplete story. I knew it to be incomplete. For nothing was said about my escape. I had not been recaptured. Instead Daria had taken my place, just as I at that time took her name, Daria, and coupled it with my husband's adopted name of Gradov.

I repeated my new name, my new identity, a hundred times a day. I am no longer Tatiana Romanov. I am Daria Gradov. As long as I clung to this new identity, I told myself, and the real Daria continued to play the role of Tatiana, the former tsar's second daughter, I was safe.

No one would come after me. No one would find me.

But the fearsome Ural Regional Soviet was implacable in its judgments, as we continued to discover from the scant news reports that reached us. The Bolsheviks in Ekaterinburg were merciless to all those they perceived to be traitors. In my worst hours I feared that in time the Red Guards would indeed come after me, find me and kill me, and Michael too. I suppose it was this fear, in part, that made our time together so pleasurable and so precious.

We were hearing that Ekaterinburg was in turmoil. Russia was indeed in a state of civil war, just as the Bayonet had insisted when he shouted at the top of his lungs in the Tobolsk town hall. The Bolshevik revolutionaries were attempting to hold onto their newfound power and the monarchists, the Whites, were attempting to take back all that had been lost since the revolution began. By that summer, the summer of 1918, a White army was approaching Ekaterinburg.

A storm was brewing, a terrible storm.

When Michael's fellow-soldiers in the newly reconstituted Fifth Circassian regiment swept through Tobolsk on their way eastward we decided to leave the safety of our remote village and join them, despite the risk we knew we were taking, hoping that the forces of the Whites would recapture the town and that my family would be freed.

We were too late. Before we could arrive in Ekaterinburg the Bolsheviks, among them the fearsome Bayonet, decided to act.

I can hardly bear to write what happened. But the world knows. The world has known for many decades. My father and mother, my sisters Olga and Marie and Anastasia and my brother Alexei, along with some of our servants, were all shot in the basement of the house where they had been imprisoned.

It was merciless, pitiless slaughter of innocent people and I know that those who carried it out are burning in hell, every last one of them.

What the world has never known until now is that Daria, Niuta's sister and my friend, was massacred too, because the Red Guards believed she was Tatiana.

I can only hope that when they died, my family cherished in their hearts the knowledge that I was not with them and the trust that I was free and alive.

Michael has told me so often that I must not feel guilty that I survived and those nearest to me did not. If your father were standing right here, Michael tells me, he would say Tania, my dearest Tania, you were right to go on ahead, to save yourself. I meant to follow. You must not mourn for me. Papa would be glad for each day of life that I have had. He would say, dearest Tania, all is in the will of God.

I try my best to remember this, as I look at the icon of St. Simon Verkhoturie that hangs on my wall, and imagine that he weeps for all that has happened, and as I look down at the gold bracelet that I wear on my wrist, the bracelet I have never taken off since the day mama gave it to me when I was nineteen years old. I have worn it, and will always wear it, in memory of my beloved mama, even though my wrist has thickened and become the fleshy wrist of a stout old woman.

From that day in July of 1918 when my family died I have carried their blood and their hopes. All the evils that were unleashed in Russia when I was a girl have now played themselves out, and the Russian people, still my people despite all my years of living in Canada, can breathe free. I rejoice in their freedom, as I have rejoiced all these years in my own. My hope is that my children and grandchildren and great-grandchildren will take pride in who they are, the descendants of emperors, and will remember with love the family they never knew. My family. The family of Tatiana Romanov, also known as Daria Gradov, daughter of Tsar Nicholas II of Russia and of Tsarina Alexandra.

And now I write to whoever reads this account of my life, remembering always my dear family, and in thankfulness that I was spared,

All is in the will of God.

EPILOGUE

When my Aunt Niuta died, I found Tatiana Romanov's story about her family and her own escape among her papers, and after much thought I decided that it should be given to the world.

I do not know exactly how or when the former grand duchess sent her story to my aunt, or how she even knew that my aunt had survived. Perhaps they corresponded. Or it may be that others from Pokrovsky who escaped the revolution and its bitter aftermath made their way to Canada and contacted the woman who called herself Daria Gradov.

Whether Tatiana would have wanted her story to be widely shared I can't say. The time she writes about seems so very long ago now, and the story itself is not easy to believe, though I believe it, every word. But my aunt often talked about the family she served—she was proud of having been a member of the tsar's household, though she did not dare say so to anyone but my Uncle Nikandr and me. Many of the small details in the story were things Aunt Niuta told me about. And the icon, the gold bracelet and the small velvet box of jewels that were bound up with the manuscript are all from the time before the revolution. I know, I had them all authenticated before returning them to Tatiana's—I mean Daria's—relatives in the town of Yellow Rain.

EPILOGUE

I do not know whether the world will care that one of the last tsar's daughters survived, but I care. For after all, as she says in her manuscript, she helped to bring me into the world, in that long-ago time before the revolution, in the Workers' Clinic in Smokestack Town, and I am grateful.

Iskra Melnikov

NOTE TO THE READER

Though in this historical entertainment the heroine Tatiana survives to a ripe old age and tells her remarkable story, the real Tatiana Romanov, sadly, did not. She was executed with her family in Ekaterinburg in 1918, and all her hopes, plans and loves died with her.

The Tsarina's Daughter is an imaginative retelling of Tatiana's story, with many invented characters and events added to the historical background. Fiction and reality intertwine in this narrative; Michael Gradov is an imagined figure, as are Daria and Constantin and others. But what I hope emerges from this congeries of invention is an image of Tatiana Romanov's world, and of the darkness that closed over it at her brief life's end. The real Tatiana was not allowed to escape that darkness, but the fictional one overcame it, and lives, in these pages and in our hearts.